PROM NIGHT FOR SLASHER VICTIMS

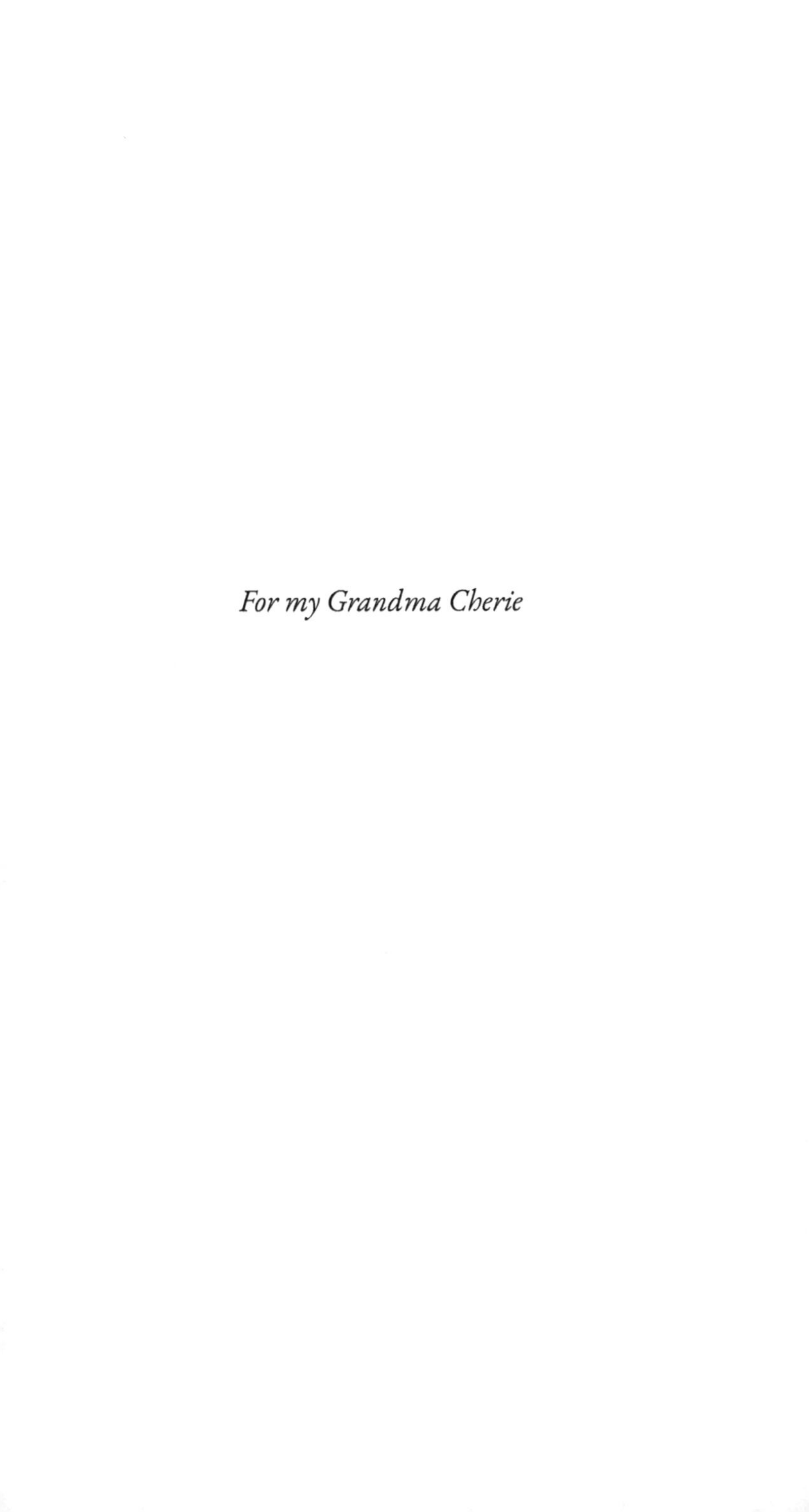

For my Grandma Cherie

" . . . I'm sure as hell not dancing with death
any time soon. Just you."

Content Warning

This novel contains graphic depictions of trauma, murder, gore, violence, and torture, including psychological and emotional manipulation. There are also explicit descriptions of nudity and sexual content. This book is not for children. Reader discretion is advised.

Contents

Prologue

"Goodbye, Mrs. Chloe!" the preschool children yelled, huddled beneath the hand-painted banner that said the same thing, with the *E* at the end of her name written backward—an error for certain, but likely played off as a stylistic choice by the teacher who would be taking Chloe's place after today, Ms. Sarah. An error like this would usually make Chloe laugh, but seeing her name spelled out with the title *Mrs.* distracted her.

She hadn't thought about it until then, but this would likely be the last time she would ever see her name spelled this way, and the same would go for hearing it from her students, considering the fact that her divorce had been finalized just the week prior—a day she took off from work to visit the courthouse, and probably the same day the students, with the help of Ms. Sarah, made this banner behind her back. It was a surreal feeling, one of many that she would have to deal with as she took her next steps moving on with her life, but what was she going to do? Correct the kids and make them call her "Ms. Chloe" after all this time? Explain the heartbreak that we call "divorce" to three and four-year-olds?

Not a chance.

What took her out of that moment was her favorite student, Johnny, running from the huddle to give her a hug as she placed her hand on the doorknob, fully prepared to walk out of the classroom for the last time.

"Don't go!" he yelled, wrapping his arms around her legs and burying his face against her thigh.

"Aww, I'm gonna miss you, too, kid." She pulled her hand from the doorknob to muss up his hair. When he pulled out of the hug, he was sniffling and doing his best not to cry.

"I made you this," he said as he reached into his pocket. Chloe tilted her head, both excited and concerned about what he could reveal, knowing that coming from a kid his age, it could be anything from a crumpled-up macaroni painting to a snot-stained ball of tissue.

When he did pull it out, it took her a second to realize what it even was and a longer second for her to act appreciative. It was a Popsicle stick painted green bearing his name, misspelled as *Johny,* written with a red marker. He held it out by the floss-like string that he'd looped through a hole stabbed near one of its tips, effectively making it a necklace.

"No way! You made that for me?" she asked.

"Can I put it on?" He held up the necklace, expecting her to bend down and lower her head.

She obliged and replied, "Please!"

He pulled the necklace over her head, which is when she discovered that the string was made of rubber, as it pulled on her hair when he forced it down. She smiled as she grabbed it from him and finished pulling it on herself, then raised her head up to face the rest of the preschoolers with that same big smile.

"How do I look?"

The kids responded with lots of noises that sounded highly positive, so she booped Johnny's nose while saying, "Thank you."

He laughed and shouted, "You're welcome!"

Riding that positive energy, she grabbed the doorknob once again, twisted it, said, "Bye, everyone," and stepped out into her new life.

Just a few hours later, she found herself reminiscing on that very moment, driving her beat-up sedan—the only real thing she kept from the divorce—as she watched the Popsicle stick necklace dangle back and forth, not hanging from her neck but from her rearview mirror—a reminder of the one good thing she was leaving behind.

She felt nervous, as anyone would, not only living alone for the first time in her life but also living in a town where she wouldn't know a single soul who lived there. However, following her nasty divorce and with a great job offer to start her career, she was optimistic for this next step in her life.

As she pulled up to the door of the one-car garage of her overpriced California condominium, she grabbed her phone from its holder suctioned to the windshield, closed the GPS app, opened her emails, and started scrolling.

"Okay, so how do I get in?" she muttered to herself, stopping at the message she'd starred from her landlord.

The subject of the email was *Arrival Instructions*.

"Let's see . . ." She started reading aloud, her voice tired from the hours of driving, "*I hope you're having a nice day . . . I can let you into the place if you arrive by seven . . . You can park in the garage, the button to open it is on the kitchen counter . . .* Oh! Here we go." She sat up in her seat upon finding the line of text she was looking for. "*If you arrive late at night, I'll put the key in the mailbox beside the front door.* Cool!" She quickly turned off her car, pulled the key from the ignition, dropped her phone into her bag, and stepped out, purse in hand. She left her car unlocked because she would be back shortly, and she assumed her new neighborhood was safe enough to leave her vehicle unattended for a minute or two.

Upon reaching her small front porch, she walked up the single step and found the mailbox nailed on the wall to the right of her door, just below the exterior light which had been left on.

"That was thoughtful," she said, opening the top flap and reaching her hand inside. But she didn't feel any keys, just the cheap, dusty metal base of the mailbox. Confused and sure she was mistaken, she stood on her tiptoes to peer inside and confirm her disbelief; there was nothing inside.

"Just my luck." She sighed and continued to complain as she rifled through her purse for her cell, "So much for a fresh start." Struggling to feel her phone, she looked down into her bag to find it faster, but something else caught her eye.

Between her feet and the door lay a welcome mat, bright blue with a yellow smiley face to the left of the word *WEL-COME.*

Maybe it's a gift? she thought, blinking hard at the mat, considering it definitely wasn't hers, and it wasn't there when she last checked out the place. "I wonder . . . "

She reached down, grabbed the mat, and lifted it. Underneath, a single key lay on the floorboards.

"I guess this was a last-minute choice," she said, grabbing the key. She inserted it into the lock, twisted it, and stepped inside. Once there, she walked down the hallway, past the staircase to the upper floor, and straight to the kitchen. She flicked on the light and watched it illuminate the room, along with the living room on the other side of the partition wall. The condo was emptier than she was used to seeing it—considering it had been furnished for staging purposes— with nothing remaining now but the refrigerator and stove that came with the unit and the garage door clicker resting on the counter beside an envelope.

She looked around the kitchen first, then wandered into the living room, imagining everything she could do with the place now that it was hers. The idea of having complete freedom of the space, designing and decorating entirely her decisions, was better than she imagined. She took a deep breath, let it out slowly, and smiled. Her eyes then darted upward when she heard a *creak* from upstairs.

"Must be the neighbors," she said, then made her way back to the kitchen to grab the clicker and enter the garage, which was somehow more eerie than the rest of the condo, given the dull coloring, concrete floor, and it being much colder. However, there was a washer and dryer in the corner—two necessary appliances that she had hoped would be included—so she raised her hands in praise and cheered her little win. Then, she clicked the button to open the garage door and after a brief pause, it rumbled awake and slid upward until she saw her car staring back at her.

She wasted no time hopping in and bringing it inside. While the garage door closed behind her, she opened the trunk and stared at her few belongings: a plastic bag containing a deflated air mattress and its accompanying pump, two duffel bags for the small amount of clothing she'd kept, her toiletries, a pair of towels, a small blanket, a pillow, and a handful of books she planned on reading over the summer. She was usually a fan of romance—leaning toward erotica—but considering her recent change in relationship status, she was feeling more self-help and true crime this time around.

It took her two trips to get everything inside, leaving it all in the living room, too tired to try to bring it upstairs. Then, she walked to her front door to make sure she locked it—you can never be too safe—and went back into the living room to unfold the air mattress and connect it to the pump. With a *flick*, the air pump roared to life and the mattress slowly inflated like a person's chest inhaling.

She watched it for a brief moment, realizing quickly that it was going to be a while before it finished. With her stiff muscles and sore back from the long drive, rather than sitting and waiting for the bed to finish inflating, she would make her way upstairs and start drawing a bath.

She took her shoes off and placed them against the partition wall, then removed her socks. Holding them in her hand, she realized that she didn't have a hamper for her dirty clothes. She sighed and raised her right arm to rub the tightness out of her neck.

"Add a hamper to the shopping list, I guess," she said, then tossed her socks in the corner of the room. She looked back at the air mattress, checking its progress, and it had finally started to look less like a tarp and more like something that *could* end up being comfortable. She walked around it to get back to the hallway and peeked up the stairs. They were dark and uninviting, as was the floor above, which was entirely pitch-black. Looking at the two light switches on the wall to her right, one of them was flicked up in the on position and the other down for off.

She flicked the latter up, and the dim light above her head lit up the small space by the front door, but the upper portion of the home remained unlit. She then flicked the other light switch down and saw the porch light shut off through the tiny window at the top of the front door.

"I was really hoping that would work," she said about the light switch potentially illuminating the top of the staircase. After one last look around the front area of the condo, she came to terms with the fact that there weren't any other light switches, then began her walk upstairs.

The carpet that lined the steps beneath her feet was soft and soothing—a distinct upgrade from her apartment's floors, which were cold hardwood. She knew hardwood was the favored flooring and that carpeting would be more difficult to clean, but she always preferred carpet. She grew up with it, so it made her feel more at home, and she thought it looked better too. Oh, and she was a rather clumsy person, so the softness was appreciated when she would trip and crash to the floor. Which is just what she did when she reached, or thought she'd reached, the landing. Stepping upward, unsuspecting one more stair, she banged her foot against the last, *hidden* one and fell forward, slamming her knee onto the floor first, then her chest, then her hands in an attempt to catch herself, and lastly, her forehead.

"Ouch, dammit!" she yelled, rolling over and sitting up at the top of the stairs. She tossed her hands around, shaking them off and feeling the soreness that centralized in her wrists. "That's gonna hurt tomorrow," she said, then brought her hand up to her head, rubbed the place of impact, and winced when she felt the bruise beneath. "And, of course, I don't have any ice."

Wait, she thought, tilting her head and picturing the refrigerator-freezer combo in her kitchen. *Did that have an ice maker?*

Before she could remember, a *creak* came from what sounded like Chloe's bedroom.

"Hello?" she asked, trying to look into the room through the banister that divided the upper floor from the staircase, but it was still pitch-black. Deciding that she was only scaring herself, she told herself again that it was the neighbors. "They probably hate me already," she said about the sound of her fall. She wasn't even sure exactly what time it was, but for someone to arrive this late at night and make all this noise when this unit had been empty for who knows how long would be annoying to anybody.

She then turned her head, looking around the upper floor, searching for light switches, but it was too dark to see any. She reached her hands back, closely behind her butt to check for another step before she rose to her feet, feeling the pain in her freshly bruised knee as it straightened.

"Ahh," she moaned painfully until she was standing tall, and carefully lifted one foot at a time up the stairs, rubbing her toes against the carpet, feeling once again for the final step—just to be safe—and once she felt confident, marched to the closest open door, reached her hand inside the room, and felt along the wall until she found the light switch. She flicked it up, lighting the bathroom and a good portion of the hallway through the doorframe, just enough for her to see the switch in the hall. She stepped to it and flicked it up, but nothing happened. Confused, she scanned the visible parts of the ceiling, noticing that there were not any installed lights for this hall *or* the staircase. She then looked down at the wall and saw the outlet in the corner, making the connection that this switch was responsible for turning that outlet on and off, so she would need to purchase a floor lamp if she wanted any light up here.

"Just another thing for the list." She sighed.

Giving up on that, she stepped back into the bathroom and inspected the room, appreciating it at first, then noticing how empty it was. Sure, there was a toilet, a bathtub, a sink, and a mirror, but that was it. No soap, no towel rack, no toilet paper, no plunger, and not even a shower curtain.

"This list is getting long," she said, stepping to the tub, analyzing the faucet, and fiddling with the handles until water poured from it. She put the toilet lid down and sat on it so she could hold one hand under the spout and use the other to adjust the temperature, taking a good thirty seconds to figure out how to work it, then another twenty to get the temperature right—just hot enough to sting. She plugged the drain with the stopper that she was glad came pre-installed—because she wouldn't have one otherwise—and made her way back downstairs, taking each step carefully and partially limping because the pain in her knee was worsening.

When she got to the living room, the air mattress was looking a lot more solid. She pressed her hand into it, testing the air pressure. It wasn't quite ready yet. She then moved to her duffels and dug through one, removing a towel before carrying the bag to the stairs and dropping it below the second step to bring up with her toiletries. Then, she took the towel to the freezer, opened it, and cheered upon seeing the functioning ice maker. With her towel, she grabbed a handful of ice and wrapped it up, forming a makeshift ice pack, and closed the freezer.

"How does the saying go?" she thought aloud, considering whether the ice or the warm bathwater would be better for her bruise. "Ice first, heat later, right?" She shrugged her shoulders and made her way back up the stairs, grabbing the duffel bag before ascending.

Back in the bathroom, she peered into the tub and found it about half full. Placing her ice pack beside the sink, she swung the door closed with just enough effort to leave it slightly cracked and dropped her duffel behind it before slipping out of her pants, first dropping them to the floor, then stepping out of each leg one foot at a time. She sat on the closed toilet, crossing her injured leg over the other to glance at her knee and wincing at the sight of the gnarly bruise. She shook her head, embarrassed by her clumsiness, and reached for the ice pack, stopping with her hand hovering over it when she heard a *bang* from a door closing downstairs, thinking, *Was that in **my** house?*

"Hello?" she called out over the streaming bathwater echoing in the room. With no response, she wanted to tell herself it was the neighbors again, but she couldn't help feeling uncertain this time. *Was it the landlord?* she wondered, then scared herself with another, more uncomfortable thought. *Did the landlord keep a copy of the key?*

Talking herself out of it, she snatched the ice pack and pressed it to her knee, peeking through the crack in the doorway. Sweat formed on her forehead, partially because of the steam from the bath but also from her newfound anxiety. After almost a full minute of looking through that crack, she heard a strange rumbling coming from her side, causing her to jump up from her seat and back up against the wall as if a monster had emerged directly from her bathwater and lunged for her. When she gathered herself, she realized the tub was full, and the rumbling came from the overflow drain doing its job.

I don't like this alone thing as much as I hoped I would, she thought, cooling herself down by wiping the now-damp ice pack against her forehead. She stepped into the tub, twisted the knob, and the water stopped pouring. Then she placed her ice pack into the sink and grabbed her shirt from the bottom, crossing both arms across her belly as she lifted up. As it went over her head, the overflow drain had silenced, and she heard something else. Something unmistakable.

Footsteps ascending the stairs—*her* stairs.

"Shit," she said, letting her shirt fall back to its original place. She then used her right hand to pull the shirt down in the front, covering her panties. "Hello?" she called out once more, louder and without the water running, so whoever was in the condo would be able to hear her—no excuse.

Then she looked through the crack once more, stepping up to it this time, and was confused as to how it looked darker outside until she recognized that the light by her front door, which should've been illuminating at least the bottom half of the stairs, had been turned off.

"Is someone there?" she asked as the footsteps stopped, grabbing the knob with her available hand and opening it wider, hoping the bathroom light would be enough to illuminate whoever should be just outside the door now. Yet, just as that gap was open enough for her to poke her head through, something shiny came flying toward her.

A knife.

Held by someone hiding behind the doorframe wearing a black leather glove, this knife brightly reflected the bathroom light and flew across Chloe's peripheral vision like a comet, until it pierced her skull, just above the bridge of her nose.

The force of it sent her falling backward, crashing into the bathroom vanity, and banging her head against the mirror on the wall above it, shattering the glass and cutting her scalp before she collapsed onto the floor.

With blurry vision, and without the mental capability of registering what was even happening, she looked up from the linoleum as the hand, still holding the knife, reached in and flicked the light switch, leaving Chloe in cold darkness.

Chapter 1

*B*uzz! *Buzz! Buzz!*

Hailey's alarm vibrated beneath her pillowcase, a usually unwelcome start to her morning, but not today. Today, she awoke excited and optimistic. She opened her eyes and rubbed the blurriness away before reaching beneath her pillow, grabbing her phone, and pulling the screen to her face.

The alarm read *Back to school*.

It was the same alarm she always set on school nights but this time, those words had a bit more meaning. Today was the first day following winter break. Meaning: she was going into her final semester of high school, and she decided she was going to enjoy this time while she still could.

She jumped out of bed and showered before rushing through her morning routine of teeth brushing, gargling mouthwash, brushing her still-wet hair, getting dressed, and putting on her makeup—usually just a quick application of lipstick, but with her extra cheeriness to get out of bed this morning, she had more than enough time to add blush and eyeliner. Then, she walked downstairs, stepping over the newest member of her household: Park Ranger Woodsby—the emotional support dog she inherited from her time at camp, currently sleeping on the floor beneath the final step. She headed to the kitchen, where she poured some Fruit Loops into a bowl and sat at the dining table, with Woodsby now lying beside her chair while she ate and scrolled through her phone.

Her adoptive mother, Alexa, and her wife, Megan, came into the kitchen one after the other, both dressed in adorable, matching flannel pajamas with their hair a mess.

"You're up early," Alexa said, grabbing the old coffee pot and bringing it to the sink for rinsing.

"And you look all ready to go," Megan said, pinching Hailey's cheek as she walked by her to take a seat at the end of the table. "Cute, even."

"Don't ruin it," Hailey said, shooing her hand away. "I've got to leave as soon as I finish eating."

"Are you excited?" Alexa asked, starting the coffee pot. Both her moms stared at her intently with smiles on their faces, as if they were more excited than she was.

"I guess," she said, downplaying her feelings as most high schoolers do with their parents.

"I bet you are. Your last semester is a big deal," Alexa said. The coffee percolated behind her as the water boiled.

"Yeah, but it's not like today is special. It's just another school day," Hailey said.

"Maybe, but I think it is more important than you realize. Your classes are gonna start speeding up as they prepare you for graduation," Alexa said.

"And you're on the prom committee!" Megan chimed in. "You're gonna have a lot more to do in that role since the dance is just a few months away."

She was right. Her friends somehow convinced her to join the committee a few months back, and her best friend and fellow Camp Safe Woods Squirrel Cabin Camper, Ale, was already bugging her about their upcoming fundraiser plans.

"Being busy isn't something to be excited about—"

Knock, knock, knock.

The knocking came from the front door. The three of them looked at each other, confused, while Woodsby let out a deep rumbling growl.

"Were you expecting somebody?" Alexa asked, looking at Hailey.

She puckered her bottom lip and shook her head.

"I'll get it," Megan offered, reluctantly getting out of her seat and trudging through the kitchen and down the hall as if she had just gotten out of bed.

"It's way too early for solicitors," Alexa said, pouring coffee into two separate mugs. "Did you want a cup?"

"No, thanks," Hailey answered.

"Really? You're almost an adult. I guess you'll be drinking it soon enough—"

"Hey, you guys! Can you come here?" Megan called from the front door. Alexa and Hailey shared a look of confusion.

"Both of us?" Hailey asked. Alexa shrugged her shoulders and led the way as Hailey took her last bite of cereal before following. Woodsby stayed behind, resting his head atop his paws.

Outside the front door stood a police officer and his partner, both pacing with their brows furrowed, expressing concern behind their sunglasses.

"Police? Is everything okay?" Alexa asked as they approached, directing the question more to Megan than to the officers.

"Hey there, I'm Officer Ronald. I was hoping to speak with Hailey," he said, shifting his head to look past Alexa to Hailey. "I'm assuming that's you?"

Hailey prepared to nod, but Alexa interrupted.

"Can you tell us what this is about?"

"I'm sure there's no cause for concern." The officer held out a cautionary hand as if trying to calm her, though he had no idea just how calm Alexa was. If she were upset in any fashion, they'd know. "Now, you are Hailey, ain't ya?"

Hailey nodded and said, "Yes, sir." Sarcasm seeped from her voice.

"All right." He stood tall and adjusted his belt. "Now, would you mind telling me where you were last night? Between the hours of—"

"She was here, at home," Alexa said, gritting her teeth as she lost her patience. "Except for about half an hour between five and six in the evening when we sent her to grab some pizza."

Officer Ronald looked at Alexa, clearly annoyed that she was answering rather than Hailey.

"Is that right?" he asked, his head tilted down so he could look at Hailey directly over the rim of his sunglasses.

"Yeah," Hailey said roughly and cleared her throat. She was telling the truth but felt nervous, regardless, because she had never been interrogated before.

"Okay, now can you just tell us what this is about?" Alexa asked.

"I'm sure whatever it is, Hailey had nothing to do with it," Megan said.

Officer Ronald cleared his throat. "So . . . we're here for . . . Well, have you ladies heard of somebody by the name of Christopher Atkins?"

Hailey's heart sank in her chest. Of all the reasons this officer would be standing outside her doorstep, this was the last one on her mind. Alexa tilted her head at the officer, as if he was close to sparking a memory, but Megan looked flat out confused.

"That name sounds . . . familiar," Alexa said.

"Really? I don't think I've heard it before." Megan shook her head.

Officer Ronald looked at Hailey. "Care to fill them in?"

Hailey sighed and said, "He's my … Well, he's a prisoner and we've been pen pals for about a year now." She held back her answer just a bit because she wasn't sure if Alexa would recognize the name or not. If she knew the full truth, she'd freak out, so keeping that from her seemed like the right choice at the time.

"You what?" Alexa asked, anger and confusion straining in her voice.

Hailey dropped her head as though she was embarrassed by her actions, but also as if she was saying, "Oh well."

"The officer raised his hand to calm Alexa down before saying, "Well, he escaped from prison last night."

So much for calming her down, Hailey thought. Alexa's eyes were opened so wide, they looked like they were going to fall right out of their sockets.

"As you can see, with Hailey being one of his pen pals, we just had to come down here as a formality. You know, make sure she didn't have anything to do with it," he said.

"She sure as *shit* didn't have anything to do with it!" Alexa said, turning back to Hailey. "A prisoner pen pal is questionable enough, but you had to go and pick the one that would break out? Really?"

"How was I supposed to know?" Hailey shrugged.

"How *did* he break out?" Megan asked.

"That's what we're trying to figure out," Officer Ronald said. "The security cameras were shut off, and the men in charge of watching the prisoners all died. On top of that, his cellmate is dead, plus four more corrections officers and the driver of one of the garbage trucks."

"It sounds like you know exactly how he got out," Hailey said.

"Well, we have our theories, but we do know that he needed help. We're just trying to find out who it was."

"Like we said, Hailey was with us, so you can go ahead and cross her name off your little list," Alexa insisted.

He smiled an unthankful smile at her and said, "Will do. Thank you." He brought his attention to Hailey. "Now, if you don't mind . . . do you happen to have any of the letters he sent you?"

She shook her head. "I . . . threw them away," she said, realizing how bad that sounded. "I didn't want them to know I was sending him letters," she added, pointing back and forth between Alexa and Megan.

"I'm sure you didn't," Alexa said.

"All right, well . . . can you tell us a little about what he would write to you about?" Officer Ronald asked.

"Just normal things. Nothing crazy," Hailey answered.

"Care to elaborate?"

"Yes, please," Alexa said. "I'd love to hear what interesting things this *prisoner* had to say to you."

"Like I said, nothing crazy. He would just tell me about his life inside. What he would eat on the daily, what kind of work he was doing. Washing clothes and stuff. And I would just, like, update him on the news and stuff," Hailey said.

"Oh my gosh, Hailey, did you tell him where you live? What does he know about us? He's not gonna come *here*, is he? I swear, if an escaped prisoner shows up at my doorstep, I'll fucking—"

"I'm not dumb, Alexa," Hailey said, not calling her "Mom" for the first time since her return from Camp Safe Woods.

Alexa stepped back with her right hand on her chest, offended. Hailey didn't care as much as she should've because she was offended herself—with Alexa questioning her like this.

"Well how am *I* supposed to know that? Penpalling a prisoner is a pretty dumb thing to do, and I can't think of a single reason that *you*, of all people, would do something like that," she said.

Hailey sucked her teeth and stalled before saying, "It's because he . . . he's my father."

Alexa stared back at her like she was betrayed. Megan gasped, and the officer pulled a small notepad from his back pocket and began scribbling in it.

"I'm sorry, did you say he's your father?" he asked, then pointed his pen to Hailey's moms. "You two didn't know about this?"

Alexa shook her head, not at him, but at Hailey. Disappointed.

"We didn't—" Megan started.

"I knew I recognized his name," Alexa interrupted. "But I never thought I'd hear it again."

"Neither of these two is my biological mom," Hailey explained. "She died. As for my father, I never met him before. He went to jail soon after . . . well, I was conceived." She looked at Alexa, "Can you blame me for wanting to get to know him?"

"Yes, I can," Alexa said quietly—too pissed to speak how she'd really like to in front of the officer. "Elizabeth kept him out of your life for a *reason*. I don't even know why you would look for him! Is our family here not *enough* for you?" Her volume raised and lowered as she spoke, as her emotions ranged from anger to sadness. The tears that swelled in her eyes made Hailey feel only slight regret.

"So . . ." Officer Ronald interjected before Hailey and Alexa would fall deeper into a fight. "You have an alibi, which is good. We aren't concerned there, and we don't want to overstay our welcome, but can we at least confirm that you'd be willing to cooperate with us, assuming any more questions come up while we look for him?"

"Of course she will," Alexa said, never pulling her tear-filled, yet angry, gaze from Hailey.

Officer Ronald tipped his hat and said, "On that note, we'll let you get back to your morning," then stepped down from the porch and made his way toward the other officer by the car.

Megan closed the door behind him while Hailey and Alexa stared each other down.

"I just don't get it," Alexa said, breaking her stillness as she brought her hand up to wipe away the first tear that fell. "Are we . . . not good enough?"

Hailey shook her head, both embarrassed and upset that they found out this way.

"Why didn't you tell me you were looking for him? Or that you found him? Hell, even then, why would you reach out to him? He could be dangerous, Hailey." Alexa reached her hand out to grab Hailey's like a concerned parent would, but Hailey rejected it.

"I didn't tell him who I was, I swear. I-I," she stuttered, "I have to go." Hailey stormed to her room. She understood why Alexa was upset, but she didn't think she would take it this badly. She thought Alexa would have known her well enough by now to respect her judgment, but clearly not.

In her room, she grabbed her purse and backpack, then slipped on her shoes before stomping back to the front door where Megan and Alexa still were—Megan hugging Alexa to comfort her as Alexa buried her tear-riddled face against Megan's chest. Hailey ignored both of them, reaching over Megan's shoulder to pull her car keys from the hook beside the door, then left.

Chapter 2

Following the abrupt end to what should've been a good morning, Hailey wasn't as optimistic about returning to Pineside High School. She parked her car and sighed, wondering if she should've stayed back to talk with Alexa about everything and beginning to regret how she'd acted. Sitting in the driver's seat, she pulled her phone from her pocket, scrolled to her messages with Alexa, and thought of what to type—some way to say what she needed to regarding her choice to reach out to her father, but also apologize and retract her behavior. When nothing came to mind, she sighed once again, dropped her cell into her purse on the passenger's seat, grabbed it along with her backpack, and stepped out of the car.

Pineside High wasn't the big and pretty school that Hailey and Ale's fellow Squirrel Cabin Camper, Billy, promised it was when he convinced them to move to his city for their senior year so the trio could stay close together following what happened at Camp Safe Woods. Apparently the occupants of the small California town,

Meadowood, voted on a proposition to spend an exorbitant amount of taxpayer money to renovate the schools in an attempt to attract people to buy property for homes and expand the town. Because of this proposition, Hailey had spent her senior year staring at a school covered in white tarps and scaffolding, plus attending a portion of her classes in trailers just beyond the main under-construction school buildings, all while listening to lectures over the roars of heavy machinery.

It wasn't all bad, though, because she *did* have her friends, which was more than she could say about any of her other years in school—a big bargaining chip for convincing Alexa and Megan to move to Meadowood. That, plus the guilt of sending her to Camp Safe Woods against her wishes and the deaths she had witnessed there, clinched the deal.

From the parking lot, Hailey made her way to the narrow walkway between the old library and art building, white tarps covering the construction on both structures eerily flapping with the morning breeze. Hailey would often joke with her friends that the walkway looked like a set from a horror film—an opinion shared by the majority of school-goers, as most opted to take the long way around the buildings to the front quad—but Billy insisted it looked great before the construction and would look awesome when it was finished. The part he seemed to be forgetting, though, was that the construction wouldn't be finished until after they graduated, and Hailey had no intention of ever coming back once she was done.

Hailey rushed through the walkway as she did every morning—just in case—but as she made it to the end, someone jumped out from behind the tarp on the right side and yelled, "Boo!"

She yelped and took a step backward, an instinct she'd developed to distance herself from a surprise attacker to give her a bit more time to analyze the situation and decide her next move. The conclusion of her not-so-quick analysis was that she wasn't actually under attack; it was just Ale with a stack of papers hugged tightly to her chest and a big smirk on her laughing face.

"You should know better by now," Hailey said. She may have only attended Camp Safe Woods for a few days, but she left with a lot more fears and a lot more survival sense. Ale on the other hand, came out of the experience the same girl she was when she went in—pretty, charismatic, funny, aloof, too oblivious for her own good. And as far as Hailey was concerned, calling Ale "funny" was debatable.

"Someone's gotta keep you on your toes, right?" Ale raised up on her tiptoes in her white Vans as if providing an example.

"The last time someone had me on my toes, they died," Hailey said, more anger in her tone than she intended, as she started walking farther into school, toward her classroom on the opposite side of campus.

"Ooh, someone's feisty today," Ale said, acknowledging that anger and following. "But you can't kill me. If you did, you'd be all on your own to pick out your prom dress, and we *both* know what kind of disaster that would be. Oh! Speaking of,"—Ale took a step forward to get beside Hailey as she handed her one of the papers she held—"the votes came in and we have our prom theme."

In neon-pink letters, the title read *'80s Prom Night*.

Beneath it were poorly placed clip art images, all representing prom with a neon dance floor and several people dancing on it, a DJ at a turntable, and a disco ball—which Hailey immediately thought was more '70s but recognized that Ale made this flyer herself, and she seemed proud.

"Eighties, huh?" Hailey asked. "I thought for sure people would've voted for the Hawaiian theme."

"It wasn't even close. Once the principal got on the intercom to make the formal announcement that girls wouldn't be allowed to wear those skimpy coconut bras, Hawaiian lost the entire male vote."

"The guys really thought girls would've worn that?" Hailey asked, swinging her backpack around to her front to stuff the prom flyer inside.

"Are you telling me you wouldn't?" Ale asked, waving at Billy ahead, who looked up from his phone and hustled to them. He wore a basic navy polo with khakis, along with a disposable face mask—the flimsy kind people wore during the pandemic, though he wasn't wearing it because of any virus. He wore it to cover the vicious scar that Oliver Vance—a.k.a. Head Counselor Nick of Camp Safe Woods—left across his face, extending his smile from his mouth to his ear.

"Hey, guys," he said, his voice muffled beneath the mask.

"Here,"—Ale handed him a prom flyer—"the votes are in." He took it and quickly looked it over.

"Eighties? I was hoping for Wild West," Billy said.

Ale raised her palm to her forehead in disappointment. "Billy, with all due disrespect, you were *literally* the only person to vote for Wild West. Seriously. I counted the votes, and it was just *one*. You."

"I thought cowboy boots, bandannas, and suspenders sounded like a fun time," he said, shrugging.

"Bullshit, you just wanted to see me in a tight corset," Ale retorted. "And will you take that thing off? I can barely hear you," she added about his mask. She didn't realize how inconsiderate she was being, knowing full well why he wore it. Hailey knew his pain because she was forced to wear an ugly scar from that night too. And while Ale spent most of their time at Camp Safe Woods injured, she somehow came out of it as the only one of the three without so much as a blemish to remember it by—her damaged ankle fully healed to its natural smooth skin just weeks after she'd made it home. However, Billy was used to this from her because she had been teasing him about his mask every day for the entire school year—so he did this time what he always did and ignored her remark, leading the way as they continued walking through the school.

"So," Billy began, breaking the awkward-ish silence, "did you guys make your preparations for the fundraiser? It's coming up pretty quickly." He was talking about the fundraiser they were in charge of, being members of the school's prom committee, for the purpose of raising money to cover the cost of prom since Pineside was reluctant to spend too much considering their ongoing renovations.

"We should be good to go. Mrs. Ivory told me she'd reserve the Meadowood Community Center over break. I'll double-check with her when I get to class," Hailey said.

"And I've got *most* of the senior cheerleaders on board. They should be enough if the others don't change their minds," Ale added.

"Honestly, I'm surprised Principal Collins is letting you guys do that," Billy said about Ale's fundraiser plan: a sexy cheerleader car wash. She left the word "sexy" out of her proposal to the principal, but it was heavily implied.

"You know he's a little pervert. Besides, if we relied on *your* idea, there'd be zero funding for prom. We'd dance to music from Principal Collins's personal playlist over the intercom speakers," Ale said. Billy's idea was a bit more tame and common: a bake sale. Having combined both ideas, the plan was for them to rent out the Meadowood Community Center and encourage townsfolk to come get their cars washed by the high school's senior cheerleaders in the parking lot while the rest of the prom committee sold cookies and other baked goods outside nearby.

"Since Eighties is the theme, the playlist probably won't be much different from his anyway. Besides, I'm sure the bake sale will earn more than your jailbait car wash scheme," Billy said.

"Hey, there's nothing jailbaity about it. The cheerleaders are all adults . . . Well, most of them. Or . . . some of them. Okay, you know what?" Ale's tone shifted from playful to aggressive. "How about we bet on it?"

"Bet on what?"

"Which of our ideas earns more money."

"Uh, sure," Billy said. "What's the prize?"

"It depends."

"On what?"

"How seriously you believe you'll win," Ale said confidently.

Billy thought about it for a brief moment before answering, "Pretty serious."

"So that's it, then," Ale said, taking an extra step to get in front of them before turning on her heels and stopping. "The winner gets to pick the loser's outfit for prom."

"Whoa, that's a lot of power!" Hailey exclaimed.

Billy looked equally surprised and excited at the opportunity. "Yeah, are you sure about that? You might end up attending prom in a pantsuit."

"Ew, I'd rather go naked," Ale said, drawing looks from an emo couple sitting against the brick wall beside the door to the 700 hallway, where Billy and Ale's first class of the day would be.

Hailey pushed the door open and stepped inside, then her friends followed. The hall was busy with kids and teachers bustling through, chatting by lockers, stepping in and out of classrooms, etc. One kid slurped water from a questionable fountain while another did a turnaround jump shot, tossing a crumpled paper ball over him and down the hall toward a trash bin, only for a rushing teacher to bust through a door and step outside, intercepting the paper ball with the side of her head. She yelled something indistinguishable beneath the hallway chatter.

"We'll have rules, of course." Ale continued with her proposition. "I mean, the *whole* outfit can't be an embarrassment, so pantsuits are completely off the table."

"Well that's no fun," Hailey said as they stopped beside the door to Ale and Billy's class.

"Wear one yourself, then," Ale said, turning to look at her.

"You're really serious about this?" Billy asked.

"As serious as a penguin with a clipboard," she said.

"What does that even mean?" Hailey asked, as something poked the back of her shoulder just enough to cause a slight spike in her heart rate. She turned to find the high school mascot— Penny the Penguin—standing too close for comfort, and with a black glove hidden on the underside of her fin, she held a clipboard with a stack of papers attached and a pen connected to it by a beady string. "What the hell?"

Penny didn't answer, only nodded her head toward the clipboard.

"You want me to take it?" Hailey asked. Penny nodded excitedly. Hailey listened and grabbed the clipboard, saying, "You know you can just talk like a regular person, right?"

Penny shook her head in disappointment. Nobody knew Penny's true identity under the mask, and they weren't supposed to know until graduation. Nobody knew except Hailey, who caught the school's lovable mascot slipping out of her costume in the girls' locker room after a football game.

The mysterious girl behind the mask was a popular blonde named Maddie, apparently a talented tumbler on the cheer squad who quit once the opportunity to put on the Penny mask presented itself. Hailey found this out earlier in the year when, after a football game that Ale dragged her to, Hailey snuck into the girls' locker room because she had forgotten a textbook she needed for homework that weekend and found Maddie changing out of the costume.

Maddie was also quite close friends with Ale, but they'd been at odds ever since she couldn't understand why Maddie quit the cheer squad. Hailey felt bad about this because after having discovered Maddie's secret, she became the only person the girl could talk to about these secret problems, making the two of them friends—an internal issue for Hailey since she now had to hear both sides of their drama. She's tried convincing Maddie to tell her secret to Ale, but she wouldn't budge, taking her role with serious pride.

Hailey scanned the paper atop the stack on the clipboard; the title read *PETITION: KEEP THE PINESIDE PENGUIN ALIVE*. Beneath that was a brief statement: *With the current renovations to improve the school, Pineside High is making plans that are both good and bad for the future of its students. At the top of the list of cons is the changing of our beloved mascot, Penny the Penguin. They want to bring a fresh new face to the city, and that just isn't right. WE ARE THE PINESIDE PENGUINS. Sign your name below to let them know you want to keep Penny!*

Below the statement were numerous blank lines and half the page was filled with student signatures.

"They want to get rid of Penny?" Billy asked, peeking at the petition over Hailey's shoulder.

Hailey scanned through the stack of papers, confirming that they were all identical pages full of signatures. "There's no way the students would ever allow this," she said. "There are so many signatures already—"

Maddie, from behind the penguin mask, lifted her stuffy arm and pointed at the pen dangling from the clipboard.

"No question," Hailey said, snatching the pen and signing her name on a blank line.

"Give me that," Ale said, grabbing the clipboard and signing her name before handing it to Billy.

"Thanks," he said, signed his name, then offered it back to Penny, who clapped her fins before grabbing the clipboard and waddling away, fully in character.

"What a weirdo," Ale said, and the first bell of the morning rang above them.

"Already?" Hailey sighed. "I've gotta run to class."

"Good luck," Billy said.

Hailey started down the hallway, then stopped after about three steps, turning back to see Billy holding the class door open for Ale.

"Wait," she said, stopping Ale from stepping inside.

"What's up?" Ale asked.

"I need to talk to you guys about . . . something," Hailey said, thinking back to her morning with the police. She wasn't sure if she wanted to vent to them about Alexa's reaction to the situation or just share how crazy of a story it was that her father would escape from prison. Ale already knew about him and Hailey penpalling, but Billy was in for the start of a crazy story.

"Is everything okay?" Billy asked.

"Yeah . . . I mean, I think so." At first she thought it was an easy answer, but Alexa instilled the unreasonable fear in her that her actions might actually have consequences here. "We'll talk later," Hailey said and nodded, affirming.

Ale and Billy shared an awkward look, as if both thinking, *What is she on about?* Then Hailey turned and hurried to class.

Chapter 3

Riiiing!

The school bell rang, declaring the first class in session and the semester officially underway. Hailey placed her purse on her desk and hung her backpack on the chair before taking her seat. She scrolled aimlessly through her phone for about thirty seconds before her teacher, Mrs. Ivory, a young lady with straight, jet-black hair, stepped through the door—not scurrying like teachers do when they're running late, but stepping confidently and proudly, as if the class should be thankful she even showed up at all. She walked in these outrageously tall stilettos that she always wore, giving an impressive stature to her otherwise small frame.

She carelessly dropped her laptop bag on her desk as she walked around it and leapt into her chair, rolling across the class a good three feet, swiveling it in a full circle before it stopped, then she leaned her head back, pointing her face to the ceiling. It was this unprofessional demeanor of hers that made her the favorite teacher of many students,

Hailey included. In fact, she was probably the only teacher in all of Hailey's years of high school that she actually enjoyed having conversations with.

"You look a little tired there, Mrs. Ivory," said Grace—honorary teacher's pet, front-runner for valedictorian, head of the prom committee, and student body president. "Are you okay?"

Mrs. Ivory dragged her head back down as if she were annoyed and said, "Yeah, I'm just"—she lowered her cat-eye glasses to the bridge of her nose to see who was asking, then nodded like it was obvious upon seeing Grace—"a little hungover." This drew a few chuckles from the class as she stood up and stepped to her desk, her stilettos click-clacked against the tile with each step. She unzipped her bag and pulled her laptop from within, then opened it and slammed it on the desk. She looked back up at all the students staring at her. "What, did nobody else enjoy their winter break?"

The class then drew their attention to the door as it swung open and Maddie came rushing in looking like an unorganized mess with frizzy hair and her textbooks held to her chest. She dropped the stack of books onto the empty desk beside Hailey—one of them falling to the floor—and took her seat, bending down to pick up the fallen book. Sure, she was late and unprepared, but Hailey was impressed with how quickly she'd stripped out of the penguin costume and made it to class.

"Glad you could make it, Madelyn," Mrs. Ivory said. She always made a point to call people by their government names, even after asking them what their preferences were. Hailey wasn't sure whether she liked teasing the students or was just too carefree to remember anything outside of what was on the attendance sheet. Mrs. Ivory brought her elbows onto the desk and clasped her fingers together, providing a self-made perch for her to rest her chin on. "Did *you* do anything special over the break?"

"Huh? Oh!" Maddie said, confused, "I visited my cousins for Christmas."

Mrs. Ivory puckered her lower lip like she was unimpressed. "All right, anybody else wanna share what they did?"

Jackson, the pitcher of the school's baseball team, who looked like he would either grow up to be a star pitcher in the big leagues or the manager of a pizza joint, raised his hand and said, "Yeah, so me and the boys . . . "

Hailey quickly tuned him out and kicked Maddie's ankle to grab her attention. "Hey, did you hear they're trying to kill off Penny the Penguin?" she whispered sarcastically.

"Really, though, can you believe that?" she said, probably louder than she intended, drawing a side-eye from Mrs. Ivory, who was pretending to be interested in Jackson's story about a ski trip.

"It's a little crazy, I guess. Do you have any idea what they're replacing her with?" Hailey asked.

"Does it matter? Penny has been an icon in this city for years! They can't just get rid of her," she said.

"I didn't think you'd get so bent out of shape over it. I mean,"—Hailey looked around, confirming nobody was listening to them—"it's not like you'll keep wearing the costume after you graduate this year."

"It's just hard to hear that this character that I, and so many others, have grown to love over time, can just be killed off so easily. It feels like such a waste"—she crossed her arms and slouched in her seat—"after all the time I spent bringing her to life."

"That must suck," Hailey said just as Jackson finally finished his story. Mrs. Ivory perked up, eager to move on to something else, then sighed when Grace raised her hand because she knew she was about to get sucked into another boring story.

"For *my* winter break, I collected canned foods from my neighborhood to donate to the local homeless shelter," Grace started, drawing a collective sigh from multiple classmates, plus a silent one from Mrs. Ivory, who slouched in her seat.

The rest of class went by quickly, as Mrs. Ivory let all the students share their winter break stories because she didn't want to "overload us with work so early in the semester." But Hailey believed it was really because she wasn't kidding about being hungover and just wanted to relax. By the time it was over, Hailey had fallen asleep at her desk, only to be woken up when the bell rang, dismissing them from class. After wiping the dried drool from her cheek, she quickly gathered her things and made her way for the door, but Mrs. Ivory stopped her before she could exit.

"Hailey, can you stay behind a moment?"

"Is everything okay?" she asked, one foot out the door.

"I was gonna ask you the same thing."

Hailey stepped back inside. "Oh, yeah, sorry I fell asleep. I had a long morning."

"No, that's fine. Between you and me, a couple of their stories put me to sleep too. I just couldn't help but notice that you seem to be upset about something."

This caught Hailey by surprise. *Did my face make it that obvious?*

"You know you can talk to me. Have you been having nightmares again?" Mrs. Ivory asked. If there was one thing Hailey gained from her time at Camp Safe Woods, it was her ability to talk to people about her problems, and Mrs. Ivory quickly became one of the only adult figures in her life she could talk to who didn't live in her home or require a phone call to reach.

"No, nothing like that. Like I said, it's been a long morning."

Mrs. Ivory chuckled and crossed her left leg over her right in her seat. "Tell me about it. And my day's just getting started. Six more classes to go, and I couldn't even get a coffee this morning." She grabbed a pen from her desk and brought it to her lips, lightly biting the end as she gazed off into the distance, irritated, as if imagining her reasoning for running late. She tapped the pen twice against her chin and looked back at Hailey. "You wanna know how I get through tough times? I like to find and isolate the cause of my problems and get rid of them. In my current case, that's a bit impossible since drinking too much the night before is what caused me to run late and miss out on my coffee, and I am *not* mentally stable enough to cut alcohol out of my life—" She stopped when she realized she was talking to a student and got back on track. "Look, whatever it is that's getting in the way of your happiness, get rid of it. Cut it out. It's not worth keeping around. I'm not sure if that applies to your situation because you haven't told me what your situation is, so I can only try to help as best I can based on limited knowledge."

"Thanks, I appreciate it." Hailey smiled to be nice, but she was failing to find how that advice would be helpful when the cause for stress at the moment was Alexa.

"You're still young. You need to enjoy that time. Take it from me, who is wasting my last good years working this shitty teacher job."

Hailey laughed.

"There's that smile." Mrs. Ivory continued. "Keep that going and you'll be all right."

"I'll try," Hailey said, glancing up at the clock to see how late this conversation was making her for the next class.

"Now, tell me. Prom's coming up . . . who's your date?" Her eyes brightened as she asked the question. Mrs. Ivory was always so interested in the school gossip that Hailey felt she probably missed being in high school herself. With her being quite an attractive young woman, Hailey assumed she would've been popular in high school, and her time there must've been amazing.

"My date?" Hailey took a step back as she noticed she spent more time worrying about planning the prom than figuring out who she'd go with. "I don't have one."

***

"What do you mean you don't have a date?" Ale asked, stepping forward in line as their fitness training classmates took turns at the diving board. Hailey walked alongside Ale, parallel to the line, excused from the diving session due to her claims of PTSD triggered by being submerged in water after the way she watched her mother die when she was a kid. While the story was true, her PTSD trigger was not; she just didn't want to wear a bathing suit in front of the other students for the same reason Billy wears his mask every day—she has a gnarly scar on her left side from a stab wound and subsequent surgery over the summer. Sure, she could wear a one-piece like some of the other girls in class, but she didn't own one, and she wasn't going to spend money on one just because of a little insecurity. Soon, the scar would start to look a lot better, and she could hop back into a skimpy, borderline dress-code violation of a swimsuit like the one Ale wore right now without feeling like everyone would stare at her in disgust. At least, that's what she told herself.

"Don't act so surprised. You don't have one either!" Hailey said, holding her hand high to block the sun from beaming into her eyes.

"*I* can go with whoever I want," Ale scoffed. "I'm just keeping myself available to see who impresses me with the most extravagant promposal." She stepped forward, following the next girl to climb the steps to the diving board. "What's *your* excuse? We both know you're gonna go with Billy."

Hailey's eyebrows furrowed. "You're joking, right? He's totally into you." The water splashed as the girl made her dive. Ale was up next.

"Of course he is. Every guy at this school is, but there's no way he'd have the courage to act on it. In his eyes, you're the attainable one."

"What's that supposed to mean?"

"Ale!" Coach Dudley yelled. He was a young heartthrob who attracted more attention from the female student body than any parent would be comfortable with. However, he always maintained a professional and sweet yet stern relationship with his students, saving his flirting for the female staff members of the school, most notably Mrs. Ivory. "Get your *ass* on that diving board!"

"Don't tell *me* what to do with my ass!" Ale said, taking steps up the ladder. "Or else you might get yourself in trouble," she added and prepared to make her dive.

"Sorry," Hailey said to him, partially apologizing out of secondhand embarrassment for her friend, but mostly for distracting her and holding up the line when she herself wasn't even participating. He just shook his head.

Ale made an unimpressive dive but compensated for it by exiting the pool and then flipping her hair back in an overly try-hard fashion, as if she were being filmed in slow motion for a 2000s-era frat comedy film.

"Are you sure you don't want to dive today?" Coach asked Hailey.

"I'm positive, thanks for asking," she said, walking to the opposite end of the pool where Ale was taking her time climbing up the ladder.

"All right, Jackson, you're up." Coach Dudley blew hard into the whistle hanging from his neck and Jackson stepped up to the diving board.

"Are you ready to go, or are you gonna sit here and wait for a guy to ask you to prom mid-dive?" Hailey teased.

"I'd tell him no before he hit the water." Ale laughed, stepping out of the pool just as Jackson dove in behind her, the water splashing high.

"Oh wow, is it that time already?" Coach Dudley asked, peeling his sleeve back to look at his watch and squinting to see through the sunlight reflecting off the swimming pool. He looked up and scanned the line of remaining students waiting to dive, then looked at the small set of bleachers where those who'd already gone were waiting and chatting. "We're running out of time here so once you're finished, you can head into the locker rooms and hit the showers. I know a lot of you are uncomfortable with the thought of showering in front of each other, but otherwise, you're gonna walk around campus smelling like chlorine all day, and that would be nauseating. Keep your suits on if you need to." He turned back to the line of waiting students. "Now, Grace, you're up!" He blew the whistle again, and she stepped up to the diving board while the rest of the class headed to the locker rooms.

"Joining us in the showers?" Ale teased Hailey, holding open the door for the girls' locker room.

"I'm sure you'd like that," Hailey said, walking inside. As she entered, to her left was a small area with poles containing four shower heads, one on each side. The walls separating the showers from the rest of the locker room were just chain-link fences that ran up to the ceiling. Through the fence opposite Hailey were the rows of lockers and benches. "You have fun in there," she said as Ale stepped into the showers. Hailey continued down the hall toward her locker.

She sat on the bench in front and leaned in to input her combination, then twisted the lock. It opened with a satisfying *click*. Although she didn't partake in the diving today, she was still required to wear her normal gym outfit. From inside the locker, she pulled out her regular clothes and changed into them. Just as she was slipping into her jeans, the bell rang above her. She grabbed her backpack from the locker and when she reached for her purse, she noticed something beneath it—the white corner of a piece of paper. She lifted her purse and saw that it was an unmarked envelope sealed tightly with what felt like a folded letter inside. She picked it up and thought, *Did I put this here?*

As she stood there examining it, Ale walked by and sat next to her, towel wrapped around her dripping wet body. "What's that?" she asked, as she opened her locker, pulled out her clothes, and placed them on the bench.

"I'm not sure. I just found it in my locker," Hailey answered.

"Oooh, a letter from a secret admirer! Did you open it?" Ale removed her towel, revealing the bathing suit she still wore underneath, and worked on drying her hair.

"No, not yet," she said, flipping the envelope over and examining both sides. "How did they get it in my locker?"

"Who cares? It was probably Billy! I'm sure he knows your combo." Ale twisted her hair up in the towel, her full attention devoted to the envelope.

"You really think so?" Hailey asked. Billy was a nice guy and a great friend, but she had never thought of him with any sort of attraction. They had been through something highly emotional and traumatic together, and from that, he'd become a figure in her life with whom she could talk about anything—a connection much deeper than a normal friend, but never once considered to be romantic. At least, not from Hailey's perspective. But one thing was for certain—someone *did* leave this envelope in her locker. Plus, given how pushy Ale was being about this, Hailey's mind started to race.

*Does Ale know something I don't? Did Billy feel some-thing **more** between us? Would I even be open to it if he did?*

"What are you waiting for? Open it!" Ale looked con-fused and antsy as she crossed her arms and leaned on one hip.

She was waiting because the contents inside had the potential to change the dynamic of a relationship she cher-ished. A change that she hadn't had the time to consider whether it would be for better or worse.

Hailey sighed. *Only one way to find out,* she thought as she slid her poorly polished fingernail beneath the flap, separating the envelope from the adhesive and tearing it open. She pulled out the paper inside.

Folded into thirds, in bright red marker the outside read *I made you a present.*

"Did a child write that?" Ale asked, chuckling. The handwriting was unfamiliar to Hailey, and it definitely wasn't Billy's. However, that could've been intentional because whoever was behind the letter clearly wanted this to be a surprise. It was written as though the marker was gripped with a full fist, leaving sharp jagged lines. She unfolded the letter to check the inside.

It read *Come to the baseball field and find it beneath the bleachers.*

"Aww, how cute! Asking you to prom with a scavenger hunt," Ale said, spewing an awkward mix of sarcasm and jealousy.

"Well, one thing's for certain. This isn't from Billy," Hailey said.

"Why do you say that? It's not unlike him to be this corny."

"Because he knows I don't like surprises." Hailey checked the back of the letter for anything else, but there was nothing.

"Well are you gonna go and find out?" Ale asked, scurrying to pick up her dry clothes from the bench.

Hailey looked up at the clock above the locker room exit door and saw that she only had three minutes to make it to class. "Not if I want to make it to class."

"But what if your secret admirer is waiting for you? This could be your only shot at having a date for prom."

"You're such a bitch. Besides, why would they be waiting for me? It says it's a present."

"Then you might want to go grab it before someone else does."

"You just want to skip class and come with me, don't you?" Hailey asked, knowing her friend too well.

Ale nodded frivolously.

"All right, but let's make it quick," Hailey said.

"Sweet!" Ale chirped, a bit too excited. "Just wait for me to get dressed."

Chapter 4

The baseball field was rather unimpressive because baseball season hadn't started yet, so nobody had taken the time to clean it up. Banners from last year still hung tattered and torn from the rusted backstop. Weeds grew tall in the outfield. Uneven mounds littered the field between the bases. The paint faded and split along the wooden exterior of the ticket booth. Graffiti desecrated the bleachers.

"This place looks like shit," Ale said bluntly.

"Not very romantic, is it?" Hailey agreed.

"That's putting it lightly. Now, which bleachers do you think?" Ale asked, looking ahead at the two sets—the larger behind the home team's dugout, and the much smaller behind the away team's.

"The large one, right? There's more shade to hide a present under them." Hailey continued walking toward the bleachers and Ale followed.

"Yeah, but people go under there to make out. Some random student would be more likely to find it there."

Ale stopped walking, silencing her shoes crunching on the gravel below. "Unless . . ."

Hailey stopped to make sure she was okay, instinctually suspecting something bad had happened as she always did, but Ale was fine.

"Unless a make-out session *is* the present," she said with a teasing grin. She nudged Hailey with her elbow as they resumed walking.

"I hope they're a little more creative than that," Hailey said, looking beneath the large bleachers, squinting to adjust her eyes to the shade. When they reached them, she crouched below a horizontal beam to get under the bleachers and Ale followed. She felt a drastic drop in temperature as she stepped out of the sunlight and into the shade. "Hello?" Hailey called out, hoping whoever was behind this scavenger hunt would step out from behind one of the pillars, but she was met only with the sound of the cold breeze picking up, blowing around the dust on the ground.

"I think I see someone over there." Ale pointed behind one of the large vertical posts holding up the bleachers, about halfway down. Hailey saw them, too, seated on the dirt, their back against the post and facing them.

Hailey stopped in her tracks. "Is that a girl?" she asked, quiet enough not to alert them if their early calling out hadn't done so already.

"Looks like it to me," Ale said, leaning in an overexaggerated, almost animated fashion to get a better view. "Which is cool, if you're into that."

Hailey crossed her arms and looked at her like she was dumb. "You know I'm not into that."

Ale threw her arms up. "How am *I* supposed to know that? You've never shown any interest in boys." She dropped her arms. "And whenever I want to talk to you about them, it's like talking to a wall."

"Well I've never shown interest in a *girl* either. Besides, whenever you talk about boys you only either talk about how frequently they come on to you, or you try to convince me that Billy has eyes for me."

"Look, all I'll say is, if someone held a knife to my throat and had me point a finger at a girl in our class who swung the other way, I might just point it at the girl who has *two moms* at home." She held her arm outstretched toward the figure on the ground as if inviting Hailey over and said, "Clearly, someone else had the same thought. Now, are you gonna keep stalling or go find out who your secret admirer is?"

"I hate you. Just . . . wait here." Hailey took a few steps toward the figure before she started to feel shaky. Then, a few more steps before a chill sent shivers down her spine, filling her arms with goose bumps. She hadn't had someone confess feelings for her since middle school, and even though the idea of it coming from a girl wasn't something she was into, the nervousness still felt the same. However, the feeling came from the thought of it being someone she knew closely and how that relationship might change when she let this poor person down. A lump wanted to form in her throat, but before she let it, she swallowed and shook away her nervousness, then marched forward the rest of the way.

The closer she got to them, the more Hailey wanted to gag with the rancid stench that formed in the air, which made her take notice of the mass of flies that were swarming the area.

Did some animal die down here? They really need to clean this place up.

She stepped around the post to confront the figure, and tried to say, "Hey," but couldn't even get *that* out before she saw them and stopped where she was, petrified.

She didn't recognize her, and probably couldn't have if she *did* know her. She wore a T-shirt but no pants or shoes. The shirt looked oversized, but only because her flesh had already decayed leaving behind these almost entirely skeletal remains. Patches of dulled blonde hair hung in streaks from her scalp past her shoulders. The flies flew in and out of the hollow holes in her head where her eyes once were, and the third hole in between them—a crack surrounded by shattered bone from the murder weapon that had clearly taken her life.

"Hailey?" Ale asked, likely seeing the multiple causes for concern from her friend's posture, but Hailey didn't hear her. All she could do was tremble until her weakened legs shook so much that she fell down to her knees, scraping them on the gravel. To try and get something, anything out, she went for a scream, but it was silenced—caught beneath the vomit that she spewed to her side. Once she got that out of her system, she heard Ale running toward her, and just as quickly heard the scream she wanted to release herself, only Ale managed to do so first.

***

"Attention, faculty and students," Principal Collins said into the landline phone on the desk, his voice echoing over the intercom. "After an extensive search, the police have determined that there is no threat. We are officially lifting the lockdown, and all classes for the day are dismissed. Please, all of you, be careful and get home safely. If you need a place to wait for your parent or guardian, meet in the cafeteria where you will be supervised by faculty until your family members arrive." He hung up the phone and shook his head, stressed.

Hailey and Ale sat across from him at the desk in his newly renovated office. Hailey trembled so much that her feet had been audibly vibrating against the linoleum since they were escorted here, and Ale still hadn't regained the color she lost in her face as soon as she saw the body.

"I'm really sorry about this, girls," Principal Collins said, looking up as the door opened.

"I take it you're the girls who found the body?" a familiar voice asked, leading Hailey to turn her head and find Officer Ronald, who she recognized from earlier this morning.

"Yeah," Ale said, her voice sounding weak. She cleared her throat and tried to repeat herself, but Officer Ronald interrupted.

"Wait, Hailey, is that you?"

She tried to force a smile. "Busy day, huh?" she joked, but it didn't cheer her up like she hoped.

"I wish it weren't." He quickly pulled out his pen and notepad from his back pocket and began writing in it.

"Wait, you two know each other?" Ale asked and turned to look at Hailey. "I didn't think you knew any locals, let alone an officer—"

"We met this morning," Hailey interrupted. "Remember when I said I needed to talk to you and Billy about something?" Ale nodded and Hailey gestured to Officer Ronald as if saying, "This was it."

"Okay, so let me get this straight," Officer Ronald said. "I was told that you girls found the body because of an anonymous letter, right?"

"Yeah, here." Hailey dug through her purse for the envelope and handed it to him. He grabbed it and analyzed the letter inside, studying every word for clues.

"Now where did you find the letter?" he asked.

"It was in my locker after our fitness class," Hailey said.

"And it wasn't there before?"

Hailey shook her head. "Nope. I'm sure of it."

"Was that always *your* locker?"

"Yeah. I mean, this whole year, at least."

"What, do you think they meant to give that to someone else?" Ale asked.

"I doubt it. Honestly, having Hailey involved in this makes this case make a whole lot more sense," Officer Ronald said.

"It does?" Principal Collins asked, intrigued.

"What, you think *he* had something to do with this?" Hailey asked.

"*He*? Who is *he*?" Ale wanted to know.

"Oh, I'm almost sure of it. Unless you can think of anyone else who would gift you a corpse," the officer said.

"He doesn't even *know* me! How would he find out where I go to school? And why would he even look? It's not like he has a reason to target me. Plus, nothing he ever wrote me made him seem violent."

"Wait—" Ale tried to interject, but Officer Ronald responded too quickly.

"Be that as it may, the trail of bodies he left in the prison suggests otherwise. We'll find the motive later, but this is a crime he is certainly *capable* of, and it would be unwise to leave him anywhere other than the top of the list of suspects, especially considering your relationship."

"Trail of bodies?" Principal Collins repeated.

"Relationship?" Ale asked. "Hailey, you're not talking about your—"

"My dad, yes," Hailey interrupted. "He escaped from prison last night."

Principal Collins threw his arms up and rolled back in his chair, while Ale simply raised her eyebrows in shock.

"And you didn't tell me?" Ale asked. "We just spent all morning talking about prom bullshit when you had some juicy tea like that to spill? I'm . . . Well, I'm disappointed."

"I just found out before school and was still pissed at how Alexa reacted to the news that I've been writing him. I was going to tell you and Billy after school—"

"Okay, sorry to interrupt, but I'm going to take this and leave," Officer Ronald said, holding up his notepad. "I'm sure the news reporters are outside waiting for someone to tell them what's going on."

"Wait," Hailey said. "Please, don't tell them about my relationship to him. I don't want that to be public information. As far as I know, he doesn't even know he has a daughter."

"Of course not. I'm not even going to say we think he's involved. I need more evidence before we begin public witch hunts." He gave a thumbs-up. "Your secret's safe with me."

"Thank you," Hailey said.

He tipped his hat and left the office.

"Wow," Principal Collins said as if gathering his mind-blown thoughts that scattered about the room. "That's some heavy stuff there, Hailey."

"Tell me about it."

"Well, are you okay? I mean, both of you. Do you need anything?" he asked.

Therapy, Hailey thought. The graphic image of that dead woman's face flashed through her mind, followed by a similar image of Oliver Vance's charred face bearing the marshmallow-skewered knife protruding from his temple. She felt cold and weak again, just like she did that night at Camp Safe Woods.

"We'll be okay," Ale said, pulling Hailey from her thoughts.

"In that case,"—he put his hands on his desk and used them to push away his rolling chair as he stood up—"you girls are free to go." He walked to the door and held it open for them. "You do have a way home, right? If not, I can drive you."

"No, thanks," Ale said, reminding Hailey of earlier when Ale said this guy was a pervert. "We can manage."

Ale stood from her chair and gave Hailey a hand, lifting her out of hers.

He smiled and nodded to them as they exited the office.

***

After Ale arranged a meeting with Billy in the quad via text messages sent during the lockdown, they went there to meet with him, only to find the place busier than anticipated. Standing at the center of the quad, surrounded by multiple formally dressed reporters shoving handheld microphones and cameras in his face with the occasional boom mic floating above him, was Officer Ronald giving his report of what went down today.

" . . . Two students stumbled upon the body after following what they believed to be a letter from a secret admirer guiding them to a present." He awkwardly glanced at Hailey and Ale as they walked past, heading toward Billy who was intently listening to the report from a bench behind the reporters, and then he went back to his statement. "We still have not identified the body, due to its decayed state, but we are working tirelessly on finding who it is. However, we do believe her to be a blonde female in either their twenties or thirties that was murdered sometime within the last five to seven months. We are already on the lookout for any missing persons reports in the surrounding counties that might fit that description. It's worth noting that her fingertips were completely removed, along with her teeth so it was impossible for us to collect any prints, and it will be impossible to match any dental records. Whoever we're dealing with is a very dangerous individual who did this for a reason we have yet to uncover. And while there are a few names of people who may be involved, we cannot disclose any suspects at this time."

"Hey," Ale said, talking to Billy over the officer. His eyes brightened when he saw his friends, as though he had been worried about them this whole time and he could finally rest knowing that they were safe in his field of view. He practically jumped out of the bunch and hugged them both, drawing looks from some of the reporters.

"I'm so glad you're both safe," he said as he pulled away from Ale.

"Don't act so surprised, like we haven't been texting you this whole time," Ale said.

"Texts aren't enough and you know that," he said. "I needed to see you to know you're okay."

Ale smiled and Hailey thought she saw her blush.

" . . . We'll update you guys as soon as we have more information. Thank you," Officer Ronald said, trying to dismiss the band of reporters, but they all followed with a roar of questions, barking over each other so none of them could be heard louder than the others. "Please, please . . . I know you all have questions, but I need to get back to work and I've already shared with you what I know." The crowd slowly quieted their questions as most of the reporters lowered their microphones and cameras, except one. She was a stunningly pretty woman wearing a soft pink mid-length skirt and a matching cropped long-sleeve vest over a black V-neck, with heels that would impress Mrs. Ivory. Hailey recognized her from a local news station that she would find Megan watching some mornings.

"Hi, Tiffany Watson from *Channel Six News*," she spoke with enough confidence to draw the officer's attention and quiet the crowd. "It's my understanding that you're also working on the investigation of the recent prison break of the dangerous fugitive, Christopher Atkins."

Hailey's neck snapped toward the mention of that name faster than the whiplash of a car accident victim. She studied Officer Ronald's face as he thought heavily about how to respond, especially noting how hard he fought the urge to glance in her direction.

"Yeah, that's right. It's been a busy week." He tried to laugh it off but looked more uncomfortable than anything else.

"Would it be irresponsible for those of us seeking answers to assume that *he* may have had something to do with this poor woman's murder?" she asked.

Officer Ronald narrowed his brows, annoyed that she made such a guess and said, "Just because I'm on both cases does *not* mean they're linked. At rare times like these, when the station gets busy, officers are tasked with multiple cases. We have no reason to connect the two crimes at this time."

"Really?" Tiffany whipped her head to send her hair flying back over her shoulder and stood up straight. "Were you aware his daughter, Hailey, is a senior here at Pineside High?"

Hailey gasped, her hand immediately covering her mouth while her friends both looked at her; Ale checking to see if she'd heard that, too, and Billy confused about the situation. Officer Ronald shot a quick glance at Hailey, redirecting Tiffany her way.

"Oh! Speak of the devil and she appears." Tiffany walked with an uncomfortable strut in her heels, holding the microphone out toward Hailey as she yelled, "Hailey, would you be willing to answer a few questions?"

The media crowd turned their heads and cameras her way, astounded by the news. Residents already knew about the Camp Safe Woods survivors who lived in their town, so as a local celebrity, Hailey assumed it would be quite a shock for them to hear that her father was an escaped convict. Camera lights flashed as the news reporters' murmurs grew into an uproar. Hailey felt overwhelmed and her head started to spin. Choosing not to answer the reporter's question, she turned her back, and just as she intended to run away, she bumped into a tall figure standing behind her.

When that person placed an arm around her back to comfort Hailey, she turned her head and ran face-first into some business-casual cleavage. Pulling her eyes upward, she saw that it was her teacher, Mrs. Ivory, and she looked pissed—not at Hailey for running into her, but at the media for their tactics.

"You should all be ashamed of yourselves," she said. "Hailey's been through enough, and she's had a long day. Unless you want it to be plastered all over social media that your platform harassed a traumatized high school student, she won't be answering any of your questions."

"We have a right to know," one reporter said above the crowd, which quickly went silent.

"And I have the right to have you removed from school premises, and rather than wait for security to do it, I'll carry you out myself and that footage will play on the news right after the murder coverage when viewership will be at its peak."

The crowd looked amongst themselves, confused and embarrassed, but Tiffany Watson crossed her arms and looked annoyed that she wouldn't get her story today. Hailey simply watched her teacher in awe, thinking, *What do I have to do to be strong like her*? Mrs. Ivory looked nothing short of intimidating, and Hailey envied her.

"Well put," Officer Ronald said as the crowd lowered their cameras and dispersed. Tiffany Watson was the last to leave after taking one final, long look at Hailey before turning on her heels and commanding, "Cut" to her camera guy.

"Thank you," Hailey said.

"Oh, don't mention it. Those people are the worst." Mrs. Ivory slouched to get closer to Hailey's height and asked, "How are you doing?"

Hailey couldn't muster the energy to say, "Terrible," so she just shook her head and avoided eye contact, hoping her teacher would know exactly what she meant.

"I know. Today's been rough—I can't even imagine." She ran her fingers down the length of Hailey's hair, smoothing out a few tangles. Hailey stepped out of her embrace. "You three have a way home, right?"

"Yeah, we'll be okay."

"Good." Mrs. Ivory reached into her breast pocket and removed a sticky note and pen. She scribbled a phone number and handed it to Hailey. "If you need anything, don't hesitate to call."

"Thank you," Hailey said. Mrs. Ivory smiled, nodded, and left them to talk with Officer Ronald.

"So . . . " Billy began as he awkwardly stepped over with Ale by his side. "Did they say your dad escaped a prison?"

"Yeah, he—"

"I didn't think you had a dad!" Billy interrupted.

"We've . . . we've gotta get you caught up," Hailey said.

Chapter 5

"Are you gonna answer that, or just let her keep calling?" Ale asked about Hailey's phone vibrating atop the shopping mall food court table. This was at least the dozenth time that Alexa had called and Hailey avoided it.

"I just don't know what to say to her."

"How about, 'I'm alive'?" Billy offered before taking a few loud sips from the bottom of his empty fountain soda.

"Yeah, she probably saw the news and is worried about you. Your face is all over the TV right now after that bitch brought up your dad," Ale said.

"Can we talk about how I had to find out from some random news lady that your dad was not only *alive* but in *prison*?" Billy asked.

"I just . . . don't talk about him." Hailey looked up from her phone as Alexa's call went to her voicemail. "Honestly, I don't even know how *she* knew. The only people who knew about that were me and Ale."

"Wait, *she* knew?" Billy gestured to Ale, his face written with jealousy. Ale stuck her tongue out teasingly at the same time Hailey's phone began ringing again.

"Okay, I'm just gonna text her."

Hailey picked up her phone and sent Alexa a text: *I'm okay, I promise. I'm with my friends and will see you when I get home.*

After sending it, she put her phone on mute and slipped it into her pocket. Billy tried taking a few more sips from his empty drink as Ale glared at him, annoyed.

"You know you're not going to get any more out of there, no matter how hard you suck on it, right?" Ale snarked.

"I'm just getting my money's worth," he said.

"Sure you are." Ale crumpled up her empty hot dog wrapper with her used napkin and dropped them onto her tray before scooting her seat back and standing. "You guys ready to go, or do you want to shop around?"

"The longer I'm away from Alexa, the better," Hailey said, gathering her things and getting up from the table.

"I still think you should call her. There's no point in stressing about it," Billy said, following them to the garbage cans.

Ale dumped her trash inside. "Hey, some of us haven't learned how to face our fears yet," she joked.

"Yeah, we didn't all get to finish a summer at Camp Safe Woods like you, Billy," Hailey added. He rolled his eyes, exhausted from the girls teasing him like this constantly.

They strolled through the mall, casually entering and exiting various stores that caught their attention. Among these was Victoria's Secret, where, Ale playfully joked, she would search for Billy's prom attire once he lost their bet. Eventually, they stumbled upon Mozart's Record Store, a hole-in-the-wall shop that had managed to survive ever since the days when albums were how people actually listened to music.

"Who even buys this stuff?" Ale asked, holding up the first vinyl record she could grab off the store's display—Michael Jackson's *Thriller*. "I mean, do people actually own record players?"

"Yes, they do, and there are some real audiophiles out there who prefer how these sound. Plus, there's a huge collector's market," Billy explained.

"It's a waste of money, time, and space," Ale said, putting the record back on the shelf. "I'm not paying for music that I can't even listen to in my car. And it's like forty dollars for one record! I can get months of a music subscription for that price."

"Careful," an employee said from behind the front counter. She sat on a metal barstool, leaning back with her combat boots kicked up beside the register. Hailey recognized her as Nia, a classmate of hers from English class. "Tell too many people and I'll be out of a job."

"I doubt that," Billy said. "This place has survived worse than the rise of music streaming."

"Only because of the porn tapes we sell in the back. Without those, this spot would be one of those sports stores that only sells bootleg jerseys." She removed her feet from beside the register and leaned forward on her elbows. "What are you guys doing here anyway? School shouldn't be out yet. I didn't think you three were the type to ditch."

"You haven't heard?" Hailey asked, exchanging surprised looks with her friends.

"Heard what? Did something happen?" Her eyebrows raised, exemplifying her confusion.

"Did you just *not* go to school today?" Hailey asked.

"Nope. My coworker called in sick and I *need* the money, so I prioritized and covered for them."

"Wow. And you seriously haven't heard? It's gotta be all over the news," Ale said.

"You think *I* keep up with the news?" Nia asked. "Just spit it out. What happened?"

"Ale and I . . . " Hailey started.

"We found a body," Ale finished. "The school went on lockdown for a bit, then sent everyone home early. There's an investigation . . . campus was filled with reporters . . . it's a whole thing. I can't believe you haven't heard."

"What, like a *dead* body?" She looked amused. "You're joking, right?"

"I wish we were," Billy said, running his fingers across a Pat Benatar record on the shelf.

"Who was it? Anybody I know? Oh! What did the body look like?" Nia stood and planted her hands on the counter, ready to leap out of her boots with excitement. Her lip piercings swung loosely, recovering from the motion.

"Uh, uh . . . " Hailey stammered and said, "very dead."

Nia's smile dropped into a more regretful expression. "Shit, I'm sorry, guys. I forgot you three have a history with . . . well, dead people. Sorry. That must've been an awful experience."

"It's okay. Corpses are a lot easier to look at when the faces are unrecognizable," Ale said.

"Easier isn't exactly a word I would use, though," Hailey said. Nia did her best to look remorseful but couldn't keep her eyes from appearing as bright as ever.

"You sure look excited to hear about it," Billy said.

"I know, sorry! Things like that just don't happen in this town. And I probably watch too many horror movies." She rubbed her eyes and moved her body as if shaking out the excitement. "So do we know who it was? Like, was it a student?"

They shook their heads.

"No, she was definitely an adult," Hailey said.

"Well, what did the police say? Do they think she was murdered?"

"Police didn't need to tell us that," Ale said. "The knife sticking out of her face was a pretty good tell."

Nia's eyes lit up again, but she used her hands to cover her mouth, which obviously wore a smile. She took a deep breath to compose herself and rid the smile from her face as she stepped out from around the counter.

"And before you ask, no, they don't know who did it," Ale said.

"Oh my gosh. So you're saying there's an actual murderer in town? Like right now, today?" She looked both excited and nervous, like a little girl getting ready for her first big roller coaster.

"Don't get too excited," Billy said. "Horror movies and serial killer documentaries are fun to watch, but you never want that stuff to be too close to home."

"Take it from us," Hailey said, waving her finger around the three of them, "once the murders start, you never know who'll be next."

***

Hailey opened her front door slowly and peeked inside, expecting Alexa to be waiting right there for her to arrive. When she wasn't, Hailey looked back at the driveway and confirmed that both Alexa and Megan's cars were there. Hailey sighed in an attempt to mentally prepare for the inevitable argument she was surely walking into.

With a "rip the Band-Aid off" mentality, she closed the door behind her loud enough for those in the house to hear, placed her bags against the wall, and charged into the kitchen where both of her mothers would surely be sitting—with Megan squeezing Alexa's hand tight, trying to calm down her hot-headed personality. Only, they weren't there.

What the hell? I thought for sure they'd be sitting here waiting. Then, she began to worry. *What if Alexa was calling because of an emergency? What if the person who killed that lady knows where I live?*

She looked down the hall to the stairs. Her heart sank as she thought of what she might find if she ascended them.

The only way to find out is to go up there, she thought. If anything, her awful experience at camp gave her a conflicted level of bravery. Sure, she was afraid of more than the average person, but she knew now that facing those fears head-on was the only way to get rid of them. Plus, facing them with a knife in hand made it a whole lot less scary. She stepped to the counter and pulled the biggest chef's knife they owned from the magnetic cutlery display hanging from the wall beside the refrigerator. It's hard to feel anything less than confident with a full grip on the handle of a weapon this size.

At the top of the stairs she felt the weight on her chest as her breaths grew heavier. She first brought her attention to the loft, which appeared empty with the lights off, but as she flicked the light switch, she heard a soft *woof* and Park Ranger Woodsby crawled out from his oversized dog bed behind the ottoman in the center of the room.

"Hey, buddy," Hailey whispered when he approached. She scratched behind his ears until he turned and presented his backside, where Hailey then scratched his favorite spot—just above his tail—as she looked down the hallway until Woodsby started kicking his leg with each scratch, making more noise than Hailey was comfortable with.

"*Shh shh shh,*" she said, pulling her hand away. "You wait in here, okay, buddy?"

Woodsby responded with a whimper and dramatically went back to his bed to lie down.

Hailey continued into the hallway to check the master bedroom. With one sweat-filled palm on the knife and the other on the doorknob, she swung the door open. The room was a mess, but not any more than usual—they weren't the most organized couple. Their blankets were thrown about the bed as if Woodsby had used them as a toy. Their pajamas from the morning—including their socks and panties—were strewn across the floor as if they'd pulled them off in a hurry and thrown them haphazardly.

Their dresser drawers were fully extended with loose articles of clothing hanging out of them. Two wet towels lay on the floor—one outside the bathroom door and the other outside the closet, which was wide open to display visible sweaters and dresses on the verge of falling off their hangers. All of this was their usual mess.

She was about to enter their bathroom when she heard the *click* of a door handle from the hallway, so she turned around to check that out instead. As she exited the bedroom, Alexa stepped out of Hailey's; they saw each other at the same time and had an awkward pause as they both struggled to find their words. Alexa was holding a stuffed animal—Lana, the Loch Ness Monster—given to Hailey by her late mother when she was a child and her most treasured material item, which she relied on for comfort when stressed or scared.

"I . . . I thought you would need her when you came home," Alexa said, as her eyes—glistening with tears—traveled down Hailey's arm to find the knife she clutched. She choked on a gasp as her mouth fell open and the tears pooling in her eyes overflowed. "Oh, baby." She hurried to Hailey, gently grabbed the knife, and tightly hugged her. "You must be so scared," she whispered.

"You guys weren't downstairs," Hailey said, returning the hug long enough for tears of her own to form. "I just had to be safe, you know?" She backed out of the hug and wiped her tears away, noticing black residue on her thumbs that made her realize she'd smeared her eyeliner across her face in the process. "So much for being pretty today."

Alexa laughed. "Are you kidding? You have your mother's genes—you're *always* going to be pretty. And you live in *my* house, so . . . " She handed Lana to Hailey, then reached her hand around to the back of her pants and pulled a handgun from her waistband—a Glock 19 she purchased when she'd heard about Hailey's experience at Camp Safe Woods. "You're always safe."

"Hailey, you're home!" Megan exclaimed, stepping out of Hailey's room. "Where have you been? And why in *the hell* weren't you picking up your phone—"

"Honey, it's okay," Alexa interrupted and Megan went silent. "Now, what should we eat while you tell us what happened at school?"

Chapter 6

A month had passed without any updates in either case—neither Christopher Atkin's escape from prison nor the body Hailey had found at school. It started to seem as though the town of Meadowood had forgotten all about them, and things had mostly gone back to business as usual—including Hailey and her friends, who were now more worried about plans for their upcoming prom fundraiser and Hailey's eighteenth birthday.

"So what do *you* want to do?" Ale's voice rang through Hailey's cell phone speaker. "It's not like you're turning twenty-one; there's nothing really crazy an eighteen-year-old can do for their birthday."

"Paintball was fun on yours," Hailey said while lying on her bed, pillow under her chest, legs bent, and her feet kicking in the air. She was browsing the Internet on her laptop for party inspiration.

"Yeah, much better than Billy's stupid escape room," Ale said, her voice muffled by the wind blowing into her car windows as she drove. "But what else is there? It's crazy, they call you an adult but you still can't do anything. No renting cars, no alcohol, hell, you can't even smoke cigarettes!"

"And I bet you're in such a rush to have that sweet, sweet smoker's breath," Hailey teased.

"Ew, no. It's not like I *actually* want to smoke, but the option would be nice. It's just frustrating that the only things that change for us are the ability to drop out of high school, move out of our parent's house—as if we could afford to do that in this economy—and watch porn without putting in a fake birthday."

"Ah, yes, a freedom I'm sure you exercise quite often."

"Hey, I'm an adult. Since I have the right, why not?"

"It says here I can volunteer for jury duty."

Ale imitated a vomiting sound. "Gross. I wouldn't even go if I was summoned—who would *ever* want to volunteer?"

"Not me," Hailey said, closing the website providing that information. She rolled over and sat cross-legged, craning her neck toward the screen and opening another site. "You know, if we want to exercise our adult freedoms, we can always go to the strip club."

"Hailey, you naughty girl. I didn't think you'd be into that," Ale said with a playful tone. "You know, if you wanted to see some titties, you can always just take off your shirt. I know you've got some nice mirrors in that bedroom."

Hailey looked at herself in her closet's sliding mirror doors. She wore only a Camp Safe Woods T-shirt—Mitch mailed it to her to replace the one she had been wearing when she was stabbed. He didn't get the sizing correct, with this one being so big that it hung down to her knees, so she added it to her rotation of sleeping attire.

"You're such a bitch," Hailey said. "You know there are male strip clubs, right? Or we can go to one of those *Magic Mike*-esque shows. You can't tell me you don't want to go to one of those."

"Me, sure! But Billy? Definitely not."

"It's a good thing it's not *his* birthday, then. And if he doesn't want to go, we can make it a girls' trip."

"Yeah, then we can bring both of your moms, too," Ale said. The wind blowing into the phone speaker was replaced with the sounds of Ale shifting the car into park and pulling the keys from the ignition. "Okay, I'm gonna put you in my pocket while I go talk to Charlie's parents," she said about the family whose house she arrived at for her weekly babysitting gig.

Hailey then noticed her phone screen light up with a call from Billy.

"Oh, Billy's—" Hailey said, then stopped once she heard the muffling indicating Ale's phone sliding into her jeans. "Okay, I'll just merge the call," she said to herself, tapping the green button to answer.

"Hey, Billy, what's up?"

"Hey, not much. I just got home from hanging out with Leo," he said with an awkward and uncomfortable tone.

Hailey narrowed her eyebrows and pursed her lips while she looked at the bottom corner of her laptop screen for the time: *8:38 p.m.* "Okay, and why does it sound like you didn't just call because you wanted to hear my voice?" She closed her laptop and lay back on the bed.

"I, uh . . . Well, I wanted to let you know that Leo's agreed to help with the bake sale," he said, though he still sounded like he was beating around the bush.

Leo was one of Billy's few friends from before Ale and Hailey came to town. He was tall with dark, curly hair and looked like the kind of person who'd not only work a drive-thru window but eat fries from your bag as he handed it to you. He's a good person at heart, though—a true gentle giant—but his dirty sleazeball aesthetic would rub anyone who judges a book by its cover the wrong way.

"He did?" Hailey asked, concerned. Sure, Leo was fun to be around, but he was a massive stoner, and somehow Billy seemed to be the only person in town who didn't realize it. "Are you sure that's a good idea?"

"What? Yeah, of course. The more people we get to help, the better," he said. What he didn't realize was that Hailey was *really* asking if it was safe to put Leo in charge of baked goods that they'd be selling to townsfolk. There was a zero percent chance that he wouldn't spike at least *some* of what he brought to the event, and if the wrong people found out . . . Well, it wouldn't be very good for anyone.

"I just don't want—" Hailey started before Billy cut her off.

"Look, I know you guys have all this stuff to say about Leo, but he's fine. Okay? You know you can trust me, right?" he asked. Hailey thought back to that final night at Camp Safe Woods and remembered the sight from just after she had been stabbed by Oliver Vance, when Billy had tackled the lunatic and beat his face to a bloody pulp, then stopped thinking about it when she remembered the feeling of Oliver ripping the knife out of her and slicing Billy's face open with it.

"With my life."

"Good. Then you should know that I trust this guy and believe he is better than you guys give him credit for."

*Than the **whole town** gives him credit for*, Hailey thought, but chose to keep it to herself. "If you say so, but don't say I didn't warn you when we get complaints from parents whose kids were served pot brownies." Hailey thought her joke was funny, but the silence on the other end of the phone meant otherwise. "So was there something else you wanted to talk about?"

"Yeah, actually." There was a shaky nervousness in his voice that Hailey wasn't used to hearing. "I need your opinion on something."

Hailey hated awkward conversations, especially with family and friends. She had lived through enough uncomfortable moments in her life, and she aimed to keep those feelings out of her everyday encounters. "Okay, spit it out," she said with a tone meant to let Billy know that he was being weird. "What is it?"

"It's about Ale. Nobody's asked her to prom yet, right?" he asked. Then, as if hearing the words leave his mouth, he said, "I mean, I doubt it because she would definitely tell us both if she did, but I was wondering if maybe someone *did* ask her, and maybe she only told you about it since you're . . . you know—"

"A girl?" Hailey asked, pretending to be offended.

"Yeah. A girl," he said.

Hailey's mouth fell into an excited *O* that quickly shifted into an ear-to-ear grin once she realized where he might be leading the conversation. "No. Nobody's asked her." She sat up and excitedly looked at her phone as though she was waiting to see if her lottery ticket was a winner.

"Okay," he said with an exhale of relief. There was a brief pause in the conversation while Hailey waited for him to continue because she didn't want to interrupt his opportunity to explain himself. "Now what do you think—" That nervousness in his voice forced him to pause once more. "What do you think about me asking her to go with me?"

"You mean as a date?" Hailey asked a bit too quickly, as the excitement she tried to hold back forced its way out. "Because if you're asking her to go as your friend, she'll laugh in your face for thinking she'd want to spend her only prom night without a proper date."

"You don't think I know that? No, I want her to be my prom date," he said with confidence in his voice this time, causing Hailey's excitement to spill further as she rocked back and forth on the bed, biting her lip.

"And we're talking about the same Ale, right?" Hailey asked, as if what she was hearing was too good to be true. Her two best friends getting together would be the most adorable thing she could think of, and they were the perfect match for each other. Ale was the thick-headed, dominant force in the relationship, and Billy was the kind of guy capable of handling that without feeling insecure or getting his ego hurt. On top of that, they both knew first-hand what traumas the other had gone through, which could only bring them closer together. The cherry on top, though, was that Ale could no longer tease Hailey about Billy being into her.

You won this time, Ale, Hailey thought—a joke she would save for later.

"What other Ale would I be talking about here? No shit we're talking about the same one. Now do you think she'd say yes or no?"

Hailey took a second to actually think about it, but it wasn't easy to come up with a solid answer. With as much time as Ale spent yapping about boys to Hailey, she couldn't think of a certain type that she might be into. The conversations with her—if you could call them that—were once simple like, "He's hot as fuck," but had since evolved into egregious declarations of horniness like, "I would ride his dick like a pool noodle," or Hailey's personal favorite, "I want to straddle his face like a donkey before a hike up Mount Everest." She got the metaphor but didn't know why she'd made it. And unfortunately for Billy, none of these statements were ever made about him. Hailey didn't know how that would effect his odds, but it couldn't be good.

Before Hailey could think of something positive to say other than, "Go for it!" Hailey heard something that made her heart skip a beat—a familiar sound on the other end of the phone.

Shit, Hailey thought, *I forgot we were still on a merged call!*

The phone was muffled for a couple seconds before Ale said, "Okay, I'm back."

"Ale?" Billy sounded both scared and embarrassed. *She didn't hear, did she?*

"Billy?" Ale replied. Her tone didn't hold any implication that she was pretending not to know he was on the call, but it wasn't enough to convince Hailey.

"Yeah, he called to talk about the bake sale so I merged it while you were gone," Hailey said.

Her phone lit up with a text message from Billy: *YOU DIDN'T TELL ME THE CALL WAS MERGED!*

Hailey felt bad. If Billy was going to ask her to prom, she wouldn't want to ruin that. Ale deserved the surprise and Billy deserved the proper chance to give it to her.

She texted: *SHIT! I FORGOT! I'm sorry!!!*

"*Hmph*, boring. How's that going for you?" Ale asked.

"It's great. Leo agreed to help out," he said.

Hailey's phone lit up with another text from Billy: *You don't think she heard, do you?*

Ale laughed and said, "I didn't realize drug dealing was allowed at high school-sanctioned events. But you must *really* want to pick my dress if you're gonna stoop that low to win our little contest. It makes me worry about what you might have in mind."

Hailey texted: *I don't think so . . . ?*

"I wouldn't worry too much. I'm sure the jailbait car wash will attract plenty of weirdos. I'm just trying my best to keep it close," Billy said.

Are they . . . flirting? Hailey thought. The two of them were always like this with each other, but she never thought anything of it. They were all close with each other, but now Hailey felt almost like she was intruding. The idea started to worry her; if her two best friends started dating, would she be pushed out? They already went everywhere and did everything together, so would Hailey just be the third wheel now? Or would they slowly start pushing her out as they wanted to spend more time alone together?

No, they wouldn't do that, Hailey told herself. *This is a good thing and I'll be happy for them.*

"I hate you so much," Ale said.

If she says yes to him, that is, Hailey thought.

"So, Ale, are you in their house now?" Hailey asked about her babysitting gig.

Then she sent Billy another text: *We'll talk more about it later.*

"Yeah, I'm waiting on their couch for them to get their snot-nosed son down here," Ale said. "I swear this kid gets more and more difficult every week."

"What, you're babysitting *again*?" Billy asked. "How is it that you manage to land a gig every week?"

"Because this couple are some freaks, and their son, Charlie, keeps requesting me."

"Freaks?" Billy asked.

"Yeah, you're making yourself sound more like an escort than a babysitter," Hailey said.

"Sorry, poor wording. But yeah, they're some freaks. I guess these two had Charlie very early in their twenties and worried their sex life was going to die. To avoid that horrifying fate, once a week they hire a babysitter—me—to watch their little brat while they get a hotel room and fuck each other's brains out," Ale explained.

"And they told you this?" Billy asked.

"Yep. Well, not really. They said they were going on weekly date nights, but what else could they be doing when they leave their kid home alone with a high schooler for a few hours?"

"You know, dating. Dinner, movie, bowling . . . anything, really," Hailey said.

"Hailey, you sweet, naive, innocent thing. Bowling is for children," Ale said as a little kid screaming in the background pulled her attention away. "Okay, I think Charlie is coming down. I've gotta go, you guys. Text me if you decide what we're doing for your birthday!" All noise from her end went silent and Hailey double-checked her phone and confirmed she left the call.

"Is she gone?" Billy asked.

"Yep, I just checked," Hailey said.

"You're a real asshole for not telling me she was on the call."

"Hey, I said I was sorry! And if she heard anything, you *know* she would've said something about it. She's not really the type to hide any emotion."

"I hope you're right," Billy said, leading them into an awkward silence. Beneath Hailey's bed, a quiet rumbling startled her. She peeked over the edge and saw Woodsby lying on the floor, growling. He was a trained emotional support dog that only growled when there was danger around or occasionally in his sleep. For a dog, he had seen a lot of terrible things in his life, and Hailey often wondered if he had nightmares like she did. It wasn't a happy thought for her, but she hoped this was what was happening at the moment. Because otherwise, it would mean that he was detecting something or somebody he wasn't used to. Woodsby settled down, and then, breaking their phone silence, Billy asked, "So what do you think?"

"Hm?" Hailey pulled herself away from stressing over Woodsby's growling and redirected her attention back to the conversation. "Think about what?"

"About me asking Ale to prom," he replied, still embarrassed to talk about his plan. "Do you think it's a good idea? Do you think she'll say yes? Or do you think she'll just laugh in my face?"

"She's *definitely* going to laugh in your face, even if she says yes. She'll never let you live it down. I can see it now. She'll be all like, 'I was mean to you every day from the moment we met, and you still couldn't resist my petite frame.'"

"I hate that you're right," Billy said. "Do you think she's expecting it?"

Hailey's thoughts immediately ran to the multiple times Ale teased her about Billy asking *her* to prom instead. "No, I don't. You know, she's actually fully convinced that you were going to ask *me* to go with you."

Billy chuckled and said, "No way. You? Really?"

"Damn, was it that crazy of an idea? I didn't think I was *that* ugly," Hailey joked.

"No, don't do that. You don't need me to tell you how attractive you are," Billy said. She wasn't exactly fishing for the compliment, but it did feel good hearing it come out of his mouth since she was always at least *slightly* curious about his opinion of her. "Now correct me if I'm wrong, but there wasn't really any of *that* kind of chemistry between the two of us, was there?"

"Who knows?" Hailey teased. "You made your choice and you'll have to live with it." Within his silent response, she could feel the energy that came from the rolling of his eyes from across town. "So how long have you had this little crush on our dear Alejandra?"

"Since camp," he said with zero hesitation.

"Wow. Love at first sight, then?"

"I wouldn't exactly call it that. To be honest, it started when she hurt her ankle tripping over that bear trap."

"What are you, some kind of sadist?"

"Um, no. I've seen a lot of pain in my life. Never once did I think, *Wow, that's hot.*"

Hailey laughed.

"It wasn't the injury itself. It was seeing someone who has such a strong and independent personality like hers showing me a vulnerable side of her that I could tell she wasn't used to showing. I think I developed some sort of attachment to her when we would help move her around camp, getting her in and out of bed, and even bodyguarding her tiny bladder's bathroom breaks in the middle of the night. Something about that whole experience really made me care for her in a way I haven't felt for anyone else before," Billy explained.

Hailey felt teary-eyed hearing him talk like this. She knew that he was speaking straight from his heart and no longer sounded embarrassed to talk about it. Actually, he sounded excited to finally confess these feelings to someone after such a long time of keeping them to himself.

"So your time spent consoling me in the showers after I found Nurse Cherie didn't have that same effect on you?" Hailey teased, to which Billy stuttered. Before she let him spend too much time thinking of a response, she said, "I'm only joking. That's honestly really sweet. You two would be perfect together."

"You think so?"

"Of course. Just promise me one thing."

"Okay. What?"

"When you two start getting serious, don't forget about me."

"Forget about you? You know we wouldn't do that."

"Of course not, but I know you two are gonna be all kissy and touchy-feely with each other, and you'll gradually want more and more alone time. I just don't want to be that annoying third wheel who eventually gets left out of everything. I want to be involved," Hailey said, then reconsidered her choice of words. "Maybe not involved with the kissy and touchy-feely, but . . . you get the point."

"Hey, I think we're getting a bit ahead of ourselves. I've gotta ask her to prom first, then she has to say yes, then we can go from there. Besides, you know the three of us are always gonna be inseparable."

"Because we're 'The Slasher Victims'?" Hailey joked. She thought up the moniker for those who'd survived last summer along with Annie, her counselor from Camp Safe Woods, but Billy never liked it.

"No. That's been stupid since you first thought of it," he said. "But we *are* 'Squirrel Cabin Campers,' and I'll claim *that* nickname proudly."

"Thank you," Hailey said. As she started to adjust her position on the bed, Woodsby suddenly barked, causing Hailey to call out a scared, "Oh!" She hadn't heard him bark with aggression like this since the night of the slaughters, so Hailey knew that something was wrong.

Woodsby rose from the floor and darted to Hailey's bedroom window where he stood on his hind legs and continued barking at the glass, as if he was ready to jump out and attack whoever was waiting on the outside. Luckily, the window was closed because old age or not, he wouldn't survive the jump from the second story of the house.

"Is that Woodsby? He sounds angry," Billy said, hearing the commotion in the background.

"Yeah," Hailey answered over the barking. She got out of bed and patted Woodsby's head, saying, "*Shh shh*. It's okay, boy." Hailey looked out the window at the street in front of her house, trying to spot what upset him. But other than a night sky, neighboring houses, cars parked along the sidewalk, and trees blowing with the wind, there was nothing out of the ordinary.

Once Woodsby quieted down, he resumed lying where he was before his outrage and closed his eyes, though he continued to growl.

"I think the wind scared him," Hailey said.

"Are you sure? That was a lot of noise for some wind." Billy sounded concerned.

"It had to be. There's nobody outside." Just as Hailey's words left her mouth, she saw the interior lights of a van down the street turn on and a girl climb into the driver's seat. Hailey couldn't recognize her in the dark, but she didn't move with the urgency of someone who just got scared away by a dog, so she thought nothing of it. She pulled her blinds shut and lay back on the bed. "He's fine now, though."

"Poor guy," Billy said.

"What were we talking about?" Hailey asked, twirling her hair around her index finger to help calm her nerves.

"A lot."

Hailey giggled. "Yeah, a lot."

"Hey, before Ale hung up she said you were planning your birthday, right?"

"Yeah."

"You have any ideas?"

Hailey thought about all the Internet's suggestions for an eighteenth birthday, then recalled Billy's words about the Squirrel Cabin Campers being inseparable, and she said, "Yeah, I have one. But I'm not sure you'll all agree to i t."

Chapter 7

"**H**oly fucking HELL, that hurts," Ale whimpered. Her whole body shivered from the pain until she let out a high-pitched scream that pierced the air like a needle on glass.

Hailey clenched her fists to brace for the pain and dull the stinging sensation that lingered. If this pain wasn't bad enough, Ale's screaming left a ringing in Hailey's ears that screeched through the sound of mechanical whirring that filled the dimly lit room.

"You're gonna be fine," Hailey assured Ale, then took a deep breath and said, "I've been stabbed by worse."

"That's encouraging and all but it doesn't make it any better," Ale complained, out of breath.

"It's really not that bad, guys." Billy swiveled on the stool between them.

"Shut your mouth," Ale said. "Don't act like we didn't see you holding back tears when you got yours done."

The tattoo artists sitting to the sides of Hailey and Ale's reclining seats laughed while Billy admired the new piece of artwork on his wrist. The girls were feeling nervous when they showed up at the tattoo shop, so Billy volunteered to go first and convince them it wasn't that bad. It was Hailey's birthday and after plenty of consideration—and even more persuasion—they all agreed to go out and get a matching piece to celebrate. The design itself was something simple yet representative of them as friends, as well as what they had all gone through: the silhouette of a squirrel—the very same icon that represented their cabin at Camp Safe Woods.

The tattoo artist working on Ale's wrist was a woman in her mid-twenties named Angel. Hailey wasn't sure if that was her real name or a nickname, but she also didn't bother asking. She had an innocent, pretty face with jet-black hair in a loose bun. She wore tight black jeans with a studded belt, Chuck Taylor Converse on her feet, and a denim jacket with the sleeves cut off exposing full-sleeve tattoos on both arms featuring a dragon in a traditional Chinese art style, its tail near her left wrist and its head breathing flames toward her right. She looked like the rough and rugged type of girl one might be afraid to talk to until she welcomed them with her bright, warm smile.

The artist in charge of Hailey's piece was the same one who did Billy's, and he was also the owner of the shop. His name was Dan Sharpe. Sharpe Needles and Inkwork was his baby. He wore a gray polo shirt with a cross necklace, tailored jeans, and a pair of Dr. Martens oxfords.

He didn't look like somebody Hailey would imagine as a tattoo artist, most notably because he didn't have any tattoos of his own. She even mentioned this to him when they first walked in. He explained that his indecisiveness combined with his perfectionism kept him from getting any work done, and while he loves tattoos—obsesses over them, even—he would continue his practice on others' bodies until he found the inspiration for a design so perfect that it would be worthy of putting on his own body.

Angel brought the needle back down to continue her work on Ale, who grunted as it ran across her skin. As Angel was leaning over, Hailey caught a glimpse of more ink beneath the collar of her vest and asked, "You have more than just both sleeves done?"

Angel replied, "Hm?" and sat up, realized what was being asked, and said, "Oh, yeah." She unbuttoned the top two buttons of her vest and held it open, exposing what she could of her chest above her sports bra, then raised the vest up to show off her midsection and pulled her jeans down at the side to show a piece of her hip. She was covered in ink from the neck down with multiple, cohesive, and beautifully colored pieces featuring a lush landscape with ocean waves, mountain ranges with the sun setting behind them, cherry blossom trees and more, all in that same Chinese style. It was clear that the art continued well below her waistline. "It's a full body tattoo," she said, buttoning up her vest. "Dan actually did it."

"Wow!" Billy exclaimed.

"It's beautiful," Hailey said.

"How far down does it go?" Ale asked, her eyebrows furrowed as she surely was imagining the hours of torture Angel had to endure to get all that done.

"To my ankles. Well, actually the left foot is done, and we're gonna do the right next. Tonight if I'm lucky."

"If I have the energy," Dan chimed in.

"You're doing more?" Ale sounded genuinely concerned.

"Just the feet and the neck left. I guess my hands could be done at some point, but I don't know what I'll put there. I won't get anything on my face, though. That's too much for me."

"Oh, *that's* too much?" Ale sunk into her seat, closed her eyes, and extended her arm. "*This* is too much. Can we get this over with already?"

They all shared a laugh and the artists went back to work. Hailey's arm both stung *and* burned, but she focused on her breathing and fought through it. Billy's phone rang with a certain ring tone that Hailey recognized as an incoming video call.

"Are you seriously getting a video call right now?" Ale asked. "If it's Leo, you are *not* answering. I am in too much pain to deal with his shit right now."

"It's not Leo," he said. "It's a surprise for Hailey." He answered the phone and held it up for her to see. It was their former cabin counselor, Annie.

"Happy Birthday!" she screamed with a big smile on her face. She sat in the driver's seat of her car, sideways so her legs were likely extended out the door.

"Thank you!" Hailey said, then flinched once Dan brought the needle back down on her. "Sorry, I'm getting a tattoo done right now."

"Billy told me. They're exciting but painful, huh?"

"Painful. Just painful," Ale said. Billy pointed the phone at her.

"Ale is being a crybaby about it," he said, to which Ale flipped him off with her free hand.

"Have you gotten one done before?" Hailey asked, and Billy brought the phone back to her.

"Yes, I did, actually." Annie brought her camera down and out of the car to show Hailey her ankle, where she had the very same squirrel silhouette they were all getting now. "I did it this morning."

"No way!" Hailey said.

"Let me see," Ale demanded, and Billy obliged.

"Yes way!" Annie said. "It hurt like hell, but once Billy told me your plans, there was no way I was going to miss out."

"Did he not tell you we were doing it on the wrist?" Ale asked.

"He did. But I thought the ankle was cuter and figured, why not let the campers have their wrist tattoos and the counselor be a little more unique?"

"The symbolism is all the same," Hailey said, and Billy brought the phone back to her. "I'm so happy you got one too. We all need to hang out soon."

"We will! I don't know when, but soon. I promise." Annie turned her attention to a voice that called her from off-screen. "That's Mitch. I've gotta go."

"Okay, we'll talk soon?" Hailey asked.

"Absolutely. Send me pictures of your tattoos when they're all done."

"You got it," Billy said, turning the phone back to himself. Mitch called for Annie once again.

"Okay!" she yelled at him. "Happy Birthday, Hailey!" She made two quick smooching noises and said, "Gotta go, bye." Then Billy's phone went silent.

Hailey looked at Billy and mouthed the words, "Thank you," because it really meant a lot that he would orchestrate something like that with Annie for her. Even though she lived far away from them, she was just as much a part of their group as the rest of them, and maintaining a friendship through phone calls alone was hard work. A gesture like this was heartwarming, and by the time this squirrel was finished being inked onto their bodies, Hailey would feel closer to all of them than ever before.

*****

"Crazy kids, huh?" Dan said about the three who had just left the shop.

"Yeah." Angel laughed. "The girl I worked on was something else. I don't think I've ever heard a client scream so loud."

"I have." Dan smiled as he poured black ink into a cap and set it on a stainless steel tray—the same kind surgeons would use in an operating room to hold their surgical tools.

"You have? Who?" She took off her right sock and shoe, then settled into the comfortable reclining chair. Whenever Angel had time after work, she would bug Dan to get more ink done, and he would usually oblige, often calling her body his favorite piece of art—his magnum opus.

"You." He focused on his tray to make sure it was filled with everything he would need for the job: tattoo gun, needles, disposable gloves, alcohol pads, aftercare ointment, bandages, paper towels, etc.

She scoffed. "Yeah, right." She reached for the hand towel hanging from the handle of a nearby storage cabinet and whipped him with it.

Dan sat on the swivel stool he used for every session, then grabbed and unwrapped an alcohol pad. He leaned in to wipe off the area atop her foot and said, "What, you don't remember when we went to your place and—"

Angel interrupted and pressed her foot against his chest, "*That* . . . wasn't a tattoo."

He grabbed her ankle, put it back into position on the reclined seat, and wiped the area. "But you *are* a client, and I *have* made you scream."

"Don't give yourself too much credit. I did most of the work." She leaned back in her seat and relaxed. "So what ideas do you have for that foot?"

"Are you sure you want me to tell you? Or should I blindfold you and surprise you once it's done?" He put the needle into the tattoo gun.

"If you blindfold me, we won't be doing the tattoo." She laughed.

Dan's ears perked up. "You don't mean—" She nodded. He considered whether he should dip that needle into the ink or scurry to find a makeshift blindfold and take her up on that offer. "In the shop?"

"Why not? I've never done it at my workplace before. Plus, these chairs are super comfortable." She gripped the headrest of the leather seat and rotated her knees outward, opening her legs and inviting him.

He looked at the empty canvas that was her foot. Then he looked at the tool in his hand, the rest of the items he so carefully prepared, and lastly, the chair he'd spent so much time sanitizing—and would have to spend *extra* time sanitizing if they went through with this—then asked, "How about after?"

She pouted and slammed her legs shut. "You're no fun."

"Come on, you know I like to work when I'm feeling inspired." He turned on the tattoo gun and dipped the needle into the ink.

"We'll see if I'm still in the mood after." She waved toward her foot, saying, "Now get to work."

***

Three hours later and Angel's foot felt raw with a tingling that stung the whole surface below her ankle. Dan wiped away the blood and excess ink with a paper towel and exposed the newest addition to the art piece she called her body. The design, a simple one: a koi fish swimming around a lily pad in a pond. Dan squirted some healing ointment on it and covered it with plastic wrap, which cooled the area and reduced that tingling sensation.

"There we go, all done," he said, then stepped to the nearby sink and washed his hands.

Angel examined her foot—as red as it was sore. "That wasn't so bad." She sat upright and leaned forward with her hands planted on the chair between her thighs. "So I guess I'll be leaving, then."

"So soon?" He wore a flirtatious smile as he dried his hands with a washcloth. "I have a better idea."

"I don't think so. You lost your chance a while ago." She slid forward in the chair in an attempt to get out of it, but Dan softly grabbed her shoulders from behind and pulled her back into it. She let out a light moan as the tension in her body dissipated.

How did he know I like being pushed around?

"You're not going anywhere."

Yes, sir, she thought, closing her eyes while he reached his hand down to unbutton her vest. She unbuttoned her pants and slid them over her ass. They came off her right leg with ease but got caught on her left shoe. She kicked her leg with urgency and annoyance, but they didn't give. Dan chuckled and stepped around to her left. She thought he would help with removing her pants but instead, he grabbed and brought them around the chair's side, pulling her leg with them, and wrapped the loose leg of the jeans around the chair's base, effectively tying her leg in place.

"Creative," she said, impressed.

He walked to the other side of the chair, reached beneath the sink, and grabbed three black towels.

"Take those off." He pointed to her panties.

"Yes, boss," she joked but hurried, moving so quickly that she heard a tear in the lace as they fell to her ankles. Just like her pants, they fell off her tattooed foot with ease but caught on her left ankle with her jeans. He ran his hands up her leg as he rose to his feet, spreading goose bumps across her nearly naked body—having only her wide-open vest and sports bra covering her. As he marveled at her figure, she wondered whether it was her body he saw or if he focused more on his own works of art that covered her; however, the answer didn't matter much. She got a good feeling just knowing that he was looking.

He took one of those towels, wrapped it around the calf of her naked leg, and tied it to the opposite side of the base of the chair's legs, spreading her open. Next, he stepped behind her and helped remove her vest. He then took another towel, pulled her arms around the back of the chair, and tied them together tightly. She felt as if she were handcuffed.

"If you acted like this more often, we'd have done it a lot more than just once," she said. The Dan she was with tonight felt entirely different than the Dan she worked with every day and also the Dan she had slept with, who was calm and reserved—polite, even—like he was afraid to touch her. This was an entirely different experience, as if his seal had finally broken and he was ready to confidently act out his fantasies upon her. She was ready for it.

"Noted," he said before grabbing her bra, pulling it up, and freeing her breasts. She felt exposed and embarrassed, but that only excited her more. His hands were freezing cold as he groped her, asking, "When are you gonna let me draw on these?" He squeezed her tits together and let them go so he could watch them drop. They were the only spots still inkless on her torso.

"I think they look good enough already," she answered.

"I guess you're right," he said, disappointed. He picked up the third towel.

"What's that for? The cleanup?"

"This? No." He folded the towel lengthwise and brought it over her face to cover her eyes. "I promised you a blindfold." He pulled the towel behind the chair's headrest and tied it, strapping her eyes shut and head against the chair. She was so excited she couldn't contain her smile. He ran his thumb across her lower lip and she reached forward to nibble on it, but he pulled away and since she couldn't pull her head from the chair, she just bit the air.

"Nice try," he said. "Now where should I start?"

Angel's stomach felt like it was tying in knots as her nervousness and excitement intertwined. She couldn't see a thing, which is why she squeaked from the surprise of a quick sting in her left nipple.

Did he bite me?

Her mind raced as she eagerly awaited his next move. She clenched her body as she braced for another jolt of pain but instead, he kissed her. Once on the lips, which felt more intimate than she expected from this type of encounter. She thought this was just another night of sex for them, but the way his lips graced hers was outright romantic.

His lips next touched her sternum and she quivered. He continued his kissing trail downward with her navel, then once more on her pubic bone. By now, her toes were curling and she was ready for him.

He placed his hand between her legs and touched her—slowly at first, but picked up the pace as she arched her back in the chair and moaned.

"I want you," she said. He responded with a flirtatious, proud chuckle and pulled his hand away. She heard him fumbling with what sounded like a plastic wrapper. "Hurry," she said once she heard a rip, certain it was for a condom as a whiff of latex entered her nose.

Just as she heard him unzip his pants, there was a loud *bang* from the back of the shop, undeniably the sound of the back door slamming shut.

"What the hell?!" Dan exclaimed.

"What was that?" Angel asked, trying to cover herself up, but she couldn't do more than bring her knees slightly closer together.

"I don't know. I'm not sure." He sounded nervous. "Wait here."

"What do you mean, 'Wait here'?!" She shook her arms and legs but couldn't break them free. As his footsteps moved farther away, she yelled, "You're gonna leave me exposed like this?"

"Just for a second," he said, from the back of the shop now. She heard him push the door open and step out, slamming it shut behind him.

With no other options, she sat there and waited for him—naked and terrified, not to mention cold, as the outside breeze from his opening of the door grazed her exposed flesh.

"Hello?" she yelled, hoping he would hear her and return. She called for him at least five times before giving up, and after what felt like forever, the door finally opened once again. "Finally! Did you find out what that was?"

He didn't answer.

"Hello?" Angel tried to move her head to wriggle out from beneath the blindfold, but he had tied it too tight. She heard footsteps slowly approaching her. "Dan, quit fucking around and untie me— Ah!" she screamed as something that felt like sharp, cold steel ran seductively down her stomach.

Did he step outside and grab some kind of toy?

"We can't just get straight back to business after a scary-ass noise like that without a word," she said. "At least take this blindfold off for a second so I can see you."

The item on her stomach turned around to run in the other direction now, with more pressure; it felt like it was piercing her skin.

"Okay, that's starting to hurt," she said, though she didn't mean it. She had gotten so much work done, this was nothing to her—and Dan would know that. But she was scared.

Why is he acting like this?

"Just say *something*, at least. Then you can do whatever you want to me, I swear."

The sharp item left her stomach, and Angel sighed, believing that he was about to untie her blindfold. Instead, with a quick slice across her stomach, she knew that the item was a knife and that this wasn't Dan.

She screamed louder than she ever thought she could as another slice went from her left hip bone, down the length of her thigh, to her knee.

"Help! Dan, where are you?! Where the fuck are you?!" She screamed and cried and choked on her tears. "God, why me?" As her assailant sliced across her cheek, she felt the ooze of her blood warm up her body as it spilled out.

She continued screaming after the slicing stopped. She thought the worst of it was over when the intruder stepped away from her, fumbled with items around the room until they found what they were looking for, then returned to the chair.

"No!" she yelled, until her mouth filled with a liquid that had a horrendous chemical taste. She spat it out, undoubtedly onto the assailant because they slapped her face right where her fresh knife wound was, causing it to sting even worse.

The attacker pinched Angel's nose shut as they poured more of that foul liquid into her mouth and down her throat. She couldn't breathe as it overflowed her airway and she choked on it. Once enough of it filled her mouth, the attacker released her nose. Angel inhaled, breathing in both air and the liquid in her mouth. She choked some more and spat out what she could, splattering it over her body, then realized what it was that they were pouring into her as the scent entering her nose allowed her to properly taste it—tattoo ink.

Just as she felt like she was getting an almost proper inhale, more ink was poured down her throat and sunk into her lungs. She felt the bubbles rise and pop in her windpipe as she gurgled on it. She felt it creep up and spew ejected from her nostrils. She was drowning and knew she couldn't do anything about it. She kicked and tugged at her binds, but it was no use. She screamed as best she could but didn't have enough air left in her lungs to make a sound. Her mind started to fade away, and her body uncontrollably spasmed soon after. The last thing she felt was the knife cutting clean and deep across her neck, releasing a thick mixture of blood and backed-up tattoo ink pouring onto her body.

***

When Dan awoke, he was in his shop with a piercing headache. The overhanging lights felt brighter than anything he'd ever seen before. His torso burned and stung. He felt dazed, and it took a few moments to gather his thoughts—starting with the tattoos he had worked on earlier in the day, followed by what he and Angel were doing, and then . . . *What happened after that?* He remembered pausing due to the sound they'd heard and going to check it out, but not much after that. He stepped out back, but it all went black after that.

Adding it all together, he knew that he was attacked, and given the tender feeling on the back of his skull, he'd been hit hard. Very hard. So much so that he was likely concussed. But if he was attacked out back, he didn't know how he ended up inside or why he was strapped naked to a tattoo chair.

At first he thought that Angel might've tied him up as revenge for leaving her inside while she was scared, but as his eyes slowly focused through the lighting exaggerated by his concussion, he could make out the blurry figure of Angel still strapped in the chair he'd left her in, and even in the same pose.

"Angel?" He felt the weakness in his voice, as though his throat muscles were as tired as the rest of his body. As his eyes focused and made out a clearer image of Angel, he knew that something was wrong. Once he realized just how wrong, he screamed as loud as he could.

Her body was covered in dark blood, with black ink pouring into the mess from her mouth and nose alike. Her head was tilted and limp. Her body was scarred with lengthy cuts here and there, most notably the one that nearly severed her head from her spine.

He writhed, trying to escape, but it was no use. His arms were secured behind the back of the chair by what felt like zip ties. He looked down to assess what bound his legs, then stopped when he saw it—a fresh tattoo on his chest. He couldn't read it, looking down with his blurred vision, but he wasn't going to stop trying until he could make out the words.

"My body," he uttered softly. "Who would do this to my body? What message could be so important that it's worthy of a spot on **my** body?"

To make matters worse, whoever did this to him was clearly unsanitary. The whole area was cherry-red and well on its way to becoming infected, not to mention the chicken scratch handwriting. Failing to read the message, he looked away once he heard footsteps. Turning his head to his right side, he was greeted with a pair of tattoo needles held by one fist, swinging directly into his eye sockets, blinding him.

He felt a soft hand grip his throat the same way he did to Angel earlier, only they didn't release their grip until he ran out of breaths to take.

Chapter 8

The next morning, Hailey heard about what happened from the local news. Not the news her moms would watch on TV, but from the news anchor, Tiffany Watson, who knocked on their door that morning requesting an interview with Hailey.

She'd closed the door in her face, but when Tiffany blurted through it, "Dan Sharpe was murdered," Hailey couldn't help but open it to make sure she heard her correctly.

"I'm sorry?" she asked, one hand on the door in case she needed to slam it shut again.

"Dan Sharpe, owner of Sharpe Needles and Inkwork, and his employee, Angel Huang, were brutally murdered last night."

Hailey fell silent as the cold morning breeze rolled up her doorstep and past her ankles. She remembered their smiling faces just the day before, their playful—borderline flirtatious banter—and their love of the craft for even something as simple as the squirrel on her wrist. She felt her knees quivering, another symptom she'd developed that happened when she felt scared, helpless, sad, anxious, or most negative emotions in general. Some things she could handle, but others just sent her body into an uncontrollable spiral and not surprisingly, death was a trigger.

"So do you think I could ask you a few questions?" Tiffany asked again, snapping Hailey back to reality.

"Um—" Hailey started, standing up straight to compose herself. "Actually, I have a question for you," she said with newfound confidence. "Why is it that someone gets murdered in this town and you come running to my house for answers? Are you that desperate for a story? Harassing minors at their home?" Her voice quieted as she finished the sentence, remembering that she wasn't a minor anymore. Adult wasn't a title she was used to, and it wouldn't be for a while.

"Are you saying that I'm wrong for making a connection here? Did you and your friends not go to their studio just yesterday to get work done?" She eyed the squirrel on Hailey's wrist as she leaned against the door, which Hailey heavily considered closing. Instead, she removed her arm and crossed it behind her back. Then, Tiffany said, "Oh, and happy belated birthday, by the way. I would stop pulling that minor card if I were you; you're bound to get somebody in a lot of trouble that way."

"Okay, so what? We got tattoos done there yesterday and what, you think we had something to do with it? If that's the case, why are *you* here instead of the police?"

Tiffany held her hands up as if proclaiming her innocence and said, "Hey, I didn't accuse you of anything. I'm just here for the story, and there obviously is one. I mean, the survivor of a brutal massacre's father breaks out of prison, and she finds a body the next day, and then a month later, the artists who did her and her friends' tattoos die the same night. Oh, and then there's the other thing."

"Yeah, and what's that?"

"There was a message . . . tattooed on Dan Sharpe's chest."

"No." Hailey shook her head. "Dan didn't have any tattoos. He was very particular about that."

"He *didn't have* any tattoos. But he does now. His assailant very aggressively left one on him—a message for you. And, judging by the way it bled and scarred, it's safe to assume that he was alive when they did it."

"What, like torture?"

Tiffany nodded. "Angel had it much worse."

"Oh my God, what did they do to Angel?"

"You don't want to know."

Hailey blinked twice, awaiting an answer.

Tiffany sighed as if to say, "Okay, fine," and stated, "They tied her to a chair, stripped off her clothes, blindfolded her, and she drowned from the tattoo ink they forced down her throat—before slitting it."

Hailey felt the nerves in her back go numb. She felt like she couldn't breathe.

"No," she said, gasping while she slid down the length of the door until her butt reached the ground. Between ugly crying breaths, she uttered, "You're lying. Who would do something like that?"

"Whoever it is, they seem to be after you."

Walking in from the hall, Alexa said, "Hailey close that door, you're letting the cold air—" She stopped short once she saw Hailey on the ground with the reporter standing in the doorframe. "What's going on?" She knelt down to Hailey and helped her up. "Did something happen?" Once back on their feet, she noticed Tiffany and said, "Hey, I recognize you."

Tiffany extended her hand. "Tiffany Watson, *Channel Six News.*"

"That's right. You're the reporter who let the world know about Hailey's father."

"I—" Tiffany tried to get a word in, but Alexa cut her off.

"A father she's never met who we've been trying to keep out of our lives for good reason."

"I apologize," Tiffany said, and she sounded sincere. "I didn't understand the extent of their relationship when I was trying to conduct that interview."

"Bullshit," Alexa said. "You 'didn't understand the extent of their relationship,' but you somehow *knew* that they had one? The only person outside of this household who knew about their relationship was her biological mother, and she's been dead for almost a decade."

Hailey winced.

"Now, tell me. How is it that you learned about their relationship in the first place?" Alexa asked in a tone that sounded more like a threat than curiosity.

"An anonymous tip," Tiffany said, crossing her arms.

"Anonymous," Alexa scoffed. "Your revelation could mean my family's in danger, so why don't you cut the crap and just tell us who it was?"

"Because I don't know. A letter was slipped under the door of my office the morning Hailey found that woman's body."

"And what did it say?"

"Something simple, along the lines of *Escaped convict Christopher Atkins has a daughter that lives in Meadowood*. Plus, it had Hailey's senior picture clipped to it with her name, home address, and school schedule written on the back."

Hailey felt naked and exposed. Someone out there has all her personal information and clearly some obsession with her, not to mention their homicidal tendencies. The biggest question on her mind now was, *Why?*

"Great, so whoever it is knows where we live," Alexa said.

"And you didn't think to report that to the police?" Hailey asked. "That's so creepy."

"Technically, I did. Just in an interview—or at least, an attempt at one."

Alexa tilted her head and glared at her.

"Hey, if I go reporting every anonymous tip I get, people are going to stop leaving them."

"I'm sorry, can you just give me one reason not to close this door on you?" Alexa asked.

"As I told Hailey, her tattoo artist from yesterday was murdered last night."

Alexa gritted her teeth and snarked, "Oh, so you're just delivering news door-to-door now? Great, thank you for your service, but I'll stick to watching any station other than channel six for my local news—"

Hailey interrupted her, saying, "Wait, Tiffany. You said they tattooed a message for me on Dan's chest. What did it say?"

Alexa looked at her with sharp concern.

"Are you sure you want to hear it from me? I'm sure *Channel Seven News* will hear about it and report it in a week or so. But you may have to stay up late. They can't report anything over there until they're done airing their Little League baseball games, soap operas, and weather reports for other states. I'm sure they'll have your story on by two a.m."

"Okay, look," Hailey said, bouncing her eyes back and forth between the reporter and Alexa, "how about we all agree to work together? You're right," she said to Tiffany. "There *is* a story here, and it's probably going to be your big break. So how about I give you your interview, and you agree to feed us any information that can help keep me and my family safe as soon as you receive it?"

"Enticing, but I want a bit more."

"Imagine that," Alexa said sarcastically.

"I want to exchange phone numbers with the two of you, and I want you to answer any questions I may have for you as they arise. Plus, if anything happens to you that might be related to this story, I want to be the first to hear about it."

"Okay, fine," Hailey agreed. "Now, what did that tattooed message say?"

Tiffany cleared her throat and adjusted her skirt before reciting from memory, "*Hailey Atkins, death dances with those around you, patiently awaiting your turn to take the floor.*"

Hailey wasn't sure what to say. The message clearly had some hidden meaning behind it. The "death dances with those around you" bit was obviously a threat of sorts. They murdered her tattoo artists, so it could be assumed that they would come for more people close to her. But what could they mean by "patiently awaiting your turn to take the floor"? Does that mean she's a target? Why wouldn't they just kill her first? *When* would it be *her* turn?

Overwhelmed, rather than asking one of these important questions, she just uttered, "Atkins isn't my last name."

Alexa remained silent, which confused Hailey because she was always outspoken, but clearly Alexa didn't know what to do here.

"No, but it *is* your father's surname. And he's still on the run," Tiffany said.

"Well people only know about that thanks to you," Alexa finally said.

"I understand that—"

Alexa interrupted with, "And blood or not, she is *not* a member of the Atkins family, and she will *not* claim that name. She's officially been a Ramirez from the moment I took her in, and she was born with the name Hailey Winter."

"Look, you don't need to convince me," Tiffany said. "Personally, I think Winter is the best name of the three, and I wouldn't claim Atkins either. But it's not me you have to convince, it's whoever did this to your tattoo artists."

"Well, I know we made a deal, but I'd be careful if I were you," Hailey said. "Since 'death dances with those' near me, you shouldn't want to get too close."

"Oh, sweetie," Tiffany said, lifting her skirt above the stocking on her left thigh to reveal a gun holstered to her garter, "I've been waiting for an opportunity to show the world how good I am at dancing."

Chapter 9

Tiffany may have been excited to dance, but the rest of Meadowood felt differently. From the moment the message that was left for her reached the local news, people would walk the other way when they recognized Hailey on the street, classmates changed seats when she sat nearby, and stores would refuse to serve her out of fear for their lives.

Today was her late mother's birthday. Before moving to Meadowood, farther away from her mother's grave, Hailey had made a promise to herself. Despite the distance, she would find a way every year to visit the site on this special day, knowing she wouldn't be as close or able to visit as often as before. Now, with Hailey's newfound notoriety *in* town, she tried her luck with a small florist just *out* of town before making her journey.

"*Meadowview Florist*?" Billy seemed unimpressed reading the sign. "Why didn't they just use Meadowood?"

"Because Meadowood Florist was probably taken. Besides, they wouldn't want to falsely advertise," Hailey explained. This trip was something she originally wanted to do on her own, but with everything going on, her moms didn't want her to go alone. Ale had another babysitting gig to go to after school, but Billy was free— as he usually was—so he volunteered to tag along. Alexa was thankful, of course, aware that he was partially the reason Hailey survived Camp Safe Woods. But she would always joke about how scrawny he was, so she put her handgun in the glove compartment of her car before they left—just in c ase.

The shop was a quaint little building that looked like it was designed to be a home but had been repurposed for the business. It had a pastel-pink wooden exterior with white accents, wind chimes by the door, a birdhouse beside the porch window, and an abundance of flowers growing in pots around the property. Hailey parked along the street outside, just behind the station wagon they assumed belonged to the owner since there were potted flowers inside it visible through the rear windows.

When they made it to the porch, the front door was open, but the screen was shut. The place had such an intimate feel to it that Hailey felt obligated to knock before entering, but nobody answered.

"Hello?" Billy called. Without a response, Hailey opened the unlocked screen, which jingled the little bell above the door, and they let themselves inside. The interior was relatively small, with a cramped vibe thanks to the numerous wooden tables inside that displayed all the colorful flower options. In the corner of what would've been the living room was a counter with the cash register, and behind it was an open door with an *EMPLOYEES ONLY* sign dangling from a crooked nail.

"It's cute in here," Hailey said.

"A bit small," Billy remarked, squeezing between the table of poppies and daisies, and the bougainvillea that lined the trellises against the window. "At least it smells nice."

Hailey stepped into the room with the register and admired the variety of roses on the table across from the counter until she heard footsteps coming from the *EMPLOYEES ONLY* door. She turned and saw a male walk in and recognized him immediately.

He was Westley "Flores" Parker, a classmate of hers from Mrs. Ivory's class and rising superstar athlete on the baseball team. Hailey wasn't into the sport, but everyone in town knew of him, especially if you went to Pineside High. He had just started playing on the varsity team this year and was already a top-five college recruit in the country, so he was a big deal. If anyone was more famous than Hailey in town right now, it was him. Standing at least six-foot-three, with impressively long arms and legs, unruly brown hair, and an unfairly handsome smile, he was easily the most desirable guy in school, but also felt so out of reach that most would just appreciate him as eye candy rather than actually pursue him. According to Ale, who, of course, *did* pursue him earlier in the year, he is so focused on his athletic success that he doesn't have time for a girlfriend right now and never had one.

"Westley? Y-you . . . " Hailey stuttered. She had never spoken to him before, aside from maybe once or twice in Mrs. Ivory's class, and only ever seen him passing by in the hallway. Up close and personal like this he was, to put it simply, intimidating. With a large yet lean frame and dripping with self-confidence, it was hard not to be in awe of him.

"Hailey, right?" he asked, showing off that smile of his.

"Yeah," she said.

Great, he knows who I am, she thought, sure the next thing out of his mouth would be a request that she leave his store.

Instead, he leaned on the counter, grabbed it with both hands, and asked, "What brings you all the way out here? You know there's florists in town, right?"

"Local stores haven't been very welcoming to me these past few days. I'm sure you've heard the news." Of course he'd heard it. They were in a class together after all, and by now, all her teachers had to publicly announce to the students that they would be safe, regardless of Hailey's attendance. And the increase in security on campus—especially in her classes—had the entire school gossiping about her.

He laughed and said, "Yeah, you've made quite the name for yourself." He stroked the petal of a small potted orchid on the counter. It was adorable to Hailey, seeing this athletic jock from school wearing a dirt-covered apron and caressing a flower. At least, until he said, "I can't believe they did that to those poor people. I mean, drowning that woman in tattoo ink? That's just . . . scary."

"I can leave if you want," she said, pointing her thumb at the door. "I'd hate for anything bad to happen to you, and I don't want you to be uncomfortable."

"No, it's okay," he said, walking around the counter and blocking the way to the exit. "I didn't mean it like that."

Hailey felt uncertain. Was he just trying to be nice and act tough in front of a fellow classmate, or was he actually not afraid of her?

"Are you sure? I mean, if you're scared, I wouldn't blame you."

"Me? Scared? No way," he said, sounding confident. "But how do you think they would do it? Shove flower petals down my throat? Or would they go biblical and give me a crown of thorns? Doesn't sound too scary to me." He crossed his arms.

Hailey giggled. "I'd be more worried about them choking you with vines." She ran her fingers across a red rose on the table and pressed her fingertip on one of its thorns until it started to sting.

He waved it off and said, "*Pfft*! Nothing I haven't done myself already."

Hailey laughed much harder this time, so much so that she wondered if she overdid it.

Are we flirting? she thought. It wasn't something she did often, outside of the harmless suggestion here and there with Billy or a cute waiter, and even less frequently would the flirting be reciprocated.

"I didn't know you worked in a place like this," she said.

"Really? Where'd you think I got the nickname 'Flores'?"

Duh. "I guess I never really thought about it. I just figured you needed a cool nickname for when they announce you at games."

"You think it sounds cool?" He took a step forward and examined a yellow rose just two pots down from the one she stabbed her finger with.

"It's a nice nickname, yeah. But I haven't heard them announce it. The only game I went to, you sat out."

He chuckled. "That's unfortunate. Coach Dudley only lets me play when scouts are watching. He doesn't want me getting hurt and ruining my chances at a career." He was fidgeting with the yellow rose now, rubbing a petal between his thumb and index finger.

"This one's so cute," Hailey said, stepping up to that same flower to smell it. It smelled fresh with a light, sweet aroma. Westley removed his hand from the rose and lightly grasped her hair that hung close to its petals.

"It almost matches your hair," he said, making her weak in the knees in a different way than she had grown accustomed to.

Flustered, she looked up at him as he loomed over her now. She glanced past him and into the other room where Billy was distracted with a Venus flytrap he was playing chicken with, sticking his finger in and pulling out before it closed on him.

"Who are they for?" Westley asked.

"Hm?" Hailey replied, not hearing him as she got lost in the moment.

"The flowers. Who are they for?" He released her hair and slid past her, their warm bodies brushing in the tight space, and Hailey felt out of breath as a sudden surge of arousal coursed through her. "Are you asking someone to prom? Or do you have a boyfriend?"

"No!" She didn't mean to yell, but she didn't want him getting the wrong idea. "I mean, I don't have a boyfriend. I'm lonelier than a stripper pole during the daytime." She regretted saying it as soon as the words crossed her lips, but his laugh and ensuing smile eliminated that regret.

"Noted." He laughed.

Looking down at the yellow rose, she bluntly said, "They're for my dead mom."

He puckered his lips and raised his eyebrows, unsure of how to respond.

"It's her birthday," Hailey elaborated.

"I see," he said, shooting quick glances around the room as though he was deciding what would be the best for her to buy, considering the occasion.

"Ouch!" Billy yelled from the other room. Hailey and Westley both looked in his direction, where he stood holding his thumb beside a cactus he must've touched. "I'll be okay," he said once he saw them staring at him.

"Sorry, my friend can be an idiot." Hailey grinned.

"Don't be sorry," he said. "I poke myself on those all the time." He walked over to the table by the window where they displayed mixed bundles of roses and baby's breath in colorful vases. "I didn't realize you brought your friends."

Is he jealous? Hailey thought, finding herself more and more enticed by him with everything he said and did. Their conversation—however brief—filled Hailey's chest with a warm sensation she hadn't felt before. *Was this what a crush felt like?*

"Just the one. He's playing bodyguard for me right now." Hailey walked to the table and stood closely beside him, letting her shoulder graze his arm, a deliberate touch to gauge his reaction. His fingers twitched like they wanted to reach for hers, but he tucked them into a fist instead.

Am I overthinking this? I think I'm overthinking this.

"From the other room?" He picked up a vase with a mix of red, purple, and white roses. "He doesn't seem very protective for a bodyguard."

Maybe I should try harder. Commit to the flirt.

"You're right. Maybe I should call him in here and tell him the big bad florist is threatening me," Hailey said, holding her hands behind her back and looking up at him like a puppy dog begging for food.

"There's no need for that." He smiled and spun the vase in his hand before setting it back down. He turned his back to her and walked down the aisle, carefully gazing across the rows of plants. "Did your mom have a favorite color?"

"Yellow and blue. She loved them both because we shared our blonde hair and blue eyes." Hailey followed closely behind him. He had a strong, distinct, spicy cologne scent that cut between the wafts of rose petals that filled the air.

He turned the corner and stopped beside the yellow roses with a smirk on his face before saying, "She sounds like she was *very* beautiful." Hailey felt herself go red. She tried to hold back her smile but couldn't help it; her lips curled all on their own.

"She was."

"So how about this?" He pulled a half dozen yellow roses from the pots and placed them on a small white table in the room's corner behind the register. Then, moving like a machine in a factory, he hustled into the room Billy was in and grabbed a handful of blue hydrangeas, then reentered the room with Hailey. "I'm going to make you a bouquet for her." He picked up the roses from the table and mixed them with the hydrangeas before placing them back on the table and looking around the room once again. "My goal is to make them resemble *you* as much as possible. It'll be like you're leaving yourself to rest with her—until your next visit, of course." He then reached beneath the table of roses and pulled out some baby's breath from a pot hiding there. "And if this bouquet resembles *you* in any way, it's bound to be stunning."

His words caught Hailey by surprise. No boy had ever talked to her like this, and especially not one that looked like *him*. She wanted to respond but didn't have it in her. Butterflies fluttered from her stomach and up into her throat, forming a lump that held her tongue down.

He brought the baby's breath to the table, mixed it with the other flowers, trimmed their stems, placed them in white plastic wrapping tied with a yellow-gold ribbon, and held the arrangement out for her to see. "What do you think?"

"Stunning," she said, reaching for them. They were perfect—much better than anything she planned on buying when she entered the shop, and her mom would adore them.

"I thought so," he said, handing her the flowers. Thinking of how she could thank him, she watched as he stepped back to the table, cleaned up, and tossed the stems he'd trimmed.

"I—"

"Did you find some?" Billy interrupted her, peeking into the room with one foot still in the hallway, pointed toward the exit.

"Yeah, I did." She spun to face him and twirled the bouquet. "What do you think?"

"They look great. If you're done, I'm gonna wait in the car. It's getting hot in here, and that added humidity doesn't help."

"Okay, I'll be right out." She watched him leave and waited for the door to close behind him before she approached Westley, who was waiting behind the register. "How much do I owe you?"

"Don't worry about it," he said. "They probably would've died if you hadn't come in."

"No—" She tried to deny his offer, but he insisted.

"Seriously. It's kind of crazy how frequently we throw out flowers here. I honestly don't know how my mom keeps this place running."

"Please, let me pay for them. It was nice enough that you made a custom bouquet; I can't just take them for free." She reached into her crossbody purse for her wallet.

"Consider it a thank you."

Hailey raised a confused eyebrow, keeping one hand in her bag gripping her wallet.

"Ever since you . . . "—he quieted his tone—"found that body, the local news has spent less time harassing me and more time following you. It's been nice, and I'm thankful."

"Are you sure?"

"I'm positive. What's that old saying? 'Your money's no good here.'"

"Okay, then how about this?" She let go of her wallet and leaned on the counter. "You've heard about the big prom fundraiser that's coming up, right?"

"You mean that cheerleader car wash thing?" He seemed interested.

"Yeah." Hailey chuckled. "Well, my friends and I are on the prom committee and are in charge of running it. You know Ale, right?"

"Yeah." He laughed. "She's a very . . . eccentric and . . . forward girl."

Hailey joined his laughter, mortified at the thought of what her best friend could've said to this man during her endeavors. "That's one way to put it." She twirled the bouquet in her hand, letting the sweet aroma release and find its way into her nostrils. "Well, we'll be running the whole show together and I think you should come." She fought through overwhelming nervousness to extend the invite, and even though it wasn't like she was asking him on a date—she'd never asked a boy to anything before—this was a big step for her. And, if Hailey learned anything from Camp Safe Woods, it was that life is too short to let nerves get in the way of enjoying it. "It'll give me an opportunity to repay you for the flowers."

"Does that mean you'll wash my car for me? That would be great, especially if you put on one of the cheer uniforms," he said playfully.

"I'm sure you'd like that," Hailey teased, still failing to hide her smile.

"Oh, definitely. But I didn't think you were on the cheer squad. Surely I'd remember something like that."

"Do you remember every cheerleader?"

"Only the pretty ones."

"Is that right? Maybe I don't meet your criteria, then."

"I'm having a hard time believing that. You'd have been a distraction for me during games if you were out there. You would've cost me a few scholarship offers by now, I'm sure of it."

The butterflies fluttered back down to her stomach, much more aggressively than before. Fishing for compliments wasn't her style, but she still wasn't certain if he was as into her as she was him, and it felt damn good hearing them. But she chose to quit while she was ahead and further her invitation without fishing for more.

"Well, lucky for you, I'm not on the squad and won't be washing your car. We're also running a bake sale at the same time, and I'll be working that. So if you have a favorite baked good, tell me now and I'll have a special one waiting for you."

"Are you sure you can't just borrow Ale's uniform?" he asked, and before Hailey could respond, his serious face swapped to a playful smile. "I'm only joking." He held his index finger to his lips and considered his options. "How about a cupcake?"

The car horn honked as Billy grew impatient, startling Hailey. She rolled her eyes, brought her attention back to Westley, and said, "Cupcake. You got it."

"Great. I'll see you there."

She shot him her best smile and started for the door. Before she left, he said, "Oh, I almost forgot!" He walked around the counter, pulled a single red rose from a vase with just two fingers, and held it out for her. "This is for you."

Chapter 10

"So, you and Westley, huh?" Billy asked, reclining the passenger seat as far back as it allowed.

"What do you mean?" Hailey asked, focusing extra carefully on the road ahead, as if making eye contact with Billy would allow him to read her mind.

"Don't play dumb," he said. "I saw you flirting with him, and your face was lit up like a Christmas tree."

"I think you're crazy," she said.

"I saw you hide that rose in the back seat."

"That's for my mom," she lied.

"Oh, really? Then why is it separate from the bouquet?"

"Okay, fine. He gave me a rose. So what?"

"So he clearly likes you. Is this a new thing, or has this gone on a while? Wait, did you go to that florist on purpose?"

"No, I didn't even know he worked there."

"So, what happened?" Billy asked.

"I don't know. I asked him about some flowers, he flirted with me, I *may* have flirted back, one thing led to another, and he gave me a rose. No big deal, okay?"

"If you say so," Billy said, closing his eyes. "Did he ask you to prom?"

"No, he didn't ask me to prom. We basically just met. Do you hear yourself?" Hailey felt herself getting flustered so she redirected. "Did you ask Ale to prom?"

Billy raised a lone eyebrow. "No. Not yet anyway. I haven't found the right time."

"Right time? Just do it. There's no such thing as a right time. Just shoot her a text right now."

"Yeah, maybe if I wanted her to reject me."

"Well, you'll run out of time if you keep waiting. Someone else might come and sweep her off her feet. Plus, you already missed Valentine's Day, and you could've even done it when we got our tattoos." Hailey glanced at the squirrel rubbing against the steering wheel.

"I wasn't gonna ask her to prom on *your* birthday."

"I wouldn't have objected."

Billy shot her an "Are you serious?" look.

Hailey took her eyes off the road to catch his gaze with a "Yes, I'm serious" deadpan stare. Looking back at the road, she had to make a small swerve to stay in her lane as the road took an unexpected curve.

Hailey drove the next two and a half hours with Billy dozing in and out of sleep beside her. When they arrived at Greenhome Cemetery, the sun was nearly set behind the hilly landscape with a bright amber and pink glow that cut through large clouds casting gloomy shadows on the grassy field that gave the cemetery its name. They went through the open metal gate and followed the thin one-way road up and around a small hill, then parked the car in a roundabout beneath the lone weeping willow tree at its center.

"We're here," Hailey said to Billy, whose eyes were cracking open.

"Great." He stretched his arms up and wide. "Did you want me to go with you?"

"No, that's okay."

"Are you sure? It's not a problem."

"I'll be okay. Thank you, though. I won't be too long, so feel free to take a nap or whatever." She switched off the ignition. "I'll leave the key here so you can use the heater, but make sure nobody jumps in and drives off."

He gave her a thumbs-up, his eyes already closed. She hopped out of the car, grabbed the bouquet from the back, and walked carefully along the grass to avoid stepping over any of the new graves that had popped up since her last visit. Her mom's wasn't too far from her parking spot—just about twenty feet down the hill from the road—but it took a bit longer for Hailey to find it now with these extra graves. When she saw it, it was unmistakable: a small silver and bronze plaque in the dirt, marked:

Elizabeth Michelle Winter

Loving Mother and Friend

"Hey, Mom," Hailey said with tears she promised she wouldn't let out welling beneath her eyelids. "Happy Birthday. I brought you some flowers." She gazed at the bouquet before placing it gently atop the plaque's corner. "The boy at the flower shop helped pick them out. He said the bouquet looked pretty, like me." Crossing her legs, she sat on the cold, semi-moist grass. "He was really nice and such a flirt. I haven't had any luck with boys throughout high school, so that was a nice change." She plucked strands of grass from the ground and sprinkled them down, watching the wind pick them up and carry them away. "But it was just a small interaction so nothing will probably come from it. I'm just stressing because prom is coming up and I have nobody to take me. Hell, even my two best friends are going together, and while I know I don't *need* a guy to take me, it would be nice if one did."

Hailey chuckled at her next thought, easing her sadness. "Alexa always tells me not to worry and that I'll 'get as much dick as I want in college,' which probably isn't the best thing to tell your high school senior daughter, but it always made me laugh, which in turn made me feel better. You'd be so surprised at how well she's done with taking me in, considering how immature she was and how much I disliked her when you were . . . well, alive." She sniffled. "She's been great. Honestly, she matured so much in like an instant. We get along great, and I couldn't imagine a life without her."

Hailey stretched her legs out wide, spreading them around the plaque, imagining it as her mother's head resting in her lap while she spoke to her. "To be fair, I never could've imagined my life going the way it is now. Everything's so—" She choked on her words. "Awful," she forced out. "It's been awful, which is probably crazy to hear because things weren't all that bad the last time we spoke, but so, so much has happened since then, so I guess I need to fill you in."

She lay on her back and stared at the sky, initially to avoid letting her tears fall, but maintained the gaze because she liked the idea of speaking to her mom up in heaven rather than down in the dirt where her mother wasn't even buried. After she died, her body was never recovered, but Alexa wanted to give Hailey a proper place to mourn, so she reserved this plot and had the plaque put in place. And while Hailey wasn't religious after the things she'd been through, the concept of her mom's spirit watching over her from a special afterlife in the sky was a lot more comforting than the alternative.

"So this past summer, I went to a camp that was supposed to be good for kids who have been through traumatic events. And it was nice at first—I met my two best friends and had some fun—but the place turned into a living hell. The head counselor, Nick—or Oliver, or whatever his name was—went on a murderous rampage, killing a bunch of counselors, the nurse, and the cook." She felt like an electric current ran through her, causing her limbs to shiver as she spoke. "I was the one who found the first body. It was a nightmare. I even got stabbed." She winced as the memory of that feeling came back, filling her scar with a sharp pain.

"But my friends and I stopped him. The counselor in charge of my cabin took his knife and stabbed it into his head. I still don't understand how Oliver could do what he did. I guess his sister, Victoria, killed the rest of his family and a bunch of other people and wanted to kill him, too, but he escaped and was put into witness protection. I guess he was jealous of the other people at camp who were all allowed to talk about their problems with each other, but he had to keep it to himself or else he'd put himself at risk. The camp owner, Mitch, said that his psychotic breakdown wasn't just a severe response to the trauma he'd endured, but I don't get it. For someone who's seen as much death as him, how could he do something like that?" Hailey sat up, uncomfortable with the moisture from the grass seeping into her hair and top. "I guess that kind of murder mentality just ran in his family.

"But from there, Alexa agreed to move us out to Meadowood so I could be with my friends from camp for my last year of school. Oh yeah,"—she smiled—"I'm a senior now, by the way. Your baby's all grown-up. I just turned eighteen, so I'm an adult now too. I even got a tattoo, though I don't know if you'd approve." She admired the squirrel on her arm. It was finally starting to look less red and more like it was supposed to be there. "Alexa said you wouldn't care, but I don't know. It does mean a lot to me, though, so maybe you wouldn't mind so much. Sorry, I'm ra mbling.

"I'm sorry I haven't been here in a while. Like I said, I moved recently, and we had to get here early enough to get used to the town before school started, and I've been really busy since then. But I promised I'd be here for your birthday every year from now on. That doesn't mean I'll only come on your birthday, though. I'll . . . I . . . I'll find a lot more time, I promise.

"But things are so hard. If you thought that camp story was crazy . . . I don't even know what's going on right now. There's so much. I guess my biological father broke out of prison—I'm sure you would've loved being here for that. Then, I found another body at school. I-I don't know," she stuttered, "I guess they might be related. I think the body was a threat, and my father might be the prime suspect." She took a deep breath. "My tattoo artists were murdered just the other day, on *my* birthday. The killer left a message for me—a threat—and used my father's last name. I don't even know how they would know that unless it *was* him, but he shouldn't even know I exist.

"There's just *so* much going on right now, and I don't know what to do. I just . . . I just . . . I—" She struggled with the words because they were always the hardest for her to get out. "I just wish you were here." She couldn't hold the tears back any longer. They trailed down her face and dripped from her chin to water the grass between her and her mother's plaque. "I don't know how I can keep going like this—without you. It's all too much, and Alexa's doing a great job at the motherhood thing—so is Megan—but they aren't *you*. No one is. And this is all just *so* hard." She clamped her hands over her eyes and held them there, letting the tears fall down for as long as they needed to, until they stopped, and until she could breathe without hiccuping. When she pulled her hands away and opened her eyes, she noticed the sky was turning dark. "I miss you."

She leaned down on her hands and knees and kissed the center of the plaque. "I miss you, and I love you, and I'll see you soon. I fear my next few months will be awful, but once I get all this stuff settled, I'll come back and give you a much happier update." She kissed the plaque once more. "I'll stay safe, I promise." She adjusted the bouquet slightly and said, "Enjoy the flowers."

She stood up and wiped what grass she could from her hair, back, and butt. "Happy Birthday, Mom. I love you."

Chapter 11

The fundraiser started off slowly but picked up quickly after the first hour. Hailey sat at one of four long folding tables, each complete with dozens of storage containers filled with baked goods made by those handing them out. Hailey took Westley's request of a cupcake to heart and spent an embarrassing amount of time and money trying to learn and perfect multiple recipes and flavors, leading to her current selection displayed: vanilla, chocolate, strawberry, and her favorite—which she chose for Westley's extra-special reserved cupcake—white chocolate with raspberry frosting.

The group in charge of the bake sale all agreed it was the best idea to settle on one baked good each, so customers wouldn't have to wait in one line for their items and could spread out to the specific tables for whatever they wanted. As such, Hailey's table for cupcakes was the second busiest, only behind Leo's for brownies, which Hailey was 90 percent sure was because he had a special batch of pot brownies hidden beneath the table that he would pull out frequently for suspicious-looking customers. Next was Grace's table for her neon, '80s-themed cake pops representative of the upcoming prom theme. Lastly, with the least number of interested customers, was Billy with his chocolate chip cookies, which Hailey actually enjoyed even though they looked basic in comparison to the other options. Apparently he had a few customers come to his table after Leo's, asking if there was weed in the cookies, then would walk away disappointed.

Hailey was surprised by the success of her table, considering the fact that most adults in town feared for their lives during even small interactions with her. But she *did* notice that it was mostly fellow students at her table. Whether they weren't up-to-date on local news, or if they were classmates who wanted to show support, or if they were just dared to risk their lives and get in line, Hailey couldn't be sure. But it was a fun day for her, and she hadn't had many of those lately.

Out in the parking lot in front of them, Ale was in her full cheer uniform, upset with how wet she was getting while squatting to wash an elderly gentleman's Chevy Tahoe. They seemed to be making a lot of money, as there was a long line of cars trailing down the street, with supportive parents, teachers, creepy old guys—much like who Ale was working for at the moment— and students who already had their licenses all coming to support the cause. So far, the cheerleader who earned the most money from donations was Henry, the most buff, masculine kid in the school who joined the cheer squad for reasons Ale and Billy would often argue. Ale thought he was gay, but Billy believed he was trying to feel up as many of the girls as he could. Whatever the reason, the moms who brought their cars would get excited if they were given the opportunity to watch him lather up their vehicles and wipe off the suds. Those moms who were sent to another cheerleader were disappointed but watched Henry work from across the lot. Ale said she wasn't doing too bad herself, but her customers were mainly old weirdos so far and not the senior jocks or hot dads she'd hoped for.

With nobody next in line, Hailey was glad to have a quick break. She looked over at Ale and saw that she was rinsing the car she was working on. She looked incredibly uncomfortable in her uniform, while Hailey couldn't have been more comfortable in her outfit: a black hoodie with a pair of red Camp Safe Woods shorts that were a bit too cheeky to wear at school, but luckily for her, there wasn't a dress code for a fundraiser. For the first time in a long time, she wanted to wear something to impress a boy and also wanted to be comfortable for the hours she had to work today. Hailey knew her legs were one of her nicest features—mostly from Ale saying how jealous she was of them whenever they were exposed, which was a massive compliment from someone who held their *own* appearance in such high regard—so she didn't waste the opportunity to wear the shortest shorts she owned and flaunt her gams. But with the weather as cold as it was, being early spring, she had to throw on a hoodie to warm up the rest of her body while her legs were left to deal with it. Considering the way the sun had been shining throughout the day, there wasn't much suffering, just a few goose bumps on her thighs that she would rub warm between customers.

Billy looked bored at his table and Hailey felt like she could use some time out of her seat, so she walked over to him.

"How are we doing?" she asked.

"Great, actually. I think we're going to earn more than the car wash because all of their customers are coming to us right after." He pointed to Leo's table, which had a line of at least a dozen customers waiting. "And who would've thought the community would love brownies so much? I don't know how he's doing it, but the people are just throwing money his way."

Does he really not know yet? She resisted the urge to laugh at his obliviousness and, instead, chose to try and convince him of his friend's methods. "You know it's because he's selling special brownies, right?"

"Special? In what way?" Billy asked.

"They're adult brownies," Hailey said.

"What do you mean 'adult brownies'? They're just brownies."

"I mean, they have something in them that kids can't eat."

He looked blank while the hamster wheel in his brain kicked into gear until he finally caught on to what she hinted at. "Oh, you mean"—he looked around to make sure nobody could hear him—"weed?" he whispered.

Hailey nodded.

"Not this again. I keep telling you guys . . . Leo's not like that."

"Okay, okay," Hailey said. "Maybe you're right. Maybe the brownies are just *that* good."

"Yeah," he scoffed. "Much better than my cookies, at least." He looked past her, toward the parking lot, and pointed. "Oh, heads up."

Hailey spun around, saw Westley getting out of his car, and suddenly she felt as though every nerve in her body went into shock, as if all her preparation for today just jumped out the window. She had thought about this moment for weeks and expected it to go smoothly, but now that she was in it, the nervousness set in. He looked even more handsome today than in the flower shop, wearing snug-fitting jeans with a Pineside High letterman jacket over a black T-shirt and his dark hair slicked back like an '80s heartthrob. When his eyes locked with Hailey, his smile was enough to make her feel like she would melt right there on the sidewalk.

She adjusted her hair and smiled back. They hadn't really spoken since the flower shop, outside of shooting flirty glances at each other in class and the occasional "Hey" when passing each other in the hallway, but Hailey's crush on him had grown exponentially over the few weeks that had passed. Billy already had his suspicions about the two of them, and since he told her about his feelings for Ale, she had let him in on this little secret of hers—including what she planned on doing today.

"Great. Wish me luck," she said, her voice trembling along with her knees as she walked back to her table.

"Good luck."

She sat down at her table just as Westley stepped up.

"Hey," she greeted and cleared her throat, scrapping the nervous stuttering before it could come out. "You made it."

"Of course I did." He laughed. "I was promised a cupcake."

"Right!" she said, remembering that she had to grab it for him.

"These look good." He went for one displayed on the table.

"Oh, not those. I baked you a special one." She reached under the table and pulled out a small, round storage container that held his cupcake.

"Special, you say?" he asked as she popped open the lid and slid it across to him. He picked it up and examined it. "How so?"

"You'll have to eat it and find out." She smiled, her words slipping between nervous lips. There was no backing out of it now; she was putting herself out there. "Just don't throw away the wrapper."

He gently peeled at the edges of the wrapper and peeked at its interior until he saw it—Hailey's phone number carefully handwritten with bubbly characters so there'd be no chance he couldn't read them across the sharp ridges.

"You're right, it is special," he said with his signature smile.

The words equally relieved and excited her. But she knew that giving him her number was just the start. Now, the ball was in his court, and she would have to wait and see if he would actually use it—a thought even more terrifying than putting herself out there this much to begin with.

"Better than a car wash?" she asked.

He laughed and took a bite, closing his eyes to focus on the flavors before nodding and saying, "Better than a car wash."

Overjoyed, she held onto her chair tightly and kicked her legs while she watched him take another bite.

"How much do I owe you?"

"You're joking, right? Nothing after you gave me that *stunning* bouquet. I told you already, this is me paying *you* back."

"I know that, silly," he said. "But this is supposed to be for prom, right? That's important enough to spend money on."

"All I need from you is a text," she said, refusing his money just as he'd done to her. "If you really want to donate to prom, buy some baked goods from the other tables. Or go get that car wash you want so bad."

"Sounds good to me. If I'm lucky, I'll get Henry to wash mine."

She let out an ugly laugh she wasn't prepared for and it made his smile spread wider. His eyes communicated that he thought it was cute.

"Come here," he said, holding his free arm out wide for a hug, and she jumped out of her seat so fast, the skin on the back of her thighs peeling away from the chair from her nervous sweats made a quick tearing sound that she ignored.

When he wrapped his arm around her, the first thing she noticed was his scent. Whatever cologne he was wearing was easily the best thing she had ever smelled, and she didn't have time to think about it before she involuntarily moaned and said, "You smell amazing."

"Oh, you like that?" He pulled out of the hug much quicker than Hailey wanted to. She wished she could cuddle up in that kind of warmth for the rest of the season. "I just bought it, actually. I think it's called Tease or Tempt or something like that. One of those *T* words."

"Whatever it is, I would drink it straight from the bottle," she said, leaning in to sniff him again.

He stepped back and laughed, nervous for the first time since she'd known him. And just as Hailey had hoped, she caught his eyes looking her up and down, with an obvious lingering on her legs. "Please don't. It was very expensive."

"No promises."

"Well, I've gotta run. Thanks for this," he said, raising the cupcake.

"Are you sure? You're not gonna check out the rest of the fundraiser?"

"Unfortunately not. I've got some errands to run, and I only wanted to stop by real quick to say hi." He took one last bite of the cupcake and neatly folded the wrapper before sliding it into his pocket.

"That's so sweet of you. Thank you for coming." She hugged him a second time, really taking in that scent again.

"I'm glad I did. And when I get home later I get to find out whose phone number is written on that wrapper."

"Exciting, right? It's like a fortune cookie, only better." She pulled out of the hug to avoid being clingy.

"I hope so. I never get lucky with those."

"My gut's telling me that this time you will," she said, feeling embarrassed immediately upon realizing she unintentionally offered up sex in a metaphor.

He smiled and said, "We'll see about that," before taking a few backward steps toward his car, taking one last long look at her. "Nice shorts, by the way."

He noticed, she thought, making every little frozen goose bump on her body worth it. She gave him her cutest, innocent-girl smile she had available and said, "Thank you."

He gave her a cool, light wave goodbye and turned to walk away before she could wave back. She watched him until he was in his car and driving off, only looking away once she realized Ale and Billy were both watching her from the cookie table. As a customer approached them, Hailey hoped to act like they didn't see her interaction with Westley and retreat back to her table, but Ale followed her.

"Sooo, what was that?" Ale asked.

"I don't know what you're talking about," Hailey said, taking her seat and bringing her attention to the mom approaching with two elementary-aged daughters. "Hey, how can I help you?"

The mom smiled and opened her mouth, but before she got any words out, Ale said, "The question was rhetorical, bitch. Billy already filled me in."

The mom's face went sour as she said, "Okay, let's check out something else," and ushered her kids toward Grace's table.

Hailey heard one of the poor girls yell, "But I wanted a cupcake!" before she focused back on Ale.

"So why act surprised?" Hailey asked.

"Because I *am* surprised. *You* and Westley? Geez, you spend all senior year practically avoiding boys, then you come out and take the best option away from the rest of us," Ale said.

"I didn't *take* anything away. I just gave him my number. I doubt he's even going to text me."

"*You* gave him *your* number? I didn't think you were a first-move kinda girl. Somehow you're still surprising me every day." She sat half her ass on the table, in the tight space between the edge and the cupcakes on display. "Still, you've got to be careful with guys like Westley. I think you'd be much better off with a 'good boy' like Billy."

Hailey raised an eyebrow as she said, "'Guys like Westley.' What does that even mean?"

"You know: athletically talented, good-looking, and borderline famous."

"And you think he can't be all that *and* a 'good boy'?"

"Please, have you ever heard the phrase, 'too good to be true'? You're reaching into that territory now. Guys with those traits always have something crazy going on. Best case scenario: he cheats on you and you leave him. Worst case scenario: he turns out to be Ted Bundy."

"And why is it that Billy's your example of a 'good boy'?" Hailey asked in an attempt to gauge her interest in him since Billy still hadn't done so himself.

"Just look at him," she said, leaning back over the cupcakes so Hailey could get a better view of Billy handing a stack of cookies to a group of women who looked like they'd just come to the fundraiser after their monthly book club meeting. The smile on his face was hidden beneath his mask but was evident by his raised cheeks and glowing eyes. That was probably the biggest sale he had made all day. "Does he look like Ted Bundy to you?"

"No. No, he doesn't," Hailey admitted. "Have you ever thought about it?"

"Hm?" Ale asked, still distracted watching him.

"You know . . . *Billy*," Hailey said with an elevated pitch to emphasize the suggestion. "Have you ever thought about it?" she repeated.

Ale snapped her head toward her as if taken aback. Then, after a brief thinking period, she said in a serious tone, "Of course I have."

"You *have*?" Hailey asked, surprised not only by the answer but by the rare blessing of an honest and serious answer from Ale.

"Yeah, I have," she repeated, looking back at him while he entertained the mother and daughter that Ale scared away from Hailey's table. The daughter looked very disappointed with the cookie she was given. "But I always just thought the two of you would end up together, so I guess I convinced myself it was more of a dream than anything else." She stood up from the table and pulled down the bottom of her shirt.

"Wow," Hailey said, almost speechless. "I don't think I've ever heard you call *any* man a 'dream.' I've heard you use 'super soaker,' 'splash zone,' 'moisture magnet,' and 'daddy third leg.' But never 'dream.'"

"That's not true. I've called my English teacher, Mr. Fisher, a 'walking wet dream,'" Ale said, proud of herself.

"Okay, but do you see how that doesn't hold the same merit as 'dream' by itself? That's big, especially coming from you."

"Is it really that crazy? I don't think so. After what we've been through together, it's hard not to feel *something*. And watching him get on top of Nick and beat the shit out of him like he did . . . Well, that made *me* want to get on top of *Billy* and—"

"Please stop before you put that visual into my head," Hailey interrupted.

"Look, the point is: Billy deserves the world, and if *you'd* rather spend your time sniffing Westley's jockstrap, then giving Billy what he deserves doesn't seem like so much of a dream to me anymore."

"I won't be sniffing any jockstrap, but you have my blessing regardless."

Ale jumped in place and clapped her hands with excitement. "You really mean it?"

"Yeah—" Hailey said, her answer cut short by a suffocating hug from Ale.

"Thank you," she said. "But promise you won't say anything to him."

Hailey peeled away from her and motioned her fingers across her lips as though she were sealing them shut.

"Great," Ale said. "I've gotta focus on winning this fundraiser bet first. After I win, I can worry about how I'm going to ask him."

"Ask him out, or ask him to prom?"

Ale looked at her, confused. "I was thinking more, 'Would you rather have me on my back or on my knees?'"

Hailey laughed so abruptly she choked on her tongue. "You're joking, right?"

"You're right, it's a dumb question. I'd obviously look better on my back. But I don't know what he's into, so I want to give him the option."

"You really are in your own world, aren't you?" Hailey asked.

"For now. But with any luck, he'll be in it soon."

Hailey smiled. She'd never seen Ale say something so honest and heartfelt before, and it was a warm feeling hearing both sides of her two best friends falling for each other. She was happy for them and excited to see how the two were going to pursue one another, knowing both of their secrets.

Ale took a step backward toward her car washing station and said, "I'd love to stay and chat, but we only have a few more hours left of this fundraiser and I've got a bet to win."

"Yeah, you'd better get on it."

Hailey pulled her phone from her pocket to check the time, only to see that she had received a text two minutes ago from an unknown number: *This really cute girl I like just gave me her number. Would it make me look desperate if I text her now or should I play it cool and wait a few days? ;)*

Hailey's smile must've been big enough to convince Ale that something interesting happened because she stepped back toward Hailey's table and asked, "Who's that?"

"Huh? Oh, no one." She tried hiding her smile, but she was just too excited. She had worried that Westley would *never* text her and that she only embarrassed herself today with her little cupcake stunt. Getting a text back this soon only further confirmed that there was something between the two of them.

She texted: *You wouldn't want to leave that poor girl waiting now, would you?*

"What do you mean 'no one'? You definitely just got a text, and it made your face warm up like a campfire," Ale said.

Hailey's phone vibrated again with another message. She opened it like an excited child opening a birthday present. It read: *Oh, well in that case . . .*

Ale leaned in and said, "Let me see."

Hailey turned in her chair to keep it out of sight from her, then it lit up with another message: *Hey, this is Westley.*

Ale caught a glimpse of it. "Westley? He's texting you already?" She wore a cautious expression and said, "There's no way a guy like that would be so desperate, so he *must* be crazy."

"He's not desperate, and he's not crazy," Hailey countered with a big smile. "He just likes me."

Chapter 12

On the Monday following the fundraiser, Pineside High was throwing a pep rally to excite its seniors as they launched into the final stretch of the school year. Hailey sat in the gymnasium's bleachers, watching the assembly with Billy. She clutched her phone tightly in her hand, glued to the ongoing text conversation with Westley that had lasted all weekend. She wished she was sitting alone with him instead of Billy—and Billy probably felt the same about Ale—but both their crushes were unfortunately involved with the rally, so they were stuck with each other.

As the senior class settled into their seats, the last people to enter the building were Nia from Mozart's Record Store and Mrs. Ivory—both of whom looked sad, though Nia's sadness seemed tinted with dread *and* anger.

Nia took the steps up to the top corner of the bleachers where Billy and Hailey sat, pointed to the empty spot beside Hailey, and asked, "Do you care if I sit there?"

Hailey shook her head and Billy said, "No, go ahead." They lifted their backpacks from the floor in front of them so she could squeeze by; the sound of her combat boots stomping on the bleachers somehow overpowered the commotion from the entire Pineside senior class echoing within the gymnasium's walls.

"Is everything okay?" Hailey asked once she sat down.

"Yeah,"—she put on a fake smile—"just some bad news."

"Aww, I'm sorry." Hailey put her hand on Nia's back to comfort her and felt just how tense she was. The two of them weren't close, but she seemed like she needed someone to talk to and Hailey was always more than willing to listen to someone in need. "Is it something you want to talk about?"

She felt Nia's back rise as she took a deep breath in what felt like preparation for her lungs to spill her troubles, and before she could say anything, the gymnasium's speaker system blared to life with a generic '80s synth beat and Principal Collins's voice yelling in a motivational, upbeat tone, "Good morning Pineside seniors! How are we feeling about our last few months of high school?" The crowd cheered some, but not loud enough to completely drown out the music. With more enthusiasm this time, Principal Collins repeated, "I said, how are we feeling about our last few months of high school?"

Hailey glanced around the crowd, who cheered even less the second time, and saw Nia's mood worsening.

"All right," he said, hurt in his voice. "Well in these last few months, we've got some exciting things planned out for you guys! For starters, let's welcome our school's prestigious baseball team!"

Prestigious was a bit of a reach, considering the team only found success when Westley was playing, which wasn't often. Apparently they hadn't won more than three games in the past five seasons before this year, which was when Westley joined the team. But this finally got the crowd excited, and Hailey wasn't going to *not* cheer him on, so she joined in on the clapping as the music through the speakers quieted and the school's marching band led the team into the gymnasium. The band lined up against the wall opposite the entrance, beneath a basketball hoop, while the baseball players grouped up in the center of the floor. Westley entered the room last with a cool strut and wave, peaking the crowd's cheering. Hailey even whistled so he could hear her above the crowd and he found her, locking eyes and winking.

He joined the rest of the team and the band stopped their song while Principal Collins stood from the center of the front row of the bleachers and walked to the baseball team. "And with a special message, allow me to introduce our very own Westley 'Flores' Parker," he said with a proud grin, as if Westley was his son. He handed the microphone to the phenom, who looked nervous holding it.

"Hey, guys," Westley said, brushing his fingers through his hair, "I just wanted to say that we are playing our final game of the season tonight. It means a lot to me because it's my last game before I'm off to college, so it would be nice to see as many of my classmates in the stands as possible to give me that real Pineside send-off experience." The audience roared, and Hailey clapped along. Principal Collins reached for the microphone and Westley said, "Thank you," before handing it to him.

"Can we get another round of applause for Westley and the rest of the team?" Principal Collins waved his arms to hype the crowd as the baseball team made their way to a reserved spot on the bleachers.

Jackson from Hailey's class, who was also on the team, grabbed the microphone and yelled, "Go Penguins!" earning more applause, then he continued on with the rest of the team.

"Now, for those of you considering going to this season's final baseball game, we've got some excitement planned to commemorate the event. First of all, it's worth noting that you can pay for your prom tickets at the ticket booth prior to the event, so if you haven't done so already, you can kill two birds with one stone. And on top of that, everyone who buys a prom ticket at the game will be entered into a raffle, with the grand prize being a special limo ride to prom for you and up to six of your friends!"

Some kids in the crowd were excited, but most of them seemed as though they were done cheering for the day.

"That's pretty cool," Billy said, clapping slowly like he was excited but didn't want to be louder than the rest of the crowd.

"And don't worry, if you already bought your prom ticket and attend the game, you can present your ticket to the student working the booth and be given a raffle ticket." The crowd responded better this time, with cheers coming from those who thought they'd missed out.

"God, wouldn't that be awesome?" Hailey asked, directing the question to Nia in an attempt to engage with her and draw her attention from whatever bad news she'd received, but it didn't work. She just stared blankly at the principal and nodded her head.

"While we're still on the subject of prom," Principal Collins said, "We have some exciting news from your student body president and head of the prom committee! Everybody give a warm welcome to Grace Nisbett!"

The crowd roared as she walked across the gym floor, especially the boys who were over-the-top because she was the most attractive, popular, and desirable girl in the entire school. With traits like those, she earned the titles of student body president and head of the prom committee, though she never actually participated in any of the programs. She ran purely as an opportunity to boost her popularity and social media follower counts, and she only performed in the roles when it came time to give speeches, like now.

She wore kitten heels and a knee-length skirt that violated the school's dress code, but Principal Collins often allowed her to break the rules, using her privileged status as student body president as a reason for her to dress more "professionally," but Ale had convinced Hailey that it was because he just wanted an excuse to see one of his students in a skirt. She grabbed the microphone from him and addressed the students, "Hello, everyone, I'm Grace," as if anyone didn't know who she was by now.

She wore her hair straight and down. Her masterfully contoured makeup was a work of serious talent and art that made even Ale jealous of her beauty. She stood tall and proud as a polished orator with a soothing yet strong voice who would do great as a public speaker or an actress, demanding popularity and she had earned it—already being the front-runner for prom queen without a boyfriend to share the crown with.

"As you should all know, my very special team—the prom committee—along with our talented senior cheer squad, put on a fundraiser for prom over this past weekend! The numbers have spoken and proved that, at the very least, we have some great supporters out there, and I suspect that many of them are in this very room!" she announced, drawing cheers from the crowd. "With that, I wanted to share those numbers so you can hear how much money we earned for our special night."

"This is it," said Billy, sitting up in his seat, his full attention drawn to Grace as he eagerly awaited the results of his bet with Ale. The entrance to the gymnasium opened and Ale leaned inside; the entire cheer squad waited behind the door with her, clearly supposed to wait for an entrance, but Ale's impatient self had to hear directly who won their b et.

"Starting with the car wash, I want to thank everyone who came by and put our lovely cheerleaders to work. Thanks to you and your wonderfully generous donations, they earned a grand total of two thousand, three hundred forty-seven dollars and sixty-eight cents!"

The crowd roared, and the cheerleaders waiting outside chimed in. Ale clapped loudly with a serious look on her face, awaiting the next total.

"Thank you, thank you," Grace said, quieting the crowd. "But they weren't the only ones who worked the fundraiser. My lovely members of the prom committee also assisted by raking in some donations with their incredible baking skills. Let's see a show of hands. Who here checked out that bake sale and got some treats?"

About 80 percent of the audience raised their hands.

"Wow, that's a lot! Weren't they good? How about *my* cake pops? To die for." She smiled as she watched the crowd react to her every word, taking it all in. "Similar to our cheerleaders, this group of talented bakers earned a whopping two thousand, *six* hundred twenty-nine dollars and fifty-three cents!"

Billy was the first to cheer this time. His voice roared above the crowd and straight to Ale, who merely shook her head and stepped out of the room. He quieted and looked at the door as if he felt bad about gloating.

"You don't think she's mad, do you?" he asked.

"She didn't look happy," Hailey said.

"The bet was *her* idea."

"Still, she likes winning."

Once the crowd quieted again, Grace continued. "If my math is correct, that brings the grand total of the fundraiser to four thousand, nine hundred seventy-seven dollars and twenty-one cents. Which is basically five grand, which means us seniors are gonna be treated to a pretty *awesome* prom night!" As the crowd roared, she spoke above them to say, "Here to celebrate with a special routine is our very own Pineside High School cheer squad!" Grace went back to her seat.

Keeping with the prom's '80s theme, Eddie Murphy's song, "Party All the Time," blared through the speakers as the gymnasium's double-door entrance swung open and the cheerleaders marched in, stomping their feet and shaking their pom-poms in unison. Ale was in the center of the line of cheerleaders as they made their way to the center and danced into a triangle formation with her at the tip. She was the only one not smiling. She danced her way through the routine with minimal effort while avoiding eye contact with Billy. When the song and routine were over, unlike the baseball players, the cheerleaders split up and sat wherever they wanted in the audience. Reluctantly, Ale squeezed between Hailey and Nia. Billy stared her down with a shit-eating grin.

Principal Collins was talking with Grace as he collected the microphone from her.

"So I take it you heard?" Billy asked.

"Shut up. I'm not talking to you," Ale said.

"She heard," Hailey confirmed.

"Fuck both of you." Ale turned her head to Nia, noticing that her mood was sour. "Hey, girl! Why do you look like so . . . terrible?"

"Ale!" Hailey said, smacking her friend's arm.

"I've had better days," Nia said.

"You and me both. What's wrong?" Ale asked.

Nia took a deep breath with an even longer exhale, holding a blink like she was holding back tears. "I, uh—" She cleared her throat and said, "I just found out I won't be allowed to attend prom."

Hailey and her friends' jaws dropped.

"What do you mean? Don't tell me you have to go to work or something lame," Ale said.

"No, but it's *because* of work." She sighed. "My family really needed me to bring in more money this year, so I've been having to cut class to pick up shifts. Because of that, I officially won't be graduating on time and lost prom privileges."

Hailey and her friends exchanged looks of sorrow, and none of them knew what to say. Hailey wanted to open her mouth to tell her that it would be okay. She wanted to tell her that she would help fix her problem and that there was no way they could just kick her out of prom, especially given the circumstances, but Hailey knew she couldn't deliver on either of those.

"That's terrible," she said, offering up the only words she could find.

"It's okay. I'll get over it," Nia said. Strong words from someone who was on the verge of tears.

Ale opened her mouth, but Principal Collins was finally back in the center of the gym, addressing the crowd and cutting her off—which was probably for the best, given Ale's insensitivity.

"Aren't those cheerleaders great? You can expect to see them give another wonderful performance at the baseball game tonight. Plus, you know who else is going to be there? Our mascot, Penny the Penguin, for her very last sporting event appearance! And during a quick break following the fourth inning, we will have a special ceremony where she will pass the torch to our new mascot, which we will be revealing here today!"

Shock and interest filled the crowd amongst the murmurs.

"Wait, they decided on a new mascot already?" Ale asked. Billy and Hailey both shrugged their shoulders, just as confused as her.

Principal Collins announced, "We know a lot of you were against the idea of a new mascot for our school. We heard about your petition and saw how many signatures you got, and we were truly impressed. But that old suit was dated and we had a great opportunity to make improvements. So please, give an electric Pineside welcome to . . . " The drummers of the marching band began a drum roll, and a pair of teachers held open the gymnasium entrance.

The crowd went silent as everyone was on the edge of their seat. The mascot sprinted straight into the room, performing a cartwheel into a backflip and landed perfectly on the high school logo at the center. It was another penguin, only this one was more modernized and humanoid, even wearing a Pineside High School T-shirt over its thin body. The original Penny the Penguin suit looked more animated with a big belly, more like a true penguin, and more like something you'd see at a child's birthday party. This one looked stale and boring.

"Our new and improved Penny the Penguin!" Principal Collins announced to mixed responses from the crowd.

Hailey spotted Maddie in the crowd, and she didn't look happy. Her time as the mascot was coming to a close anyway, but being forced to pass the torch to a design as bad as this must've felt awful, especially after she tried so hard with the petition to keep the old one around. Sure, Principal Collins *listened* to the petition and kept Penny, but the redesign was arguably worse than replacing her altogether.

Hailey pulled her phone out and sent a text to Maddie: *Looks like Penny lost some weight.* She intended for it to be a joke and hopefully lighten her mood a bit.

The new Penny waved and blew kisses to the crowd, then ran to the Principal and gave him a big hug, lifting him off the ground and dropping him back on his feet.

"Whoa, I'm happy to see you, too," he said, nervous and relieved that he didn't fall on his butt. Penny continued waving as she made her exit from the gymnasium.

Hailey's phone vibrated with Maddie's response: *She looks like she's on meth. I'm not passing her any torch.* Hailey smiled and put her phone back into her pocket, happy that Maddie at least had a joke in her.

"That's all for today's assembly. Be safe getting back to class and don't stray too far from your teachers," Principal Collins said, waving the crowd off.

Hailey's phone vibrated once more. It was a message from Westley: *You should come watch me play tonight. It'll be fun.*

She texted: *I wouldn't miss it :)*

Chapter 13

Seeing the new mascot at the pep rally was a surprise for Maddie and not a good one. On top of that, she knew this would be her last sporting event where she could wear the costume. She already dreaded the idea, and if the powers that be expected her to spend that time passing the torch to something as horrid as *that* design, they were out of their minds.

After the rally, she was asked to meet with Pineside's cheer supervisor, Coach Dudley, in a private meeting with the new Penny the Penguin, Hassina. She was a petite and athletically gifted girl who was a sophomore flyer on the cheer squad, but she jumped at the opportunity to take up the mascot mantle.

"Maddie?" she asked surprised, in a thick Persian accent. "You were Penny the Penguin this whole time?" Then, as if a light bulb clicked in her head, she said, "That's why you quit the team!"

Maddie explained to her the importance of anonymity with the role, and Coach Dudley added his bit about how not even your closest friends can know you're behind the mask. Otherwise, rumors would spread and the magic would be gone. This reminded Maddie how lucky she was that Hailey didn't spoil her secret to anyone, but it also got her reminiscing about those friends of hers who treated her differently after she left the cheer squad without a solid explanation. But her time spent behind the mask was some of the most fun she'd ever had, and she wouldn't trade that for anything.

Coach Dudley explained to them both the procedure for tonight—how Maddie would act normally behind her mask, and between the fourth and fifth innings, Hassina would come out in the new costume. Maddie would act surprised about seeing the new penguin, give her a hug, then wave goodbye to the home crowd and leave the field. Hassina would cheer for the rest of the game in place of Maddie. Obviously, Maddie wasn't going to follow things *entirely* according to plan.

As soon as school ended that day, she snuck into the locker room and made sure nobody was inside. In the corner of the room, behind an office, was a storage closet that had been used exclusively for storing the Penny the Penguin costume. She took her keys out of her purse and opened the door, holding her breath in the hopes that her plan would work.

Once she saw the hideous, deflated, new Penny costume hanging beside hers, she exhaled in relief. She pulled the sad costume, which felt like something a cheap Halloween store would've designed, from its hanger and folded it into a small compact shape capable of fitting into the tote bag she got from a local bookstore that she used for carrying her textbooks around school. The helmet of the costume was a bit more spacious than the bodysuit, but it was malleable enough for her to squish it into the bag with one of her textbooks and keep it out of sight. After closing and locking the door, she walked to the opposite side of the locker room and tossed the key over the gate for the showers. That way, when people realized the mascot suit was missing, they couldn't blame her since she'd lost her key. They would just assume some other student stole the key from her and used it to take the costume.

Feeling as though she'd just stolen a baby from a nursery, she clutched the bag tightly to her chest as she walked through the school to the back of the parking lot where her sedan waited. Inside her car, she tossed the tote into the back seat, closed her eyes and took a deep breath, then exhaled.

"Okay," she said, her voice shaky. Before today, she had never done *anything* mischievous before, and she didn't like how it felt. Her nerves were going haywire, her stomach was turning, her forehead was sweating, and her arms wouldn't stop shaking as she grabbed the steering wheel for stability. She cleared her throat and tried again, confidently yelling, "Okay!" *It's just a senior prank*, she told herself, convinced it was a solid excuse to keep her out of trouble for theft if she got caught.

She pulled down the sun visor and opened its vanity mirror to look herself in the eyes when she relayed the plan. "Just go home, drop it off, and get ready for the game tonight." She opened her phone and confirmed that she had just under two hours to get home, center herself, and get back to school. After leaving her phone in the cupholder, she pushed her key into the ignition, put the car in reverse, backed up, then slammed on her brakes when she looked into her rearview mirror and saw it—Penny the Penguin. *Her* Penny the Penguin, standing in the parking lot behind her car and facing her.

What the hell?

She glanced briefly at the tote bag with the stolen costume in the back seat, then decided there was no way someone already knew she'd stolen it.

*So why are they standing behind my car? And more importantly, why are they in **my** costume?*

"Hey, asshole," she yelled as she stepped out of her car and stomped to them. "Don't you see me backing up?"

Penny the Penguin just tilted her head as if she were an animal taking interest in Maddie.

They must've seen me throw the key and changed into the costume.

"And what do you think you're doing wearing that?" Maddie whispered, not wanting to give up her identity to anyone who might be listening nearby. Luckily for her, the only people in the parking lot were already in their cars and on their way out. Had it been later, the place would be packed with students and locals alike coming to watch the big game. But for now, if the need arose, she could berate this mascot impostor without much risk for drawback. "You and I both know you're not supposed to be wearing that." She stared at Penny, expecting a response.

What looked to be a pair of female eyes stared back at her, visible from the sun illuminating the thickly netted eyeholes on the costume's helmet. They showed no clear emotion.

"Okay, enough of this," Maddie said, fed up and offended that someone else would *dare* to put on *her* costume. She stepped forward and reached with both hands to pull Penny's head off and reveal the asshole behind this terrible prank, when all at once Penny grabbed Maddie's face, their palm covering her mouth while simultaneously turning over their opposite fin and revealing a shiny chef's knife they had concealed. As soon as Maddie realized what it was, the cold steel pierced her navel and ripped downward, stopping at her pelvic bone where Penny pulled out the blade. Maddie's screams were muffled by the attacker's palm. She watched her blood spill onto the asphalt between them.

Maddie looked left and right as if checking the parking lot for witnesses, and there were none.

Why did I park in the back?

When screaming didn't work, she bit the impostor's hand, which only pissed them off. They pulled their palm from her mouth and smacked her across the face with their knife-wielding hand. Maddie fell onto the ground, realizing that her assailant's grip was the only thing keeping her standing at that point.

Penny stepped up to Maddie's car and popped open the trunk, then stared silently while she pointed inside it, commanding her to climb inside.

"What? No!" Maddie yelled. Penny put her hands on her hips and shook her head in disappointment, then wiggled the knife carelessly with one hand while pointing into the trunk with the other.

Maddie looked down at her wound—blood profusely poured through her ripped shirt and onto the pavement. If she had to make a choice, she decided on the one where she *didn't* get stabbed again. Biting her cheek to help withstand the pain, she held her hand against the gash, putting as much pressure on it as she could handle because she had seen in movies that doing so could help slow the bleeding. Hoping that someone, anyone would take one look in this direction, she crawled slowly, as quickly as her weakening body could manage, toward the car.

Penny waved the knife furiously, urging her to hurry but she couldn't move any faster. She scraped her arms, ass, and back on the asphalt until she bled. When she made it to the car, she tried raising up and straightening her arms, but that motion made it feel like a thousand knives ripped through her pelvis all at once. She screamed in pain, which only caused Penny to react.

She rushed to her side, covered her mouth once again, and dug her other hand into Maddie's open wound, which sounded like boots squelching through swampy mud. Using the gash as a handle, Penny lifted her off the ground. Maddie, already struggling to breathe, choked on the scream that forced its way out of her. The pain too much to handle, her bladder spilled and dripped down her dangling legs. Disgusted, Penny tossed Maddie into the trunk like a bag of garbage and slammed it shut.

She heard Penny open the driver's-side door and felt the car shift with her weight as she sat in the seat. Maddie then reached into her pocket for her phone, only to remember that she left it in the cupholder. The car's engine roared to life and reversed out of the spot.

"Fuck," she muttered, then recalled that cars nowadays are usually built with an emergency trunk latch in case anyone ever got locked inside. Her problem, though, was that she didn't know *where* it was located, and it was far too dark for her to see anything. Her fingers explored around the trunk lid, only to feel the carpeted interior, then decided it wouldn't make sense for the latch to be on the lid. Growing delirious from the rapid blood loss, she knew she didn't have much time left. As the car picked up speed, she couldn't even imagine where she was being taken. All she could do was use what little energy she had left to find the latch. She felt around the outside walls surrounding the lid, and when she came across the hard plastic of the latch, she grew confidence.

"Oh, thank you, God!" she yelled, or at least tried to, her voice failing to sound anything like her—raspiness and wheezing taking over. She opened her hand to properly grab the lever, but just before she could, the car screeched to a halt, and she rolled deep into the trunk, hitting the back of it hard. A pair of textbooks from her junior year that she never got rid of slid with her, and one of them crashed into her wound.

"Ah!" she screamed but didn't give up hope. She felt like she could remember where that latch was if she could just get back there. Crawling in the trunk with her injured abdomen on the floor, the car started moving once again, shifting her enough to feel a rip in her wound. She screamed in pain, using the last bit of energy she had, until she couldn't anymore. When her voice gave out, she closed her eyes and didn't hurt much longer.

Chapter 14

Hailey took extra time getting ready because she wanted to look top-notch when Westley looked for her in the crowd. She originally put on a nice button-down shirt with a knee-length skirt, but Alexa warned her how cold it was going to be when the sun went down, so she changed into dark jeans with a soft gray cardigan. Feeling like she didn't look much different than her usual school outfits, she knew there was more work to do.

She'd spent the following hour blow-drying and straightening her hair and the half hour after that putting on her makeup. She tried to keep it simple at first, with just some eyeliner and foundation, but then she saw her peach eye shadow. She knew how much it made her eyes pop, and Westley loved her eyes. Once that was applied, mascara was needed. And since her eye shadow was peach, the obvious choice was peach blush to match. With all that color accenting her eyes, her brows looked underwhelming, so she used a soft taupe pencil to darken them enough to not get lost on her face. With everything else done, bare lips wouldn't cut it, so she used her favorite cherry-red, matte lipstick to complete the look.

On her way out the door, Alexa stopped her, took note of her appearance, and joked, "I thought you were getting ready for a baseball game, not prom." Hailey took it as a compliment. "Go get him, girl." Alexa knew she was trying to impress a boy tonight, and she would *not* let her leave the house if she didn't look flawless.

"Thanks," Hailey said, feeling Alexa watching her walk all the way down the driveway to the sidewalk where her car was parked. "Don't wait up!" she teased as she hopped in the driver's seat. They both knew Hailey wasn't the type of girl to do anything crazy or stupid, but she liked feeling like she could make Alexa worry, if even just a little. Then again, Alexa was probably the only parent who wouldn't be mad if Hailey slipped up and did something stupid for once. Megan, on the other hand, would worry until her head fell off and never let her hear the end of it.

When she got back to the school, it was very close to game time and the place was packed. The line for tickets and the crowded bleachers were visible from the parking lot. Just outside the fence that lined the field were news vans and camera crews that Hailey knew were there to see Westley. However, it reminded her of when the news harassed her, not just here at the school when she found the dead body but also when she got out of the hospital after Camp Safe Woods. If Westley was the phenom everyone insisted he was, he'd have to get used to camera crews like this, if he hadn't already.

*Maybe he and I **do** have something in common*, Hailey thought as she got in line to buy her ticket. There already looked to be too many people for what the bleachers could support, and Hailey was anxious that she arrived too late. What made her even more nervous were the groups of students she saw leaving after they made it to the ticket booth. Among those students was Grace, who Hailey stopped as she walked past, saying, "Hey, Grace."

"Hailey? What's up?" Grace asked, looking up from her phone.

"Where are you going? Please tell me they didn't sell out of tickets."

"I don't think so. I just came to get a raffle ticket for that limo."

Hailey let out a breath of relief, then gestured to the scads of other students walking away from the ticket booth. "I'm guessing they did the same."

Grace shrugged her shoulders and said, "Most likely. I think you're safe, babe." Then she looked back down at her phone and kept walking.

When Hailey finally made it to the front of the line, she was pleasantly shocked to see none other than Billy working the ticket booth.

"Hailey?" He was equally surprised to see her there.

"What are you doing here?"

"Grace asked me for a favor. Are you here to buy your prom ticket and enter the raffle?"

"Believe it or not, I'm here to watch the game," Hailey answered.

"Since when do you watch sports?" he asked, confused. Then after a sudden realization, he said, "Oh, you're here to watch Westley play. I see you." He grabbed a ticket for the game and slid it across the counter. "Things must be going well with you two."

"Nothing's going on between us. We're just . . . talking."

"That's how it starts. Talking. Then you start going to his baseball games, and next thing you know . . . you're wearing his jersey around school. After that, you'll start making out and letting him squeeze your ass in the hallway while us single folks watch in disgust."

"Sounds like an exciting future for me," she teased. "You know, you don't *have* to be single, right? You could always just *ask* her to prom like you said you would."

He rolled his eyes and said, "Not this again. You're holding up my line. It's twenty dollars for that ticket."

"Don't students get a discount?" she asked.

"If you have your school ID."

She stared at him blankly until he broke.

"I'm only kidding. Fifteen dollars."

Hailey looked at the poster on the wall behind him advertising the limousine ride she could win if she got a raffle ticket.

"How do I enter the raffle?"

"You'll need to buy your ticket to prom here."

"And how much is that?"

"An extra eighty dollars."

"Yikes." She didn't want to spend that kind of money yet, but the limo sounded exciting enough to convince her. "Okay, I'll buy a prom ticket, too, then."

"Just one? I'm shocked you and Westley don't have plans already."

"Just one, and like I said, we're just talking."

"Sure you are." He reached under the counter and grabbed her ticket, then ripped a raffle ticket off the long red roll behind him and slid both across the counter beside her game ticket. "That'll be ninety-five dollars, Mrs. Flores."

"Gross," she said nonchalantly, handing him her debit card from her wallet. He charged the card and printed a receipt for her.

"There you go. Have fun," he said, placing the receipt with her tickets. "Oh, and if you leave the game early, they'll be announcing the winning ticket number over the intercom tomorrow."

"Thanks." She put the tickets and receipt in her purse and headed for the bleachers.

It was such a strange feeling for her—seeing this place so loud and lively when just a few months ago it was all worn down and dead-looking, and that was without mentioning the actual murder victim she'd found here. The grass in the outfield had been cleaned up, the baseball diamond had fresh paint for the foul ball lines, new banners finally replaced the old tattered ones, and the wooden frame that lined the base of the fence had a fresh forest-green paint job

.

She hadn't thought about the baseball game taking place in the same location where she'd found the body, and it made her feel uncomfortable. Especially considering the fact that she would be sitting in the larger, home team bleachers—the very ones the victim was hidden under. The alternative would be to sit in the much smaller away team bleachers and be separate from *anybody* she would know. Not that she was sitting with anyone in particular, but she knew Ale would be sitting in the front row with the rest of the cheerleaders who were required to attend tonight, and Hailey could try to find a seat near her so she wouldn't be entirely alone.

She justified her decision by telling herself that as far as she was aware, the murder didn't actually happen here, and if she was comfortable stepping over buried corpses at a cemetery to talk to her dead mother, she should be comfortable stepping over a place where a body *used* to be to watch her crush play a game of baseball. The thought of the bleachers being haunted by that poor woman did cross her mind, but she immediately scrubbed that idea and tried not to think about it, deeming it a silly thought to begin with.

The home team bleachers were on the side of first base, along with the small dugout just inside the foul line fence close to home plate. The away team's dugout was on the opposite side, with the players already inside receiving a warm-up speech from their coach. Between the bleachers and fence was a sizable concrete walkway, just big enough for people to comfortably pass through without hindering the view of those in their seats. To the right of the dugout, just behind the fence, was a small bench reserved for the cheerleaders, who were already present and wearing their long-sleeve uniforms, though they still looked like they were freezing in their pleated skirts. All except Henry, who was wearing a matching tracksuit.

As Hailey approached, Ale was flirting with a non-reciprocating Henry—as she usually did. Henry saw Hailey approach from behind Ale and escaped the potential group conversation as soon as Hailey whispered into Ale's ears, "Did you move on from Billy that soon?"

Ale jumped, frightened, and quickly forgot about Henry. It was all a game to her anyway.

"Don't *fucking* scare me like that," Ale said, holding a pom-pom to her chest as she caught her breath.

"You do it to me all the time."

"That's different," Ale said.

"How so, exactly?" Hailey asked.

"Hey, and don't talk about . . . " Ale leaned in when she whispered, "*Billy*." Then, in her normal voice, she said, "At least not in public. Rumors spread like peanut butter and jelly in this school." She looked at the other cheerleaders to make sure they hadn't heard anything.

"Did you know he's here right now?" Hailey asked.

"Watching the game?"

"No, he's working the ticket booth. I guess Grace asked him as a favor."

"He doesn't even like Grace," Ale said quickly.

"Whoa, is that jealousy I hear?"

"Shut up," Ale said, then air horns blared around the stadium. "That means the game's gonna start in about five minutes. You should probably find a seat."

"Good idea. I'm gonna try to find a spot in the front row, so just find me when you have free time." Hailey turned to walk away but stopped upon seeing a monstrously large, shadowy figure by the stairs for the bleachers. It was Maddie in her Penny the Penguin costume, staring dead straight at Hailey.

"Geez, you scared me," Hailey said, approaching her. She had no response aside from pivoting to keep her eyes on Hailey. "Right, you're in character, sorry." She patted the penguin's head as she stepped up the stairs, then squeezed through the front row of people to a vacant spot. When she looked back at the penguin, she was still staring at her, almost lifelessly, which started to freak her out. The air horns blared once again, startling Hailey. She watched as Penny the Penguin walked from the stairs to the cheerleader bench and waved to the crowd, hyping them up.

The field's speakers came to life with a familiar female voice that yelled, "Good evening, and welcome to Pineside High School, everyone!" She sounded like she was trying hard to be enthusiastic, but it was clear she wasn't. Hailey turned and looked up at the small press box at the top of the bleachers and saw that it was Nia inside with the microphone in her hand. "Are you guys ready for some baseball?"

The crowd's enormous response drowned out the sorrow hidden beneath Nia's voice. Hailey felt bad, knowing what she was going through, but she wasn't going to let that ruin her evening. She clapped loudly with the crowd while the cheerleaders shook their pom-poms and did a little dance as the home team came pouring out of the locker room and ran onto the field. Westley led the charge with an outpouring of energy that Hailey never thought she'd see from the guy. He was in his element, looking so much cooler than even *she* thought he could, and the screaming crowd was eating it up.

While players from both teams began their session of quick warm-ups, Journey's "Any Way You Want It" played through the speakers while the cheerleaders gave the crowd a rousing, energetic performance. To say Ale looked like she was in her natural habitat wouldn't do justice to the effort she was giving. She had better rhythm than the other girls, didn't miss a single step, kicked higher than everyone else, and, though Hailey would never tell her to boost her ego, she wasn't just a part of the show—she was the *star*.

But it wasn't Ale's performance that had Hailey overheating and sweating in her seat despite the cold breeze, it was seeing Westley's stretch routine in his baseball gear that she always thought looked ridiculous on guys, yet somehow it worked on him. The tight pants emphasized just how long his legs were and how toned his thigh and calf muscles were. When he pulled his arms high above his head, his sleeves fell and exposed his biceps that had so much definition Hailey could see veins popping all the way from the bleachers.

When he moved on from stretches to a warm-up game of catch with Jackson, the pitcher, she felt like she was going feral. She crossed her legs and bit her lip to remind herself that she was in public. The way his body moved so effortlessly but with such focus and precision was overwhelming her. To keep herself in check, she looked away, only for a moment but long enough to spot something that would freak her out and make her wish she'd never taken her eyes off him. Across the field, through the fence by the away team bleachers, Penny the Penguin was watching her. It was hard to tell, of course, because the mascot had big, indirect eyes on its helmet, but the way its full body faced her felt intentional and strange.

Hailey pulled her phone from her pocket and sent Maddie a text: *You good?*

She knew Maddie was upset about the passing of the torch tonight, and Hailey started to think that maybe she wanted to tell her something, and this weird staring was the only way to get her attention. But she also knew that Maddie wouldn't be able to check her phone while in costume, and she didn't want to worry about her when she was supposed to be having fun tonight—however uncomfortable the staring made her.

Following another air horn, both teams had a quick huddle with motivational speeches from their head coaches and their team captains—for Pineside's team that was her classmate, Jackson, who she knew was the pitcher. She couldn't make out anything they said from this far away, but she could feel the energy and see how emotional it made the team. Most of them were seniors, and with this being their final game of the season, not only would it be the last time they'd all be playing together, it very well could be the last time some of them played baseball *ever*. Hailey could understand why that would make somebody emotional.

When they were done, the school band came onto the field. The teams lined up along the baselines and removed their caps while the audience stood for the band's performance of the National Anthem. When they finished, the band marched off and the teams took their places in the dugouts and on the field.

Westley took his place at shortstop, which he had just recently explained to Hailey meant he would be positioned between second and third bases. He told her it was a pretty important role, fielding ground balls, catching line drives, and acting as the middleman for throws from the outfield. It all sounded very exciting to her, which was shocking since it seemed like he had more action in the one position than she had ever seen in an entire game of baseball. But her late-night phone calls with Westley could make just about *anything* exciting to her.

The top of the first inning went by quickly. Jackson struck out their first batter in four pitches with just one foul ball on the third pitch. The second batter had a nice swing, but the runner didn't get far. The ball flew fast and low, bouncing just once on its path to the right fielder before he caught it and threw it like a dart to the first baseman before the runner could tag the bag. The third batter hit the very first pitch with a loud *crack*, sending the ball straight over the pitcher's head toward Westley who made a leaping catch, landing on his back and breaking the fall with an improvised backward somersault.

Following the umpire declaring the batter as out, Nia announced, "That's three outs!" and the crowd roared. The cheerleaders cheered and did a small dance to the upbeat song that played while the teams switched places.

Penny waved her arms like she was *trying* to be excited, which was unlike Maddie's usually enthusiastic performances, but Hailey knew she was not happy about what was going down tonight. Hailey, on the other hand, was having the time of her life.

"Batting first for Pineside High, please welcome our pitcher, Jackson Grady!" Nia announced before he stepped to the plate with his walk-up song, "Till I Collapse" by Eminem, playing over the speakers. The away team's pitcher was a slim, cocky boy with a full-of-himself attitude that Hailey didn't like, and he held the gum in his mouth in his lower lip like it was a wad of chewing tobacco, which really ticked her off. He spit on the pitcher's mound as Jackson readied his bat, and Hailey almost gagged. Disgusting.

The first pitch came out and fell low near Jackson's ankles, but he held the bat high, not swinging at it. The second ball looked like it was coming straight down the middle, and Jackson swung for it, but it curved just out of the bat's range before making contact.

The umpire called, "Strike!" and the away team's bench started clapping.

Someone in the bleachers to Hailey's side yelled, "Come on, Jackson!"

Coach Dudley yelled, "Focus!" from the dugout. Jackson twisted his foot in the dirt and raised his bat. When the third ball came, he was ready. With a *crack*, the ball flew deep into left field and the outfielder had to run for it. Jackson sprinted down the baseline and ran through first base just as the ball was picked up. The left fielder threw it to the shortstop, who missed the catch, leaving the second baseman to step off, pick up the rolling ball, and race Jackson to the bag.

Jackson was forced to slide to avoid getting touched by the incoming baseman and was deemed safe by the base umpire. Hailey found her heart racing with the excitement.

Was baseball always like this? she thought.

"Please give a warm welcome to our second batter, Westley 'Flores' Parker!" Nia announced. The crowd went crazy, making Hailey recognize just how popular this guy really was. When he stepped out of the dugout, she snapped her head like a magnet to watch him walk up to the plate. He waved to the crowd, hyping them up even more during his walk-up song, "Toxic" by Britney Spears, making Hailey and the other members of the crowd laugh because it was blatantly unserious.

Hailey was *so* excited to see him bat that she was leaning forward and gripping her seat, scratching her nails against the rough metal. By now she had forgotten all about the fact that she had found that dead body roughly twenty feet from where she was sitting.

The first pitch flew blindingly quick toward Westley, but that didn't stop him from nailing it. As the ball soared through the air, she wasn't sure if she should watch him running the bases or watch the ball for its potential to land out of the park. She tried to keep her eye on the ball but lost it when it crossed between her and the stadium lights, so she watched Westley and Jackson instead—both running with so much motivation, Hailey was in awe. Then the home crowd let out a collective groan when the ball landed inbounds. They cheered again once Jackson crossed home plate, but Hailey felt very anxious watching Westley try to make it to third with the ball flying in from left field.

When the baseman got hold of the ball, Westley was about 80 percent of the way to the base, so he had to turn and run back to second. This prompted a funny game of hot box as the second and third basemen kept throwing the ball back and forth, closing their distance to him with each pass while he tried to safely reach a base. Unfortunately, he was tagged out when he tried to pull a fast one and sneak past the third baseman, but he didn't fall for it. Hailey was still proud of him because he ran Jackson in at least, and the smile on his face told her he was having fun.

The game wasn't always that entertaining, though—the pace slowed after the first few batters and seeing only a few hits here and there from both teams prompted some small bursts of excitement for Hailey when the ball would go Westley's way. He tagged a few people out and even assisted in a double play during the third inning, which had Hailey clapping like she'd been a fan of the sport her whole life.

By the time the fourth inning came around, Pineside was just barely losing, then Westley finally stepped up to the plate again. This time, though, the away team knew better than to let him hit a ball. They threw four consecutive intentional balls out of the strike zone, walking him to first base where he stayed until the next batter struck out, sending them into the fifth inning. But not before Nia announced that they'd take a quick break for a special ceremony.

Chapter 15

Both teams headed to their respective dugouts to have discussions with their coaches while Penny the Penguin, accompanied by the Pineside cheerleaders and Principal Collins, walked to the pitcher's mound.

Principal Collins pulled an index card from his jacket pocket and tried to read into a microphone, but no sound came out. He smacked the mic and looked up to the press box, confused and annoyed. Hailey also looked at the press box and saw Nia make a face implying that she'd just remembered her task and clicked a button on the laptop in front of her.

Then Principal Collins spoke loud and clear over the speakers, "Good evening, everyone." He waved at the away team bleachers. "For those who don't know me, I am Principal Collins of Pineside High School." He looked back at the scoreboard, where the unimpressive score was displayed:

Home - 1

Away - 2

"How about that game?" he asked, prompting claps mostly from the away side. Then, under his breath, he uttered, "I'm sure that score will turn around soon enough. Now where was I?" He looked down at the index card he held and said, "Oh, right. How many of you recognize our school's very special mascot, Penny the Penguin?"

The crowd cheered, but Hailey didn't. She knew what was about to happen—as did all of the other seniors who attended the assembly that morning—and she wasn't happy about it. Moreover, she felt uncomfortable because even out there in the center of the baseball diamond, with all eyes on her, Penny the Penguin was staring at Hailey.

She didn't know what to do. Was her friend desperately reaching out to her? All her instincts told her that this was something else, but she couldn't tell what. The behavior raised red flags in her brain, and she felt crazy for it.

It's okay, she told herself. *Maddie's just upset about the mascot.*

"I'm sure most of you have heard by now, but for those of you who haven't," Principal Collins started—a voice for Hailey to focus on while trying to ignore the big creepy penguin that was shooting darts at her with her eyes—"tonight is the end of the road for this legendary penguin." The crowd was mostly silent. "But that also means that it is time to bring in our new, iconic mascot. Give it up for the revamped, improved, and freshly designed version of Penny!"

Charging out of the dugout, like anything *other* than a penguin would, was the new mascot. They did a series of cartwheels and flips as they approached the center of the baseball diamond while some energetic tune played over the speakers. The crowd roared, watching the new spectacle, but Hailey was too distracted to notice anything other than the old Penny mascot leaving the field. As she left, she headed toward the locker rooms and out of sight.

Hailey sent Maddie another text: *Hey, are you okay? You're kind of freaking me out.*

When she looked at the field, Principal Collins looked confused as to where the old Penny went, but he played it off like it was all part of the plan. The new Penny finished their routine and hyped up the crowd, waving her arms as the song ended.

"All right, how was *that?*" Principal Collins asked the already excited crowd before saying, "This new Penny will be here all night and at every school event moving forward. Now, let's get back to some baseball!" He put his hand on the new Penny's back and guided her outside the fence while the away team's players rushed the field and took their defensive positions.

The next few innings weren't great for Hailey because she couldn't shake the jitters she got from Penny the Penguin. Maddie hadn't messaged her back, and she didn't know what to think about it. On top of that, the game was starting to bore her; the score hadn't changed and she was getting hungry, but she knew if she left her seat, she would lose her spot and wouldn't get one nearly as good again. Plus, it was getting dark outside, the breeze was picking up, and she was getting cold. But she knew Westley was going to bat again pretty soon, so she tried her best to stay excited.

To help with that, right before the seventh and final inning came around, Nia spoke over the speakers, "Can I have the attention of all Pineside seniors, please?" Hailey's ears perked up. "I know you've been waiting all night for this, so I'd like to announce the winning raffle ticket for the limo ride giveaway." It was obvious she was reading off a script, but clearly she was ignoring the directive to sound excited about it. "I'm gonna call the winning ticket now, and you can either bring it to Billy at the ticket booth to redeem your prize or bring it to the office at school tomorrow. We will also announce the winning ticket number during the morning announcements at school tomorrow if the winner doesn't come forward tonight. If it isn't redeemed by the weekend, we will pick another winner and announce it the following Monday." She sounded out of breath, getting all that info out as fast as she could.

Hailey dug her raffle ticket out of her purse as Nia announced, "And the winner is . . . "— she paused as if she was pulling the ticket herself—"ticket number ending in one seven three eight." And just like that, Hailey forgot all about Penny the Penguin. She won.

She wanted to scream and jump out of her seat, but she also didn't want to draw attention to herself. She felt like she had won the lottery. She'd never won a raffle before, and it felt great.

"Again, the winning ticket ends in one seven three eight." Hailey double-checked her ticket and confirmed, pulled out her phone and took a picture of it, then slipped it back into her purse.

The mom sitting next to her noticed her excitement. As Hailey felt her eyes staring at her, she answered the question the woman hadn't asked yet, saying, "I won."

"Aww, that's awesome, honey," she said. Hailey didn't know if this lady meant it or not, but she didn't care. It *was* awesome.

She sent the picture of the winning ticket to her group chat with Ale and Billy with the caption: *Hey Billy, where's my prize?*

Her phone buzzed almost instantly with a response from Ale: *Fuck you, that's not yours.*

Then Billy's response: *No way! If that's yours, it's definitely the winner. Just bring it over here so I can confirm and sign you up.*

She smiled and replied: *After the game.*

As Nia announced, "All right, now let's get back to the game," Hailey spotted Ale on the cheerleader's bench, giving her a "Come here" wave.

Hailey sent her a text: *I don't want to lose my seat.*

Ale replied: *The game's basically over. Who cares?* She looked up from her phone and saw Hailey's displeased face, then looked back down and sent a follow-up text: *Just sit over here.*

It was a much better seat, and the bench was almost empty, so Hailey obliged.

"Where's the rest of your squad?" Hailey asked about the empty bench.

"It's cold, so they left. Now, quit your dillydallying and show me the ticket," she said, holding her hand out like a bartender asking for payment.

"'Dillydallying'?"

"See? You're still doing it." She took the index finger of her other hand and pointed it into the palm of her open hand, directing Hailey where to put the ticket.

"I'm not pulling it out. With my luck, the wind will blow it away or someone will steal it." The away team's first batter of their final inning stepped to the plate.

"With your luck? That's funny coming from someone who claims to have just won a raffle."

Jackson threw out his first pitch. A strike. Hailey tried her best to pay attention to the game, but Ale was too much of a distraction.

She better not talk this much when Westley's batting, Hailey thought.

Ale must've noticed Hailey not giving her full attention to her, so she said, "So are me and Billy joining you in that limo ride or is it just gonna be you, Westley, and all his baseball jock buddies that you're suddenly so interested i n?"

"I don't know. Are you and Billy going to prom together or is he bringing Grace?" Hailey teased, then felt bad immediately after. Ale wasn't the type to be insecure about things, but she also hadn't ever seemed as emotionally attached to another boy before Billy. Ale and Billy were tiptoeing around a genuine relationship that Hailey knew they were *both* heavily interested in, and she felt like the secret was going to burn out of her throat at any given second. She just wanted to find the best way to organically push the two together and finally make it happen.

"Billy could bring a tiara-wearing fuck doll to prom and it wouldn't stop me from getting in the limo with you guys."

I guess she wasn't going to be insecure about it after all, Hailey thought, relieved she didn't cross a line with her remark. She went quiet as she brought her full attention to the game. The away team failed to put any points on the board before their three outs, leaving it up to Pineside's final attempt to flip the score.

Down by one, they had to start the inning with the last guy in the batting order, a junior named Franklin. He'd gone to the plate twice in the game and only hit one foul ball, so Hailey wasn't optimistic.

The first pitch came in—strike. Then the second—another strike. On the third, to Hailey's surprise, he managed to hit the ball—a pop fly straight into the air for the pitcher to catch, sending him back to the dugout shaking his head. One out.

It was Jackson's turn again and he looked motivated. As he stepped to the plate, Hailey clapped along with the home crowd in the bleachers behind her. He hit the second pitch that came his way, after the first one went out of the strike zone. His hit flew between second and third, forcing the opposing shortstop to chase after it. Jackson slid into second base and stayed there as the ball flew into the baseman's glove.

Now it was Westley's turn.

With the game on the line, Hailey could only imagine how nervous she would be if she were in his position—but he wasn't. He walked calmly to the plate and even noticed Hailey through the fence. He smiled, so happy she came, then gave her a cool wave.

"You got this!" she yelled. He nodded and took his place, readying his bat.

Hailey clasped her hands like she was praying for him to knock it out of the park. With this being his last game before college, Westley had told her that scouts were going to be there tonight and scholarships would be on the line. He didn't seem nervous about it when he'd said it because he already had so many options available to him, but Hailey wasn't sure how any of that worked. He hadn't really done anything when batting, but the opposing pitcher didn't give him many opportunities. He did look good on defense, though, but only so many balls came his way. The game was so slow, she couldn't imagine how scouts could watch and pick out which players were the stars, especially when they only got a few opportunities presented to them.

Was losing a scholarship offer possible from this one game? She worried, then told herself that if Westley wasn't worried about it, neither should she be. *Just do **something** to show them you're worth it.*

It felt like it all happened in slow motion as the pitch came flying in, clearly out of the strike zone.

"They're going to walk him again," Hailey said, continuing to stress.

"What? Since when do you know *anything* about baseball?" Ale asked. It was a good question. She learned bits and pieces, looking into it online to learn more about what Westley *does*, but she also loved asking him about it when they talked on the phone because he seemed so passionate and knowledgeable. She'd also learned a lot today just by bringing her full attention to the game in its entirety.

"Doesn't everyone know how baseball works? It's basic stuff," she said, deflecting.

The pitcher readied up and threw another one. It flew in an almost identical path to the last ball, only this time Westley was ready for it. He stepped and leaned into it, smacking the ball with the most satisfying *crack* that echoed through the air, inciting an uproar of emotions from Hailey and the home crowd.

"Go!" she yelled to him, though he was already sprinting down the baseline. The ball arced over the entire field as though it was riding over a rainbow. The center fielder sprinted for the back fence, but he wasn't prepared to keep up with a hit that deep—not that it mattered because the ball would've never been caught. It disappeared behind the scoreboard, somewhere into the night. "Oh my God!" Hailey said, not realizing she had literally jumped out of her seat. And Ale was jumping and excited with her, really boosting Hailey's enjoyment of the scene. Both friends ran up to the fence and watched Jackon and Westley run the bases and wave goodbye at the away team's bleachers as they ran from third to home plate.

"And that is an out-of-the-park home run by Westley 'Flores' Parker to close out this one!" Nia announced, genuinely excited for the first time all night.

Once Westley crossed home plate, he immediately looked at Hailey and started walking toward her, but the home team had already left the dugout and charged the field, surrounding him and chanting his name.

"Oh wow," Ale said, as the team lifted him off the ground and carried him all the way to the pitcher's mound. While atop the crowd, he looked as happy as he was embarrassed. He pointed to Hailey and waved for her to come onto the field as they put him down. "Oh, he wants you!" Ale said, excited. Jackson and Franklin both ran toward the dugout, where Jackson went inside and Franklin held open the gate beside it for Hailey to enter through.

Her stomach flipped over with nervousness. She walked down the fence line as the team formed a semicircle around Westley at the mound as though making way for some big theatrics.

"Oh, what's this?" Nia asked over the speakers, drawing attention to them.

Hailey entered the gate as Jackson stepped back onto the field with a rolled-up poster in his hand and jogged back to the team.

"What's going on?" Hailey asked Franklin.

"Go find out," he said, urging her toward Westley.

She felt all eyes on her as she took the long walk across the field.

What is he doing?

I hope my hair looks good.

Am I walking funny?

These thoughts all ran through her head as the walk felt like it took forever. She focused her eyes on Westley, who was now holding the poster from Jackson, and he had this big, nervous smile on his face.

When she *finally* made it to him, he said, "Hey," followed by an awkward and nervous but cute chuckle.

"Hey," she said, letting out a nervous giggle of her own.

"I don't know how to do this. I'm not usually one for spectacles," he said. She laughed. "But I have a pretty important question to ask you." He began unrolling the poster, handing one edge of it to Jackson to help him hold it up.

In big, blue letters, a shade similar to her eyes, which she *knew* had to be intentional, the poster read *Will you be my date to prom?*

Beneath it was a giant empty square beside the word *YES*, and beneath that was a much smaller box beside the word *no*.

And as if the poster wasn't enough, he asked her, "Will you be my date to prom?"

She felt like her stomach would explode from the dangerous combination of nervous excitement. Her knees trembled like they were going to crumble beneath her. Jackson offered her a red Sharpie. She grabbed it with shaky hands and pretended to be confident in that moment, uncapping the marker and holding it to her lips, then crossing her other arm around her stomach as if she needed to consider the offer.

"There's only a *ton* of people watching you. No pressure, though," Jackson joked, yielding an elbow smack from Westley behind the poster.

"Hurry up and do it!" Ale yelled through the fence.

Hailey looked back at her with a "Don't rush me face" and saw Billy standing there beside her, eager to find out what she was going to mark.

Finished with her pretending, she stepped in and drew a big heart in the box beside the word *YES*, prompting the baseball team to explode with cheers and teasing of Westley. The audience somehow cheered even louder than the team, and Ale cheered the loudest of them all. They even got some claps from the away team's dugout. Westley let Jackson take the poster away so he could hug Hailey. She felt so warm in his grasp, and when he lifted her off the ground, she screamed—but not because she was afraid, because she was beyond happy. He spun her around in a circle and she felt like she was flying.

For one last announcement, Nia said, "Look at that, folks . . . he gets the home run *and* the girl. Talk about a storybook ending."

Chapter 16

Hailey was the first student in class the next morning, revitalized with newfound excitement for going to school. She wasn't even tired like Megan warned her she would be after staying up until almost four in the morning on the phone with Westley, talking about anything, everything, and nothing all the same. On the other hand, Alexa was so proud of her, telling her to enjoy herself because romantic guys like him are rare. Then she made a joke about that being why she chose to go with women instead.

At class, Mrs. Ivory greeted her with a comment about how cute the promposal at the game was, and it made Hailey feel all giddy just thinking about it again. She couldn't believe that something so exciting happened to *her*, and it all just felt so unreal.

When Westley got to class, he took the seat beside Hailey that Maddie usually sat in, which reminded her about how strange she was acting in costume at the game and that she never got a response from her. But that thought quickly passed when Jackson walked in, pointed at the two of them sitting together, and yelled out, "Look at those two lovebirds!" to which the crowd laughed.

Class went on as usual, with Mrs. Ivory lecturing about their latest assigned reading of Shakespeare's *Romeo and Juliet* for about twenty minutes when Hailey's phone vibrated with a text that made her heart drop. It was from Tiffany Watson—who she was happy not to have heard from in a while—and it read: *Do you happen to know a senior at your school named Madelyn Bennett?*

She means Maddie!

Hailey's eyes darted to the seat Westley was in, where Maddie was supposed to be, and he took notice of the fear in her eyes.

If she's texting me, something must've happened!

She looked around the classroom and confirmed that Maddie never showed up, and without her Penny the Penguin responsibilities, she would have no real reason to be this late to class today.

She typed anxiously, having to fix multiple misspellings before sending her response: *Yes, I know her. Please tell me she's okay.*

Then she swiped to her conversation with Maddie and sent: *Please just text me back.*

She gasped out loud, drawing looks from the whole class—most importantly, Mrs. Ivory—when she got the follow-up from Tiffany: *Her parents reported her missing this morning. They were expecting her to come home late after that baseball game. She never did.*

"Hailey, put your phone away, please. You may be living in your own version of *Romeo and Juliet* right now, but that doesn't excuse you from the lesson," Mrs. Ivory said, drawing snickers from the other students. Westley didn't laugh, though. He looked as concerned for Hailey as she was for Maddie.

Before slipping her phone into her pocket, she received one more text from Tiffany: *Word hasn't gotten out yet, but I'm sure it will in the next few hours. Prepare yourself for a heavy news presence on campus.*

Great, she thought, gritting her teeth and closing her eyes until Westley tapped her shoulder.

He offered her a folded note: *What's wrong?*

Hailey grabbed her pen from her desk and wrote: *Maddie was reported missing this morning.* She handed it to Westley while Mrs. Ivory continued her lecture, walking between the rows of desks.

Westley mouthed, "Are you serious?" The note, lying open on his desk, was snatched by Mrs. Ivory as she walked by.

"Now, unless this correspondence speaks of exile and poison, it is irrelevant to our lesson and therefore disrespectful," she said, adjusting her glasses to read the piece of paper, which quickly shifted her attitude. She looked around the class—a room full of kids staring at her, eager to hear what the note said. A room without Maddie.

"Read it!" Jackson said with a fake cough to cover that it was him.

"Is this true?" she asked Westley, who looked confused, then turned to Hailey. "Hailey, did you write this?"

"No," Westley said, lying to defend her from getting in trouble.

Mrs. Ivory seemed annoyed and disappointed when she said, "Westley, if you're going to lie, at least don't be obvious about it. Come see me after class." She brought her attention back to Hailey. "Now, Hailey, is this true?"

Hailey swallowed the saliva welling in her mouth and nodded.

"Okay, then. I'm not sure where you might have gotten this information, but I hope you understand why it might not be a good idea to tell the whole school about it. So please, no more rumor spreading, no more note passing, and no more phone usage. You can do whatever you want in your other classes, but not mine. Class will be over shortly."

***

By lunchtime the news had spread—not only of Maddie's disappearance but also of Westley taking Hailey to prom, for those who hadn't been at last night's game. Everywhere she looked, she would either hear people spreading rumors about what happened to Maddie—from Christopher Atkins holding her hostage to Hailey being behind the disappearance herself—or hear students gossiping about Westley finally having a "girlfriend," which really annoyed Hailey, because she didn't think she'd earned a title other than "prom date." In fact, they hadn't been on *any* date yet, and she was worried that if he heard someone call her his girlfriend, that would run him off, especially considering the fact that he'd never had one before. Besides, she was enjoying getting to know him, and the fact that she'd be on his arm at prom was enough for her. She didn't feel the need to rush into anything else.

But all of that tension she felt from every eye on her reached its limit when she met with Westley in the cafeteria to share her worries about Maddie, and a female student she didn't even recognize snapped a picture of them with the flash on—not only embarrassing her but drawing even more attention to them.

Hailey stepped toward her, just seconds away from cussing this girl out in front of everybody while giving her a life lesson on privacy and human decency, when Westley grabbed her by the hand, calming her immediately. It was the first time she'd ever held his hand—which, to her surprise, was alarmingly soft for an athlete of his caliber—and the comfort it provided made her never want to let it go.

"I know a place we can go and be alone," he said, leading her by the hand and she followed him without question, like a child holding their parent's hand in a scary neighborhood. In that moment, she would've followed him anywhere.

He took her to the side of the school that had been mostly abandoned for reconstruction and remodeling. There, they entered the old library slated to be demolished over the summer.

"Have you ever been in here?" he asked, escorting her to the central area where there were desks nailed to the carpet without chairs to accompany them. The bookshelves surrounding them were mostly empty, but some still contained various reading materials. The room was dark; the electricity in the building had been shut off before the school year began, so the only light entering the room was from large windows behind the bookshelves and the double doors they'd entered through. Most importantly, it was quiet.

"No. I didn't realize this place would still be open," she said.

"It's not. Well . . . not really. They keep it open during school hours because they still haven't transferred all the books to the new library yet. Everything's still in their system, though, so when people want to check out books and can't find them, they send people in here to look."

"Really? That's interesting. How'd *you* find out about it?"

"I needed a book for social studies and the librarian didn't have any copies, so she told me. She's a nice lady," he said, taking a seat on the floor and resting his back against a bookshelf. He patted the floor next to him, gesturing for Hailey to sit down.

"Must be nice," Hailey said, "having people be pleasant to you. Lately, I'm lucky if people aren't outright rude when they tell me they have a right to refuse service."

"You're joking," he said, but neither of them were laughing.

"I wish I was. People are afraid to be near me. They're worried about 'death dancing with those around me,' or whatever that psycho lunatic running around Meadowood said, and honestly, I can't really blame them for being scared. I'd want nothing to do with me either." Westley just looked at her, listening. "You don't have to, you know."

"Hm?"

"Be around me. I would understand if it scared you. It scares me. It *horrifies* me. I don't really know what's going on, and I'm still not 100 percent sure that the message was really intended for me, but I think there are enough coincidences and bullshit happening around me that leaves me wondering who might get hurt next." Tears welled in her eyes. "I just . . . I would hate to be putting you in a situation you didn't want to be in—"

"Hey," he interrupted, "*I* asked *you* to prom, remember? Not the other way around. I did that of my own free will, because even through everything going on, I want to spend that night dancing with *you*. And I'm sure as hell not dancing with death any time soon. Just you."

She laughed, releasing the tears and her overwhelming emotions flowed down with them. "Thank you. You have no idea how excited I am for it. I just hope all of this other stuff passes by then so we can enjoy it."

He reached his arm across her shoulders and pulled her in. "We're going to enjoy it no matter what is going on. I can promise you that. After everything you've been through, you deserve to have the best night of your life."

"You're not just taking me to prom because you feel bad for me, are you?" she asked jokingly, but there was some true insecurity there. Everything felt like it was happening so fast, and she wasn't used to being this happy. She oftentimes felt like she didn't deserve happiness.

"Of course not," he said. "I'm taking you for a few reasons, but that's not one of them."

"Is that so? Tell me, what are some of those reasons?" She leaned her head on his shoulder and closed her eyes while she tried to calm herself. It was working.

"Let me think . . . " he started. "I guess the first and probably biggest reason is that I haven't been able to stop thinking of you since you walked into the flower shop."

"You haven't?" she asked. She felt her whole body tingling—as if every one of her nerves was reacting to his words individually. This is what she imagined ecstasy would feel like.

"No, I haven't. I always thought you were beautiful, but something in me just switched that day. I didn't just like looking at you anymore. I liked *you*, and I wanted to have you."

"Well, now you do." She twisted her head on his shoulder, attempting to move even closer to him. "What's another reason?"

He chuckled and thought for a moment before saying, "You're the only girl who never felt fake to me. They always see me and see that I'm popular or see the potential money I could make playing baseball. They have a look in their eyes that's real similar to the look of someone with a crush, only it's not for me—it's for the money and success. It dehumanizes me, and I hate it. I never got that look from you."

Hailey felt like he was speaking from the heart. He knew he had a future linked with money and fame, and he had to learn how to cope with people around him who didn't see him as anything more than that. Sure, the money and fame had crossed her mind—it would for anybody—but she never looked at him as only *that*. She was glad that he took notice of it. "Then what *do* you get from me?" she asked. A serious question on her mind since he sent his very first text to her.

"A little bit of everything." His grip on her shoulder tightened. "Starting with the way you look at me—it's unlike anything I've ever experienced before. It's a mystery to me, honestly. It makes me feel wanted, among other things."

"Other things?" she asked, opening one eye to read his nervous face.

"Well, it makes me feel like the person I was before I made the team. I haven't felt that in what feels like forever." Hailey smiled and closed her eye again. It wasn't what she expected to hear; it was so much better.

Wow, I do all that for him?

The double doors swung open, and purposeful footsteps filled the library. Hailey lifted her head from his shoulder and he unwrapped his arm from around her, moving quickly as if they'd just been caught in a deep make-out session.

Mrs. Ivory stepped into the central area they were in, surprised to see them there. It didn't help that they both looked guilty.

"Uh, whatcha doing?" she asked awkwardly.

"Just getting away from all the noise," Westley said. "You know, rumors . . . gossip."

She looked Hailey up and down, as if she could see the stress blowing off her like steam blowing off a sweaty body in the snow. "I can only imagine." Minding her own business, she walked to the bookshelves across from them and started piling books into her arms from the *RELIGION*, *OCCULT*, and *MYTHOLOGY* sections.

Hailey and Westley exchanged awkward looks, not knowing what to do.

"What brings you here?" Hailey asked, cutting the silence.

"I'm teaching an Anthropology of Religion course over the summer for the community college, and I need some reading material to reference historical beliefs involving human sacrifice. Most of these haven't been moved to the new library yet, so here I am." With about six books in her arms, she looked at the shelves disappointed. "I was hoping they'd have more, but I guess I have to remember that it's just a high school library." She shrugged her shoulders and started for the door. Before turning the corner to exit the central area, she stopped. "Ooh! They probably mention sacrifice in this." She extended her arm, struggling to grab a lone copy of the Holy Bible from the shelf beside her. "Catholics are into some real crazy shit. Oh, and you both probably know that you're not supposed to be in here right now, but I'll let it slide." She held up the Bible. "You two don't do anything in here that God wouldn't approve of, okay?" She smiled like she thought she was hilarious, then added the Bible to her stack of books and left.

"Wow," Westley said.

"Right? For a teacher, she is *so* unserious," Hailey said.

"She's kind of awesome."

"Oh, didn't you have to see her after class? I hope you didn't get in too much trouble," Hailey said.

"With her? What, are you kidding? She didn't even really want to see me. She said she just wanted to make it look like even *I* could get in trouble so people took her class more seriously. That way, she wouldn't have to dish out actual punishments."

"Wow, she really is awesome," Hailey said. Then the lunch bell rang.

Chapter 17

"Thanks for coming, guys," Hailey said, holding her bedroom door open for Ale and Billy. "This week's been so stressful." With everything going on, Hailey's moms suggested that she invite her friends over for a sleepover.

"Ugh, tell me about it," Ale said, throwing her overnight bag on the floor beside Billy's before jumping onto Hailey's bed like it was her own. "I had the cops questioning *me* about Maddie's disappearance. Can you believe that? I haven't talked to that girl in *months*."

"That's odd," Billy said, taking a seat in Hailey's computer chair at her desk.

"I thought so. Surely, she had closer friends than *me*, but I guess it's good they're checking all avenues."

"They questioned all the cheerleaders," Hailey said, sitting on the bed beside Ale.

"I don't know why. It's not like she was on the squad anymore," Ale said.

"Well, she kind of was," Hailey said matter-of-factly.

"What do you mean?" Ale asked.

"Nobody really knew this, and she'd probably kill me if I told you, but I guess given the circumstances, it's probably okay now," Hailey said, nervously twirling her hair. Ale just stared at her, waiting for her to elaborate. "She left the cheer squad for . . . a reason. *She* was Penny." Ale's face went sour, as though she was betrayed by her friend.

"The penguin?" Billy asked. Hailey nodded.

"Wait," Ale said, looking as though she were connecting all the puzzle pieces in her brain that suddenly added up. "So you mean—"

"Hey, you two," Alexa said, cutting her off as she stepped into the bedroom's doorway, "good to see you guys!"

"Good to see you," Billy said, getting out of the chair to give her a hug. Ale stayed on the bed and continued with her train of thought, ignoring Alexa completely.

"Wow," she said. "I was *such* a bitch to her. Why didn't she just tell me? And why did she tell you? It's not like you guys were close."

"She didn't really *tell* me," Hailey said. "I found out. I accidentally walked in on her changing out of the costume."

"And you didn't think to tell me?" Ale asked.

Alexa sensed the awkwardness and did her best to change the subject before the air in the room became too heavy, saying, "That's not so bad. I walked in on Hailey's mother when she was making Hailey."

"That's *so* gross. I didn't need to hear that," Hailey said, then turned back to Ale. "Maddie wanted to keep her identity as Penny a secret. She took the role very seriously."

"But more seriously than our friendship?" Ale asked, hurt.

"It's not like you *had* to cut her off for leaving the cheer squad."

"I think we should let Alexa tell the story of Hailey's conception," Billy joked, trying to change the subject before Ale got offended. It didn't work.

"Okay, you know what?" Ale hopped off the bed and grabbed her bag. "Fuck this. I'm gonna go wash my face before the anger sweat makes me break out."

As Ale crept past her in the doorway, Alexa said, "I thought *you*, of all people, would want to hear *that* story."

"Another time," Ale said, stepping into the bathroom and closing the door behind her.

Alexa turned to Billy. "Okay, so her mom and I were roommates in college—"

"You can stop now," Hailey interrupted.

"Right, sorry. I'll wait for Ale to get back," Alexa said.

"Or just, you know . . . don't."

"You're no fun," Alexa said. "Billy, do you like lasagna?"

"Of course," he said, smiling. Without the mask he usually wore on his face, the scar on his cheek made him look happier than he intended. Hailey was used to the look by now, seeing him often enough, but she was proud of Alexa for doing such a good job at pretending she didn't notice it, though she definitely did.

"Megan makes a great homemade lasagna. The whole thing from scratch—sauce, pasta, all of it." She made a chef's kiss gesture. "I think she's putting it in the oven now. I'll let you guys know when it's ready."

"That sounds amazing," Billy said.

"Great." She smiled at him and stepped backward out of the doorway just as Park Ranger Woodsby ran through, almost taking her out at the knees. "Whoa!" Woodsby ran right up to Billy and pounced on his lap.

"Hey, buddy! I missed you," he said, scratching behind the dog's ears.

"You kiddies have fun." Alexa patted the door jamb on her way out. Woodsby turned and rubbed his backside on Billy's legs, demanding targeted scratches, which Billy obliged.

"It's like he hasn't seen you in years." Hailey laughed.

"Weeks, years, what's the difference?" Billy brought his other hand to the dog's chest to scratch there too. Woodsby growled with overstimulation, which was funny at first, until he had enough and walked away, hopping onto the bed where Ale had been sitting. Hailey reached over to pet him. During a brief period of silence, they could hear Ale splashing water in the bathroom sink.

"She seemed really upset," Billy said.

"She'll get over it."

"You think so?"

"Yeah. She doesn't usually dwell on things."

"True, but she also doesn't usually get that upset."

"I know how you could cheer her up." Hailey smiled.

"How's that?" he asked, then quickly realized she was hinting at asking her to prom. "Oh, no way. Not while she's like this. If there's any chance she's gonna say no, I at least want her capable of making a joke about it. If it happens while she's upset, she'll probably just call me an idiot."

"Well if you don't ask her soon, *I'll* call you an idiot. She's not gonna say no, just trust me," Hailey said.

"How do you know that?" He was on to her. "Did she say something?"

"No," Hailey answered, but her voice cracked. She was a terrible liar, but Billy was an even worse people reader.

"Don't tell me that *you* said something to *her*," he said, agitated.

"Of course not!" she exclaimed, her voice working this time.

"But you *do* know something. That much, I can tell." He leaned back in the chair.

"Maybe I do, and maybe I don't. Just ask her already," Hailey insisted, just before the sink water stopped running.

"I'm going to, okay? Can you just keep it down so she doesn't hear you?"

"Yeah, sorry." She leaned in so she could keep her voice low. "How about we make a bet? If she comes in here, and she's already over the Maddie situation, you ask her to prom tonight."

"And what if she *isn't* over it?"

"Then you ask her anyway? See? It's a win-win."

"I don't think you know how bets work."

"Well what did you think I'd say? If she comes back in here still upset, we'll take our tops off and make out while you watch?"

"Was that an option?"

"No, you little perv!" She grabbed a pillow and tossed it at him. "Now cover yourself up. You can't ask her to prom with a visible erection."

"What? I'm not—You know what? I'm not even going to respond to that," he said, but still put the pillow on his lap and laid his arms over it for comfort. The bathroom door opened, and they heard Ale's footsteps in the hall. Billy pointed at Hailey and said, "Not a word."

Hailey mouthed the words, "Do it," as Ale entered the room dressed in cute, soft-looking, cow-patterned pajamas. She looked at them both like she sensed they were talking about her but couldn't discern what about.

"Those are so cute," Hailey said—something simple to judge Ale's mood through her response.

"Not ideal for eating lasagna," Billy said about their white color.

"Are we having lasagna?" she asked, then noticed the pillow. "Why are you covering your lap? Don't tell me you have a boner," she said, sitting on the bed behind Woodsby.

"No, I don't—"

"He said he wants us to get topless and make out," Hailey said.

"That's not—"

"It was only a matter of time until it happened," Ale said, unbuttoning her top button without hesitation. "Come on, Hailey," she said, urging her to join. "Let's see those titties." Hailey lifted her shirt high enough to show her navel, stopping just before exposing the scar on her side. Billy was loosely covering his eyes with his hand, and completely red in the face.

"Look at him!" Hailey said. "He thought we were actually going to do it." She laughed.

"Were we not?" Ale asked, with enough seriousness in her tone to have Hailey questioning if they weren't actually in on the joke together. She had unbuttoned three buttons—enough for Hailey *and* Billy to see she wasn't wearing a bra.

"Okay, you can stop before Billy stains my pillowcase," Hailey said, recovering from her laughter.

"Hey, I'm just saying I'm willing to go the distance to make him uncomfortable," Ale stated, now fully buttoned up.

"Well, you succeeded." Billy crossed his legs beneath the pillow.

"Speaking of going the distance . . ." Ale started, sprawling out on the bed. "Have you and Westley?"

Hailey raised an eyebrow.

"You know . . . gone the distance?"

She raised her other eyebrow as if saying, "Are you really asking me that?"

"Do you need me to spell it out for you?" Ale asked. "Has his penis entered your vagina?"

"I understood the question. I'm just surprised you asked," Hailey said, then backtracked. "Actually, no, I'm not."

"So answer the question, then!"

Hailey smirked. "Yeah, we do it all the time. Super messy stuff, right on this bed. Now that you mention it, he popped my cherry right where you're sprawled."

"Gross," Billy said while Ale scrambled to get off the bed.

"I'm kidding." Hailey laughed. "You think I'd do something like that without talking to you about it first?"

Ale reluctantly got back on the bed.

"Besides, Megan has a strict 'No boys in the house' policy for me," Hailey informed, still amused.

"Hey, what about me?" Billy asked, offended.

"You don't count," Hailey said. "Who knows what will happen on prom night, though?" Alexa's planning on taking Megan out that night, so I'll have the place to myself for a few hours."

"Your moms aren't dumb," Ale said, skeptical. "They wouldn't let you have the place to yourself on prom night because they most assuredly assume that you'll bring him over."

"Megan's the prudish one. Alexa did it on purpose with a wink and a nudge. She told me the worst thing that could happen is I become the mother of a superstar athlete's baby."

"And you'd be okay with a prom night pregnancy?" Billy asked. "That's low, even for you."

"It's not like I'm planning it! Like I said, I don't know what's going to happen. But one thing's for certain—he's not fucking me without a condom." She looked back and forth between the two of them. "What are you guys worried about it for anyway? Instead of worrying about my post-prom plans, shouldn't you worry about your *own* plans?"

Billy's and Ale's eyelids both twitched.

"If you don't find your dates soon . . . Well, you don't need *me* to tell you how much that would suck," Hailey said, pulling out her phone, pretending to have received a text. "Oh, Megan needs my help with the lasagna." She typed a message to show Billy, then got up from the bed.

"What does she need help with? Pulling it out of the oven?"

"She didn't specify, see?" She showed him the message she typed for him: *I'm giving you a chance to be alone with her. Make your move.*

He looked confused at first, then looked up at her, annoyed.

"I'll be back in a bit. You two get comfortable," Hailey said. Woodsby hopped off the bed and left the room before her.

"When you come back, can you bring me something to drink?" Ale asked. "I'm having a throat drought right now."

"There's no way that's an actual saying," Hailey said. "I'll see what I can find." She closed the door on her way out.

***

When Hailey went downstairs, she found Alexa and Megan cuddled on the couch and watching some reality TV show she didn't recognize, with Woodsby lying at their feet.

Alexa noticed her and asked, "Hey, sweetie, you guys doing okay up there?"

"Yep, everything's great." Hailey plopped on the love seat beside the couch. On the TV, a couple were arguing over something that seemed minute, but they were making an over-the-top big deal about it.

"Where are your friends?" Megan asked.

"I locked them in the room. I'm giving them some alone time," Hailey said, not realizing how bad it must have sounded. She looked at her moms when their silent response made her question what she'd said. "Oh, not like that. They've both confessed to me that they like each other, but neither of them has asked the other out yet. I set the mood and pressured Billy, so now I'm just letting that marinate, and hopefully one of them will crack and do it before I go back up there."

"No way!" Alexa exclaimed. She was a sucker for gossip.

"That's awesome," Megan said, reluctance in her voice. "But they're keeping their clothes on, right?"

"I sure hope so. If they've gone this long without coming clean to each other, I think they can go a few minutes without stripping down," Hailey said.

"Okay, just . . . How long were you planning on leaving them up there?"

"Until they either come down cheering with the good news or the lasagna is ready. Whichever comes first."

"That'll make for good dinnertime discussion." Alexa grinned.

"I hope so," Hailey said. "Otherwise, I'm just gonna spill the tea to both of them."

"Who do you think you are? Cupid?" Megan asked.

"Cupid's arrows make people fall for each other, and they've already been shot. If I'm anyone, I'm Eros, pushing them close enough to breathe in the love that's already in the air."

"Just don't ruin it for them. Think of how excited you were when Westley asked you to prom. It's not something you can rush, no matter how frustrating it can be as the middleman watching it all unfold. Some things just need to happen organically," Megan said, and Hailey agreed—to a point. The way Westley asked her to prom was something she'd remember for the rest of her life, and she would never want to take that from her friends, but she knew neither of them was making extravagant plans for popping the question, and it was maddening seeing them let so much time they could be spending together pass them by.

Woodsby growled and Alexa joked, "It sounds like Woodsby disagrees with you, babe."

Suddenly, his growls intensified and he got up to run to the sliding glass door. Immediately, Hailey went to check it out.

"Do you see someone out there, boy?" she asked, flicking on the back porch light. There was nothing out there.

"Do you see anything?" Alexa asked, getting off the couch.

"Nope. Nobody."

Then Woodsby simultaneously barked while the timer in the kitchen buzzed. Hailey hated the alarm because it was loud, dated, and annoying. On top of that, every time it went off, it scared the hell out of her. Combined with Woodsby's bark—a telltale sign of actual danger—Hailey's fight-or-flight response kicked in, and flight sounded really great at that moment.

"The lasagna's ready," Megan said, heading to the kitchen and not taking the situation as seriously as Hailey was. Alexa, though, knew that Hailey was on edge, and she wouldn't take that lightly. She locked eyes with her, and they both knew that each other was on alert.

"What is it, boy?" Hailey asked Woodsby, whose low, rumbling growl grew quieter and quieter until they heard something shatter upstairs.

Chapter 18

Billy sat awkwardly in the chair with his stomach turning in knots. As hard as he tried, he couldn't come up with the *perfect* way to ask Ale to prom, and Hailey was right—he was running out of time. And there they were, alone in Hailey's room, with Ale looking as irresistible as ever—her loose-fitting pajamas allowed a peek at as much of her skin as he'd seen since their one day at the lake at Camp Safe Woods, her makeup having been freshly washed off gave him what felt like an intimate look at her that he didn't see often, the freshly applied lip gloss that only made him want to taste her lips the more he stared at them, and the way her hair lay in a messy pile beneath her, unlike its usual perfectly coiffed state.

He hated to admit it, but Hailey knew what she was talking about. He didn't want to go any longer without locking this down. And why shouldn't he? What would be more important: the way he asked her to prom or the event itself, including all the time they'd have together in between? Plus, given how confident Hailey was that Ale would say "Yes," why shouldn't *he* share that same confidence? He wasn't going to wait any longer.

It's time to man up and make this happen, he told himself, sitting up straight.

"Ale—" he started, stopping when his voice cracked.

Not a great start, he thought.

"What's up?" she asked, rolling over onto her stomach so she could reach into her bag on the floor beside the bed. Billy couldn't help but notice the way her shorts rode up and the bottom of her cheeks peeked out. He wanted to look away and respect her privacy, but something about it felt like she was doing it on purpose, teasing him.

He left the chair and took a seat on the edge of the bed, turning to face her. "What do you think about what Hailey said? You know, about us running out of time to find dates. Is that stressing you out at all?"

She rolled onto her back, her phone now in hand. Once again, Billy found himself distracted as her breasts settled into place. They had never been particularly large—a detail that had never mattered to him—but today, unrestrained and natural beneath her pajama top, with the subtle outline of her nipples visible through the fabric, they were perfect.

Settle down, Billy told himself. *Don't make her uncomfortable before you do what you're doing.* But, working up the courage to ask her out was harder than making *her* uncomfortable. With quick, subtle glances, she noticed his eyes, followed their trail down to her chest, and without speaking, cracked a flirty smile.

"Stress *me* out?" she asked like it was a crazy thought. In one swift motion, she sat upright against the headboard, sweeping her hair back as if she wanted him to look. And for a moment, he indulged—just long enough to catch a glimpse of the soft curve of her breast through the slight gap between the buttons of her top, which had parted as she moved. "I'm not the type of girl to stress over a guy. I'm just waiting for the right one to ask me—and either he will or he won't. *If* he does, I'll have fun and make it worth his while. If not, I'll have my own fun."

So, basically, I have the ball to play or pass, Billy thought.

"What about you?" she asked, rubbing her right foot on her left ankle as though scratching an itch. She wore a cute, thin, rose gold anklet on her right ankle that Billy absolutely loved. It jingled as her foot moved. Her smile hadn't changed. "Are you stressing out?"

"I wouldn't say that," he said, scratching the back of his neck—something he did when he was stressed. He noticed this and stopped, then shifted on the bed so he was sitting against the headboard beside her. She crossed her legs at the ankles and kicked her feet with rhythm. "I have a plan. Or at least, I wanted to come up with a plan, but I was having trouble there."

She laughed. "What does that even mean?"

He was falling apart. Being this close to her, she smelled amazing . . . like roses grown in a lingerie store. Her skin looked so soft that he wanted to dig his hands in her thighs like a little kid playing with sand on the beach. But to contrast his excitement, he found himself more nervous than ever. He felt like he was free-falling, like the bones in his skin weren't his own, like he couldn't control the words that spilled from his mouth.

"Well, I was waiting for the perfect time to do this, but I'm honestly sick of waiting." He turned to her, confident but nervous all at once. Locking eyes, he couldn't help but notice hers were glossy like her lips. She was excited, too, he could tell. There was no doubt in his mind that she knew what was about to happen, and she also looked just as nervous as he was. "Alejandra . . ." He cleared his throat. She laughed. "Would you go with *me* to prom?"

Her smile opened wide, and she said, "Finally."

Before he could move, she had rolled on top of him. Her hair hung down over his face, which she grabbed and pulled up to hers. Her lips tasted like raspberries. Goose bumps raced across his body when her breath poured into his mouth between little kisses. When her tongue slipped into his mouth, it felt monumentally better than he'd ever imagined. He wanted to try his tongue next but didn't know how—it was his first kiss after all—and he didn't want her to feel like he wasn't into it, so he tried anyway. He aimed for the inside of her top lip, but she had a different idea, opening her jaw to bite his lip. When she got his tongue instead, all they could do was touch foreheads and smile.

"That's a *yes*, by the way," she said.

Instead of giving a vocal response, he pulled her close and kissed her again. He couldn't get enough of the taste—not just of the lip gloss, even her saliva tasted like heaven. The whole experience was so unlike anything he'd thought possible. All he wanted to do was get closer to her. Nothing could've ruined that moment for them. Until it did.

Suddenly, the window in the room shattered. Ale screamed, and Billy's excited piece of anatomy softened.

***

"What the hell was that?" Megan asked as Alexa and Hailey ran past her and up the stairs.

Hailey made it to her room first, and Alexa ran past it to her own bedroom, shouting, "I'll grab the gun!"

When Hailey opened her bedroom door, she noticed Ale on top of Billy on her bed before she noticed the broken window and rock amid shattered glass on the carpet.

"What happened?" she asked while Ale got off of Billy.

"How should I know?" Ale answered.

"Whoa, Mrs. Ramirez," Billy said to Alexa, who entered the room behind Hailey, pistol held high.

"Nobody's up here?" Alexa asked.

"No, but someone broke the window," Billy explained.

Then Woodsby started barking, followed by an ear-shredding scream from Megan in the kitchen.

"Call the cops," Alexa said before running downstairs.

Hailey already had her phone out, typing a text to Tiffany Watson that an attacker was at her house. Tiffany had a gun, and Hailey believed she would arrive sooner than the police. Hailey repeated, "Call the cops" to Ale and Billy before sending the text and following Alexa.

Woodsby's barking was as loud and rampant as ever. Pairing that with the horrified, tear-filled face of Alexa as she aimed the gun into the kitchen, Hailey feared what she'd see when she turned the corner.

"Please, let her go," Alexa pleaded. "God, please just let her go."

When Hailey looked into the kitchen, she saw Megan standing with her back to them, holding the lasagna she'd just pulled out of the oven.

Hovering over her, with one arm wrapped around her abdomen and the other hand pressing a chef's knife against Megan's spine, was the original Penny the Penguin.

Penny's head snapped toward Hailey as soon as she saw her, then she lifted the knife-wielding hand and waved to her.

"Let her go, you sick fuck!" Alexa yelled, shaking the gun pointed desperately at the penguin. Penny quickly brought the knife to Megan's rib cage, threatening to stab her.

"Maddie, is that you?" Hailey asked, but Penny only stared back like she did at the baseball game.

"Did she say Maddie?" Ale asked, picking up her pace as she started running down the stairs with Billy. This pulled the attention of Hailey and Alexa to look their way long enough to hear Megan's scream followed by the lasagna dropping onto the floor. When Hailey looked back into the kitchen, Megan was on the linoleum with the knife lodged in her side, almost identical to where Hailey had a scar of her own. The scene looked *extra* graphic at first, like something out of a low-budget, practical effects splatter film, until Hailey recognized that she couldn't tell the difference between her mother's guts and her homemade meat sauce.

While Alexa was busy screaming at her fallen wife, Penny charged them. Hailey didn't know how to react, because she didn't have a weapon, but neither did Penny. Before she could move her feet, Penny crashed into the two of them, pushing them both to the floor and turning the corner toward the living room where, just minutes ago, Alexa and Megan were peacefully watching the show that still played on the TV.

"Oh shit!" Billy yelled. "Is that Penny?"

Alexa raised her gun and fired a shot at the penguin, which breezed right over her shoulder and hit the TV, causing sparks to fly as the screen went dark. Hailey rose to her feet as Alexa fired another shot, which shattered the sliding glass door as Penny escaped outside. Woodsby chased her, barking nonstop.

When Billy saw Megan on the floor in the kitchen, he ran to Alexa, took the gun from her, and told her, "Go check on Megan."

Alexa nodded, Ale helped her up, and Hailey followed Billy to the back door where Penny had vanished. Just like the last time Hailey looked out this way, nobody was there, only Woodsby barking at their back fence. Penny was gone.

The two friends joined the others in the kitchen, where Megan's blood was staining Alexa's hands as much as it was puddling on the floor. Alexa cried, holding Megan, whose skin was turning pale, rocking her back and forth like a baby.

"Try not to move her too much," Billy said. "We don't want the knife to do more damage." Megan already looked like she was gone, and Alexa was an emotional wreck, but Hailey knew he was right.

Hailey, Ale, and Billy all turned their heads at the sound of glass crunching in the other room. Billy raised the gun, keeping it pointed at Tiffany as she stepped into the kitchen, her own gun raised, Woodsby following her closely

, sniffing her leg. Tiffany lowered her gun when she saw them and stepped forward.

"What are you doing here?" Billy asked, his hands trembling while pointing the gun, warning her not to take another step.

"It's okay. I told her to come," Hailey said, her hand on his wrist, lowering the gun.

"What happened here?" Tiffany asked, hovering over Alexa and Megan. She looked relatively unshaken, considering the stab victim beneath her, as if this was something she saw often.

"Someone in the old Penny the Penguin mascot costume broke in and attacked us," Hailey explained.

"You mean the costume the missing Maddie wore?" Tiffany asked.

Ale looked pissed, saying, "Even wannabe Gale Weathers knew about that, but not *me*?" The comparison seemed to annoy Tiffany.

"Now's not the time," Hailey said.

"It's my job to know things," Tiffany asserted, assuming that would settle Ale. It did not.

"Did you guys call the police?" Hailey asked.

Billy nodded. "They're on their way."

***

The night felt like it would never end. They spent the first few hours at the hospital, each giving their own account of what happened during the attack to the cop on duty, Officer Ronald. Hailey told him everything was normal until Woodsby barked like he did, followed by the diversion of the broken window upstairs, which was when Penny entered through the back door and caught Megan taking the lasagna out of the oven, causing her to scream, so Hailey and Alexa ran back downstairs and saw the rest of it happen. Officer Ronald questioned Woodsby's alertness, and Hailey explained how he was trained for his role at Camp Safe Woods to detect danger, which made Hailey remember the few times she'd been alone in her room and Woodsby acted up, making her question if whoever was behind the mask had been watching her before tonight.

Officer Ronald took note of this and tried to reassure her, saying, "Well, it's safe to say that we've finally got a lead suspect in this case."

"You do? Who?" Hailey asked.

"Madelyn Bennett. She's been missing for about a week now, and suddenly the mascot costume she was last seen wearing shows up at your house and attacks you guys? I think it's a safe bet."

Hailey didn't believe him. Why would she do something like this? It didn't add up.

"No, you're wrong," she said. "She wouldn't do something like that; she doesn't have *any* motive."

"Do you have any better ideas? We've gotta start some-where, kid."

"Well, if you start there, you'll be chasing nothing. I'm telling you, it couldn't have been her," she insisted. Then she had a sudden epiphany. "Wait, you said she was the last one seen wearing the costume?"

He nodded. "At the baseball game. Congratulations, by the way."

She shook her head, offended that he would bring up something so irrelevant at a time like this. She paused, getting back on track before asking, "What if it wasn't her? She always kept her identity a secret, and it's not like peo-ple are watching her change into the outfit. At the game, I noticed the penguin staring at me all night, and it was really weird. I thought Maddie was upset because it was her last time in costume, but what if it was really the fucking weirdo who's been following me wearing the costume?"

Officer Ronald thought about it for a second before saying, "Well, I suppose it's possible. But you do realize that if it wasn't her in the costume, either she's working with your stalker or—"

"Yeah, I know," Hailey said, cutting him off before he could say that something terrible must have happened to Maddie. She was hoping for the best and didn't need a cop putting something so horrid in her brain—even though it had already crossed her mind—when she had enough problems to worry about.

"Okay." Officer Ronald sighed. "We'll keep investigating. Just . . . be careful."

She forced an exhausted, agreeable smile and watched him leave through the hospital waiting room, where she joined her friends and Alexa, who had fallen asleep.

Hailey sighed. "Officer Ronald thinks Maddie might have done this. I told him no way."

"Yeah, that's bullshit," Ale agreed.

"I know I said she'd kill me if I told you her secret, but I didn't mean it literally." Hailey thought it was funny until she realized it wasn't. Then she pointed to sleeping Alexa. "How long's she been out?"

"Just a few minutes. The doctor came with some updates and said Megan would be in surgery for a few hours," Billy said. "She fought it for a while but once her eyes closed, she was out."

"What kind of updates?" Hailey asked.

"A bunch of shit," Ale said.

"She has a fractured rib, punctured lung, potential nerve damage, internal bleeding . . . you name it. That knife did some serious damage," Billy said.

"Ouch," Hailey said instinctively. She rubbed her own scar, which felt like it was burning. "She got it worse than me."

She felt her phone vibrate with a text; it was from Westley and read: *Are you okay? The news is saying you were attacked?*

"Wow, Tiffany works fast. I didn't even realize she left, and she's already reporting what happened."

Hailey texted Westley back: *I'm okay. I'll call you in the morning.*

"I'm not sure why you trust her. She's a bit crazy," Ale said.

"I mean, she came ready to shoot. She scored points with me for that," Billy said.

"But did you see how fast she got there? How do we know she didn't just take off that stupid costume and hop back over your fence with a gun?"

"Because she didn't shoot us when she came in," Hailey reasoned.

She received another text from Westley: *It's already morning. Two in the morning, but morning is morning.*

She smiled. He was worried about her, so she couldn't be annoyed with his persistence. It was cute.

"Girl, who are you texting at this hour?" Ale asked, then noticed Hailey's smile. "Oh, it's Westley. Dumb question."

"You're right, it was," Hailey said, slipping the phone back into her pocket and taking a seat beside Billy. "So, I have a question for the two of *you*. How did *Billy* get some of *your* lip gloss on *his* lips?"

Billy licked his lips self-consciously, and Ale went red in the face.

"I'm not usually the type to kiss and tell," Ale said. "Just kidding, I *totally* am. And if a rock hadn't come flying through your window, he *probably* would've had that lip gloss in *other* places."

"I would?" He raised his eyebrows.

"Maybe. But I guess now you'll just have to wait until marriage."

Chapter 19

Just like the other attacks, everything went quiet for weeks following this last one. It was finally prom week, and instead of stressing about her mother still recovering in the hospital or the crazed, murderous stalker that was still out there, Hailey had a new priority: getting ready for prom.

Alexa offered to take Hailey and Ale to get mani-pedis, which wasn't something Hailey normally did, but Ale convinced her to go, saying, "Alexa's been spending weeks in the hospital with Megan. She just wants to do something nice for you and get out of that gloomy environment." Hailey couldn't say no to this; her current baby-blue polish was all cracked and sad, so it would be a definite improvement.

Alexa brought them to Lush & Luxe Nail Lounge, a high-end, fancy salon she and Megan would go to at least once a month. It was the kind of place that didn't offer anything special when compared to basic nail salons, but they had a posh interior and spoiled you with an experience.

When they walked in, Hailey suddenly felt extra-classy as the lavender aroma breezed into her nose. The receptionist escorted them to a private room behind a curtain, where they sat in three of four available massage chairs, complete with jetted pedicure spas. The nail technician mixed some essential oils and rose petals in the basins before the girls submerged their feet, then they were given warm towels to wrap their hands in and told to relax.

"I needed this." Alexa deeply exhaled, releasing all the weight she felt on her shoulders from her family being in danger for so long.

"*We* needed this," Hailey said, letting her know that she, too, was enjoying herself, in the hopes that it would make Alexa feel even better about bringing them.

"Yeah, we did. If we're wearing heels at prom and letting the dogs out, we might as well make them look nice," Ale said, clearly not as stressed as they were, considering she was more excited about how her toes would look than relaxing.

"Did you just call them 'dogs'?" Alexa asked, amused.

"Don't encourage her," Hailey said with secondhand embarrassment.

The nail technician reentered the room, asking, "How are you girls doing? Can I get you anything? Champagne, perhaps?"

"No, these two are only eighteen," Alexa answered.

"I'm so sorry. In my home country, we don't care about those things," she explained. Hailey seemed confused, though, because she didn't think the woman had a foreign accent.

"Where's your home country?" she asked.

"America."

"That adds up," Alexa said, drawing a chuckle from Ale. "I'll have a glass."

"I'll take a nice herbal tea," Ale said, as if she already knew that was an option.

"Just some water for me, please." Hailey smiled.

The employee returned quickly with the drinks and asked them what type of nails they would all be getting done.

Alexa told her, "The usual," and the technician didn't ask any questions. Ale requested French tips, but Hailey was unsure. She didn't want to do anything *too* fancy because it wasn't really her style, but it *was* for prom, so she asked for their suggestions.

Ale said, "Do a classic white. Guys go crazy for white nails."

"That's so basic," Alexa said. "At least make them shimmer."

"Shimmering and white?" the technician asked Hailey, confirming.

"Sure, why not?" she agreed.

Before she knew it, two hours had flown by, her nails looked great, and she felt confident Westley would like them. What she didn't feel great about was how much a place like this would cost for the three of them. Not that her mom was worried about the price, but the place couldn't have been cheap.

To their surprise, though, when Alexa went to the reception desk to pay, they didn't want her money. They said they knew who Hailey was and that she was going to prom with a hometown hero, so all they wanted was for Hailey to tell people she went *there* to get her nails done if anybody asked. It felt off to her, but it was much better than being denied access and refused service, which was her experience after what had happened at the tattoo shop.

With the girls having much more to do to prepare for prom, Alexa left the two of them to go back to the hospital, and they met up with Billy for dress shopping. They traveled to multiple stores over the course of a few hours but couldn't find what they were looking for. Everything was either cleaned out by other seniors, or they were too formal a place to carry something that might scream '80s prom. On top of that, Billy was determined to find something that made his bet with Ale worth making. Since he'd be the one to choose her dress, he didn't want to settle. So he had spent the entire day commanding their dress-shopping trip, which had been entertaining for Hailey, watching the two of them bicker with Billy looking through stores and vetoing everything available without ever telling the girls what he was actually looking for. Ale tried to pry it out of him, but he would threaten to put her in something that would make her look awful—as if that was even possible—prompting her to sigh, roll her eyes, and give up until they made it to the next store.

One thing Hailey did recognize, though, was that all the stores were joyously welcoming her—with most offering a free dress—all because she was attending prom with Westley, and they wanted their dress to be seen by the public. This put the thought in her head that whatever she wore would likely be seen on the local news and plastered all over social media in the future when Westley made it big, but she wouldn't let that influence her decision of what she wanted to wear to her only prom.

Eventually they ran out of dress stores in town, and that's when Billy had the idea to go to Valentina's Retro Clothes, a store located in the mall that sold retro clothes, as the name indicated. His idea was a logical one: since they were looking for '80s dresses, this was the obvious place to g o.

The store was impressive in square footage, considering it was located in a shopping mall, but it was still smaller than they wanted it to be, given the low likelihood that a place this size would have what they were looking for. It was lined wall to wall with hanging racks of clothes in small sections labeled *MEN*, *WOMEN*, and *KIDS*. The men's section was on the left, the women's on the right, and the kids' was in the back center of the store, split down the middle by a walkway with *BOYS* and *GIRLS* on their respective sides. Against the walls of each section were shoe racks, and beside the security scanner at the entrance was the register counter. The fitting rooms were in a small area between the boys' and girls' shoes.

They hurried to the women's section, not optimistic about what they'd find, and with even less hope when they saw there were just three six-foot-long racks of dresses. But Billy quickly went to work.

"What size are you?" he asked.

"You know it's offensive to ask a girl that, right?" Ale remarked.

"Not when they look like you," he said, sweeping the dresses across the rack. "And not when I'm picking out your dress."

"Aww, thanks, babe," She smiled. "I'm a size 1."

"Gross and gross," Hailey said, scrolling through the dresses on the sizes 3 to 6 rack. "Billy, you do know that your 'babe' is the prime example of unrealistic beauty standards, right?"

"You hear that, *babe*?" Ale asked, putting emphasis on the nickname to gross Hailey out more. "That means if you fuck this up, you'll never find someone as good as me."

"Or as narcissistic," Hailey said, holding out a hot-pink dress. It was a soft satin with plenty of ruffles that fit the

'80s theme, but she'd look like a Barbie doll wearing it, so she put it back and kept looking.

"Well, I don't plan on fucking anything up," he said, distracted while he was trying to focus on the dresses, "which is why I need to find you the perfect— Here!" He pulled a dress off the rack and checked the tag to confirm the size. "Do you think this will fit?" He held it up, and it was beautiful—royal blue, satin, low-cut back, ruffled skirt, sleeveless, with a sweetheart neckline.

Ale, impressed with his surprisingly great taste, grabbed it and said, "I'll go try it on." She looked at Hailey as she walked to the fitting room and mouthed, "What the fuck?" in awe at how perfect it was.

"Okay, Billy, why don't you find me one now?" Hailey asked.

"No, no way," Billy said, watching Ale while she walked. "If I find you a better dress, she'll be jealous."

"Fair enough," she said, pulling out a pretty, magenta-colored satin dress. It had an above-the-knee, frilly skirt, glitter throughout, and puffy sleeves. It definitely fit the vibe, and it wasn't as loud a color as she assumed most girls would show up in. Given the theme, the majority of them would likely be wearing neon. "I'm gonna try this one."

When she got it on, it hugged her body snuggly, and though she was showing more leg than she was used to, she knew she looked good. And once she found some matching heels and got her hair and makeup done, the look would be jaw-dropping.

Ale looked stunning in her dress, as usual. It was much shorter and more flirty than the magenta one, and Hailey was thankful for that. The blue dress was tight on Ale, though, which she complained about, but it hugged her perfect curves in all the right ways to make the uncomfortableness worth tolerating.

"Can I come look?" Billy asked, standing outside their shared dressing room.

"No!" Ale insisted. "You know it's bad luck if you see me in the dress before prom, right?"

"Isn't that for weddings?"

"Maybe I'm treating this like a wedding. But if you won't partake in my superstitions, then you can't partake in the consummation either."

"Wait, you mean—"

"I mean, you'll see the dress *on* me when it's ready, and if you can wait that long, you can take it *off* at the end of that night too. Now shoo."

"Yes, ma'am," he said, and his shadow quickly disappeared from beneath the fitting room door.

"You're serious about that?" Hailey asked.

"About what?" Ale slipped out of her dress.

"Well, sleeping with him after prom. Are you sure you're ready for that?"

"Ready? I've been ready since Camp Safe Woods. If it weren't for everybody around, he could've taken me that night while Nick's corpse burned in the fire beside us."

"What the *fuck*?"

"You're right. The crowd didn't matter; I would've let him even with the audience," she said, casually putting her pants on.

"While his face was sliced open? Do you hear yourself?" Hailey said, looking at her reflection in the mirror.

"Hey, he got that wound saving *us*. Who am I to judge if he got a little blood on me?"

"Okay, you've said some crazy, demented, overly-horny stuff in the past, but this takes the cake."

"Surprise!" She waved her arms like she was popping out of a cake at a surprise birthday party before grabbing her shirt and putting it on. "Horny girl says horny things. But we're way past that. I'm not just thirsty anymore, I'm *dehydrated*. He's lucky I'm waiting until prom."

"How does that make him lucky?"

She smirked. "Because once we start . . . no brakes. He'll be begging me to stop."

"Somehow this conversation keeps getting worse." Deciding this dress was the one, she started removing it to change back into her clothes.

"Hey, you asked. And don't act so surprised. I know you're feeling similar things about your boo, Westley. You even said you were gonna give it up on prom night."

"I just said that to tease you two about not having dates. Don't forget, if it weren't for me pushing you two together, you'd both be going to prom alone."

"Bullshit, it would've happened eventually. And what does that mean? That you don't really intend on sleeping with Westley?"

"Well, I haven't really thought about it."

Ale looked more confused than ever. "How have you not thought about it? You mean to tell me you pulled the most—sorry, second-most—attractive guy in school, and you haven't even *thought* about sex, let alone, *had* it?"

"I've kinda got a lot of stressful shit going on in my life right now," Hailey said, sitting on the little bench in the room to slip on her shoes.

"Exactly! And you know what's the best thing to do when you're stressed?"

"Probably not what you're about to say."

"Have an orgasm!" Ale yelled, loud enough for the whole store to hear.

"Okay, let's keep it quiet."

"What? Everybody has orgasms! Don't you masturbate?"

"Sure, but—"

"No 'buts'!" Ale interrupted, opening the room's curtain. "Just stop stressing about everything and consider the idea that prom night can be a blessing of an opportunity."

Hailey sighed, collected her items, then stepped out of the dressing room with Ale. Billy was standing just around the corner and definitely heard their entire conversation, but Ale had no shame as usual, so she just gave him a flirty smile. He looked at Hailey, overwhelmed.

"Good luck with her," Hailey said to him.

"Are we all ready to go?" Ale asked.

"Uh . . ." He cleared his throat. "Not yet. We need to find your shoes and some fishnets."

Ale sighed and checked her phone. "Shit, it's getting late!" she exclaimed. They'd been out for hours, and Hailey had completely forgotten that Ale had to babysit that night. "You two have fun doing that. I've got to get going." She hurried to the register to purchase the dress, turning back to them halfway through the store. "You'd better not buy me any *fugly* shoes. I will send you right back here to return them."

***

Once Ale was gone, Hailey and Billy found matching shoes for both dresses and paid for their stuff. They had one more errand to run for the day, and luckily for them, it was at that very same mall. They stopped for food at a Mongolian restaurant before heading to Mozart's Record Store.

Inside, a middle-aged man with a bald head and leather jacket was working the cash register. He was intimidatingly large and had a mean expression on his face, but when they approached him, he welcomed them with a genuine smile.

"How can I help you kids today?" he asked.

"We, uh, uh—" Billy stammered.

"We're looking for Nia," Hailey finished.

"You are? I don't think she's ever had friends stop by before. She's in the back, reorganizing the porn."

"Awesome. Thanks," Hailey said, stepping away before he stopped her.

"Wait, are you old enough to go back there?"

"Do you need to check my ID?" Hailey asked.

"No, just— Don't steal anything."

"Steal? I won't *touch* anything back there." She continued on with Billy right behind her and stepped through the bead curtain that separated the fun, cool part of the store from this dimly lit, gross part.

The walls were lined with cheetah-print wallpaper and purple LED strip lights. The speakers quietly played corny music that sounded like the backing track for a '70s porno. There was a shaggy couch against the wall and a glass coffee table in front of it with open nudie magazines covering every inch of the surface. Against the wall opposite the bead curtain was a row of bookshelves lined with porn VHS tapes and DVDs. On the wall beside the bead curtain was a display of sex toys and condoms that Billy stared at with equal confusion and interest, like a tourist trying to read directions in a foreign country.

All Hailey cared about was the fact that Nia *wasn't* in the room. This room was the sleaziest place she'd ever set foot in, and she wanted out. She turned to exit, but Nia came walking through the beads, almost bumping into her while holding a box of cassettes.

"Shit, you scared me," Nia said. "Usually there's nobody in here."

"I can't imagine why," Hailey snarked.

"What are you guys doing here anyway?" She set the box down beside the bookshelves and saw Billy admiring the condoms. "Buying condoms? You know they sell those like . . . everywhere else, right?"

"What? No," Billy said, scrambling to turn away from them, embarrassed.

"Probably not a bad idea, though," Hailey said, referencing her conversation with Ale in the fitting room.

"Wait, are you two hooking up?" Nia asked. "I thought you were dating Westley? Oh my gosh, did I just catch you cheating?"

"No!" Hailey said. "Billy's taking Ale to prom, and she's—"

"Whoa! Yeah, rubber up, buddy," Nia said, not needing an explanation. Billy's cheeks went red, which looked even worse with the purple lighting.

"You really think so?" he asked, looking back at the condoms.

"Unless you plan on getting her pregnant," Nia said.

"I do *not* want a little Ale running around. The one is already too much, so you can exclude me from your list of babysitters," Hailey said.

"Okay, just stop. I'm not getting her pregnant."

"We know, but it's funny seeing you get all flustered," Hailey smirked.

"Well it's not so funny to me."

"Okay, sorry," Nia said, though she was smiling.

"It's just a touchy subject. I already know Ale's got all these expectations for that night, but I've never done *that* before. I mean, what if it's not good enough? I don't want to have some great night at prom, then jump into bed and just embarrass myself," he said, looking down to avoid eye contact.

"What? You're a *virgin*?" Hailey asked, emphasizing her sarcasm. "No way."

"Yeah, who would've guessed that one?" Nia winked.

"Guess what, Billy?"

He looked up and met Hailey's eyes.

"She's a virgin too."

"She is?"

"Of course she is! I mean, have you *heard* how she talks about sex? I've never heard somebody who's actually done it talk like that."

"I just assumed she was a big fan," Billy said.

"Who would she have even slept with? I only ever see her with you two," Nia said.

"Exactly. Besides, she even told me she's a virgin, so you've got nothing to worry about. She can't expect *any-thing* from you when she doesn't know what to expect. Whatever you do that night will be the best she's ever had."

"I guess you're right." His posture shifted. He reached for the rack and pulled down the first box his hand touched, which was labeled *Xtra-Large*.

Nia's eyes widened as she grabbed the box from him and put them back on the shelf. "Okay, maybe not those ones. If *those* fit you, you'd be a better fit for one of the girls in these sticky VHS tapes than a girl with Ale's experience." She grabbed another box, one having a more basic label, and handed it to him. "There you go, big guy."

"Thanks," he said awkwardly.

"Now, what are you guys *really* doing here? Or are you the type of friends who always go shopping for sex-related items together?" Nia asked.

"Oh, right!" Hailey exclaimed, bouncing on her tiptoes. "We were thinking about prom and had a question for you."

Nia's face went sour. "You *do* know I can't go to that, right?"

"*As a student*," Billy said.

She looked at him, still annoyed, as she waited for them to finish.

"But the prom committee is in charge of finding the DJ for the event. We can't think of anyone more qualified than our school's very own sports announcer and respected employee of Mozart's Record Store," Hailey explained, proud of herself. She had the idea the night of the baseball game, then brought it to the committee's attention that week. They were all for it, especially considering the horrible predicament Nia was in.

"Wait, are you serious?" Nia asked. "You'd better not be fucking with me."

"Of course not. We wouldn't do that," Billy said. "We will just mark that we have *someone* from this store working the event, and when *you* show up, it'll be too late."

"Not too late for them to kick me out, though."

"And what, leave a prom without music? I don't think so," Hailey reasoned.

Nia thought about it, nodding as if making it make sense in her head. "Do you think anyone would get mad if the DJ showed up in a dress and danced to the music she was playing?"

"I think the prom would be boring if it went any other way." Billy smiled.

"Then you can go ahead and sign me up!"

"Not so fast. Just so you know, the music will need to fit the prom's theme. Do you know anything about '80s music?" Hailey asked.

"Girl. I'll make a playlist of seventeenth-century sea shanties if it means I can go to prom."

"Damn," Billy said. "Now I wish we had a pirate theme."

Hailey yelped when something vibrated against her ass, drawing concern from Billy and laughter from Nia. When she realized it was just her phone receiving a text in her back pocket, she exhaled a sigh of relief. This room skeeved her out so much, she was on edge.

"Sorry, my phone vibrated and scared me," she explained.

"Is it Ale?" Billy asked.

"No," Hailey answered, thinking it was cute how he was publicly crushing over her now. "It's— Oh fuck."

The message was from Tiffany Watson: *What happened with your friend, Ale?*

Chapter 20

When Ale arrived, the porch light wasn't on like they normally left it. She was a bit late but knew they wouldn't have left before she got there. She leaned back from the porch step to peek at the driveway and confirm that both of their cars were, in fact, still there before knocking on the door. When they didn't answer, she knocked again. And again.

After a couple minutes of waiting, she thought, *Fuck this*, and just used her key to the house to let herself inside.

"Hey, guys, I'm here," she said, hanging her purse on the coatrack by the door. She didn't let herself in like this often because she just felt uncomfortable walking in on a family like that, but she spent so much time there anyway, she knew they wouldn't have a problem with it.

Nobody responded to her arrival announcement, but she heard the kitchen water running, so she assumed Naomi was washing some last-minute dishes while James was upstairs prepping for their night out.

Turning the corner to the kitchen, she announced herself again, "Hey, Naomi, I'm here." She stopped just outside the threshold when she saw blood dripping from the sink into a puddle on the floor in an otherwise empty kitchen.

"No, no, no," she said, rushing straight back to the house's entrance, ripping her phone from her back pocket, and dialing *911* as she pulled her purse from the coatrack. She didn't even look back before she opened the door and got into her car.

"Nine-one-one, what's your emergency?" the dispatcher asked as Ale turned the key in her ignition.

She told the woman she was at her babysitting gig, gave her the address, and said, "There's a pool of blood on their kitchen floor, and I think they might be hurt."

"Is there anybody in the house?" the dispatcher asked.

"I'm not dumb enough to stay and find out. Just get over here. And tell the officers that I'm Hailey Ramirez's best friend," she said, knowing that would put the case on high alert.

"Okay, just please stay calm and—"

"Wait, wait," Ale interrupted when she saw him. The little boy, Charlie, whose personal well-being she was being paid to watch tonight was upstairs banging on the bedroom window and screaming for Ale's help. "The kid, Charlie, is in the house. He's screaming for me from the window."

"Do you think you can reach him? Get him to safety?"

"You want me to go back in the house?"

"Does he look safe in his room? Can you tell him to come outside to you?"

"How the *fuck* should I know that? He's all the way upstairs! The attacker can be anywhere in that house!"

"Okay, just calm down. I cannot tell you to do anything that can end up getting either one of you hurt. All I can do is advise you to wait for the officers to get there, and they are already en route."

"But that could take too long! You know what? I—" Giving up, she hung up on the dispatcher, swallowed her fear, took her pepper spray from her purse, and ran back into the house. This time upon entering, she could hear Charlie banging on the window and screaming upstairs. She assumed this meant that he was hiding the first time she entered. Then, after hearing her go in and out of the house, he came out of hiding to try to get her attention. This confirmed that her decision to run back to him was the right one, since he was risking disclosing his location to someone who might still be in the house. By the time police arrived, it would be way too late, so it was up to her to help him now.

Going straight for the stairs, knowing that his bedroom door was right across from the top step, she stopped before ascending. First, she noticed Penny the Penguin waiting at the top between the stairs and door, standing as menacingly as a fluffy penguin mascot could, watching Ale and waving with her head tilted. Then, she noticed the trail of blood staining the carpeted steps and followed them down to the trail which led back to the kitchen.

How did I miss seeing that before?

Ale took her time weighing her options—which weren't many—until Penny took one step backward toward Charlie's room. She knew the penguin was compelling Ale to come up the stairs and confront her, or else she would go into Charlie's room and hurt him.

But Ale didn't have any weapons, and Penny's hands were hidden behind her back, so she didn't have a clue what to expect if she *did* approach. Upon deciding that her best course of action was leaving Penny to enter Charlie's room, and then coming back quickly with a weapon for the encounter, she sprinted to the kitchen and heard the heavy steps of the penguin rushing to the bedroom above her. Charlie's screams became clearer and more fearful as the bedroom door opened, and Ale hurried to the knife block to grab the biggest one available. Then she raced back upstairs, where she paused at the horrific sight of James and Naomi, bloodied, beaten, and piled on top of one another in the open bedroom directly to her right.

Focusing on what she deemed most important in the moment—Charlie's safety— she faced the bedroom where the boy was on his bed, curled up in the corner against the wall, while Penny stood menacingly in the center of the room, facing Ale with her back to Charlie and her empty hands at her sides.

"You'd better leave him alone," Ale said, shaking. She held the knife out, pointing it at Penny as if it were a gun she was threatening her with.

Penny looked at the knife, and Ale could've sworn she saw offense taken through the mascot's expressionless face. Penny looked around Charlie's messy room and settled on a dirty plate covered in syrup and waffle crumbs beneath his TV on the entertainment center. Penny reached toward it, grabbed the syrup-covered butter knife from the plate, and brandished it.

"What do you think you're gonna do with that? Make us PB&Js?" Ale asked smugly. Penny shrugged and Ale raised the chef's knife high and brought it down into Penny's shoulder.

That was easy, she thought, about how smooth the knife went into her, only to realize that she hadn't actually connected with the person inside, just the fluffy costume. Penny took a step back and admired the knife in her shoulder, then took her butter knife and jabbed it into Ale's navel. It didn't penetrate her skin, but the pain was *horrific*. It was all the worst feelings of getting your belly button poked turned up to the max—the deep, nauseating pressure, bladder shock, and nerves firing off like missiles.

With Ale bending to ease the pressure on her stomach, Penny brought the butter knife up and shoved it into her throat, just below her jaw, crushing her windpipe, making her gag and wheeze all at once. As her body responded with saliva rushing into her mouth to prepare for the vomit, she fought the urge, spitting the saliva onto the carpet. Then, unable to lift her head and spot what Penny's next move was, she held her hand out to brace for whatever came next. Expecting the butter knife to come for her ribs, she was surprised when Penny simply swung it down at her hand, shattering two of her freshly manicured nails and creating a blunt, immeasurable, shocking pain against her knuckles. She screamed—once at the pain and once again when she looked at her hand and spotted the broken nails. When she looked up at Penny, she spotted the reflection of the police lights on the blade protruding from the penguin's shoulder.

Penny noticed where Ale was looking, dropped her utensil, and reached across her body for the chef's knife handle. Ale took this opportunity to pull out the pepper spray from her pocket and unload it on the penguin, who simply shifted one arm so her fin blocked any mist from entering her eyes. However, the sheer amount of spray that filled the room was enough to make Ale and Charlie cough profusely.

With the more deadly weapon in hand, Penny charged Ale, gripping a handful of hair and yanking her upward. Ale braced, watching her lift the knife-wielding hand and bring it up to her throat, only for Penny to avoid stabbing her and instead rub the pepper-spray-drenched fin onto her face. Immediately, she became overwhelmed with the burning sensation. She felt as though her face were pressed directly into the sun.

Her eyes closed to mask the pain, which only made it worse, yet she couldn't open them. Her breath came in short, incomplete spurts. Mucus poured from her nose into her mouth making her gag, triggering the worst vomiting session of her entire life—compounded by the intense bruising in her throat.

She felt a heavy push into her chest, which sent her falling backward out of the room, off-balance and tumbling down the stairs. At the bottom, with every bone in her body surely bruised, her face on fire, and feeling the absolute worst pain she'd ever been in, she heard Charlie's screams get closer and closer. She felt the weight of Penny's presence come down the stairs, step over her, and fade away, taking Charlie with her. Then the front door busted open. Help had arrived.

***

When Hailey and Billy showed up at the police station, Tiffany was waiting outside.

"Is she okay?" Hailey asked.

"It's hard to say. She's alive, at least," Tiffany said.

Hailey wanted to ask her what happened, but Billy was already hurrying to enter the building, so she followed him. Inside, the police recognized them immediately and escorted the trio to the interrogation room where Ale was held.

"You guys are interrogating her?" Hailey asked upon hearing where Ale was.

Officer Ronald answered, "No, but it was the most private room they could give her, considering the potential for a news presence," then glared at Tiffany with annoyance.

"She's okay," Hailey said, trying to vouch for her.

"Okay with you guys, maybe, but we won't allow her in there. This is an active investigation."

Tiffany started to object, but Hailey assured her that she would let her know what was going on.

When they entered the room, Billy immediately hugged Ale. Officer Ronald dismissed the cop who was watching her in the room.

"I'll be right outside," he said to Hailey before closing the door.

"I'm so sorry I wasn't there," Billy said to Ale.

"It's not your job to protect me," she said. "Well, not *all* the time." She looked terrible, which was unheard of for her. Her face was beet red and her eyes were even worse. Any exposed skin was bruised. Worst of all was her body language. She seemed more terrified than Hailey had ever seen her before, and she looked like existing was excruciatingly painful. Billy finally recognized this and released his embrace.

"Are you okay?" Hailey asked, knowing the answer but giving her an opportunity to explain what happened.

"Of course not," she said. "But I'm alive and the burning is starting to fade."

"The burning?" Billy asked.

"Pepper spray didn't really go as planned."

"Ouch," he said, wincing as if he felt the pain too. Hailey wondered if he actually did after hugging her.

"Not to mention falling down the stairs and getting stabbed in the throat."

"What?" Hailey asked, confused as ever.

"You were stabbed?!" Billy exclaimed, looking her over as if he would see the wound, though all that was there was a bruise that resembled what would happen if a seat belt caught your throat in a car accident.

"Yeah, with a fucking *butter knife*. Can you believe that? And worst of all,"—she held out her hand for Hailey to see the damage done—"bitch broke my fucking nails."

She's okay, Hailey thought.

"I don't think that's the *worst* that happened," Billy said, still focusing on her throat.

"Of course it is. The doctors said the bruising should clear up before prom so not to worry about it. But these nails were fucking *expensive*."

"What happened to Charlie?" Hailey asked, changing the subject to something more important.

"*She* took him."

"She? Did you see who did it?"

"Of course I did."

Hailey was surprised and eager to hear who.

Ale broke her spirit when she said, "It was Penny."

Hailey rolled her eyes. She thought they finally had an answer.

"Okay, what about the parents?" Billy asked

"They're dead." Ale shook her head and sucked her teeth. Hailey could see she was fuming with anger.

"I should've fucking killed that damn penguin," she said as Officer Ronald reentered the room.

"It's not your fault," Billy consoled, though it didn't really help.

"No, it's not," Officer Ronald agreed. "And I want you to hear me loud and clear when I say that. But I *cannot* stress this enough. *Be careful*. Whatever is going on, whoever's doing this, it's obvious that you are all in danger. I recommend lying low and waiting for us to figure this out. I know you guys have prom coming up, and that's exciting, but if I were you, I wouldn't go."

"You can't be serious!" Ale exclaimed, her anger showing.

"I am serious. I know this sucks and it's not your fault, but to be honest, anyone who associates themselves with you three is in *danger*. And, while we don't have any leads, we do know one thing. The message that killer left for Hailey, 'death dances with those around you, patiently awaiting your turn to take the floor,' we believe they were referencing prom. This lunatic clearly has a flair for the dramatic, and if they're coming up with dancing metaphors, I can't think of a bigger grand finale than prom night."

"Fuck that," Ale said. "They've taken lives, they've taken my job. I'm not letting them take prom away from me!"

"Look, I can't tell you what to do. I'm just recommending what would be best for everyone involved," Officer Ronald said.

"Well, I agree with Ale," Hailey said. "They've taken enough from us. If their grand finale is gonna be that night, I suggest *you* police officers prepare accordingly. We're going to prom, and the only people I plan on dancing with are my friends and Westley."

"Tell 'em, girl," Ale said.

"Please, just think about it. We'll increase the police presence at Pineside High from here on out and will make sure officers will be all over prom. If you don't change your mind, don't say I didn't warn you."

Chapter 21

With just one day left before prom, everyone was making their final arrangements. Hailey took Ale back to Lush & Luxe to fix her broken nails, and Billy took Leo to pick up their rental suits. Afterward, Leo told Billy he had one more errand to run—buying alcohol to spike drinks at prom—and asked Billy if he could take him.

"How do you plan on buying it? Do you have a fake ID?" Billy asked.

"Nah, I know a guy," Leo explained.

Billy proceeded to follow Leo's directions to a very sketchy side of town—a side he knew to avoid if at all possible.

"Take the next right," Leo said as Billy approached the stop sign. He did as instructed, turning down a residential street filled with dead grass, houses with windows that were either boarded up or secured shut with bars, and cars in parking lots with smashed windows, keyed doors, and spiderwebbed windshields. One house had a swing set in the yard, though one of the two swings was detached from a chain that was missing so the loose seat just hung to the ground while the other swing swayed with the wind. There was not a child or other civilian in sight.

"Are you sure this is the street?" Billy asked, sweat seeping from his armpits.

"Yeah, dude. I come here all the time," Leo explained. Hearing this, Billy started believing his friends' accusations about Leo's drug usage. "It's the house there on the corner. Park along the sidewalk and leave the car running."

"So, this guy you know," Billy asked, doing as Leo instructed, "how do you know him?"

"Oh, we go way back—he's a family friend," he said, holding his cell phone to his ear. Billy heard it ring until the automated voice message system picked up. Leo said, "I guess he's busy. I'm gonna go knock on the door."

"So, he's a family friend . . . and he sells alcohol to you—a minor?" Billy asked.

Leo seemed more confused than Billy was as he opened the passenger door. With one foot out, he said, "Dude, he sells me drugs. What makes you think he'd have a problem selling me booze?"

Billy just stared blankly as Leo walked up the cracked concrete step to this guy's house, feeling so dumb that he hadn't noticed sooner or believed his friends. Worst of all, he'd have to admit he was wrong to Ale, and she'd die laughing at him.

Leo knocked on the door and it creaked open from his touch. Billy watched nervously, wondering if being a getaway driver for what looked like a drug deal would get him in trouble.

"Hello?" Leo called into the house, looking inside carefully, then looking back at Billy. "I don't think anyone's home."

"Are they the type of person to leave their door unlocked when they're not home?" Billy asked through the open passenger window.

"Not at all." Leo turned back to the door.

"He's a family friend, right? Just walk in," Billy said.

"You think I'm crazy?" Leo asked, whisper yelling across the front yard. "You don't just go walking into dealers' houses without invitation."

"I wouldn't walk into one *with* an invitation," Billy muttered to himself, tightly gripping the steering wheel, ready to leave as soon as he could.

"Anybody home?" Leo called into the house again.

"Just make it quick, dude. I wanna get out of here," Billy said, his palm sweat making the leather steering wheel slippery.

"Yeah, yeah." Leo nervously pushed the door all the way open and stepped inside. Disappearing around a corner, Billy heard him call out, "Hello?" once again, followed by a quick, alarming, "Oh shit!"

Billy, alert as ever, shifted the car into drive and eagerly stared into the doorway, waiting for his friend, tapping his left foot on the floor mat to calm his nerves, when Leo suddenly came running from around the corner, slipping on the welcome mat and falling down the single step, hitting his face and scraping his forehead on the walkway.

"Let's go!" he yelled, getting up and sprinting to Billy's car. Before his seat belt was on, he shouted, "Get out of here!" Billy obeyed, burning rubber as he stomped on the gas pedal and sped down the street.

***

At Lush & Luxe, Hailey was relaxing in a massage chair while Ale was on her last nail that needed to be repaired when Billy and Leo came bursting in through the doors.

Hailey heard Billy ask the receptionist, "Are Ale and Hailey here?" and hurried to slide open their private curtain when she noticed how out of breath and scared he was. Leo looked more shook-up than Billy. He was the kind of aloof, goofy guy who was high on life—if not other things—and was pretty much never fazed. This look was something knew for Hailey to see, and it scared her.

Ale looked up, wide-eyed. "Billy?"

"What are you doing here?" Hailey asked.

"I need to talk to you," he said, then saw that Ale was in the middle of getting her nail worked on. "Er, just one of you. Privately."

Hailey exchanged looks with Ale, they both nodded, and Hailey said, "I'll be right outside," then followed Billy and Leo to the parking lot. "What's going on? Did you have problems getting your suits?"

"What? No, that went fine. But Leo wanted us to run an 'errand' afterward—"

"I wanted to buy alcohol for tomorrow," Leo interrupted

"Hailey was surprised Billy would enable him in that endeavor, but she let them continue telling their story.

"Yeah, so he took me to some *sketchy* fucking neighborhood—"

"To my dealer's house," Leo interrupted again.

Billy seemed annoyed with the constant interruptions, but Hailey was more shocked to see that Billy wasn't shocked to hear Leo mention having a dealer.

"Just tell her what happened," Billy said.

"Yeah, so I go in there, and they— They're all fucking dead."

Hailey's heart skipped a beat. "What? Who was?"

"My fucking drug dealer!" He looked around at the pedestrians walking around them, giving them side-eyes. "Him and a few other goons at his house. Shit was bloody, man." He held out his hands, and they were trembling.

"I'm still shaking. I've never seen shit like that before." Then, like he suddenly realized something important, he shouted, "Fuck! Where am I gonna get booze now?"

"Did you go to the police?" Hailey asked—the logical first response, ignoring his booze dilemma.

"And tell them what? My drug dealer's dead? Nuh-uh, no way," he said, shaking his head. "I don't want any part in that." He rubbed his forehead with both hands as if he was stressed while thinking. "I'm gonna have to see if my cousin can hook me up with some liquor. I promised people alcohol."

Hailey understood that Leo wasn't used to this kind of pressure, so she ignored him, looked directly at Billy, and asked, "Do you think this is related to everything else?"

He shrugged his shoulders. "It's hard to say, but . . . maybe not. I didn't *see* the bodies. Leo did. And unless you have relationships with those kinds of people, I can't see why they'd be targeted."

Hailey listened and considered this, nodding along. Then she asked Leo, "Did this guy have any enemies?"

"How am I supposed to know? We exchanged money and drugs, not life stories and shoulders to lean on."

"Okay, but it is possible, right?"

"I guess," Leo said while Billy nodded in agreement.

"All right, here's what we're gonna do. Leo, you're going to join us in the nail salon and use their phone to call the police. Tell them you'd like to remain anonymous if you *really* need to, but let them know what you saw and where it was. *I'm* going to sit back in my massage chair and hopefully release some of the tension you just added. And Billy, you're gonna go tell Ale that her nails look nice and that her throat bruise looks like it'll be gone by morning. If the cops think this has anything to do with us, they'll let us know. If not, I'm going to pretend it never happened and get through prom."

***

That night, Hailey stayed up late with her stomach churning like she was on a roller coaster creeping up slowly before a big drop. And like it usually did, that nervousness faded as soon as she got a text from Westley. It read: *Hey, sorry if you're sleeping. What color dress are you wearing? I'm making you something and I want it to match.*

She replied: *I'm surprised you're still awake. And I waaas going to keep it a secret, but it's magenta :)*

She tossed her phone to her side on the bed and stretched her arms up high, bending her back at an odd angle so it would crack, and then took a deep breath, exhaling as his next text arrived: *Of course I'm still awake. I'm too excited about tomorrow to sleep. Now what color are your shoes?*

She replied: *Same as the dress.*

His response: *Okay, that doesn't help. How about your nails?*

She texted: *White :)*

His quick reply: *Beautiful.*

Then, another text followed that read: *Since the secret's already out, how about you send me a picture of you wearing the dress so I have an idea of what I'm looking forward to?*

She replied: *Without my hair and makeup? Nice try. You'd have a better shot asking for nudes.*

Once she hit send, she felt embarrassed. The implication she *wanted* to make was that it simply wasn't going to happen because the odds of her sending him nude photos were just about zero. But since he wasn't *her*, he might have assumed she was making an offer.

She watched nervously, watching the three dots indicating that he was typing his reply pop up, disappear, and repeat as if he was struggling with finding his response. Her stomach now felt like she was back on that roller coaster, and the drop finally came, sending her into a sinking free fal l.

Why would I send that? she thought, telling herself that spending so much time around a constant, overwhelming, ferally unhinged horndog like Ale must've started to wear on her.

Feeling too ashamed to backtrack on her text and overwhelmingly anxious waiting for his response, she called

Ale, who answered sounding like she was waking from a month-long hibernation.

"Hailey? Do you know what time it is?"

Too nervous to pay her rhetorical question any mind, Hailey skipped to the point and asked, "Has Billy seen you naked?"

"Okay, *fine*, I'm awake," Ale said, suddenly rejuvenated. "What's going on?"

"Has Billy seen you naked?" she repeated. "Or any boy, for that matter."

"Oh, that was a real question? Look at you, being all invasive and stuff."

"Just answer the question," Hailey said impatiently. She felt like she was backing herself into a corner and was unsure what to do if Westley *did* ask for a picture.

I can't suggest it and back out, can I?

"Okay, geez. No, he hasn't. At least, I don't think so. I wouldn't exactly *blame* him if he had peeked through my window in the middle of the night. And *obviously* no other guy has deserved a look at *this*," she said, followed by what Hailey assumed was a demonstrative ass spank.

"Hmm," Hailey said, considering her options.

"What's this all about?" Ale asked, then let out an excited gasp. "Wait, are you finally thinking about 'doing the do' tomorrow night? Oh my gosh, I'm so proud of you! First thing in the morning, I have an appointment for a Brazilian wax. I'm not sure if they'll have another appointment available, but maybe you can come piggyback off mine?"

"What? No!" Hailey said, somehow still finding the things that came out of Ale's mouth shocking.

"Oh, you're right. It might hurt too bad after to screw, huh? See, this is why I'm glad we talk about these things. Razor it is."

"No, that's not it. But I *am* calling about something embarrassing and could use your honest opinion."

"Well you'd better spit it out before I either fall back asleep or think of more ridiculous shit to talk about."

"What's your opinion on sending naked pictures?"

"Hailey Mae Winter-Ramirez, prudish girl turned naughty nympho. I like it. You're taking after me, you know? It's like you're my own personal protégé."

"Ale—"

"That's 'Mistress Alejandra' to you!" she interrupted.

Hailey chuckled. "More like 'Madam Libido.'"

"Hey, I like that. As a matter of fact, can you make sure that's on my tombstone?"

"I'm already setting it as your name in my phone," Hailey said, updating the contact information. "Now, back to your opinion on nudes."

"Right. I love the idea. Haven't sent any myself because I'd rather him see the real thing in person first."

"That's . . . really good advice," Hailey said, surprised to hear that even Ale could show restraint, making her realize she might be jumping the gun.

"But! If he's bugging you for pictures and you're not opposed to it, I'd say tease him. It could be something simple like thigh cleavage and a belly button, or you could go crazy and do a full-body nude silhouette shot in the mirror. If you're feeling *really* frisky, send him a selfie wearing nothing but a hand-bra, with just a peek of areola so he can at least know what color they are. Even if he's expecting a nude, he'd be a fool to complain about any of those."

"I knew you were the right person to call, but I didn't realize how oddly specific you'd be with your advice," Hailey said.

"That's what I'm here for, right?"

"I guess it is. Thanks."

"No problem. If you need anything else, I'm getting my beauty sleep, so text me. But I better not wake up to any naughty Hailey bits on my phone. Once you take those pics, you're on your own."

"Darn," Hailey said sarcastically. "See you tomorrow."

"Bye." Ale hung up, leaving Hailey alone with her phone in her hand.

She went back to her conversation with Westley, prepared to back out of her accidental offer, and saw the typing dots, driving her decision to just wait and see what his response would be. The text that arrived said: *Where would the fun in that be? No thanks, I like to unwrap my gifts in person.*

Hailey felt herself grinning from ear to ear. Once again, Westley knew just the right thing to say.

What was I thinking? Hailey thought before getting startled upon seeing Alexa standing in her doorway.

"God, you scared me," Hailey said.

"Sorry about that. I just saw you smiling so hard and didn't want to interrupt." She walked into the room and sat at the bed's edge, placing a hand on Hailey's knee beneath the blanket. "Is it Westley?"

Hailey went back to smiling and nodded.

"You really like this boy, don't you?"

"I *do*. I've never really felt like this before. He just makes me . . . well, smile," she said, laughing.

Alexa laughed along before taking a deep breath and saying, "My baby girl's all grown-up!" She turned around and gave her a big hug. Hailey couldn't help but realize the tears in her mother's eyes.

"Are you okay?" Hailey asked.

"Yeah, I'm just emotional right now. I came in here because I couldn't sleep. I haven't really slept at all since Megan's been in the hospital." Alexa pulled out of the hug. "Our bedroom just doesn't feel the same without her in it."

"I'm sorry. I know it's hard." Hailey lifted an arm to rub Alexa's back for comfort.

"It is. And I heard you still awake in here, so I thought I'd come see what you were up to. I just think it's so crazy to me that you've grown up so much. I remember how you hated me when you were just a kid." She laughed. "We've come so far."

"We hated *each other*."

"That's not true. I always loved you. You were like a niece to me. I hated how you pulled your mother out of her promiscuous lifestyle, so I had to go through that myself, but when she passed and I had to take you in . . . Well, let's just say it was time for me to leave that life behind anyway. I had no idea what I was doing raising a child, and I was sure you were going to turn out awful, but look at you now."

"Look at *us*," Hailey said.

"Yeah, look at us. Watching you grow into this beautiful, smart, strong woman and growing alongside you has been the best experience of my life. And I know I'm not your *real* mother, and neither is Megan, but I want you to know that we both *do* very much consider you *our* daughter, and we've done our best to raise you as such."

"Biology aside, you're both mothers to me, and you've both done great. I'm just sorry for everything we're going through right now."

"No. Don't be sorry for something that isn't your fault. Never apologize on behalf of someone else because you'd be blaming yourself for something out of *your* control. Instead, we need to find a way to make the person at fault take accountability for *their* actions. Megan isn't hospitalized because of you. There is only one person who put her there, and under no circumstance should you ever think that person is you. Do you understand?"

Hailey nodded. She felt empowered hearing Alexa give strong, good-willed guidance like this. "I understand."

Alexa stood up. "You'd better get to bed. You've got a long day tomorrow."

"Are you sure?" Hailey asked. "You know, if your bed's too lonely, you can join me in mine—at least while Megan's away."

Alexa smiled. "Thanks, but that's okay. I'm gonna make some tea before bed, though. Would you like some? We can sip on it while you tell me more about this boy."

"Sure, that sounds great," Hailey said, her smile growing ever wider.

Chapter 22

Billy was the first at Hailey's house that evening, where they were all meeting for photos before the limo was scheduled to arrive. He let himself in as instructed via text message while Hailey was upstairs doing her makeup and Alexa curled her hair. To fit the theme of prom, both she and Ale agreed to wear their hair extra-curly and big. Ale canceled her wax appointment and squeezed her way into a salon to get hers done, while Hailey took the opportunity to bond with Alexa and have her do it.

"Whoa," he said, entering the room and spotting Hailey who was just about ready to go—complete with her dress on and getting her finishing touches done. He seemed stunned, seeing her. "You look . . . pretty."

"Don't you mean beautiful? Drop-dead gorgeous, even!" Alexa said, defending her daughter. But Hailey thought it was sweet. This was the first time Billy had ever sincerely complimented her in that way.

"Thanks. You don't look too shabby yourself," she said. He was in a standard black tuxedo with a suit jacket and white dress shirt. He was sporting a royal blue bow tie to match the dress he'd picked out for Ale. Hailey didn't want to mention it, but he wasn't wearing the usual mask he normally wore to cover the scar on his face. Ale had talked to her before about how much she hoped he wouldn't wear it and ruin their prom photos because of a "stupid" insecurity, but she didn't want to ask him and risk offending him.

Then, as Ale was wont to do, she had made a real, emotionally honest, adult conversation flip to an outlandishly inappropriate one, asking, "Do you think he'd take it off if I sat on his face?"

It made Hailey happy that he chose not to wear it of his own accord and that he looked great without it. Better even. The scar provided a uniqueness to his face, aging him in a way a beard normally would—if he could manage to grow one—and he needed it because he had a baby face.

"You kids are terrible with compliments," Alexa said. "Billy, you are quite the handsome young gentleman. 'Not too shabby,' my ass."

"Thanks. Both of you. Has anyone else arrived?" he asked.

"Nope, just you," Alexa said, just before a car door closed outside. She stood on her tiptoes to view out the window and said, "Never mind, Ale just got here." She gave Billy an impressed look of approval. "Lucky guy."

Ale soon joined them in the room, and Billy looked awestruck as she entered the doorway. Wearing the dress he'd picked out for her, sheer neon-blue pantyhose, matching fingerless fishnet gloves, royal blue wedge heels, and hair big, curlier, and shinier than Hailey's, she looked like a stunning caricature of how we envision '80s prom attire today.

"Oh my God," Billy said, prompting Ale to twirl to not only show off the outfit but to hide the fact that she was blushing.

"You like it?" she asked, peeling her skirt outward.

"You look amazing!" he said. Once she was done fishing for compliments, she looked at *him*, biting her lip as if staring at a buffet spread. Then she noticed his maskless face.

"You're not wearing your mask!" She bounced on her heels with excitement and let out an annoying, happy squeal.

"Did you think I would?" His awkward chuckle was interrupted by the doorbell. Hailey felt a sudden shift of nervousness throughout her body as she applied her final touch of mascara.

"Right on time! Your date is here, and you are all ready to go," Alexa said, taking one last look at her. "I'll go get the door." She left them in the room and headed downstairs.

"Who knew we could all look so *fine*?" Ale said.

"Right?" Hailey got out of her chair and admired her finished look in the mirror.

"Who am I kidding? *I* knew. Of course we would. Still, Hailey . . . I'm impressed. I didn't know you could be so cute with so few curves," Ale said, playfully spanking Hailey.

"Ah!" she screamed. "You're thinner than *I* am."

"I know, I'm just projecting. Now, are you ready to see your date?" Ale asked as Westley's voice joined Alexa's downstairs. Hailey thought about it and realized that this was the first meeting between the two of them. Under other circumstances, she was sure Alexa would embarrass her, but tonight was special, and she trusted her not to.

"Ready."

Billy held his elbow out for Ale to take and escorted her out the door and downstairs. She kissed him on the neck before taking the first step down. Hailey heard Westley and Alexa cracking up before she followed her friends.

"Ah, Hailey, your mom is *hilarious*," he said, hearing their footsteps, then stopped mid-sentence when he laid eyes on her. To her surprise, he looked as nervous as he was handsome, which was *very*.

He wore an all-white suit with black accents, black tie, and black dress shoes. His hair was gelled back, and he wore an icy-blue boutonniere on his lapel—she knew it was to match *her* eyes. Hailey wanted to cry seeing him like this, thinking, *How could I be so lucky?*

"Look at you," he said, approaching the steps. Speechless, all Hailey could do was giggle. He waited for Billy and Ale to leave the stairs before he lifted Hailey up and off the last step, making her feel as light as a feather as he did a full spin before setting her back on her feet.

Alexa sighed and said, "Young love . . . Can't relate." She reached to the decorative table beside the stairs and grabbed her digital camera. "Okay, the limo will be here soon, so let's get some pictures!"

She guided the two couples to stand beside each other and told the guys to grab their dates by the waist. Westley stopped beforehand, saying, "Oh! I almost forgot." He stepped to the same decorative table and grabbed an item off of it. "I told you I was making you something, remember? Give me your hand."

Hailey listened as he revealed it—a beautiful wrist corsage with two roses, one white and one magenta.

"That's so beautiful!" Alexa said.

"It really is," Hailey agreed, placing her newly decorated hand on his shoulder. "Thank you."

"A girl as beautiful as you deserves flowers that match," he said. "You're welcome."

"Barf," Ale said, but Hailey thought it was sweet.

Alexa guided them through a lengthy session of both couples together, separate, and with each of them individually as if she were a professional photographer, until Ale said, "Okay, either the limo's here for us or the president's outside."

Alexa took one last photo and said, "I can't wait to show these to Megan."

"Are you still going to see her tonight?" Hailey asked, partially curious but mostly wondering if she would actually have the house to herself tonight. Alexa saw right through this, of course.

"Yes, I am," she said, squinting her eyes, then diverting them to Westley. "If you don't wear a condom, I'll slit your throat."

"Whoa, I wasn't planning on—" he started.

"Cut the crap. I'm not some overprotective father badgering you for your intentions. All I care about is you showing her a good time and keeping her safe. Check those boxes and you can do what you want." Her stern, lecturing face then switched to a happy one. "Okay, kiddos, have fun!"

***

Neon light strips lined the luxury passenger compartment of the limousine while '80s pop hits played on the speakers. There was a mini-bar to fit the theme of a party limo, but any alcoholic beverages had been replaced with bottles of sparkling cider. Billy knocked on the tinted window that separated them from the driver to let him know they were all ready to go, and they were off.

Westley started their party, grabbing a bottle of sparkling apple-grape juice and popping it open like champagne before carelessly pouring it into four glasses, spilling the beverage on the limo's carpet flooring.

"Hey, watch it!" Ale yelled, lifting her feet up and rolling her legs over Billy's lap to keep the liquid from staining her shoes.

"My bad," Westley said with an unforgiving chuckle as he passed out the glasses. The four of them spent the short ride dancing in their seats, posing for blurry cell phone pictures, laughing, and having the most fun they'd had in the entire year. It was the much-needed break that the Camp Safe Woods survivors deserved, and Westley was happy to be a part of it—blending right into the friend circle as though he'd been there from the beginning.

The limo pulled up to the school's entrance where hordes of students—some as couples and plenty alone or with their friends—were entering, handing their tickets to the school's security guard. The entrance was surrounded by a beautiful archway of neon balloons with a banner that read *Neon Lights and a Memorable Night – '80s Prom.*

As Westley opened the door, stepped out, and offered a hand to help Hailey exit the limo, she couldn't help but notice everyone's heads turning. She felt like royalty, and not just because of the literal red carpet and roped walkway along the sidewalk to the entrance.

"I can get used to this." Ale beamed as she exited behind Billy.

"I'm not so sure," Hailey said. She was never the kind to seek attention, and it often made her uncomfortable. But tonight she planned on soaking it all in and relishing it. She was here with the most popular, attractive, and desired boy in school, and the attention she would receive throughout the night would only serve as a reminder of that.

From the school's main entrance, they were guided by a walkway decorated with scattered rose petals, neon strobe lights, and random posters from popular '80s films like *Heathers*, *The Breakfast Club*, *E.T.*, *Top Gun*, and more. She noticed the increased police presence as cops walked about the whole area. About halfway from the entrance to the gymnasium where prom was held was a cute set-up with a photographer—a sophomore Hailey recognized from Ale's cheer squad named Hassina—where couples were getting their pictures taken.

"Do you want to?" Westley pointed to the setup.

"Oh my gosh, can we?" Hailey asked.

Jackson and Grace were posing for their picture at the moment, so they had to briefly wait.

"Were those two always dating?" Hailey asked, not re-membering the two of them ever spending time together.

"Nope. But Jackson told me Grace offered him a hand job after prom if he went with her to boost her odds of winning Prom Queen, and that she'd blow him if they won," Westley explained, making Hailey realize she hadn't even thought about prom royalty titles this whole time.

"No way," Billy said. "That doesn't sound like her."

"It doesn't?" Ale asked. "She's been kissing ass to get ahead all year. What makes you think she wouldn't turn it around and kiss the front side for once?" She crossed her arms. "Not that it matters. Hailey and Westley will have those crowns once the night ends."

"You really think so?" Westley asked, scratching the back of his neck.

Of course, Hailey thought, dreading the idea of being put on a pedestal in front of her whole class.

"Duh! You two are the clear front-runners. And anyone who *wasn't* going to vote for you will have to when they see Hailey in something other than hobo clothes."

"Keep it up with the backhanded compliments and you'll get backhanded for real one of these days," Hailey joked. "How do we even know if our names are on the ballot?"

"Oh, they are. I put them there, right above mine and Billy's," Ale said.

"Why wouldn't you at least warn me? And are you even allowed to put your own name on the list?"

"Sorry, I thought you would've assumed, considering who you're with. And when you look like this,"—she stretched one leg out to the side and placed her hands on her hips—"you can do whatever you want. As long as I get one vote, I'll be happy."

Grace and Jackson finished with their photo, then Jackson yelled, "Westley, look at you!" though his eyes were focused on Ale's legs in her pose.

"We clean up well, don't we?" Westley asked as they high-fived. He then nodded at Grace and said, "You look nice."

Grace slightly blushed and said, "You, too," before turning her face to a more competitive one. "Good luck with your royalty votes." She looked at Hailey like she was an enemy in this competition that she didn't exactly sign up for.

Hailey only smiled back.

Once the two of them continued to the gymnasium, Westley and Hailey posed for their picture with a funny back-to-back finger guns pose. After them, Ale and Billy readied for their picture, where he surprised her by lifting her off her feet. She screamed until she was held sturdy in his arms, then embraced him around his neck for an adorable photo.

"Warn me next time," Ale said when he put her down.

"But that wouldn't be as fun."

Both couples gave their phone numbers to Hassina for the photos to be sent to them and they continued on to the gym.

As they approached the doors, they could feel the lively energy in the air. "Party All the Time" by Eddie Murphy blared through the night sky from within the building. The doors, surrounded by white drapes to hide the fact that it was a gymnasium, opened and they walked in through a crowd of people who were hanging out just outside of the dance floor.

Hailey's fellow classmates all looked snazzy in their attire and luckily, they all mostly fit the '80s theme so she didn't feel out of place. Plenty of vibrant dresses, sparkly heels, big hair, puffy sleeves, and ruffles everywhere. A lot of the guys wore their hair like the Greasers from *The Outsiders*, which Hailey thought was hilarious considering the movie actually took place in the '60s.

Ale started the dancing, bouncing her head and shaking her hips while dragging an embarrassed Billy onto the floor with her, and Hailey was ready to let loose. When the song transitioned into Michael Jackson's "P.Y.T (Pretty Young Thing)," she turned to Westley and said, "I *love* this song," and without another word, he followed her and they danced beside Ale and Billy.

Hailey's feet were already starting to hurt, not used to being in heels, but she couldn't care less. She stepped and stomped on every beat, dancing back-to-back with Ale while their dates across from them tried to match their energy. Westley was a good dancer—naturally, as Hailey realized he was good at just about everything—while Billy looked like he had two left feet every time Hailey spun around and spotted him; she couldn't help but laugh as he shamelessly stumbled his way through the song. After another ten minutes of nonstop dance tunes keeping them busy, the boys needed a break.

"If I'm gonna keep up with you, I'm gonna need a drink. Can I get you something?" Westley asked.

"That sounds great," Hailey said.

"Hey, I'll go with you." Billy followed him as they disappeared into the crowd.

"God, isn't this great?" Hailey turned to Ale.

"I am having *so* much fun. And who knew Billy could dance like that?" Ale asked.

"Like what, a newborn fawn?" Hailey joked.

"*Exactly*! And he's *just* as adorable."

Chapter 23

Billy and Westley found the punch table against the wall where the bleachers would usually be, and Leo—wearing a tux similar to Billy's—was hanging around with a suspicious look on his face until his eyes brightened upon seeing his friend.

"Hey, dude, why aren't you out on the dance floor?" Billy asked.

"Dancing's not really my thing, especially not after the shit I saw the other day," Leo answered.

"Yeah, that's rough," Westley said, having heard about what happened with Leo's drug dealer from Hailey.

"I just don't know how you do it, Billy. I mean, you've had people die around you your whole life—no offense."

"None taken," Billy said, wishing he was back with Ale where he wouldn't feel obligated to cheer his friend up on an otherwise joyous night.

"That shit was downright *scary*. I'm only *here* out of obligation as the only student able to sneak alcohol into the place. If it weren't my civic duty to do so, I'd be home drunk off my ass right about now."

"Wait, you snuck alcohol in here?" Westley asked.

"How'd you end up getting some?" Billy wanted to know.

Leo opened up his suit jacket and brandished a large flask from its inner pocket, saying, "This was all I could manage. I had to steal some rum from my dad's liquor cabinet. I'm offering people one shot per cup of punch until it's gone, but the cops here are freaking me out."

Billy and Westley looked about the room and noticed just how many of them were there—at least half a dozen, with one in each corner of the room, plus two standing at what would normally be the half-court line. They all seemed very focused, with none of them looking toward the punch table.

"I'll be honest, I think you're good," Westley said, taking a cup and scooping some punch from the bowl with the ladle provided. "Just keep an eye out and make it quick."

Billy followed in his footsteps.

"Do you guys want some?" Leo asked. "Break the seal."

"I'm good, thanks," Billy said.

"Sure, why not?" Westley stepped forward, holding out his cup. "Billy, come here." He motioned for Billy to stand beside him so they could form a tight circle for Leo to pour the shot out of sight before he took a swig straight from the bottle.

"*Man*, I needed that," Leo said.

Westley raised his cup and said, "Cheers."

***

When Billy Idol's "Dancing with Myself" started to play, Hailey's eyes darted across the gym to the DJ booth where Nia stood with a proud smile, watching the crowd dance to *her* playlist. She wore a short, black, layered tulle skirt with a zipped leather jacket. Her hair was shiny and shoulder-length with natural coils. She was gorgeous.

Just as Hailey was feeling so good about finding a way to get Nia to prom—and lacking any regret thanks to her perfect taste in music—the two of them locked eyes. Nia mouthed the words, "Thank you," to which Hailey smiled and nodded.

Hailey and Ale had fun dancing through the song until the boys came back with the drinks. Parched, they both gulped their punch and Hailey followed her swallow, voicing a satisfied "Ah!" and a "Thank you so much."

"Of course. I hope we didn't take too long," Westley said.

"Not at all." Hailey smiled.

"We were having our own fun." Ale winked, already backing her ass up on Billy.

"Careful, you'll get us thrown out of here," he joked, trying not to spill his drink.

"That wouldn't be *so* bad," she said, turning around and wrapping her arms around him, then biting his lip as the song ended.

Nia picked up the microphone and made an announcement, "Attention, Pineside Prom attendees!" The entire class looked her way. "This place is finally starting to fill up, but we've got some more heads still walking through the door. We'll be here partying all night, but the voting window for your Prom Queen and King will be over in about an hour and a half. The voting booth is up here with me, so come and vote before you're out of time." Then, with the press of a button, ZZ Top's "Sharp Dressed Man" played over the speakers and the crowd went right back to dancing.

"What do you think?" Westley asked. "Check a box next to *our* names? I think a nice tiara would *really* fit that dress of yours."

Hailey still wasn't sure about the idea, but he wasn't wrong about the tiara. It *would* complement the outfit, and she'd never have another shot at something like this. "Fuck it, why not?"

He took her hand and started the walk through the crowd on the dance floor, only stopping once when Ale asked, "Are you guys going to vote?" Hailey nodded as Westley continued pulling her along. Ale yelled, "We'll vote after one more song," and she disappeared behind another dancing couple.

The voting booth consisted of two small, square tables with little foldable walls around their edges to prevent people from seeing who was voting for whom. Hailey waited for less than the duration of a full song, then saw Ale and Billy get in line as she stepped up to the tables with Westley. There, they were greeted by Principal Collins, who handed them each a single red envelope with a sheet of paper.

"There is a pen on the table. Mark your choices, seal your envelopes, and drop the ballots here," he said, pointing to a box seated atop a wooden stool. "Feel free to vote for yourselves." He smiled.

Hailey took her ballot to one of the tables and went over her options. From the top down, the choices beside little checkboxes were: *Hailey Ramirez and Westley Parker, Grace Nisbett and Jackson Grady, Amani St. James and Curtis Frank, Alejandra Vasquez and Billy Thompson,* and lastly, *Sophie Jennings and Henry Walker.*

Hailey was shocked to see her name first, but given the fact that Ale made the ballots, she was more surprised that she and Billy were so low on the list. Though to be fair, she probably didn't want to make it too obvious that she snuck herself on there. Hailey didn't recognize the girl, Amani, but she knew Curtis Frank was the school football team's quarterback, so she felt proud being on the list with other members of school royalty. Still, the biggest surprise on the list was seeing the male cheerleader, Henry, and that he actually had a date.

For the fun of it, and so as not to feel like a narcissist, Hailey checked the box beside Ale and Billy's names, sealed the envelope by licking the awful-tasting adhesive, and joined Westley at the box, slipping her ballot inside just behind his.

"Two votes for us?" he asked optimistically.

She gave him a fake frown and said, "No, I figured we'd win without them. I wanted Ale to get a vote that wasn't hers."

"A woman who cares for others," Westley said. "How did I get so lucky?"

"Hailey!" a familiar voice called out. She turned and saw Nia waving her over to the DJ booth.

"I'll be right back," Hailey said.

"I won't be here." Westley smiled.

"You won't?"

"Nope. I'm gonna be out there," he said, pointing to the dance floor. "Maneater" by Hall & Oates was playing, and the crowd was loving it. "This is my *jam*. Don't take too long, or you might miss out on some *serious* fist pumping."

She laughed as he walked out to the floor, dancing by himself. Then Hailey approached Nia.

"Are you having fun?" Hailey asked.

"Are you kidding? For me, this is honestly *way* better than regularly attending. I honestly owe you so much for thinking about me for this," Nia said, the happiest Hailey had ever seen her.

"Oh, don't mention it. I'm just glad you could come. Nobody deserves to miss out on a night like this."

Nia looked like she could cry. Unexpectedly, she ran to Hailey and gave her a big hug, lifting her off the floor. Hailey almost fell upon being set back down, still off-balance from her heels.

"Seriously, I love you so much for this," Nia said. "I know you've got Mr. Flores waiting for you out there, but I want a dance before the night ends."

Hailey smiled. "You got it."

***

At the Meadowood Emergency Hospital, Alexa sat in the small, uncomfortable, plastic chair at Megan's bedside. Her visit was about as long as Hailey had been at prom—leaving the house as soon as the limo drove away—but it felt like forever at this point, especially considering the total number of hours she'd been there since Megan was attacked. They were watching reruns of some '90s sitcom that Alexa only vaguely recognized on the small TV that jutted out from the wall via a white mount arm. Alexa hated this show, not because it was particularly bad, but with the amount of time she'd spent watching it here in this place, it gave her the same horrible feeling as smelling the cheap soap in the hospital's bathrooms or the mind-numbing lighting in its hallways. It made her feel u neasy.

Alexa entertained Megan while she could on her visits, but she was constantly tired. She lasted longer than usual this time, while they went over the prom photos and discussed just how grown-up Hailey had become. It wasn't long before Alexa heard Megan's light snoring beneath the whirring of the machines monitoring her vitals.

Hungry, she let go of her wife's hand and whispered, "I'll be right back," before leaving the room and walking down the long, dreary hallway to the snack vending machine in the waiting room. With scarce options, the only two she had to choose from were sour cream and onion kettle chips—her favorite—and dry, crunchy mini cookies. The choice was easy until she looked beneath the chips and saw that it was three dollars for the tiny bag.

She uttered, "Robbery," before pulling her wallet from her purse, inserting the cash into the machine, and watching the spiral holder unwind and stop just before the chips fell. Alexa stared at the machine, blinking heavily. She stepped forward to shake the machine but saw the security guard watching her. "It ate my money," she said. "Help a girl out?"

"I didn't see you put the money in. As far as I know, you're just a thief."

Alexa felt offended and wanted to call him on his bullshit. "You're kidding, right? I'm the only person in this room, and you've certainly had your eyes on me since I walked in."

His serious face broke and he laughed. "I am," he said. "Kidding," he added. Alexa didn't find it funny. "Here, let me get that." He approached the machine and pulled out his key to unlock it. "Are you here visiting a boyfriend?" He pulled out a bag of chips *and* a packet of cookies and handed them to her.

"Wife," she said, taking the snacks. He looked like a deer in headlights upon hearing her response.

"Wow, sorry, I didn't think—"

"Don't worry about it. Keep flirting with the guests and you might eventually get a widow to fall for it. Oh, and thanks." She smiled at him and walked toward her wife's room. From the hall, she could hear the beeping that indicated something was wrong with one of Megan's vitals, scaring Alexa enough for her to run to the room, shouting, "Nurse!"

When she turned the corner of the doorway, she found the room empty, with the light bedsheet Megan slept beneath carelessly tossed onto the floor. The RN on duty came running in just behind Alexa and gasped at the sight.

"Where is she?" Alexa asked, her heart pounding.

"I don't know," the nurse said before running back to her desk and picking up the phone, alerting the hospital that a patient was missing.

"Call 911!" Alexa yelled at her while trying to call Hailey, who was too preoccupied to answer. The nurse nodded, dialing the number as nurses started scurrying up and down the halls alongside the few security officers in the building.

Giving up, Alexa sent Hailey a text: *Get somewhere safe and call me ASAP.*

As she began the call on her own phone for Tiffany Watson, she recognized the security guard who helped her at the vending machine didn't seem to move as urgently as the rest until he locked eyes with Alexa and realized it was *her* wife who was missing. He then picked up the pace, going room to room looking for any sign of Megan.

Tiffany picked up the phone with an urgency in her voice. "What's wrong?"

"They kidnapped Megan from the hospital. Can you get to Pineside High and make sure Hailey's okay?" Alexa asked, her voice unbreaking as she forced herself to remain calm and collected in the dire moment."

"I'm on my way. Keep me updated," Tiffany said, hanging up the phone.

***

Hailey sat at a white cloth-covered table with Ale, Billy, Leo, and Grace while Westley, Jackson, and other members of the baseball team were tearing up the dance floor to AC/DC's "You Shook Me All Night Long." The girls needed a break from the hours of dancing in heels, and Westley was making it clear that he and his athletic friends had the stamina to keep going. When the song ended, the instrumental version of "Time After Time" by Cyndi Lauper played quietly and the lights dimmed, making the spotlight focusing on Nia in the DJ booth the focal point of the room. Hailey felt her stomach drop because she knew what was coming. She glanced over at Grace, who looked as hopeful as Hailey was nervous.

"All right, Pineside Prom guests! It is *that* time of the night," Nia said into her microphone. Principal Collins handed her an envelope just like the ones they'd sealed their ballots in earlier, reminding Hailey of award ceremonies where the emcees are handed envelopes with the award winners listed on a card inside. Hailey wondered if there was any chance Nia would say the wrong name like she'd seen done on the Internet. "The votes are in, and you have made your choices for Prom Queen and King!"

"Hey," Westley said, sliding into his chair beside Hailey. She hadn't seen him approaching because she was so focused on Nia.

"Hey," she replied with a smile, but she felt herself trembling. *Will I freeze if I hear my name called? What if I slip and embarrass myself? What if I—* She looked at her dress to make sure she hadn't spilled any punch on it that people would notice and laugh at. *Just give it to Grace*, she thought with her fingers crossed beneath the table. Westley gripped her thigh; that settled her enough to stop the trembling.

*Get a **grip**,* she told herself. *I **want** this.*

Nia opened the envelope.

"This is it," Ale said, turning to Billy and giving him a kiss. He pulled her in close and rubbed her shoulder.

"Are you ready?" Jackson asked, approaching Grace, blocking the view.

"Get out of the way," she said, leaning to see past him and waving him away.

Hailey looked at Westley, and he was *focused* on Nia. She could tell this was something he wanted, and that made her feel better about it.

Nia pulled a tri-folded sheet of letter paper out of the envelope, and with the glow of the spotlight, even from this far away, Hailey could see that the winning couple was written on the page in blue ink. Nia smiled and held the paper close to her chest while raising the microphone to her lips.

"Are you guys ready?" she asked, and the crowd clapped.

"Hurry up!" Grace yelled, disguising her voice to make it sound deeper than her own.

"Your Prom Queen and King are . . . " She paused for dramatic effect before raising her pitch and screaming, "Hailey Ramirez and Westley Parker!"

Chapter 24

The crowd cheered while Hailey stared blankly in disbelief. She looked at her best friend, who was clapping until she motioned her hands for Hailey to stand up.

"You won!" Ale cheered.

"We won?" she asked, then looked at Westley for confirmation. He was already standing, offering his hand to help her out of the chair.

"Where is the lovely couple? Nia asked, which resulted in the spotlight moving to their table. She waved for them, then yelled, "Come on up and claim your crowns!" Principal Collins approached the DJ table with two red velvet pillows—one with a yellow crown fit for a king and one with a pretty, sparkly rhinestone tiara.

Hailey finally smiled, taking Westley's hand and standing. The first pair of eyes she felt on her was Grace's, who clapped sarcastically with a pouty face. Then, Hailey noticed every eye in the room on her, and not just as a group but felt them all individually, locking eyes with most as they made their way to Nia. Suddenly, her new biggest fear was one of her heels snapping beneath her, sending her face-first to the floor while everyone watched. She took a quick, calming breath when they finished their walk unscathed.

Principal Collins said, "Congratulations, you two," as he lifted the crown.

"Thank you," Westley said, lowering his head enough for it to be placed on him.

Hailey tried to say, "Thank you," but nervously choked on the words, and made a noise that sounded something like a frog's croak getting interrupted by a sudden boulder squishing it. She'd hoped the instrumental playing was loud enough that nobody heard her, but the big smile on Nia's face wasn't a great tell—either she'd heard and was trying not to laugh, or she was genuinely happy for Hailey in the moment. Principal Collins then placed the tiara atop her head, and she readjusted it so it wouldn't fall off.

"Don't forget this!" Nia said, holding out a big white sash labeled *Prom Queen*, opened wide for Hailey, who stepped into it. "Are you two ready for your dance?" Nia asked into the microphone, drawing cheers from the crowd.

Hailey's jaw dropped, immediately thinking, *We **have** to dance? In front of everybody?*

Before she could reject the proposal, Nia pressed the button to start the track she had cued up, and Westley was already leading her out to the dance floor.

Thankfully, the spotlight was blinding enough from this spot to keep most of the eyes in the crowd hidden, but that didn't stop Hailey's feet from feeling like they were going to fall right off at the ankles.

The song playing was the *Back to the Future* rendition of "Earth Angel (Will You Be Mine)" by the fictitious band Marvin Berry and The Starlighters, and Hailey thought it was beautiful. Her legs took her by surprise and moved on their own, paving the way for Westley to follow her lead. He held one hand on her waist and grasped her hand with the other, holding it high as they swayed with each other. The only eyes she felt on her in that moment were his as they looked into hers.

Lost in the moment, she hadn't heard when Nia announced the rest of the guests could join them for what would be the start of the "Slow Dance Hour." As couples surrounded them and moved at the pace *they* created, Hailey felt like she and Westley were alone in their own little compartment of the universe. In what felt like the best moment of her entire life, he spun her around, then pulled her in close, guided her into a slow, graceful dip, where they shared their first kiss, and Hailey felt like she was in love.

She thought fireworks were going off around her, and it sounded like it too. She didn't realize until their lips pulled apart that the sound was from all the couples who surrounded them and witnessed the moment—and those cheering loudest were her friends, Billy and Ale.

She felt as red as her cherry-tinted lips, a mixture of her blushing and the warmth in her body from that kiss. When she looked into Westley's eyes, she licked her lips as if she could taste it once again, and he smiled a nervous smile of his own.

"I've been wanting to do that for a while now," he said. "Did you know that was my first?"

"That makes two of us," she said, wrapping her arms around his neck and swarming him with a hug. As the song ended, it quickly segued into the next, "Africa" by Toto. Still hanging from his neck, she slowly swayed to the song. "I don't ever want tonight to end."

"Me neither," he said. "It's *too* perfect."

She smiled and buried her head in his chest, rubbing her forehead on it in an enamoring fashion before pulling it back up so her nose was just below his chin. "Prom King and Queen . . . can you believe it?"

"No, but it makes so much sense. That tiara wouldn't look right on anybody else."

She laughed. "I could do without the attention it brings, though."

He frowned slightly. "You know that won't go away, right? With me, I mean. If it's not eyes on you, it's gonna be cameras. If I'm as successful as everyone's predicting I will be, that is."

"Of *course* you will be! And I'll get used to it. It's just—I've been through a lot. And I'm not used to stares of envy and happiness. Ever since my mom passed, when people stare at me, it's always been because they felt bad for me or because they're waiting for me to act out—as if someone who's seen death is different from them. And I'm *not*. But those stares have only become more frequent and more aggressive since last summer, and now with everything that's happened these past few months, those stares have become looks of disgust and fear." For the first time that night, she found her happiness trailing, thinking about that stuff. Her tiara slipped, falling down her back, where Westley caught it and placed it on her head, bringing her back to the moment. "But being with *you* has changed that. You've given those uncomfortable stares a whole new meaning, and *that* is something I can get used to."

He grabbed her by the hips, pulled them to his, and stared deeply into her eyes. "How about this? I can't save you from those eyes for the rest of our lives together, but we *can* avoid them for tonight. I can make it just the two of us."

"Oh? How would you manage that?"

"You remember that old abandoned library I took you to? I kind of convinced the janitor to keep it unlocked for us tonight."

Hailey threw her head back and laughed. "No, you didn't!"

"I did." His grip on her waist tightened. "The guy's a little weirdo. I told him I'd send him a signed hat from whatever MLB team drafts me. He was so excited, he didn't even think to give me his contact information to make it happen."

Hailey kept laughing while thoroughly considering the proposition.

Is this how it happens? Am I going to lose my virginity on prom night with this hunk of a man? Where would we even do it? On the floor? That could be hot . . . But is **that** *how I want my first time* ever *to go?*

Screw it.

"Okay," she said, to *his* surprise, based on the way his eyebrows jumped. "Let's do it." She led the way, pulling him by the hand through the crowd until they reached Billy and Ale who were slow dancing, foreheads touching. She put her free hand on Ale's back to get her attention. "Hey, you guys." The couple turned their heads to face them.

"What's up?" Billy asked, still swaying.

"We're gonna get out of here," Hailey said.

"So soon?" Billy asked, but Ale knew what she meant.

"Yeah. But we won't be taking the limo home. They never asked which of us was *me*, so if you want, you can take it back to my place. I won't be there till late, and Alexa won't be there until the morning so . . . have fun."

Billy looked concerned and speechless, as if he was thinking, "Is this really happening?"

Ale let go of Billy and hugged Hailey, squeezing tightly and screaming, "I love you!" When she pulled away, she looked at Westley and said, "Take care of her," then looked back to Hailey and told her, "Have fun, yourself."

"Thanks," Hailey said.

Walking away from her friends felt like something out of a coming-of-age film, like they all knew the next time they'd see each other something would be vastly different about each of them. By age, they were all adults, but this passing moment felt more monumental than any birthday ever would. This was the first time Hailey truly felt like they were all coming into adulthood, and it was exciting.

On their way to the back of the gymnasium where they'd make their exit onto the school grounds, Hailey wouldn't have felt right without saying goodbye to Nia, so they made a stop at the DJ booth.

"Hey, guys!" Nia said. "Are you having a good time?"

"The best!" Hailey exclaimed.

"Yeah, you're seriously killing it. Announcing for a high school baseball team is one thing, but you've got some *serious* talent here." Westley meant every word.

"*And* great taste in music," Hailey added.

"Aww, stop. You guys are gonna make me blush." Nia smiled sheepishly.

"We mean it. Tonight's been perfect," Westley said.

"Then you'd better hire me to do your wedding," she joked.

"Oh, for *sure*," Hailey agreed, taking one step toward the exit, preparing her goodbye. "We—"

Cutting her off, Mrs. Ivory, chaperoning the event, stepped into their conversation, saying, "Well look at that! If it isn't the Prom King and Queen." She wore a formal, black, short-sleeved blouse with white ruffles on the collar and sleeves, paired with a just-above-the-knee black leather skirt, and her signature cat-eye glasses. Her black, sling-back, peep-toe stilettos were higher than normal, making her still stand taller than Hailey, even wearing heels of her own.

"Hey, Mrs. Ivory," Westley greeted nervously, looking toward the exit, ready to go.

"You look so good! Love the outfit," Hailey said.

"Me? Look at you! I would've brought my own tiara, but that would've just made me look like a bitch."

Hailey laughed. She never could get over her teacher's informality—it was something special and *always* hilarious.

"Now, if I'm not mistaken, I'd say it looks like the two of you are getting ready to leave this place," Mrs. Ivory said, taking them both by surprise.

How did she know? Hailey thought, then noticed her posture was obviously leaning toward the door.

"Us?" Westley asked. "No, I'm just escorting Hailey to the bathroom."

"Yeah," Hailey said nervously. She wasn't the best liar. "All that punch just runs right through me."

Nia's eyes widened. "I forgot about the punch! You know, I haven't had a drink all night," she said.

"Really?" Mrs. Ivory asked. "That's not good.

"You'd think the principal would at least offer, but nope. Not a lick."

"Can't you just go grab some?" Hailey suggested.

"And let one of these students come up here and play trash music? Not on my watch. Besides, I think the punch is just for the guests, *not* the workers."

"Bullshit. I've been drinking it all night. You wait here and I'll go grab you some," Mrs. Ivory said.

"You will?" Nia asked, her eyes bright and thankful. "That would be so awesome. You have no idea."

Mrs. Ivory smiled. "Of course! And if you need more, you just let *me* know."

Nia nodded and they watched Mrs. Ivory walk away. Then Hailey turned back to Nia.

"So, we kinda lied to her," Hailey said. "We *are* taking off early and didn't want the attention."

"What? You can't!" Nia exclaimed. "We haven't had *our* dance yet."

"Hey, it's like you said. If you walked away from the booth, someone might play some trash."

Nia sighed. "True. Rain check, then. And you two *lovebirds* have fun."

Chapter 25

With her head on Billy's chest and her hips having swayed for what felt like forever now, Ale was growing restless. The dancing had been all good and fun, but the bust seam of her dress was digging into her ribs with every breath, and her heels were so tight, her feet felt like sausages bursting out of designer casings. Plus, Hailey had given her the opportunity of a lifetime. All she wanted to do now was get out of her uncomfortable outfit and either help Billy out of his or rip it off him.

Without waiting for the song to finish, she peeled away from him and said, "Screw this. We're leaving."

He looked nothing short of nervous. Breath shaking and sweat glistening on his forehead, he asked, "What, are you not having a good time?"

She smiled. "Oh, I'm having a great time." She leaned up close to his ear and whispered, "I want to make this the best night of my life," then nibbled his earlobe before stepping back. She gave him her best puppy-dog eyes and said, "Unless that's not something that interests you."

He took a breath as though he was coming to terms with fate and said, "Yeah, *let's do it.*"

She then took her first step leading him to the exit. That's when the panic set in. She'd spent so much time thinking about, talking about, and imagining the act of sex, and her time to finally experience it was about to come.

Is there any way it could live up to the hype at this point? she thought, causing a string of worries as they exited the gym. *I've had so many people warn me that guys don't know how to make girls finish. If that's true, then what hope is there for Billy, who has never done this before either? Would the fact that it's with* **him** *make it easier to happen? Or would I have to accept the fact that it* **won't** *and just enjoy the ride?*

Then her insecurities shifted. *What if* **I'm** *bad at it? Sure, I'm hot, and maybe that could be enough for him, but what if it's not?* She shook her head at the thought. *No. Billy's not that type of guy . . . right?*

When they reached the parking lot, they found the limo triple-parked perpendicular in three spots. Ale knocked on the tinted window and the driver inside, an older, rough-looking white guy, rolled it down. He seemed confused.

"We're ready to go," Ale said, pretending to be Hailey.

"Just the two of you?" he asked.

"The others are finding their own way home."

He shrugged. "The school's paying me either way. Hop in, the back's unlocked."

Billy helped her in, then they buckled into their seats, and as soon the car started Billy was kissing her neck. She released small moans to let *him* know that she was in the mood and also remind *herself* that this process was meant to be enjoyed. His lips traveled up her neck, to behind her ears, then once on her cheek before meeting her lips, where she was waiting for him. Ever since the first time their lips touched, kissing him became her favorite thing to do. She could never get enough. As soon as she got her seat belt unbuckled, she crawled onto his lap so they were facing each other and she could feel closer to him. Things took off from there.

She was pulling at his hair. He was biting her lip. She was sliding her tongue into his mouth. He pulled her hair to tilt her head back so he could kiss her cleavage—and if she wasn't so unsure as to whether or not the driver could see into the back seat through the privacy partition, she would have pulled her dress down and let him explore her *whole* chest. They couldn't wait much longer to arrive at Hailey's, but they were so caught up in the moment that they didn't realize the limo was taking them somewhere else entirely.

When the car suddenly stopped, Billy said, "That was fast."

"Not fast enough," Ale said, opening her eyes as the volume of the music playing raised to an annoying level. She recognized the song: "Love Is A Battlefield" by Pat Benatar.

"Was it always this loud?" Billy asked, borderline yelling over the chorus, but Ale was more concerned with their location. She couldn't see well through the tinted windows, but she could tell they were in some creepy back alleyway.

"Hey!" Ale yelled toward the driver, hopping off Billy. "I think you brought us to the wrong place!"

"What?" Billy finally looked out the window and realized the same.

Ale crawled to the partition and banged on it.

"Can you turn down that music?" She paused for just a second to see if he heard her, then banged on the window again. "Hey, asshole, you brought us to the wrong place!" Giving up, she turned to Billy and gestured to the door in the back. "Can you go out there and get this guy?"

"Uh . . ." He looked out the window, and it was clear that he was uncomfortable. She felt bad having him go because this whole thing just felt wrong, but someone had to go out there to solve this, and if they needed to run, at least *he* wasn't wearing heels. "Yeah, I'll be right back."

He opened the door, took a step outside, and as soon as his head left her visibility, she watched his body convulse as his initial scream was cut off with a lengthy, garbled grunt. From her time spent watching reality crime television, she knew he'd been tased. When his body fell to the ground, his one foot remaining inside the car was all she could still see of him.

"Billy!" she yelled, already regretting sending him out there. She knew the person responsible for killing all those people was behind this attack, and she needed to act fast to prevent them from killing *her* and Billy too. Her hands immediately reached for a bottle of sparkling peach cider, which she grabbed by the neck and slammed onto the limo's floor, cracking it into a makeshift weapon. The liquid staining her prom dress was the least of her worries, though the bit that splashed her hand made her concerned that she wouldn't have a great grip on the glass.

Billy hadn't been touched since the initial attack, and he wasn't tased for very long, so she was pretty confident that he was still alive. But she couldn't see *anything* through the windows that gave away their attacker's position. The tint was bad enough, the night only made it worse. She thought she might've heard some gravel crunching outside—footsteps—but Pat Benatar was yelling too loudly for her to tell.

Holding the bottle outward with one hand, she used her other to quickly unstrap her heels and kicked them off in case she needed to run, then backed up along the seat as far as she could get from the doors, so she would have the maximum amount of time to react to whoever entered the vehicle. She felt bad leaving Billy on the ground where he was, but she knew this psycho was ruthless and killed victims violently. Meaning: they had used a taser for a reason; if they wanted Billy dead, he already would be. If they wanted Ale, they would have to come get her. Unfortunately, the one thing she didn't consider was that the partition window she had been banging on earlier was right behind her, and the driver was finally rolling it down. Thanks to Pat Benatar, though, she couldn't hear it happening.

The jolt from the taser shocked her, *literally*, when it met her neck. Her body convulsed until she collapsed.

***

Hailey always wanted to wait to do it. Not necessarily wait for marriage, but she wanted to wait. Be it a special guy, a special time, or for a special reason, she knew it was a special moment, and she wanted it to be just that. Special. With a night as magical as prom was, she couldn't think of a better time, so she was ready.

The library was unlocked, just as Westley said it would be.

"You don't think that janitor will be waiting here for you, do you?" she asked, her hand on his chest as she hung off his arm while he led her to the same spot in the center of the library where they were before. It was emptier this time around, with a few bookshelves missing and more books having been relocated to the new library.

"No, I don't." He laughed, then took her to a bench along the wall they hadn't seen last time because there was a bookshelf blocking the view of it. She could still see the rectangular dent in the carpet from the years the shelf had spent sitting there. He sounded like he was going to say something else, then stopped himself and watched Hailey as she unstrapped the velcro on the Prom Queen sash and let it fall to the floor, creating a ring around her feet as she pulled off her heels one by one.

He loosened his tie but not to take it off. It was more of a dramatic I'm-having-trouble-breathing gesture. She stepped over the sash; the old carpet was a soft relief for her aching feet. She kissed him for the second time now, and it was just as good as the first, but in a different way; as magical as the first was, this one matched with a not-so-romantic descriptor. Hot.

There was a lot more saliva swapping this time around, which she was shocked she'd found herself enjoying. The taste was sweet from the fruit punch with a hint of . . . was that alcohol? Didn't matter. She wanted more of it, opening her mouth wide, inviting his tongue in, and he accepted. She didn't realize as she pushed herself against him that he was losing his balance, and rather than stumbling to the floor, he grabbed her hips, spun her around, and plopped her ass on the bench while he stayed on his feet, leaning down over her.

Their lips separated while she laughed at the absurdity of the moment. He untucked his shirt and Hailey started unbuttoning it from the bottom while he leaned in to kiss her more. When she got to the top, she undid his tie and pulled it through his collar, as though she was taking off a belt, before undoing that final button. Feeling like she wanted to take something off herself, she reached beneath her dress, pulled down and kicked off her panties, letting them drop from her feet to the floor before standing up to catch his mouth once again. She ran her fingers up his chest, feeling his body for the first time ever. It was shockingly warm for a cold night and was solid like a cinder block.

He let out soft, stifled gasps between kisses, as if her fingers sent ticklish tremors through his chest. Meanwhile, his long arms found their way traveling downward, hiking up her dress. She felt the cold air graze her bottom when it became exposed. Nervousness at an all-time high, her knees felt weak. His palm met the soft underside of her ass with a firm, upward *smack*, sending a ripple through the whole cheek, taking her by surprise and causing her to yelp and lose her balance, pulling him down by his neck as they fell onto the floor laughing. Her tiara slipped from her head and bounced along the carpet.

He was on top of her, and her hands were moving by themselves. They moved straight for the button on his pants now, struggling with it at first, thinking, *Why do they make the button so big and the hole so small?* Then, choosing to allow her fingers to hurt, she forced the metal button through and unzipped his pants.

This is it, she thought. *I'm about to see my first in-person penis! What if it's small? That won't matter, right? At least it would hurt less. Wait, is this going to hurt? Oh my God, what if it's* **huge***? Am I about to regret this?*

With all these thoughts racing through her head, she chose to rip off the Band-Aid and dug her hands into his boxer briefs, grazed over his pubic stubble, and grasped. It was very smooth, squishy, and . . . flaccid? She pulled it out of his pants and rather than standing tall, it just flopped out and hung loosely over the waistline of his boxers, looking unimpressive and sad.

I thought he'd be ready to go, she thought. ***I** sure am. Wait, is he not enjoying himself?*

Then, disrupting her train of thought as she stared at the one-eyed creature looking back at her, Westley slapped her. It confused her at first, which only deepened when he went in for a kiss.

Okay, tough guy might want rough sex? Not exactly what I had in my mind for my first time, but let's see how it goes. She opened her mouth to return the kiss, but their teeth clashed just before he bit down hard on her lower lip, breaking the skin. She started tasting the blood in her mouth as soon as he pulled away.

"Ouch," she said, licking the cut on her lip. Then not wanting to take too much away from the moment, she reached for his penis, taking the whole thing into her one hand, expecting it to harden up after his rough acts, but it did not. So, she started to stroke him.

"No," he grunted, reaching his hand down to slip his penis back into his pants.

Was I not doing it right? she thought, her self-consciousness at an all-time high. *No, it must be that alcohol I'm tasting! That can give guys problems, right?* She didn't know how much of it he'd had, or where he even got it from, but she was sure *that* was the problem. He brought his hand up slowly, then grabbed her neck as they kissed. Gently at first, then he wrapped his thumb around the front side of her throat and tightened his grip.

Choking? That's a bit much, right? Oh well. If it helps, I guess, she thought, at this point, on the verge of getting this part of the night over. *I'm gonna have a hell of a story to tell Ale after this.*

She tried moaning, pretending to enjoy the feeling, thinking that it would excite him if she did, but all he did was tighten his grip more and more until she struggled to breathe.

"Wait." She coughed. "That's too much." The last thing she wanted to do was embarrass him for something that turned him on, but she couldn't take it anymore.

He pulled his mouth away from hers and sat up straight, keeping his hand wrapped around her throat and letting all of his weight crush onto her stomach. That only made her breathing worse.

"You know," he said, his demeanor flipping entirely. No longer did he seem excited or flirtatious. He was annoyed. "*She* wanted me to fuck you. I tried talking *her* out of it, but she insisted. And I tried. I mean it, I tried. I really did. But the only woman *I want* to fuck, is *her*." His grip tightened.

She wanted to ask, "Who are you talking about?" But all she could croak out was, "Who?" As he brought his other hand to her throat and squeezed, the added pressure had Hailey fearing for her life as she gasped for air.

No way. She wondered, *Is* **he** *the murderer? And is this woman he's talking about an accomplice?*

"But as you felt,"—he looked down at his groin—"there's just nothing there for you. Only for *her*." His grip tightened, and he leaned in, putting more weight on her throat. "And *she's* gonna give it to me *so good* when we're all done with this. I don't know what her plans are, though. I'm hoping she lets me fuck her while *you* watch. I've suggested it a few times, but she thought it would be better if *you* and *I* did it instead."

Hailey was fighting him, clawing at his arms with her freshly manicured nails, scratching them as best she could because she knew there was no way she could overpower him. But she felt herself weakening with every second her breathing was obstructed. During the scuffle, her breasts slipped out of the top of her dress.

Westley took one hand off her throat to grab her dress and pull it up, aggressively covering her, shouting, "Nobody wants to see that!" Then he brought his hand back to her throat and sighed like this whole thing was just some big inconvenience for him. "Now where was I? Oh, right! I was thinking, *How about you and I don't do anything and just pretend we did?* That would be best for both of us."

Something he and I agree on, Hailey thought, hating that something he said was making sense.

"She knows just how much I love choking, so this is perfect. She'll see these bruises on your throat and all the stars will align."

Speaking of stars, Hailey was seeing them—visions of the stars falling from the roof of the gymnasium as she danced in Westley's arms, having the time of her life. She saw it happen in slow motion, replaying it back in her head as he spun her around, then dipped her. Only this time, instead of a magical kiss, everything just went black.

Chapter 26

"So Hailey and Westley left?" Mrs. Ivory asked, placing Nia's punch cup on the table.

"Hm?" Nia said, picking up the cup. "Oh yeah, they're going to the bathroom, right?" She wanted to keep up the facade for her friend. It was the least she could do, considering that she wouldn't have even gone to prom without her. And though they were both adults and could do whatever they wanted, she could only imagine how awkward a relationship with a school teacher might be once they knew you were having sex. And the last thing she'd want is to start spreading rumors about Hailey, who gave her the opportunity of a lifetime. But Mrs. Ivory wasn't your average teacher. She was the type who saw through bullshit and already knew what they were up to.

"They're *not* going to the bathroom. They're being naughty."

Nia almost spit out her drink trying to down it, but she avoided doing so after Mrs. Ivory went through the trouble of grabbing it for her. Not to mention, red fruit punch would definitely stain, so with all the fancy outfits in the room, it was best for everyone that she kept her composure. "You think so?"

"I *know* so. But that's exciting, right? I remember *my* first time."

Nia looked at her, not as a teacher but as an adult talking to her as another adult. It was such a strange feeling for her, seeing someone who she'd normally look up to speaking to her as an equal. This night made her feel like she finally crossed the road from childhood into adulthood, and not just in her own eyes—because she'd felt that way for a long time, working so hard, making tough decisions no high schooler should've ever been faced with to keep her family and household afloat—but in the eyes of the adults around her. Like Principal Collins, who'd spoken to her like an employee he'd hired, which she was, rather than a fellow student. And like Mrs. Ivory now, who no longer cared to put up a professional face as she normally would—as little effort as she did anyway.

Mrs. Ivory continued. "Young love, I envy it. But she'll learn soon enough that it usually doesn't last."

"I don't know, the two of them looked really happy together. I'd even say they were in love."

"You think so?" She shrugged. "Maybe. Either way, I guess it beats dying a virgin."

Nia felt offended. *Was being a virgin that bad?* And she didn't think her offense taken was showing, but as usual, Mrs. Ivory saw through it.

"Oh, are you— I'm sorry, I didn't mean anything by that. I'm sure your time will come."

"Uh, yeah," Nia said awkwardly, lifting her cup and sipping slowly, hoping that by the time she finished the punch Mrs. Ivory would be gone because this was a weird conversation to be having with a teenager.

"How's your drink?" Mrs. Ivory asked, causing Nia to gulp it down quickly so she could answer the question without making the situation more awkward.

"Ah, it's good. Thanks for grabbing it." She held the cup up for emphasis, but it slipped out of her hand. She looked down at it as if making sure it didn't splash on the floor, even though it was empty. She felt dizzy staring at it, like her depth perception was off. The cup seemed so far away, as if she were nine feet tall standing over it. Her fear of heights kicked in, making her wobble at the ankles.

"Are you okay?" Mrs. Ivory asked, her head tilted.

"Yeah, I—"

Interrupting her, the crowd gasped as someone violently spewed vomit onto the center of the dance floor. She recognized him as Henry Walker from the cheer squad. His date looked disgusted at him for getting it all over her shoes, until his body started spazzing out. He fell face-first into the vomit, still shaking on the floor, splashing the mess around even more.

With distorted, colorful vision, she watched a police officer force his way through the crowd.

"He's having a seizure!" the officer yelled, turning Henry onto his side. "Call 911!"

As Henry shook violently, his vomit turned to foam. Nia felt her own stomach curdle, but she didn't know if it was watching him that made her sick or if whatever caused her sudden lightheadedness was doing it.

Then, the entire room erupted, as one by one, other students and chaperones alike joined Henry in the vomiting. Within seconds the room smelled terrible. Everyone who wasn't puking was screaming, and those who *were* puking were collapsing one after the other by the dozens.

Then Nia joined them.

She heard Principal Collins scream out, "What is happening?" while she lost control of her stomach contents. When she fell to the floor, she felt him come to her side and embrace her, though he stayed behind her to avoid getting vomit on him.

"Please," she said between puke sessions, reaching up to Mrs. Ivory who looked down on her, disgusted at the sight.

The feeling of her chest heaving to push out an already empty stomach was awful and violent—unlike any time she'd ever gotten sick before. She was afraid.

To scare her even more, she heard the police officer at Henry's side yell out, "He's dead!" sending the room into an even bigger panic, making Nia worry for her own life.

This isn't how tonight was supposed to go.

Her eyes felt sensitive to the flashing lights in the room, but she didn't have the energy to tell anyone about it. She was going to pass out and she knew it, but what she didn't know was whether or not she would wake up. To avoid drowning in her own vomit, she crawled along the floor, lying with her face downward so gravity would take her vomit away from her throat. And with a face full of it, feeling more uncomfortable, disgusting, and scared than ever, her brain shut off, and she started to seize.

***

Mrs. Ivory watched as Principal Collins gave the girl CPR, but it was clear he didn't know what he was doing. He shoved his hands aggressively onto her chest with no pattern or direction, hurting her more than helping.

"I won't let you die!" he yelled, though it was no use. She was already gone, along with anyone else who drank enough of that punch in the last ten minutes.

Mrs. Ivory approached him and placed a hand on his shoulder.

"Do you know CPR?" he asked, looking up and seeing her reach under her skirt. "Chloe, what are you doing?"

It was rare for her to hear that name; it only happened every now and then from faculty members—who she often avoided—or from the annoying student who thought he was either cool or had a romantic shot with her by simply knowing her first name. What they didn't know, though, was that it *wasn't* her name, but a name she'd stolen from some poor woman who made it all too easy for her. That poor woman was escaping an old life, moving to a new city, and picking up *this* job, hoping for a bright future, only for it to end on her first night in town, without anyone even knowing to look for her or expecting her to look like someone else entirely when she showed up for her first in-person meeting with her new boss at Pineside High School.

She detached the hidden knife from her garter and in one fluid motion, pulled it out, slitting Principal Collins's throat. He fell atop Nia's body, his blood pouring into her open mouth. With everyone screaming and distracted by those dying around them, nobody saw it happen.

Nobody but her *least* favorite student, Grace.

Her eyes were open wide with fear as she got up from the table where she'd spent the last hour sulking about her Prom Queen loss and ran for the exit, leaping over the body of another teacher, whose name she'd never cared to remember, who held the door open. Her heel snapped on landing the leap, sending her falling to the floor. Struggling to remove her overly complicated heels, she was easy to catch up to.

Mrs. Ivory grabbed her by the hair, twisted it to get a nice grip, and dragged her along the concrete, bringing her behind the flowy drapes that decorated the doors of the gym.

Grace, screaming the entire time, had road rash all over her otherwise beautiful legs by the time they were hidden behind the drapes. The woman swung her knife straight toward her face, but Grace caught it by the blade before it reached her, slicing her palm and fingers open.

"Ahh!" Grace screamed, mouth agape as she looked at her trembling hands in terror.

Both women heard a male voice yell, "Hey!"

They turned and saw Jackson, Grace's date, fists ready as he stared Mrs. Ivory down.

"Let her go," he said menacingly.

Using the opportunity, she swung the knife up and through, piercing the roof of Grace's mouth. Her eyes rolled to the back of her head as blood drained down and out of her mouth, dripping like a coffee pot. With the knife stuck in her, the woman let her go and watched her body drop.

"Grace!" Jackson screamed, then charged the killer.

Already having it planned out, she lifted her right leg and removed her heel, stepping awkwardly to the floor, losing a few inches of height on her right side. As Jackson closed in, he tried to throw a punch at her, which she sidestepped away from, slamming the stiletto into his eye socket.

He fell to the floor, screaming. While she stepped out of her left shoe, he tried to pull the right shoe out of his eye, but the eyeball came with it. He screamed violently as it dangled from the socket with the shoe still attached. She'd seen a lot in her years of doing what she does, but that was perhaps the most ridiculous. To shut him up, she went back to Grace's body, gripped the knife handle, and put her foot on Grace's throat to keep her head steady while she pulled the blade from her skull. Then she walked back to Jackson and put the knife through the back of his head.

With more people sprinting out of the gym now, she wanted to go back inside and see her work. She stepped in the doorway and scanned the room, checking for bodies *and* witnesses. At the punch table—where she'd *just* spiked the drinks with an insanely lethal dose of fentanyl stolen from the local drug dealer she'd murdered—she saw a student's shoes peeking out from under the tablecloth. Without certainty that they didn't see what she had done to the principal, she approached them.

Pulling up the tablecloth, she saw another of her students, Leo. She wasn't sure if his eyes were frightened because he'd witnessed what she had done or if he was paranoid with all the death around him. She played it cool.

"Hey, Leo, are you okay?"

He gulped. "I'm freaking out, man. Er, ma'am. What-ever. *Fuck this.*"

"Come on, let's get you out of there. This place smells, and the floor is *gross.*" She offered him a hand, which he took. *Gotcha.*

As she pulled him out from under the table, she gazed around the room and confirmed that all the police officers had left to check on the students who ran outside, intend-ing to save them before it was too late.

"Thank you, Mrs. Ivory," Leo said as he rose to his feet. "I've been drinking all night, and with the edible I ate, I'm fucking—"

Before he could finish, she grabbed his head and brought it down into the punch bowl. Luckily for her, he was so fucked-up that he was all ready close to passing out, so holding him face down in the spiked punch bowl until he drowned didn't pose a challenge. He *did* do a lot of splashing, though, which made her fingers annoyingly sticky. When she let him go, his body slid down the table, bringing the punch bowl with him as he flopped onto the floor.

As she made her way for the exit, Officer Ronald was escorting the recently arrived pair of EMTs into the gym-nasium, telling them, "Check who you can and see who's still alive." Then he spotted her and said, "You should *really* get out of here. We don't know what the cause of this is."

"Fentanyl overdose. I spiked the punch," she said calmly as she walked past him, quickly pulling the gun from his holster.

"What— Hey!" he shouted as the three shots went off, one in his head and one in each of the two EMTs. Then she tossed the gun beside the officer's body and left the gym. It was finally time for the moment she'd long awaited.

Chapter 27

When Hailey awoke, her throat felt like she'd tried to swallow a roll of sandpaper that scraped every surface on its way down. A piercing pain shot through her brain as though the hamster that usually ran the wheel that energized it was scratching its way out. Cold air breezed over her, making her limbs feel numb and her bruised throat pound even harder. The vision was blurry and unclear when she opened her eyes, as though both were traveling in different directions and avoiding meeting in the middle, like two magnets with energy that didn't match.

As she came to, she could slowly make out a figure on the ground before her. It was definitely a person, but they were dark and fuzzy. Then she started to notice small things around her. *Pineside High School* was painted on a wall above a set of bleachers beside the painting of a cartoon version of Penny the Penguin. A streetlight hung over the fence, aimed at the street; its bulb flickered like it was dying. Behind her was the school's diving board.

Am I at the swimming pool?

As she analyzed her immediate surroundings, she realized that the chair she was in was only inches from the pool's edge. She tried to get up but found that she was tied down—restrained to a plastic chair by her Prom Queen sash wrapping around her torso and tying her hands together behind the chair, along with a rope binding her thighs to the chair's seat. The feeling gave her immediate flashbacks to that night at Camp Safe Woods, finding Annie and the others at the campfire bound and restrained while Oliver Vance told them his sob story that he used as an excuse for killing innocent people.

With her vision more clear and focused, she identified the blurry humanoid figure laid out before her as somebody small—a child—in a body bag. It scared her at first, until she realized their chest was moving as they breathed.

Alive, thank God.

"Hello?" she called to them, or whoever else might be listening, her voice hoarse, raspy, and weak. The vibrations from her vocal cords only caused more pain.

She heard screams in the distance and saw the faint glow of ambulance lights shining over the roof of the school. Screaming wasn't an option—her throat was too damaged for that.

"So . . ." The voice startled her. "You're finally awake." It was Westley, walking through the opening fence gate with another adult-sized person in a body bag. She hated the sight of him. Everything they'd ever talked about, every flirty moment, every secret they ever shared, every feeling he declared for her, and every memory they made—it was all a lie. She felt awful. Violated. She'd shared bits of herself she never shared with anybody, both physically *and* emotionally. And it wasn't like he was just some asshole boy lying to get into her pants, because clearly he didn't want *that*, but he was a killer, doing the bidding of some unidentified woman who had it out for her, for some reason unbeknownst to her.

He plopped the body onto the ground like a careless delivery driver dropping a fragile package. Hailey flinched at the sound their head made when it cracked against the concrete. She tried wiggling out of her bindings, but the knot was tight, and while the material felt a lot better than any zip tie or rope, she could tell her circulation was impeded.

"Let me go!" she grumbled.

"And spoil the fun? No, *she'll* have my ass for that." He pulled a knife from his suit jacket pocket and Hailey shivered at the sight of it.

Was that in there all night?

She shook violently in the seat as he approached, then as he brought the knife to her hands she had a glimmer of hope that he was going to cut her free. But he didn't. Instead, he cut the corsage that he had made custom for her, in a sense severing any tie that still bound the two of them. He stepped in front of her, lifting the knife and letting the corsage dangle from it, the roses blowing in the w ind.

"I can't believe I made this for you. It wasn't my idea, by the way. It was *hers*. She's always been a romantic at heart, believe it or not. And having you fall in love with me was a huge step in her plan, so I guess she knows what she's doing because it *definitely* worked."

She conjured up what saliva she could in her dried-up mouth and spat at him. It landed on his tie.

"Nice try," he said, "but this isn't even my suit. It's a rental. Trust me, it was *much* worse when you got all that spit in my mouth earlier." He chuckled. "You're a very wet and sloppy kisser, which isn't a good thing."

"Fuck you," she said as the corsage finally fell from the knife. He watched it slowly float down until it hit the ground between the two of them.

"You tried, remember? Now look at you." He looked at his reflection in the knife. "As if I would ever."

"Saddest experience of my life," she said. Figuring her time was up, she would at least use the last bit of fight in her to throw insults. "Staring at your shriveled, tiny dick."

"And what did you expect? Don't tell me you thought you were worth more than a flaccid cock." He laughed. "You're lucky I even let you *touch it*. No amount of make-up, hairdos, flashy dresses, expensive manicures, or sparkly high heels would *ever* make me give you a second look, if it weren't for her."

"Her. Her, her, her. Just *who* is the woman you are so ever-fucking in love with? Please, tell me. Because I'd like to see what kind of woman could convince someone who has everything in life going for them, including a future of fame and fortune, to throw it all away to do her bidding for some batshit crazy murder plot. And why, of *all people*, was *I* involved in this scheme?"

"Who says I'm throwing anything away for her? Ever since we met, I've seen nothing but *gain* and *progress* in my life. She showed me the secrets to getting what you want, and it's all worked. Why do you think I had my sudden athletic success start up this year? Why do you think college scouts have come and seen me play and deemed *me* the best prospect of them all when I've been riding the bench for three years straight? Why do you think I was capable of convincing a stupid, *broken* girl like *you* to fall in love with *me* when I didn't even have a *shred* of attraction to you?"

She wouldn't let his words hurt her. He wasn't worth it. She'd shed so many tears in this life, she wouldn't allow any to fall for him. Instead, she looked at him, awaiting the answer to his rhetorical questions.

He answered, "Because *she* showed me how." The door from the girls' locker room creaked open, and Westley smiled. "And here she is."

Without any suspects on her list, she was thoroughly surprised when Mrs. Ivory approached them, hardly noticing her at first. Something in the way she carried herself made her feel bigger, scarier even—which was strange, considering she was a few inches shorter than she'd normally be, barefoot without her stilettos.

"Mrs. Ivory?" Hailey asked, puzzled, as if she were trying to connect the pieces in her head, but there weren't any to connect.

"That's not my name," she said. Westley approached her as if expecting a hug, but she denied him by pushing him away. "Don't think I don't know that you did not fuck this girl before tying her up," she told him. "My plans are thorough and purposeful. When you don't follow them, they don't work as well."

"But I—" he began, but she held a silent finger to her lips and he shushed immediately, like a well-trained dog.

"The plan still works the same, I guess. Just on a lesser scale. I saw that kiss at the dance. She *definitely* fell in love with you, and just looking at her, I can tell she's heartbroken." The breeze picked up, blowing the corsage on top of the woman's feet. She looked down at it and kicked it away, annoyed. Hailey noticed that her arms had blood splatter on them.

"But . . . why?" Hailey asked. "If you're not Mrs. Ivory, who are you?"

"We'll get to that in due time. But right now, we have a game to play." She held out her hand, and Westley put his knife in it. "I'm sure you noticed the bodies, right?"

Hailey stared on, gritting her teeth.

"Of course you did. You're not blind." Then she held the knife to her chin, looking up to the sky as if she were thinking. "Well, blind to the truth, I guess. But not *blind* blind." She brought her attention back down to the bodies. "Now, for this little game, I want you to know that the two people in these body bags are very much still alive. Unless they suffocated, of course. But at the very least, they *were* alive when we put them there." She kicked the smaller body. "Now, the rules are simple. You make a guess—just one guess—of who is in each bag. If you get it right, we move on. If you get it wrong, well . . ." She waved the knife.

"No," Hailey said.

"I don't think you have a choice, really. If you don't guess, they both die, so I *suggest* you play along," Westley insisted.

"Now, let's start." The woman formerly known as Mrs. Ivory squatted beside the smaller bag, gripping the knife tightly in one hand above where Hailey assumed the person's head would be.

Okay, I'll play along, she thought, understanding that if a child were inside, there was only one she was aware of who had gone missing. But of course, there was the off-chance that they were playing tricks on her, and if she guessed wrong another kid would die. *But do I know any other children in town?*

"Guess," Former Mrs. Ivory said. "No pressure. The blood will be on *my* hands."

"It's Charlie, isn't it?" she asked, hoping she didn't mistake the name of the kid Ale would babysit.

It wasn't Charles, was it?

"That was too easy!" Westley yelled. "Tell us his last name!"

Fuck, she thought. She didn't know it.

"Ignore him," Mrs. Ivory said. "He just likes the power in his hands and *really* dislikes *you*. But can you blame him? I mean, spending so much time with a broken girl like you has got to be draining."

"Fuck you," Hailey uttered.

"Hey now," she said, "that's no way to talk to the woman holding a knife over a child's head, is it?" She stood tall. "But rules are rules. You guessed right, so the kid gets to live. Now . . . "—she slow-walked to the side of the other bag—"guess again."

I think I've got this! Hailey thought. It was easy. Only one other person on her radar had gone missing recently, so she eagerly said, "Maddie. Maddie Bennett. Or Madelyn Bennett, whatever fucking name you want it to be, I know you psychopaths kidnapped her, and I *know* she's in there."

Westley looked as though he was holding back a smile, but Mrs. Ivory only looked disappointed. "Now, deary. Did you think I'd make it *that* easy?"

"Should I go grab it?" Westley asked.

"I'm surprised you haven't already."

"Hey, things are moving quickly tonight, okay?" Westley walked excitedly, practically skipped to the locker room, where he disappeared for a brief moment. Mrs. Ivory stared at the door, annoyed that he was taking his time or that whatever he was grabbing wasn't already in place.

When he returned, he struggled with keeping the locker room door open as he dragged something large, fluffy, and black out to the concrete. When he got close enough, Hailey realized that it was the original, missing costume for Penny the Penguin. It looked banged up, with a stab wound in the shoulder where Ale said she got her, and it was heavy, as if someone was inside.

"You're gonna love this," Westley said. Somehow more happy than he'd looked the entire night, like a toddler on his birthday. He pulled the oversized mask off the penguin, and Hailey screamed as Maddie's cold, pale, dead head was revealed.

"Oh my God! You fucking *killed* her, you psychopaths?" Hailey asked.

"Not *us*. *I* did," Westley clarified. "In case you were wondering."

"It doesn't matter *who* did it. You're both fucking crazy!"

"No, we'd be crazy if we didn't have a reason for it, but we sure do. Because things in life have a cause and effect, right?" Mrs. Ivory asked. "For example, the cause: you guessed Maddie was in the bag, but she wasn't! Now here's the effect." She brought the knife down like an ice pick, stabbing it into the head of whoever was inside the bag. The body jerked once as the blade entered, then remained still. Dead.

Hailey screamed, knowing that it *must* have been someone she knew—or even worse, someone she loved.

"Why are you screaming?" Westley asked. "You don't even know who it is!"

"Let's find out," Mrs. Ivory said, unzipping the bag. Hailey didn't want to look, but she *needed* to. Whoever it was, she didn't want their death to be in vain.

*As soon as I find a way out of here, I am going to **kill** these two*, she thought.

She saw the light blonde hair fall out first, and Mrs. Ivory pulled the knife from their head so she could lift the body and pull the bag down, revealing them. Hailey could barely recognize the person with the blood that trickled down their face, but another part of her just didn't want it to be true.

"Look at that, it's Megan! One of your many mothers! Though she's perhaps the *least* important one," Westley said, confirming her fear.

Now, against all her wishes, she let the tears fall. She disagreed with him, though. Sure, Megan came into her life later than Alexa did, but she would *never* put one over the other, especially after Megan spent so many years loving her and raising her as her very own child. She didn't deserve this. None of the victims did.

For perhaps the first time in her life, she *wanted* to see blood. She *wanted* to see these two dead at her feet. And she knew that all she needed was one opening, and she would make it happen.

"Now, there were supposed to be a few more bodies for this game, but we might be having some difficulties on that front. I'm sure we'll have them around soon enough, though."

"Why?" Hailey asked. "Why all the charades? Clearly, you want me to suffer, and you've shown yourselves capable of that. But why me? And why all of this?" She looked straight at Westley. "Why fake an entire relationship? What the *fuck* is the point of all this?"

"Because I want you to suffer," Mrs. Ivory said. "You've taken something from me that you'd never understand, and simply killing you isn't enough to pay that debt. You need to watch those closest to you perish. And when I thought even *that* wasn't enough, I decided that you needed to fall in love and watch it get ripped away from you. In the *worst* way. I thought having him take advantage of you without you knowing would've deepened that bond, and it would've, but I guess I picked too much of a *fucking idiot* to get *that* job done." She stood up, letting Megan's body drop to the ground, her head cracking against the concrete once again. "They say: 'If you want something done right, do it yourself,' but unfortunately for *me*, I don't think you have a thing for women in their early thirties, so I had to settle. And now, watch this. Westley . . ." she said, getting his attention before tossing him the knife.

He snatched it out of the air by the handle—showing off his athletic ability, even at a time like this.

"Kill yourself," she said. He looked at her, questioning her decision fearfully. She simply nodded at him, and without a word, he stabbed the knife straight through his Adam's apple, squirting blood over all of them.

Hailey gagged. It was hard to watch, even though she literally wanted to see exactly *that* happen, it was so unexpected she didn't know how to respond. She was speechless.

How could he just listen to her like that?

"Do you see?" Mrs. Ivory asked. "*That's* how insignificant *you* are. Just a few hours ago, you were all excited, waiting to see him in that stupid suit, and not even two hours ago, you were madly in love and making out on the dance floor surrounded by your peers. And yet, all it took was a few words and my pretty smile for him to just end it all. You thought you were important to him, but you'll *never* be valued or loved by *anybody* as much as *he* did *me*. Because how would *anybody ever* be capable of loving a *broken* girl like you?"

"Okay, I get it!" Hailey yelled with all her might, which wasn't much. "Nobody loves me. I'm broken. Now what?"

"Hailey. Hailey, Hailey, Hailey. Don't you remember? 'Hailey Atkins, death dances with those around you, patiently awaiting your turn to take the floor.' I mean, I thought the message was pretty clear when I carved it into his skin. But somehow, you didn't heed the warning. Wasn't it *pretty* obvious that prom was where we'd have our dance? I mean, how stupid can you be?" She laughed. "Well, guess what? It's almost your turn! Death just has a few more in line before it can reach you. If they would just hurry up!" she yelled into the night sky.

"How did you do it?" Hailey asked. "How did you convince him to . . . kill himself just like that?"

"Do you want the simple answer or the more complex one? Can your brain handle complex? Okay, you know what?" She cleared her throat. "Let's start with simple. Sex. Sex is powerful. You wouldn't know since you haven't had it, but it is one of the strongest powers *we* have. Especially with boys *his* age." She took the knife from Westley's body. "Find someone his age in the mall, lead him on, and you can almost convince him of anything. Don't give it up too easy, though. That's where you went wrong. At least, where you would've went wrong if he didn't already have plans of watching you die." She laughed at the irony. "Oh well, so much for those plans. To be honest, I wasn't planning on making him do that—and I wasn't even certain he would. I'm glad he did, though, because he was getting on my nerves."

"So that's it, then? You fuck high schoolers so they do your bidding?"

"No!" She pointed the knife at Hailey. "See, now I need to explain the more complex side of things." She tapped the knife on her temple. "I show people what they're capable of. I convince them that the world is dying to give them anything they want, at the cost of a little . . . sacrifice. In *his* case, *I* was a piece of what he wanted, and I did what I had to do to convince him to help me."

"Sacrifice?" Hailey asked.

"Yes, sacrifice. *Human* sacrifice. I showed him that with the low cost of a human life, the world would repay him with *whatever* he wants. I set the example first with a Mrs. Chloe Ivory, a young preschool teacher, moving away from her troubled past, picking up a job as a high school teacher in a new town where she didn't know *anybody*. I showed Westley what he needed to do to take her life and ask the world for a request—something worth *killing* for. And he did, requesting athletic success with the whole package of money and fame included. He saw those results immediately, going to the batting cages for weeks after, hitting better than he ever had before. He moved up from the bench to the starting lineup, knocked balls out of the park, made defensive plays, felt healthier, ran faster, lost fat, toned muscles, you name it. It worked.

"And I, on the other hand, took over the Chloe Ivory persona, slipping right into her new job as *your* teacher like a chameleon taking on a new color. That body you found beneath the bleachers? That was the *real* Chloe Ivory, and nobody ever figured it out!"

She pointed the knife at Maddie's corpse.

"Then, it was time for another move to be made, and Westley was eager to make a second sacrifice. He killed that poor woman and made another wish. He kept it a secret from me this time, and given how enamored he was of me, I knew he had asked for something stupid like my love. So *yes*, I *did* give it up in order to keep him by my side, and even *that* worked."

"Sounds like a placebo effect to me," Hailey said. "You told him he'd be successful if he killed that poor woman, and he convinced himself it would happen. With his new-found confidence he *became* more successful, but it wasn't due to some hippie, earth-blessed reward for sacrificing a human life. I mean, come on. You *cannot* believe in that stuff."

"Of course I do. You think I would go spreading bullshit around if I hadn't done it before myself? This isn't my first rodeo, girly. I've wished for many things in the past, and I've acquired them all, including the opportunity to make *you* suffer, here, as you are. And look! Just one of my many gifts, happening right before my very eyes! And wow, I cannot wait to see what I will be rewarded with upon your death. Maybe I'll ask the earth for a big, juicy *cheeseburger* because that's all a shitty life like yours will be worth. The dozens of your fellow classmates I killed tonight are surely worth more, and maybe, just *maybe*, I'll finally be given my prize that *you* took from me without even knowing it."

"I didn't take anything from you! I don't even know what you're on about, you *crazy psycho* bitch."

"Of course you don't. It was hidden from me, too, for many years. And yet, you and the others at that cursed summer camp found it and took it from me!"

"Camp Safe Woods? What do you think we found there? We were only there a few days before that fucking *asshole* started killing us!"

Mrs. Ivory pointed the knife at her, but Hailey didn't feel threatened as she looked like she was preparing to finally give her an answer. Until the locker room door opened once again, and Hailey heard two distinct voices muffled and screaming from inside.

Chapter 28

The screams came from Ale and Billy who emerged from the locker room. Their mouths were gagged with hand towels, and their arms were bound behind their backs as they were being led by a man Hailey immediately recognized, even though they'd never met in person.

Her father, Christopher Atkins.

"I didn't have time to bag 'em up," he said, struggling to keep them both walking in the right direction. They both realized that Hailey was tied to the chair and freaked out—trying to wiggle themselves free but it was no use. "There's police activity all up and around the area. We're honestly lucky I got them here." When he reached Mrs. Ivory, he shoved them both onto the concrete, then took in the scene, analyzing each corpse on the ground. He looked horrified, especially when he saw Westley, who Hailey assumed he knew since they'd all been working together. "U h—"

"That's fine. I wish you were faster, but at least you got them," Mrs. Ivory stated.

"Sorry, just one second," he said. "What the *hell* happened here?" He approached Westley, pointing a frantic finger his way. "Why is *he* dead?"

"Calm down. Everything's going as I planned; there's nothing to worry about."

"Did you plan for *him* to die? That's just . . . wrong." He shook his head. "This is all too messy. I can't go back to jail. Can we hurry up here so I can wash my hands of all this?"

"Hey!" she yelled, snapping him out of his panic. "*I* got you out of prison, didn't I?" She looked at him like a parent helping a child realize they already know the answer to a problem. "Didn't I?" she repeated.

"Yeah, but—"

"Then *why* would I send you back? Come on, think." She smacked the handle of the knife on her forehead like a facepalm. Ale and Billy were still squirming on the concrete with their muffled yells. Mrs. Ivory pointed the knife toward them. "Ungag them so they'll shut up."

Hailey's father obeyed, ungagging Billy first.

"Let us *go*!" he yelled but was promptly ignored. Then he ungagged Ale, who rather than yelling pointless words at them, lunged forward and bit his hand, chomping hard on two of his fingers.

"Fuck!" he yelled, raising his hand like he was going to hit her, then held back once he realized it would probably hurt him more with his newly injured digits. "I should gag you again for that." He rubbed his fingers, wincing at the touch.

"You'll get bit again. I drink a *lot* of milk, so my teeth are strong," Ale said.

Mrs. Ivory laughed. "You always were my favorite, Ale. You remind me a lot of myself if I'm being honest."

"Screw *you*, lady," Ale said.

"Hailey," Billy said, noticing the corpses one by one. Maddie. Westley. Megan. He was speechless, but she knew he was trying to find the words to ask multiple impossible questions at once, like "Are you okay?" and "What happened here?" and "How do we get out of this?"

Ale, as loudmouthed as ever, blurted out the first thing that came to mind when she took in the scene, yelling, "Holy shit, they killed Westley?"

Hailey stopped her before she could express her condolences about it, saying, "That was the only good thing to happen tonight. He was with them."

"Oh, then fuck him," Ale said.

"So did we miss it, then?" Billy asked. Mrs. Ivory and Hailey both looked at him, confused. "You know, the climax? The big reveal? When the big, bad, conceited— No, the narcissistic, full-of-themselves asshole who spent all this time traumatizing us can't help but reveal their purpose behind it all. Because they would feel incomplete if everything they did, all the work they put in, was just passed over without their target victim at least *hearing* how much of an asshole they are before killing them."

"We were in the middle of it," Hailey said, proud of him for dishing out disses in the same fashion Hailey strived for.

Mrs. Ivory laughed. "I could just kill you now if you'd like."

"No, you can't. It would be against your nature," Hailey said. "Every fiber of your being is seeking recognition from us. Killing us wouldn't satisfy you enough."

"Fair enough," she said, waving the knife about carelessly. "You know, you guys would make great therapists. Oh!" She got all excited about her realization. "You would actually make great counselors at that little camp of yours. You know, since you know people so well. Now, on *that* note, Hailey, what do you think?" She gestured to Christopher. "Kinda cool, right?"

Christopher looked very confused, like he wasn't in on the joke.

Hailey nodded in an unamused fashion. "Sure. Very thorough. Congrats. Did you have to fuck him, too, so he'd do your bidding?"

"*Tsk tsk tsk*." Mrs. Ivory shook her head. "Now, Hailey, that's no way to talk in front of your father."

"What? Father?" he asked, lost. "I don't have any kids."

"Sure you do!" Mrs. Ivory pranced to him and hugged him from behind, her hands wrapping around his stomach, the knife dangling from her fingertips. "Eighteen years ago, you met a blonde-haired, blue-eyed bombshell of a college student at a bar, followed her to her dorm room, and made that beauty over there."

"No, it can't be—" He stopped and stared at her as if looking at a vision of himself. Hailey could see the gears spinning in his head as he played back the memory of her mother and connected the dots. "But I— Why didn't she—"

"Because *you* were in the wrong place at the wrong time and got sent to jail for something you didn't even do! Isn't it *funny* how the world works? You, an innocent man, lost access to your freedom *and* a life with your daughter!"

Innocent? Hailey gasped at the word. *Was he really?* She looked around at the bodies laid out on the ground and scratched the word out of her mind. Any innocence this man ever had was far beyond gone by this point. There was no time to get caught up in sentiment.

"I didn't know . . . I-I . . . " he stuttered, like he felt bad about it, so much so that he couldn't find the right words to make things right—as if *any* words could get the job done.

"Aww, don't be upset," Mrs. Ivory said, then grazed the knife across his cheek as though she was wiping away a tear. "It's not like you *completely* missed out. Hailey here found you and has been writing to you for a while now."

"Hailey . . ." he said as if etching the word in his brain. "You were one of my pen pals?"

"It's a little late for emotions, dickhead," Ale said.

"Look around," Billy said. "All these people died because of you. People who *actually* mattered in Hailey's life. You took them from her."

Hailey remained silent as her friends poured out the words she couldn't manage to speak herself. If she tried moving them past that lump in her throat, it would open the crying floodgates and she wouldn't let him see those tears.

"What? No! I didn't do this. I've never killed anybody." He looked around at the bodies, panicking. "That wasn't me. I had no idea!" He stepped out of Mrs. Ivory's embrace. "I didn't know *anything* about this. I was only instructed to kidnap a couple high school kids as payment for getting out of prison. I wouldn't kill anybody!"

Hailey didn't care. One way or another, he was an accomplice willing to kidnap people for his own selfish reasons. Even if he *was* innocent and shouldn't have been in prison to begin with, he wasn't her father and never would be after what he'd done. She regretted ever sending him a letter, ever searching for him to begin with.

Mrs. Ivory looked bored, as though she was regretting this part of her plan. As if it was taking *too* much attention away from her. "Christopher," she said calmly, "don't play innocent now. What did you think would happen when you brought them here? We'd have a surprise birthday party? *Of course* they are going to die!"

"What? No, Vicky, I—"

She stopped him, holding the knife to his throat.

*Did he say **Vicky**?* Hailey thought, remembering the name. *No, it can't be . . .*

She flipped the knife, holding it by the blade now as she offered it to him to take.

"Now, grab the knife and prove to me that I can still trust you," she said.

Reluctantly, he grabbed the handle and looked at it like it hurt him to hold it.

"What do you want me to do?" he asked.

"You decide." She stepped away from him. "Look at that, your first taste of *real* freedom! *You* get to make a choice! You can take that knife and go cut your daughter free, and who knows? Maybe live a very happy, very short life together that will be ended *almost* immediately by yours truly. *Or*, you can take that knife and pick between your daughter's two best friends—Billy, the white knight with the hideous, scarred face, and Ale, the girl who's as annoying as she is pretty—and murder them in front of her. Then, you won't owe me *anything* anymore and you can walk away from here." She crossed her arms. "The choice is yours."

Hailey felt her heart pounding out of her chest as she watched her father look between his options. There was nothing she could do at this point but watch. Even if she got her hands free, she would still have to untie the rope around her thighs. Her friends were just as helpless watching him choose their fate.

"Just fucking kill *me*," Billy said, deciding that he'd rather die than either of his two best friends.

"What? No! Don't say that, you idiot!" Ale yelled at him, then taunted Christopher as if it would make the choice easier for him, shouting, "Hey, pussy! Kill me, instead!"

The two of them then argued with each other, shouting for their own deaths back and forth, trying to save the other.

Christopher, just as helpless as the rest of them, turned to Hailey and said, "I just want you to know that I didn't mean for any of this to happen. I never would've hurt you, and if I only knew you existed, I think our lives would've gone a lot differently." He looked down at the knife, then took a single step toward her before a loud *pop* sounded off, dropping him to the ground, sending the knife sliding across the concrete to her feet. She looked down at it with her eyes only, not wanting to shift her head in its direction and alert Vicky.

"There she is!" Vicky yelled. Hailey used the sound of her voice to mask the act of using her foot to slide the knife beneath her chair.

Great, another guest, Hailey thought, hoping this person was someone on her side, but unsure since this addition seemed to be part of Vicky's plan. While she started working twice as hard to pull her raw, stinging hands from their binds, Tiffany Watson stepped into the area from the fence gate, her gun raised high and pointed at the former Mrs. Ivory.

"I figured you'd be here eventually," Vicky said, making Hailey feel slightly better about her odds, though still questioning if this was another of Vicky's tricks. "So, what now? You gonna arrest me?" She pointed to Christopher's corpse. "He is living proof—er, *was*—that I know how to get out of a cell."

"You're right. You need to be put down," Tiffany said, pulling the trigger. The gun clicked. Empty. She looked at it, confused, while Vicky laughed at her.

"Did you forget to *reload* it? That has *got* to be the *dumbest* thing I've ever seen. Not to mention, you shot the guy who was about to free Hailey! He was walking over there to cut her ties!" she said, holding her sides as if laughing so hard was hurting her.

"I don't use this thing often, okay?" Tiffany said, then faced Hailey. "Sorry about your dad."

Suddenly, Vicky stopped laughing and approached Hailey. "If you don't mind, dear, I'm going to take my knife back."

Damn, she noticed!

As Vicky bent down to pick up the knife, Hailey kicked her in the face, knocking her glasses off, shattering the left lens.

"Yeah!" Ale yelled, cheering her on. But Vicky still reached for the knife, and as she gripped the handle, Hailey's right hand ripped free from its bind, loosening the knot enough to pull out her other, just in time to yank her by the hair.

It was no use, though; her hands were free now, but she was still stuck in the chair. Vicky sliced Hailey's wrist, spraying a small amount of blood over them—the cut wasn't deep enough to sever any major vessels. Hailey released Vicky's hair as an involuntary response to the pain and saw Tiffany fly in, tackling her to the ground, mounting her, then slapping her once with the empty pistol before Vicky responded by digging the knife into her belly. Astonished, Tiffany looked down, her mouth agape. Vicky took the handle with both hands and used it for leverage to push Tiffany off of her, leaving it lodged inside as Tiffany fell to the concrete, screaming and writhing in pain.

While Vicky rose to her feet, she dusted off her skirt, saying, "Things are getting complicated and annoying now, so I'm going to make the rest of this quick."

Hailey was clawing at the knot in the rope beneath the seat, doing her best to untangle it, but she couldn't find any give.

Vicky looked between the three Squirrel Cabin Campers and asked, "Any ideas yet why I'm doing this? Feel free to guess."

"Fuck you." Ale rolled her eyes, clearly done with the games.

"He called you Vicky," Billy said, nodding his head toward Christopher's body. "If I had to guess, I'd say you're Victoria Vance."

So, he suspected the same thing, Hailey thought. *But still, why?*

"Nick's sister?" Ale asked.

"No," Vicky said. "His name *wasn't* Nick. It was Oliver. My little brother, Ollie."

Chapter 29

"**I**t *is* you!" Hailey said, still struggling with the rope. She smiled. "Yep."

"I knew you weren't a real teacher!" Ale yelled. "Only porn stars in shitty high school scenarios wear glasses like those!"

"I still don't get it," Hailey said, using her nails now, pulling at the rope's fibers, clawing her way free. "Why would you dream up this whole revenge scheme when you tried to kill Oliver yourself? You were the reason he had to take up a different name and go to Camp Safe Woods in the first place!" Hailey yelled, enduring the pain as her throat bled releasing the words. At the taste of pennies, she spat blood onto the concrete.

"You're right. I *did* try to kill him."

"But why?" Billy asked, aggression in his tone, hurrying her to get to the point.

"That's the part you missed when *her* father was taking his time bringing you here," Vicky said.

"Are you going back to that whole human sacrifice bull-shit story you were telling?" Hailey asked.

"Yes, I am. But it's not bullshit!" she said passionately. "That night, all those years ago, I was *trying* to complete a ritual."

"Ritual? What the fuck are you talking about?" Ale asked.

"As I was telling Hailey before, there is power in killing. Feed the earth some blood, and it will repay you with favors. But if the favor is too big of an ask, you need to make some *real personal* sacrifices."

Ale and Billy exchanged confused, concerned looks, sharing the same feelings Hailey felt when hearing it the first time.

"Yeah? And what kind of favor were you asking for that required the deaths of your entire family?"

"I'm glad you asked." Vicky smiled. "I wanted eternal youth. To never have to worry about my face developing wrinkles, or my tits sagging, or my ass losing its shape, or my eyes bagging, or my hair graying, or most important-ly, never worrying about death. A request as large as this demands a lot—severing every blood tie you have on this planet, cursed to walk the earth alone for eternity."

"And you *actually* believed you'd be granted that wish?" Hailey smirked.

"Yeah, where did you come up with that idea?" Billy asked.

"Did you rub a genie out of a lamp?" Ale snickered.

"Where I get my information doesn't matter. What does matter is the proof. Since *you* took my brother's life before *I* got the opportunity, I was forced to cash in my request with my parents' lives as my payment. Rather than the gift of youth, I was given the gift of a silver tongue. The power of persuasion—the ability to convince those beneath me to do my bidding and see that *I* am a *goddess* walking among them." She waved around the scene, highlighting their predicament. "And look what it brought me. Tell me that my wish didn't come true."

"You're no goddess, and you have *no* power," Hailey said. "You're an aging woman of declining attraction with a slim figure and a loose vagina who used it to convince a dumb high schooler to kill for you." Her nail beds hurt now, and she wasn't making adequate progress on the rope. She was losing hope.

"If *he* was dumb for following *my* convincing, what does that make *you* for following *his*?" Vicky sighed and approached Hailey but stepped past her to grab her broken glasses from the ground and put them on her face.

"You know what's funny?" Hailey asked her.

"What's that?"

"You did all this for revenge on us for killing your brother, but *we* weren't even the ones who did it!"

"You think I don't know that?" Vicky laughed. "Oh, that is *hysterical*! Of course you three didn't kill him!

You're all far too weak for that. Don't you worry, I know *all* about your little counselor, Annie, who dealt the final blow." She chuckled. "Do *you* want to know something that's *really* funny? It's that *you* think you're the main character in this story! *You* three are just the warm-up. If you think *you've* suffered, just wait until I go after her! I'm doing all of *this* as a warning! Once you're all cold and dead, I'll be carving a personalized message for her into each of your backs that the news outlets will pick up and spread her way. Then, *everyone* in her life will die. I've already got the plan in place, and trust me, she's going to get it ten times worse."

She stepped in front of Hailey, who now felt off-balance so close to the swimming pool.

"You know, being your teacher and all, I had access to your file. I saw a neat little detail in there: watching your mother die in the loch gave you a lifelong fear of water. It made me realize, what better way to kill this girl than by her greatest fear?"

"Nice try," Hailey said. "I fabricated that story so I wouldn't have to wear a bathing suit at school."

"Is that so?" She adjusted her glasses. "Then I guess *you* tricked *me* for once. No matter, drowning is still a pretty shitty way to die." Her hand flew at Hailey's chest with lightning speed, sending the chair falling straight back.

She heard both her friends yell her name as she fell.

The weight of the chair was enough to drag Hailey downward slowly—even with her arms free, she couldn't fight it. Her legs were in too awkward a position to help, and paddling her arms wasn't doing anything. If she couldn't free herself from the chair, she was going to drown.

She panicked, clawing at the rope, but as it became saturated, the knot only grew tighter. She gulped in water in a poor attempt to catch her breath. The chlorine burned her already wounded throat. She screamed, but the muffled voice that emerged only sounded weak. She looked up at the surface, praying that someone would jump in to save her, and while she knew the likelihood was slim to none, she *did* find something to help her. The knife that she last saw lodged in Tiffany's gut was now in the water, floating toward her. This meant two very important things: Tiffany was still alive *and* she risked bleeding out to pull the knife from her wound to save Hailey.

Knowing she was on a time limit now to return the favor and save Tiffany, she reached for the knife, hopping on her toes against the bottom of the deep pool until she could grasp its handle, then pulled it down and sawed at the rope until it gave way—slicing her thigh open in the process. And while the pain was electrifying and amplified by the chlorinated water, she didn't have time to care for herself. She kicked her feet and paddled upward, surfacing quietly to assess the situation before making herself known.

Tiffany was growing pale in the face. Her head was tilted toward the pool, playing dead so Vicky wouldn't come back and finish her. When her eyes met Hailey's, she closed them, satisfied that her job was done.

Meanwhile, Vicky was continuing her lecture for her friends, saying, "*She* was supposed to watch you two die, but that's what happens when you piss me off. Now *I'm* faced with the task of deciding: Which of you two would have the most trouble watching the other die? *And* what would be the best method to make that happen?"

Vicky turned toward the pool when she realized that Hailey was no longer struggling in the water. Ducking her head quickly to hide beneath the concrete lip, Hailey remained unseen, keeping her ears open.

"Do you hear that?" Vicky asked. "Silence. That means Hailey's time has finally come and the last of her air has escaped her."

"You, *bitch*," Ale muttered quietly, talking herself into the anger. "I swear to God, if I survive this, I am going to *piss* on your grave! And while I'm squatting there with my panties at my ankles, and you're down in hell, staring up at my asshole, *please* feel free to come back up and kiss it!"

Vicky smirked, saying, "I might have to take you up on that. Regardless, it won't bring Hailey back from the dead."

"What?" A familiar female voice screamed from somewhere beyond the swimming pool's fence. "No, you didn't! Not my daughter!" Alexa had come to save her. "Tell me you didn't kill my daughter!"

"Alexa, get out of here!" Billy yelled. "Go, get help!"

"Ah, ah, ah," Vicky said. "How's this for a family reunion?" She stepped to Megan's corpse and kicked her. "First, your *wife*." Then . . . She pointed to the swimming pool, where blood swirled from Hailey's thigh and wrist wounds. It looked like somebody was attacked by a shark. She could only imagine what Alexa thought upon seeing it.

"Megan," Alexa's voice broke. "How *could* you? Tell me! Tell me, Hailey's not really dead!"

"Why don't you come and see for yourself?" Vicky asked, stepping backward toward the pool.

Damn, I'm going to be seen if she turns around, Hailey thought, carefully watching every step Vicky took.

"Don't do it!" Ale yelled.

"Go, get help!" Billy repeated.

"My baby girl," Alexa said, her voice shattered. She opened the fence gate and stepped through, trembling at the knees.

Vicky took another step backward. "She's right over here. Just under all this water," she said, taking another step. Her feet were at the edge now, towering directly over Hailey.

It's now or never, Hailey thought before raising the knife and slicing it across the Achilles tendon of Vicky's right ankle.

She screamed bloody murder as her ankle collapsed, and she fell into the pool beside Hailey, who quickly tossed the knife toward her friends, shouting, "Mom, cut them free!" Then she placed her palms on the pool's edge and tried lifting herself out of the water, but Vicky got a hand on her ankle and yanked. She swallowed another big gulp of water, screaming on her way down.

Beneath the surface, she fought, kicking at her hands, her face, her torso, whatever she could reach, while Vicky grabbed at her legs and dress, pulling her underwater as she tried to escape. Vicky's foot looked dead inside the cut Hailey inflicted and blood poured from it. The water around them was maroon and started to taste more like copper than chlorine.

When Vicky finally got above Hailey, she tried to kick off of her to approach the surface, but Hailey caught her by the injured ankle, where she dug her nails into the wound until she felt the loose tendon and ripped at it like she'd ripped at the rope that bound her. Vicky screamed and kicked as more blood hemorrhaged from the wound.

Deciding the water wrestling was futile, she forced herself away from Vicky enough to swim up on her own. When they surfaced at about the same time, Alexa was running poolside, knife in hand, while her now-free friends hugged each other.

"Hailey!" Alexa yelled, drawing the attention of Ale and Billy, who ran toward her.

Vicky found her way to the ladder to climb out, but Alexa was quick to point the knife at her, threatening her to stay in the water. Billy offered Hailey a hand, which she took and climbed out of the pool, her soaked dress weighing her down. If she could spend the rest of her life *outside* of water, she would in a heartbeat.

"Are you okay?" Ale asked.

"I'm fine. Help Tiffany, she's still alive," she said, coughing up water and pointing urgently. "Stop the bleeding."

Ale nodded and ran to Tiffany's side. She pulled up her blouse, exposing her cruor-covered abdomen, blood still pouring from the gash. Ale looked around frantically for something to use to stop the bleeding; she settled on ripping off a layer of ruffles from her dress, then firmly held it to the wound—the royal blue staining to a pretty, deep purple.

Billy walked Hailey to Alexa, who still pointed the knife at Vicky in the water.

"So, what's next?" Vicky asked. "You're gonna kill me, right?"

"Shut up!" Alexa yelled. Hailey had been saved, sure, but she'd still lost a wife and was having to cope with that.

"At least have fun while you're doing it," Vicky said. "I usually do. I sure did when I stabbed your wife."

"Hailey, baby, I can't do this," Alexa said, tension leaving her shoulders as she placed the knife in her daughter's hands. "I'm sorry."

"Great parenting," Vicky said. "Giving your daughter a murder weapon. That's good stuff."

"Don't be sorry," Hailey said, ignoring Vicky. "It's not your job to do anyway." She brought her attention to Vicky. "Now, Victoria Vance. What do *I* do with *you*?" She felt confident for the first time since she'd woken up in that chair. "If I kill you I get a wish granted, right? Is that how this works?"

"Now you're getting it! Maybe you're smarter than I took you for." She leaned her head on a ladder step. "How about you humor me and tell me what you're gonna ask for when you get it done?"

"Humor you?" Alexa asked, amazed, stepping away. "I can't with this woman."

Hailey held the knife firmly and focused, ready to strike at any sudden movement.

"Oh, I don't know. Killing's not *usually* in my nature, so this might be the only wish I'm ever granted. What do you think, Billy?"

"I think it's a bunch of crap."

"Agreed, but what if she's right? I'm thinking a life of peace sounds like a good ask. But I think I'll already have that, knowing the entire Vance bloodline will be wiped off this earth. I'm thinking I should ask for something *real* serious. But maybe not. If the quality or personal relevance of the sacrifice changes the quality of the wish granted, then I don't think *your* life would be worth much."

"Funny," she said, unamused.

"How about this? After I end your life, ridding this planet of the last of your *horrible* family, I think I'll use my wish on a big, juicy *cheeseburger*."

"With no pickles, of course," Billy said.

"Right, of course. Fuck pickles," Hailey said.

"If that's the case, I'll use the wishes I've been granted for all the blood I've spilled tonight to forever curse *you* with a lifetime of misheard fast-food orders, constantly receiving extra pickles every time you buy a burger."

"Oh, the terror," Hailey said. "What a shame. At least I'll live long enough to find out if your wish was granted."

"Touché—" She stopped, startled as the corsage Hailey had worn that night—having blown into the water from the wind—floated against her cheek. With the slight distraction, Hailey lunged, planting the knife into Vicky's temple, just like Annie did with Oliver. Letting go of the handle, she watched as her body sank beneath the bloodied water. In an instant, the nightmare was over.

Epilogue

A few months had gone by and things had gone back to normal—or at least, the *new* normal. Hailey and her friends graduated from Pineside High School with a very somber ceremony, complete with a moment of silence for the students who'd lost their lives and a PowerPoint presentation of those victims showing how happy they all were and highlighting the bright futures they had in front of them.

Hailey barely attended the ceremony, feeling as though it was *her* fault that they had all died, but she was glad Alexa convinced her to go, claiming it would be disrespectful of her to skip out on such a monumental moment in her life, and that the victims who wouldn't be able to make it to that stage wouldn't have blamed her or wanted her to miss out on it too.

When school was out, she wondered what she would do next with her life. Then, one day she got a call from her old Camp Safe Woods counselor, Annie, saying that the camp was reopening, and they would love it if she and her friends would join them as counselors. She wanted to say no, at first, for two reasons. The first: she wanted *nothing* to do with that camp after everything that happened because of that place, to which Annie said she understood and reassured her that the place was being rebuilt to be compliant with much safer standards now, including that *everyone* would be allowed to have their cell phones on them at all times. Plus, there would be armed security on the campgrounds, just in case. The second: she felt *horrible* about the idea of leaving Alexa alone in this big house without Megan around anymore. Her mom told her that she would be fine, was only a phone call away, and could use the time to find herself once again. Plus, she told her Megan wouldn't want her to miss out on an opportunity because of *her*—and that ended the discussion there.

With both Vance siblings dead, there was no reason to believe that there would be any danger there, and spending a whole summer at a camp with her friends sounded like it would be the kind of break from life that she needed after a full year of terror after terror.

Now, for the first time since prom night, Hailey sat in the car with Billy and Ale, holding bags of McDonald's cheeseburgers they'd been avoiding since the threat of Vicky's pickle curse. It was the day before they would head off to their new jobs as counselors, and they wanted to rip off the Band-Aid and put the Vance family behind them.

They felt they had two important jobs to do before doing that, starting with this—the pickle test.

"Okay, here we go," Hailey said, pulling her burger from the bag.

"You said, 'No pickles,' right?" Ale asked.

"Yeah. I mean, I think. You heard me, didn't you?" Hailey asked Billy.

"Yes. You definitely did," he said.

She stared at the wrapped sandwich in her hand, afraid to open it.

"This is ridiculous, right?" Hailey asked. "Am I crazy for being afraid of this burger right now?"

"Crazy? No," Billy said.

"Hey, pickles or not, the bitch is dead. Deader than dead. If you have to peel some pickles off your burgers for the rest of your life, it was worth it. Hell, give *me* the pickles. I love them," Ale said.

"You're right," Hailey said before sighing. "Okay, let's get this over with."

She peeled away the yellow wrapping, revealing the burger, which felt thicker and juicier than she was used to from McDonald's. She held it up for her friends to observe. "What do you think? Did *my* wish come true?"

"Looks like it. Now open it up and let's see if hers did," Billy said.

Hailey's hand shook as she grabbed the top bun and peeled it away like turning the page of a book. Upon seeing the open-faced sandwich, she closed her eyes and took a deep breath.

"No way!" Ale exclaimed.

"It can't be!" Billy added.

There were six pickles seated atop the cheeseburger.

"It's gotta be a coincidence," he said.

"I'm gonna go have a talk with those employees," Ale said, reaching for the door handle.

"No." Hailey stopped her. "If *this* is my fate, I'll gladly accept that she isn't alive to end any more lives or have any more wishes granted. Ale, the pickles are all yours. We should get going. We have another job to do."

Ale relaxed in her seat and nodded. "Then let's go."

From the McDonald's parking lot, they drove an hour out of town to the location provided by Tiffany Watson, who'd only spent a few days in the hospital recovering from her wounds. The sun was setting on them as they parked the car and walked through the woods for about fifteen minutes, following the GPS to a set of coordinates rather than an address.

"We're almost there," Billy, their guide, said. "Ale, are you sure you want to do this?"

"I've never wanted to do anything more." She beamed, taking Billy's hand in hers. "Besides *you*, of course."

"Gross," Hailey said. By now, she had gotten used to being the third wheel of their relationship. Seeing the two of them happy together almost made up for the hole in her heart left by Westley. They deserved what they had with each other.

"Hey, a girl can dream, right?" She gave Billy a peck on the cheek. "He's still keeping me waiting because he wants our first time to be special, but he doesn't realize that he can just take me anytime, anywhere."

"You do know I'm listening, right?" he asked.

"You're listening but you're not hearing me! I mean it, we could do it right here, and Hailey could either watch—"

"I'm *not* going to do that," Hailey interrupted.

"—or she could go wait in a bush until we're done! The point is, I'm *all* yours!"

"Trust me, this is the last place on Earth that I would *ever* want to do that," Billy said.

"You're *no fun*, you know that?" she teased.

"Okay, there's fun, and then there's crazy. Offering to do that right *here* is crazy."

"Crazy for you, baby."

"Yeah, I've gotta side with Billy on this one. Nothing about this place screams sexy at *all*," Hailey said.

"Now, hush. We're almost there, and I don't want to miss it." Billy focused on the ground as they walked. They were looking for the unmarked grave of Victoria Vance—unsure whether it was actually findable or was just a dirt mound somewhere in the middle of the forest. Either way, Ale had told Vicky she would piss on her grave the night of her death, and she wanted to keep that promise, so here they were.

"What, this doesn't excite you?" Ale asked.

"Not in the same way it does you," Billy answered. "But I *do* think it's hilarious that you're so adamant on doing the deed."

Ale turned to Hailey. "What do *you* think? Care to join me?"

"You know what? I wasn't going to, but after I had to eat that damn cheeseburger with leftover pickle essence tainting it, I might as well."

Ale bounced with excitement. "Yay! I'm so proud of you. What do you think, Billy? We could even cross streams!"

"Stop," he said, his tone serious.

Ale looked offended and hurt, like a dog that got caught eating out of the trash. "Okay, did I cross a line? I'm sorry—"

"No. Both of you, look." He pointed beyond a bush up ahead, and they all saw it. "There it *is*," he said. Victoria Vance's grave. Or at least, it *was*, but now it was just a big hole beside a pile of dirt and a shovel.

"No!" Ale exclaimed, leading them as they all ran forward to check it out. The hole was empty. "This can't be it!" she yelled, turning to Billy. "Tell me this isn't it."

He scratched his head and looked at his phone. "This *is* it. The coordinates are exactly as Tiffany gave them to me.

"Then she got it wrong!" Ale insisted. "Call her up and ask her to check again!"

"No, we need to get out of here," Hailey said. "We can call her in the car."

Her friends looked at her, knowing she had more to say, and she did.

"If somebody dug up *her* body, I don't want to be here long enough to find out who did it."

Acknowledgements

Shoutout to the slasher genre for keeping me inspired enough to not only attempt, but complete and publish five books. As far as inspiration goes, I studied films that take place in and around high school for this project. Here is that list:

Carrie (I watched them all, but 1976 was the best)
Scream (The whole franchise.)
Halloween (1978)
Prom Night (1980)
I Know What You Did Last Summer
Jennifer's Body
Mean Girls
Superbad

I'm sure there are dozens more, but the ones lifted above were a huge part of what made this book what it is.

Next, I'd like to shoutout my wife, Natasha, because without her, I'd have nothing. Exactly one month following the publication of Summer Camp for Slasher Victims, she gave birth to our first child—and coming from somebody who surrounds every moment of their life with horror, I've never gone through something scarier. I could only imagine what that time in the hospital felt like for her, but she, as strong of a woman as she is, made it through beautifully. Watching her transition into motherhood and seeing how great she is with our son has been the absolute best experience of my life, and I can't wait to see what's next on this journey through life for us.

Speaking of our son, I have to give him the biggest THANK YOU in the world for being the best baby I could have ever asked for. Seriously, it's unbelievable just how calm and collected he always is, and without that, I don't know how I would have ever finished this novel—so you should all thank him, too. I love you, Levi.

While I'm still on the subject, shoutout to all of Levi's grandparents. You're all so great with him and watching how excited you all are whenever you're around just about melts my heart.

Now, back to the book. I have to thank my beta readers for stumbling your ways through a 90,000 word, error-filled script and giving me necessary advice and opinions that helped shape this final project. You guys rock.

I need to thank my editor for her work, even more this time around, for dealing with my poor organization after my schedule collapsed on me. She does her job so well, and I owe all of my success to her. THANK YOU.

As always, thank YOU for reading. Being able to entertain you guys with these thoughts and stories that bounce around in my head all day is such an awesome thing, and the amount of people reading my work now is just crazy to me.

Last, I need to thank my Grandma Cherie, who I've dedicated this book to. According to my mom, I get my love for horror from you. She loves to tell me about how you'd always have the TV set to a station that would have horror films on, and I regret I don't remember ever watching one with you. I was far too scared back then. It's ironic, though, how my obsession with the genre began right around the time you passed. I'd like to think that it was something that you passed to me on the way out, but who knows? Within this novel, there is a scene where the main character Hailey visits her mother's grave and breaks down while updating her mother about all the things she missed out on. If there is an afterlife, then I'm sure you would have found the familiarity of when I did the same at your grave. Well, more time has passed since I've last visited you, and I thought I'd use this opportunity to update you once again.

As I mentioned before, I had a son—meaning your two youngest grandchildren are both parents now. Crazy, right? You just died so young, it will always be one of the hardest things in the world for me to know that you'll never get to meet my wife or child, but I just know you would hate the title of "great-grandmother." Still, Levi is such a warm little bundle of joy and happiness, and Natasha is just such a drama-free individual. You wouldn't believe that they were a part of our family now. You would love them both so much.

I named a character in my last book after you, because I originally meant to dedicate it to you, but with my wife being pregnant, I thought dedicating my first novel to my first child just made more sense. That character died, but only because I knew you'd think it was cool and wouldn't have it any other way. Still, I'm sure your name will appear in more works of mine, but I promise I'll keep giving it to characters worthy of it.

I promise I'll come around to see you soon. If the cemetery will allow it, I'll bring along a Pepsi and dark chocolate Milky-Way for you, along with a horror movie so we can finally watch one together. I couldn't really think of a more fitting place to watch one than a cemetery, to be honest. But, until then, just know that I love you, and I miss you. We all miss you.

Afterword

I've been dying to write a high school-based horror story for a while now, because Scream is my favorite franchise of all time, and I just love the vibes and aesthetics you can build with the setting. Some of the best horror works of all time are based around high schoolers and for good reason. I wanted this to be that. The idea of writing a prom story also proved to be an exciting challenge for me because I graduated early and never attended the event myself.

When I created Hailey as a character for It Came From the Loch, it was my intention of having her grow up into a kick-ass, powerful Final Girl-esque character, and I could finally get the ball rolling on that with this project. I'm sure a few people might be confused at first when reading this, since Annie was the main character of the first book, and I switched it to Hailey for this one, but that was always the intention for this trilogy. Book three will feature the two of them both prominently, and I wanted each of them to have their own full-length novel's worth of being the lead before the finale.

I also worry that some will be upset that this trilogy won't take place entirely within Camp Safe Woods, but hopefully those people—if any—will see the vision by the time it's all said and done. I wanted this trilogy to explore the slasher genre in its entirety, and I think it's safe to say that summer camps and high schools are pretty equally used as settings within.

With just one more of these planned for the series, I'm very glad I had this opportunity to explore Hailey and her friends as characters for such a lengthy novel because they're my favorite cast that I've developed to date, and I kinda hate that I only get to work with them for one more book. I hope you all enjoyed getting to know them as much as I did.

I would also like to mention how difficult of a book this was for me to write, and how much I've learned from it. Following the success of Summer Camp for Slasher Victims relative to my other works, I was thoroughly convinced that writing can one day become an actual career for me. I was motivated going into this book to give it everything I had; treat it like a full-time job, increase attention to details and production in every aspect, spend more time researching and plotting than I usually do, and write the best book I possibly could have.

While I believe I achieved that, it wasn't easy. I spent months brainstorming, organizing my thoughts, and outlining, which I normally don't do. For the first time ever, when I officially began writing the project, I already had the story, the characters, the story beats, and what felt like everything I needed. I thought it would make the writing easier and quicker. It didn't.

I think it made the story better, which is great for the final project, but what it also did was make the book longer because there was just so much content I had to write, rather than just making stuff up as I went along until it was finished. While I had all of these small ideas, I still had to thoroughly flesh each of them out while trying to connect them all together during the writing, and it just took forever. On top of that, I had a baby and needed to pick up more hours at work, amongst other life changes, so for the first time ever, I struggled to meet my deadlines and stressed out over one of my projects.

Not that I'm complaining or anything. As I mentioned earlier, I learned so much from this project—as I always seem to. What's exciting about these lessons, though, is now I know what I like for my writing process, and I can better schedule all the non-writing things that go into publishing around that. If all things go correctly, you'll see a second book out of me this year, before the Slasher Victims finale next summer. I've got so many stories in my head right now, and I've got a lot of work to do. But, I'm *so* glad and *so* thankful for all of you who are following me on this journey. It means the world to me, and hopefully these stories can find you a sliver of the entertainment I'm giving myself with them.

I'm not sure if authors get as personal in these afterwords or acknowledgements as I like to, but I feel like everything I do in this writing space is unorthodox, so oh well. If you're interested in more of what I've got going on, follow me on Instagram, where I'm most active. My username is @matthewmercerauthor.

I also have a mailing list and blog on my publishing website where I ramble about my writing projects, review books and movies, and plenty more. I have a lot of short stories I want to write, and I'm thinking about posting them there every once in a while, so it might be worth a subscribe/follow if you like what I do.

The website is https://www.aspectsentertainment.com/

Thank you.

Nia's Prom Playlist

Careless Whisper – George Michael

Take My Breath – The Weeknd

P.Y.T (Pretty Young Thing) – Michael Jackson

Your Love – The Outfield

Africa – Toto

Tainted Love – Soft Cell

Physical – Dua Lipa

Heaven is a Place on Earth – Belinda Carlisle

Kiss – Prince

Sharp Dressed Man – ZZ Top

Maneater – Daryl Hall & John Oates

Rock You Like a Hurricane – Scorpions

Time After Time – Cyndi Lauper

Dancing With Myself (RAC Remix) – Billy Idol, RAC

My Kink is Karma – Chappell Roan

Love is a Battlefield – Pat Benatar

Revenge – Ministry

Lady of Namek – Tory Lanez

You Shook Me All Night Long – AC/DC

About the author

Matthew Mercer is a published author and owner of the self-publishing company, Aspects Entertainment, who resides in the California Bay Area with his wife, son, and two dogs. He has published five works to date, including three novellas from the *It Came From Anthology* and two novels from the ongoing *Slasher Victims Saga*.

Find more from him on:

https://aspectsentertainment.com/

Facebook and Instagram: @AspectsEntertainment and @MatthewMercerAuthor